# SEEING THROUGH DOORS

## THE EARLY YEARS OF GLORIA STEVENS

ELLE RENEE

Seeing Through Doors
Copyright © 2022 by Elle Renee

All rights reserved. No part of this publication may be reproduced, distributed, or transmitted in any form or by any means, including photocopying, recording, or other electronic or mechanical methods, without the prior written permission of the author, except in the case of brief quotations embodied in critical reviews and certain other non-commercial uses permitted by copyright law.

Tellwell Talent
www.tellwell.ca

ISBN
978-0-2288-7808-7 (Hardcover)
978-0-2288-6897-2 (Paperback)
978-0-2288-6898-9 (eBook)

This book is dedicated to all my loving family and friends. Thank you for your support on this new and exciting journey. My loving husband Ryan, for putting up with many meltdowns. My sister, best friend, and soon to be agent Hayley, for putting up with me in general. My fur baby Wally... and Princess Savvy. My parents John and Sandra for always pushing me to pursue my dreams, no matter how outrageous. My soul sister Jasmine for keeping me on the level.... Daily lol..... And my second parents Barry and Fran xoxo. My band family Always on Friday!! (Hayley and Ryan, and of course Carolina and Tim) Gabi! (You Gotta Get Gabbi'd people...) My Hacks family. And of course all my family friends whom I cherish every day! Steph, Shawn, Shannon, Rob, Nancy, Brent, Sarah, Noel, Jenn, Sean (Sheila), Nat, Brook, Crystal, Sue, Judy, Meredith, Jutte, Jenn+Mike, The entire Ordiway Clan.... The re-recording of HnF MUST happen... and I'll be first in line for the live screening of Mall Security... JLP...... The Nige.... All my Houlachan family. Also a little shout out any friends I did not mention, and to those who have come and gone out of my daily life but are still in my heart and always will be.

Trust me, in my next instalment... this dedication list will have some more honorable mentions xoxo.

# TABLE OF CONTENTS

Prologue ................................................................. vii

| | | |
|---|---|---|
| Chapter 1 | Trip to Kitchener | 1 |
| Chapter 2 | Memory (Halls) Lane | 11 |
| Chapter 3 | The Regus | 21 |
| Chapter 4 | Veronica | 32 |
| Chapter 5 | The Beginning | 44 |
| Chapter 6 | Canada Day | 63 |
| Chapter 7 | Fireworks | 96 |
| Chapter 8 | Don't Ask | 114 |
| Chapter 9 | Moonlight and Discovery | 121 |
| Chapter 10 | Looking for Answers | 139 |
| Chapter 11 | Labour Day | 145 |
| Chapter 12 | Secret Allies | 151 |
| Chapter 13 | A New Beginning | 171 |
| Chapter 14 | Back to Kitchener | 181 |
| Chapter 15 | Off to School We Go | 194 |
| Chapter 16 | The Martini and The Memory | 212 |
| Chapter 17 | First Parent-Teacher Night | 221 |
| Chapter 18 | The Real Lesson Plan | 233 |
| Chapter 19 | The New Teacher | 241 |
| Chapter 20 | A Lesson in Darkness | 257 |
| Chapter 21 | Protective Mothering | 270 |

| Chapter 22 | Night Terrors | 279 |
| Chapter 23 | A New Best Friend | 286 |
| Chapter 24 | The New Veronica | 299 |
| Chapter 25 | Girls' Night Out | 316 |
| Chapter 26 | The Field Trip | 343 |
| Chapter 27 | Year-End BBQ | 370 |
| Chapter 28 | The Aftermath | 401 |
| Chapter 29 | Awake | 410 |

Epilogue ... 421

# PROLOGUE

Richard stared at the computer screen with a blank expression. *Where should I even start??* He thought to himself while sitting in the basement office. He looked around the room for some sort of sign—anything to point him in the right direction.

The last council meeting was weeks ago. Him and all the elite were there. Even the deepest and most powerful of minds didn't know where to begin. They looked to Richard for his expertise in psychology. He was being relied on by some of the top in their field. Those who'd gone public, and those still concealing what they were. No one could explain why they couldn't see anything. Not one. They all knew it was something obvious they were overlooking, but that was how these things worked sometime.

His office space was not his favourite room of the house, not by far. When it came down to where in his home he'd rather be, he preferred his billiard room on the second floor. That room. Yes that room is where he spent hours on end playing pool, and where he liked to read. He'd hosted many late night poker tournaments for his friends. They would play cards while he would busy himself with darts or other games of coordination. A game room was something he insisted on having. A place for games of skill or chance. He wanted to decorate it as he saw fit, and Linda couldn't touch a thing in it. Originally, the office was supposed to be on the second floor, and his game room in the basement, according to Linda's plan.

"A man cave is supposed to be in the basement!!!" Linda cried out during one of the many tiffs they'd had while they were designing their new home.

But he stood his ground and eventually got his way. It didn't come easy; it cost him. He had to agree to let her decorate the rest of the home to her taste. He didn't always like her taste in home decor as he thought it was very boring and dull. But, it was because of her the home felt like a home. Her warmth and energy. He really did love her. As the thought of winning that argument came to his mind, a tiny smile came across his face. *Happy wife, happy life, right?* Richard was proud he convinced her fair and square. No tactics. Just reasoning.

Down in the office, he had no such luxuries that one would even consider fun. The walls were painted off-white, the colour Linda chose. He didn't care for the cold unwelcoming feeling he got looking at the walls. They certainly were not helping him right now. He needed some stimulation. Something to get things started.

His eyes drifted around the room out of sheer frustration. Over in the corner under the window, he looked at all his books in more detail. Most of them were medical books from his profession. There were some textbooks for reference, and some on his studies from his days in Stanford. Those books helped in many cases while he was doing his residency. Some were for show, but he still liked to have them. Some were hardcover, some soft. A few you could tell he read in detail by the piling of the book's binding. Some had clearly never even been opened.

As he continued looking as his books, his eyes shifted to his diploma.

**Richard Matheson**
**Stanford University**
**Master of Science in Psychology**
**Class of 1999**

*Wow*, he thought. Sometimes, he was even impressed himself by how successful his professional life had been. So many people he had helped, so many lives saved.

He brought his attention back to his computer screen.

"Focus, Richard," he blurted out.

He couldn't keep getting distracted. This was his path. He didn't choose it, but it was where he was meant to be. It was what he was supposed to be doing at this time. A person would never choose to be in this position. He was not going to let one more day go by without doing something, ANYTHING to at least try and help. The world needed him, the council needed him, and so did she.

He passed a few hours on Google, mostly looking at photos of her life and career. He needed to see something. Nothing was working yet. What came up first was photos of some of her greatest achievements. Her majorly public attributes. Where she started to gain a name for herself. Joining the FBI, solving the Coleman case. Pictures of crime scenes from cold cases she'd solved. Some of the world's most wanted that were now in custody paying for their crimes, or were made to start helping solve even worse ones. Then older photos started to come up. Some clearly from people in her past who sold them to make a buck. People that had no place in her life now. A few from high school, at Forest Heights. He noticed some taken in LA in the midst of her high school years. Then a few fan photos and pictures from the paparazzi. The public loved her. At least they did. She gave up a life of research and goodwill for a life in the public's eye. Television. Her show had been on for over ten years, and she hadn't gotten close to the quality of work she was capable of in her prime.

He noticed nothing come up about her youth. Nothing before the age of thirteen. *That's odd, I've never noticed that before.*

Continuing throughout the sea of pictures, Richard couldn't help but marvel at her life in the public eye. He'd always admired her. She used to help the medical profession as well as the law. Research to help explain the unexplainable. She loved solving mysteries about disease and anatomy. *What caused this kind of cancer? Why could one woman conceive and not another?* Helping people used to give her purpose. What she taught the medical world changed all our lives. We all could live longer, and she made history.

She helped police, military and the FBI. She helped with scientific breakthroughs on a few dozen research missions. One could go on and on about all the areas in which she'd been involved.

She made a difference. Well, she used to.

Now? Since she sold out to TV, she hadn't done anything monumental in the last decade or so, except to generate high ratings. She was signed at a time when it was extremely common for celebrities to have a talk show. Some producer out there decided *why not?* Her fame had exploded all over the globe. Her show ended up being a massive success that was still running today.

Richard look disgusted at his computer screen. *Really, Gloria? That's what it's come down to? You would never have settled for that before.*

*What was it?* Richard started to rub his temples in frustration. *Why did she allow herself to change?* he thought. *Coleman.* The thought of that name gave him shivers. After the Coleman case files, she was never the same. He could always sense it. What she had to do, what she saw—it would change anyone.

"Think, Richard, think!" He yelled out loud, knowing he could.

No one was in the home. Linda was in the yard gardening, and his children had long since grown up, and now had families and lives of their own.

Slumping deep into his chair, his anxiety grew. He knew he had missed something. But what? *Richard. You're better than this. How can you do this???* Suddenly, Richard sat forward in his chair. It all came into focus in his mind.

For a basement room, his office got a lot of natural light. This was something he had never been fully grateful for until right now. The sun moved into the room as the day went on, and a beam of sunshine was now cast on his desk, hitting a picture frame. The picture was of Linda and his boys. Richard loved this picture. He remembered taking it.

The photo was taken at their cottage. Their cottage was a sight to see, much like their home. But, the lakefront property was exceptionally breathtaking. He bought it for him and Linda when they moved for his new practice in Toronto. It was a gift to celebrate his pay raise. Not to mention the status he now had. Going from working intake in a psych ward for his residency to running a private practice in one of the largest cities in the country held every right for bragging. Not a lot of new doctors get a private practice right away. But given his circumstances, he excelled in the field like no other, and earned quite the reputation. He already had a lineup of high profile and wealthy patients that were going to start to work with him.

He looked in detail at his framed picture, and the memories came rushing back to him. One warm August morning in 2012, he woke up at their summer home in Northern Ontario. He woke up in a good mood, knowing today his whole family had planned a long hike—they all enjoyed hiking so much.

The kids were young then, and doing things as a family was easier. The kids were not allowed any TV at the cottage. Just outdoor actives. A rule Linda insisted upon from her being raised until the age of eleven on a farm. Her parents subsequently sold their farm in Brantford and moved to Cambridge. Richard didn't mind. He found the rule was good for him too. It let him really unwind and unplug from all the news and horrors going on in the world.

That morning was a particular beautiful sunrise. An hour into the hike, he was walking behind his wife and two boys as the sky filled with colours of pink and light amber before the sun reclaimed the sky from a starry night.

Linda looked so beautiful that morning. Her auburn hair picked up on the sunlight and started to shine like copper. He remembered how much he loved her red hair since they had met in the hallways of their high school.

He saw the true beauty in her features on their first date at Charlie's restaurant. That unforgettable night.

*What a great picture this would be.* He yelled ahead to his family to stop and turn around. Linda's face lit up when she saw the camera. She loved pictures of any kind, but especially ones of the family.

The boys huddled into their mother, being about four and six at the time. She kneeled down to their height and wrapped her arms around them. She smiled a pure, vibrant smile that let Richard know how happy she was at that moment. He didn't need anything but his eyes to see that. The boys smiled cheek to cheek too. You could tell they loved their mother so much.

"THAT'S IT!" Richard yelled as he stood up from his chair. "Why didn't I think of this before?!"

He walked around his desk with pure vigor, pacing and trying to put the pieces together. He laughed to himself and was enlightened to be able to tell the council what they all knew. They were missing something. He was the one meant to figure it out. They were right.

*How will I find her?* But he knew all too well the pieces would come together easily for him. Things like this always did since he was young.

A wave a calm took over him for the first time in weeks. He knew what he had to do and where to start. A start. That was it, but at least it was a step forwards. A change in the right direction. If he could get to her, he could get to Gloria. Eventually.

Richard sat back at his desk and entered a new subject in the search field.

**Southridge Public School** in Kitchener. He scrolled past the links to the current website until he found what he was looking for.

**SOUTHRIDGE SCHOOL. Home of Gloria Stevens 1972-1979.**

Of course, reference to Gloria was one of the first things that popped up. Anything, any place or anyone she ever was linked to, always took advantage of the publicity from having a tie or connection to her.

There were only three known photos of her at the school that were ever released to the public. She kept it that way. But why? He had to dig deep on the internet to find them. Even they were questionable that it was even her, or even that school? But he knew what he was looking at.

He quickly looked up the teachers listed for the school year of 1977-78. With only a few years dig into, he felt this was the year to look up. Mrs. Kropf. He was right. There she was. A few more clicks and he found a few listed honourable mentions of her teaching career, and the last listed item was that she retired in 2018. Links started popping up from a posting in *The Record*. This was a local paper from the city of Kitchener where Gloria went to school in her youth.

The article read:

*Southridge Public School is saddened to announce the retirement of one of our favourite teachers, Mrs. Samantha Kropf. Mrs. Kropf is a tenured teacher of our school, having started teaching with us in 1972 when the school was still fairly new. She will be missed and never forgotten. Mrs. Kropf was not only a teacher here at Southridge, but she also ran the drama and music club for the last twenty-three years. Her shoes will not be easily filled. We would like to thank Samantha for her forty-six years with us. Enjoy retirement with Greg!*

*Love, all the teachers and staff at Southridge Public School in Kitchener.*

With that, Kitchener, Ontario became his place of interest. Despite the fact that Gloria hadn't lived there since the late 80s, Richard knew this was the right direction.

After refocusing in his office, Richard made a long phone call to his lawyers and got a few things in line. He logged off his computer and headed upstairs. The top of the stairs led to the hallway that took him outside where Linda was busy in the garden. He passed his game room. What he wouldn't give to just stay in there. But he knew that he wouldn't have that pleasure, not today. Not for a long time.

He opened the back to door to see Linda just to his right. She had been busy! The garden was beautiful. She always took the time at the end of each season to properly prepare the land for snow. It was the end of May, and spring had finally arrived in full. Linda never liked to plant until she was sure no frost would come and destroy all her hard work. She had a natural green thumb, and all the knowledge to care for any plant life came with it. Being raised on a farm outside of Brantford taught her well. Even though they had more than enough money to hire a gardener, it was one of her passions. They had a team come take care of the lawn and outside maintenance as the property was huge, and Richard never cared to do it. He did all those chores as a teenager and figured he earned the right to hire a landscaper. But, the hired company had strict instructions never to touch the back gardens. The back garden was Linda's pride and joy.

He took a deep breath, not sure how Linda was going to take the news. Linda looked up at him and sighed. She knew the expression on his face all too well.

"Linda, honey, I have some business I need to attend to right away. I have to go to Kitchener ..."

# CHAPTER 1

# Trip to Kitchener

Richard was eager to be off the road. The trip was only about a two-hour drive from his home in Toronto, but he couldn't wait to get started

*Finally,* he thought. *I'm going to get some answers.*

The navigation system in his new Bentley Infinite Platinum SLX was state-of-the-art. The voice command was incredible. He also enjoyed the auto-pilot feature that was a new standard on luxury cars. He put the car in auto-pilot mode to free his hands for him look up some information on his device. He knew he was on the right path but needed to know where he had to start.

About an hour later, Richard found an address and a phone number. All the information looked to be current. There wasn't much information you couldn't find about a person in 2032, if you knew where to look. As a licensed doctor, Richard had access to the personal information listed on someone's health card. Any Canadian who had been to a doctor or hospital was traceable. It was an advantage that Richard had access to this information, being a psychiatrist.

"Now entering Guelph," the friendly audio-engineered voice said.

*Thank God.* Kitchener was just thirty more minutes from there.

His car drove down the familiar paved highway, and a rush of memories came to him. He grew up in a city named Cambridge that was just outside of Kitchener. As his car drove past Guelph and entered Cambridge, the more vivid the memories came swimming into his head. He and Linda drove to Cambridge often, years back when her parents were still alive. But, the trips never extended into Kitchener.

With the car in total control, he was able to see so many good times in venues and businesses long gone. He was coming up to the Sportsworld highway exit. It was named after a popular water park he liked to go to as a kid. It had a huge arcade which he would spend hours in. It was probably the time spent there that led to his love for video games. A love Linda didn't understand then, or now.

Richard laughed to himself. *God, she hated the arcades.*

His mind drifted to their first date when they were kids. He met Linda at Galt Collegiate Institute in Cambridge during the 80s. He thought he'd impress her by driving out of town to somewhere she'd most likely never been to. He took her to Charlie's Restaurant, a very popular Italian restaurant in downtown Kitchener.

He remembered how excited she got that he was taking her out of town. She'd never done that with anyone but her parents. On their first date, she fell in love with him. For years, she would always tell him that was one of her happiest memories. At least, the part until he took her to an arcade after.

Richard shrugged his shoulders and shook his head. *What was I thinking?! Oh well,* he thought. *I must have done something right.* Of course he did. They were married now for almost forty years.

As the car passed the exit, he noticed the attraction had long since been torn down. Once, it was a huge water park with a brightly-coloured waterslide you could see from the passing highway. The wave pool, the mini golf. All were gone and replaced by half-empty shopping strips. For lease signs on most of the windows.

He smiled as he noticed another restaurant he fondly remembered.

**The One, The Original. Moose Winooski's.**
**Come see us today and enjoy our famous wings!**

He had some great memories at that restaurant. You didn't go to Sportsworld without at least a visit into this rustic, country cottage themed atmosphere. It screamed Canadian stereotypes. But that was its charm. He just couldn't imagine being there without all the attractions everyone once enjoyed.

His sense of nostalgia temporarily distracted him from the fact that he was getting hungry. A large grumble in his side made him realize he should probably eat. His nerves were getting the best of him. There was a lot riding on all this. Who knew how this was all going to go. Not knowing was unfamiliar territory to him. Luckily, he was almost at his destination.

To distract himself from his growing hunger pains, he switched back to self-drive mode. As he pulled his car into the downtown core, he felt another grumble from his stomach. *Hmm, I guess I am getting a little hungrier than I thought.*

"Turn left on Ottawa," his dashboard blurted out.

"Really? That doesn't seem right," he said aloud. *I thought the hotel was straight down this road.*

Well, his new navigation system had never been wrong before, so he thought he should follow it. It better be right, given what he had spent on the car. Since he had lived close to here for years in his youth, he thought he'd know his way around without a hand from his navigation system.

Then suddenly, he could see why his car had told him to go this way. Since leaving Cambridge for university in the 90s, the neighbouring town of Kitchener had changed. New developments and high rises were everywhere now. He barely recognized it with some of the new architecture. The city also put in a massive new train system all over the city. It tore up the streets that he knew as a young man. Richard then recalled reading about it online. He always kept up a little on Kitchener and its development, yet always wondered why it had an appeal to him. He didn't even keep up on Cambridge (where he really grew up) as much as he did with Kitchener.

Looking at the new metropolis that the city was clearly trying to achieve, the trains seemed fitting now, given how much the city had grown. The pictures he'd seen online didn't do it justice. He felt he was in a city he'd never been to before.

He pulled into the front of the Crowne Plaza hotel right in what he remembered being the heart of downtown in its hay day. He chose this hotel for a few particular reasons. He got out of his new flashy car, and looked around. He barely recognized the area. What was once a bank across the street was now a sports bar. Next door was a vacant building that he had memories of going to for Oktoberfest for souvenirs and tickets. *Oktoberfest*, he thought. Kitchener was known for the annual fall celebration that lasted ten days. Kitchener was founded by many German settlers who brought this tradition over from Germany. The festival used to be the biggest of its kind outside of its native country. Now, the old headquarters sat empty with a *For Lease* sign. Such a shame. Another casualty of the pandemic of 2020.

Across another street in front of the hotel was a tower of green glass that sat empty. A former shopping complex called Market Square. For decades, developers had been in and out of projects to do with this once popular mall. It had sat empty since 2022 or so. The nostalgia of past lifestyles always seemed to intrigue him, especially the 80s and 90s. Perhaps it was because he lived through those decades. *Wow, has it been this long?*

He shut his car door and grabbed his luggage from the trunk. He felt a sense of pride seeing some other guests stare at his car—it was the newest model you could buy in this part of the continent. He pulled some strings to be able to be the first to get it. But, he always seemed to get his way. He smirked a little smirk. He didn't always use his gift of persuasion to acquire material things, but *a man needs some toys, right? Right*, he convinced himself.

A man standing by the hotel doors looked at it in shock. "Hey! Is that—"

"The new Bentley? Yes. I just got it," replied Richard with a smirk.

"But . . . you can't—"

"Get it yet? Well, you can. You just have to know the right people. And you have to know how to talk to them. And—before you ask . . . yes, it's street legal . . . barely." Richard's smirk then turned into a full smile.

The man looked at Richard like he was at the hotel for business. Richard gave a cheeky wink to the man and walked into the hotel.

He looked at the inside of the hotel in shock. This was his first time being in the space since the 90s. It was once a place called The Valhalla. One of the hottest spots in the city. Back in the day, it would hold massive parties and weddings. For both business and pleasure, it was the go-to meeting place for so many in the city. He remembered a few nights of Oktoberfesting in the late 80s in the iconic establishment.

The renovation of the hotel was stunning, yet Richard felt more attached to the way it used to be. It was a literal shell of what it once was. While beautiful and modern, it lacked the original warmth he felt the place once had.

"Can I help you?" a friendly young woman said from behind a podium.

"Ah yes, I'm sorry. I haven't been here for many, many years. I'm just taken back by how much it has changed."

"Well welcome back to Kitchener, Mister . . ."

"Oh, where is my head. My sincerest apologies." Richard walked over to the desk from his trance in the center of the lobby. He set down his luggage at his feet. "I'm Mr. Richard Matheson. I have a reservation."

The young woman behind the desk began frantically typing on her computer.

"Ah yes, here it is. It says you will be with us for a few nights, checking out on Sunday. Are you here for the reunion?"

"No, I am here on some business I hope to have wrapped up by this weekend. Is my reservation for a meeting room on the conference level confirmed for this weekend as well?"

"Oh, my apologies. I just assumed since you said you haven't been here for years that you'd be with the reunion." The woman was young, probably in her 30s, and she nervously typed on her computer.

Richard noticed her constantly making corrections, looking up shyly at him every few seconds.

"Let me see, yes. Here it is. We have you in Suite 234 for your stay. You use the elevators located just behind you. Head to your left and follow the signs. And as for your meeting room, all the details are listed here, and it says everything has been finalized with our sales team. Did you need to make any changes?"

"No, that will be fine. I have a copy of the contract in my email. That will be everything."

"Ok, sir. We are so happy you've decided to stay with us. Sir, if I may. Your room is rather close to the group events this weekend. There is a high school reunion here, and these types of events can get rather loud. Could I suggest we move your room to our tower?"

"No. That will be fine."

"Are you sure? It's no trouble at all. I can—"

"Vanessa, right? No, it's ok. I like my reservation as is." He saw a slight crimson hue flushing on her cheeks when he spoke her name.

"Oh, a-a-alright then, s-sir. May I have your keys to give to our valet?"

"Actually, I have to run to Grand River Hospital on some business. Could you have my bags taken to my room? I should be back this evening."

"Right away, sir. Let me know if there is anything else I can do."

\* \* \*

A few hours later, Richard returned to the hotel. He pulled his car into the front laneway and shut off the engine. While he was exhausted, the day was a complete success. He got what information he needed for tomorrow. He got out of his car and headed into the lobby.

"Welcome back, Mr. Matheson." The young woman smiled warmly at Richard. "I have Jack here available to valet your car."

"Vanessa, you are an angel."

"Oh, please." A huge smile came over her face. "It's my pleasure." She turned to a young kid maybe a few feet away by the entrance. "Jack?" she said while looking to the valet desk. "Can you please park Mr. Matheson's car in the VIP section of the garage?"

He looked terrified. "Me? Drive that?" Jack was nervously looking out the front bay windows at Richards's $3,000,000 car.

"Young man, Jack was it?" Richard spoke sternly while walking in his direction.

Jack was almost shaking. "The new Infinite Platinum SLX?! I can't drive that! What if I hit something?!"

"Jack, it's ok. I trust you." He looked at Jack with a deep intense gaze. "Don't worry, I know it will be just fine." He walked over to the valet desk and placed the key in the trembling valet driver's hand with a $50 bill beneath it. "Good night, you two. Thanks again, Vanessa. I'll see you—"

"Tomorrow," she blurted out and looked shocked. "I'm here tomorrow, and all weekend. If you need anything, just ask for me by name, Mr. Matheson."

"Please, call me Richard." He smiled and turned around and headed to the elevators.

As he got on the elevator, he could hear them talking.

"I'll be right back, Vee. Or is it Vanessa now?" Jack looked at her sarcastically as he walked around his valet desk and headed to the doors.

"Shut up, Jack! He was nice. I am just doing my job."

"Ok, whatever you say, VEE."

"Jack, knock it off, ok! He must have read my name tag or something. Besides, I think a man of his stature can address me by my full name. It sounds more professional, don't you think?"

"Oh for sure," Jack said, almost out the front doors. He quickly turned around to get the last word. "But, seeing as you don't have a name tag on, try and think of a better story by the time I get back? I can't believe he's letting me drive this thing! Ok, wish me luck." Jack was out the doors before Vanessa could think of a witty comeback.

Then, in a moment of thought, she realized something. Vee looked down at her blazer and noticed that Jack was right. She didn't have a name tag on.

# CHAPTER 2

# Memory (Halls) Lane

In his room, he found his bags waiting. His room was gorgeous. A suite on the second floor, right near the conference area just as he requested. He had some business to attend to on the weekend. While it was not how he remembered it, the hotel was simply gorgeous. They spared no expense updating everything in the building.

He gave Linda a check-in phone call, as he had only been updating her with text messages all day.

"Honey, have you eaten today?"

"Yes, Linda, I'm fine. I had lunch with an associate for this case around 1 p.m. I'm in Kitchener, Linda, can you believe it? It's been so long."

"Richard, we used to go to Cambridge often to see my parents, and you never expressed an interest to go to Kitchener."

"I know, Linda, I'm just saying. You wouldn't believe how different it is. I'm going to go explore a little."

"Ok, hun, but get some rest too. I can't wait to hear about this trip, but I still don't know why I couldn't come with you."

"I told you, Lin, it's business. You more than anyone understand why I have to work and stay focused. I love you so much it can distract me. My first ground work had to done at the hospital. You know you're not allowed in the hospital with me." Richard hated keeping the details from her. But he did it to keep her safe.

"I know. I just don't like when you go on the road, and you know that. And I could have gone shopping or gone to see some friends in Hespeler."

The phone went silent for a moment. Richard didn't know what to say.

"But, who am I to stand in the way of my dashing husband off to save the day for someone who needs help."

Richard laughed. "Linda, you always make me feel good. I love you. I'll message you later. Good night."

"Love you, call me in the morning."

Richard hung up the phone and quickly freshened up.

He left his second floor suite and headed down the hall. He opted out of taking the elevator and instead took the stairs down. He didn't want to have to make small talk in the lobby. He made his way down a staircase and saw a fire exit. He walked out the doors and just started down the connected laneway.

*Oh, if these streets could talk*, he thought. He had memories of him and his buddies crashing spring formals in this very hotel. The girls in Cambridge never interested him and his boys, so they would come to Kitchener for the high school formals of Kitchener high

*Seeing Through Doors*

schools. Well, no girls interested him at G.C.I. (Galt Collegiate Institute) until Linda started there in his senior year.

He could remember drinking for the first time with friends at night clubs down the streets that no longer existed. Sneaking into bars in Cambridge would have been too risky. Running into parents was a huge risk. He and his friends drove the twenty-five minutes to enjoy nights out before they were of legal age. It was the 80s, so a fake ID was easy to make.

Parties and events were at every corner, it seemed. Again, he wondered why the draw to Kitchener over Cambridge was always there. He shook his head and kept walking.

So many other businesses went under after the recession in 2022–2025. He read about it on the webpage for *The Record* while researching about Gloria. The new and vibrant urban life that had sprung into the shell of what the area had been was quite impressive. It reminded him of a smaller version of his new home in Toronto. His practice was right downtown in the massive city. In a strange way, it felt like a home away from home.

Richard turned right out of the hotel. Directly across from the hotel was the start of Halls Lane. A strange small road that once was used to connect main arteries of the downtown core. While walking straight down Halls Lane, a few blocks up he turned left on Ontario Street.

Not even a half a block down Ontario Street, he looked up. Charles Street sign was fifteen feet above on a light post. He couldn't believe he was actually looking at it. Of course, he knew why he'd headed straight there. Curiosity. Nostalgia. He knew it was long gone, but he wanted to see the location.

Turning right on Charles, he walked up the half block and stood in front of the building, now a local office. His mind shifted to picture what is was oh so many years ago.

Charlie's Restaurant. His first date with Linda. He smiled and closed his eyes and took in the flood of images and happy memories of getting Linda to agree to go out with him.

1985. Linda was new to G.C.I. She just moved to the city from their family farm in Brantford. Her family sold the farm after her grandparents passed on. Her mother and father were never much into farming, so they celebrated the chance to move and make a new start.

He first saw Linda walking down the halls of their high school. Her bright auburn hair was so unique, it caught the attention of many boys at school. It made a lot of girls jealous, and they would tease her about being so plain and simple. Her beauty was what most people looked at first anyways. He felt so lucky she agreed to the date. He saved up for three weeks to take her to dinner; he wanted to go all out.

His mind shifted to the big day. Friday night at Charlie's Restaurant. The natural brick wall, the stripped awning over the salad bar, brass pole details at every corner. Ah, that was the era. He remembered the waiters and waitresses in their white button-up shirts and black bowties. He swore he could smell the garlic! Linda did look so beautiful that night. They were so young. How badly he wanted to impress her!

Linda enjoyed the dinner so much. She ordered the spaghetti and he got the pasta primavera. While up at the salad bar, he overheard two women having a serious conversation. A memory he hadn't had since it happened.

*"This isn't helping you, not one bit!"* one of the women said to the other, grabbing her forearm in concern.

*"Don't you think I know that?"*

Richard nervously grabbed his salad plate and turned his attention back to Linda who had just said something to him.

*"Sorry, what?"*

Linda was staring at him, clearly annoyed. *"It's rude to eavesdrop on other people."*

*"You're right, I'm sorry."*

They both stacked up piles of delicious salads and starters on their plates.

*"You look so pretty tonight. Did I tell you that?"* He embraced her arm like a true gentleman and led her back to their table.

*"Yes, like a million times."* Linda blushed. *"Come on, I can't wait to dig in!"*

Richard spent the rest of that night devoted to Linda.

*Funny that memory should surface after who I saw today at the hospital.* Richard could still appreciate serendipity after all these years.

Richard's mind came back to the present day, and he thought it was best to keep moving. He walked a few more blocks and stopped at a small independent diner somewhere on King Street. He didn't bother to get the name. It was brand new that year. It was on the corner of City Hall in the centre of downtown.

As he sat in the diner, he looked up at City Hall. Richard didn't care for the new City Hall like many residents in the area. The original City Hall in the city was a tremendous monument compared to this. While he had always opposed the new building, he knew the old one had become a safety hazard. Once it was the heartbeat of the downtown area. Huge columns, lush gardens. The local farmers market once had its home there every Saturday morning.

With a brief sigh, he spoke to himself. "Well, in time everything changes." Then added in thought, *whether we like it or not.*

He ate quickly and walked back to the hotel.

The next morning, Richard woke up and felt refreshed. Knowing that things were at least in motion allowed him to get a good night's sleep for the first time in weeks. He had a hot shower and got dressed. He went with his black suit that held a slight crimson sheen to it in certain lights. He didn't know designers as Linda dressed him mostly. He looked at the tag—*Alexander Amosu Dormeuil Vanquiss ll*. Was he even pronouncing that right? He didn't care. He liked how it looked.

*Seeing Through Doors*

Richard was not vain but did take his appearance to heart. After all, he knew more than most how a first impression was made. He knew that firsthand in ways not many ever could. He splashed a little Chanel Egotist on (Linda's favourite scent) and headed down to grab a bite before heading to Waterloo.

When he arrived downstairs on the main level, he entered the lobby. A young man was working the desk and was busy with a few guests. He walked straight past them and decided to explore the hotel a little before heading for breakfast.

He walked down a main hall to a wall of glass. One side held the onsite business centre, a typical thing you'd find in almost any hotel. High-speed computers, printers and scanners. A traveller didn't really need them now. Not with technology in portable devices. But in recent years, having an IP address for some documents was mandatory for security. Things that travel across a signal can be read and stolen. A lawyer, for example, would need access to one for their profession. High-end hotels always catered to major professions.

Richard looked over to his right and saw the pool area. Or what was left of it. It saddened him to see the shallow ground they passed as a pool. Nothing of its original character was present. The pool used to have windows in the deep end. Parents could go down to the fitness centre on the level below and see their kids frolicking in the water. The pool had been filled in and made a lot shallower as well.

Such a shame. He was *seeing* parties and events. The pool area would host massive parties, and the elegance in that area was breathtaking when done right. A fountain in the pool. He focused and could see more. Portable bars on every corner. A massive buffet set up on the deck. There used to be access to the lobby bar and patio seats outside so people could have a drink and watch their kids swim. Now, just a wall of plaster.

In the corner was a large set of wooden doors that led to offices. Richard focused. *Was that always offices?* Then a bar that used to be Schatzi's bar came into clarity. He could hear the parties that went on in there. Live music. Years after that, a bistro-style restaurant.

He looked up and through the roof above the pool. Now, it was a ceiling with lovely skylights allowing natural light in. Before? An open space that hotel rooms above could look down into.

"Things change, Richard."

Richard looked and took in more of the surrounding area, but decided to get something to eat. Today was a big day and he didn't have time for this. But how he enjoyed seeing the past.

Richard went to the restaurant bar, looking around at things present, and past. He saw a sign that said PLEASE WAIT TO BE SEATED. He waited patiently and was greeted by a warm welcoming lady.

He didn't need to see her name tag, and so he blurted out, "Good morning, Carol."

The waitress smiled. "Good morning, sir! Just grab whatever table you like and I'll grab some coffee."

Richard sat down at the closest table, still in awe of seeing many past stages in the hotel's history. While

*Seeing Through Doors*

relishing in the hotel's diverse appearances, Carol was back at his table with a small pot of coffee and a menu. She flipped over the elegant coffee mug on the table and poured him a cup. He looked up at her and knew she had a history with this place.

"Thank you, Carol. I'll just have your eggs benedict. Say, have you worked here a long time?"

"Long time? I'll say. I've been here longer then some of the furniture!"

Richard shook his head, not knowing just how long she'd been there.

"Wow, you must have quite the stories, I bet!"

Richard scanned her memories of the different places she'd worked in the hotel. She bartended and served at all the business ventures the hotel had tried over the years. Night clubs, Oktoberfest halls, Christmas parties, bistros. Too many to go into detail in such a short time.

"Oh honey, that could take its own lifetime to get into. I'll get the kitchen started on your breakfast right away." She grabbed his menu and placed the small coffee pot on the table.

Richard was so glad to meet her as he got to see an unique perspective of the local landmark.

After he finished eating breakfast, Richard knew he shouldn't drive today. He'd be better to take a taxi. While his vehicle did have self-drive mode, that didn't matter. He knew a fine scotch was coming his way.

He paid for his meal, and headed toward the lobby. The young man working the desk was no longer busy. He saw the guest agent start to smile as he walked toward him.

"Well hello, Mr. Matheson. Anything I can help you with today? Should I have your car brought around?"

*Mr. Matheson? Oh*, he smiled, *apparently I've been talked about.*

"Hello, Keith, thank you, but I won't be needing my car today. Would you please call me a taxi?"

"Certainly, it would be my pleasure." Keith quickly picked up the phone and called a local taxi company. "Is there anything else I could help you with, Mr. Matheson?"

Richard noticed how eager the staff seemed to be around here.

"No, thank you, have a lovely day."

"Absolutely. I am here until 3 p.m. today if you need anything else. After that, Vee is on duty this evening to assist you."

"Great, I appreciate that."

Richard turned to the front door and saw there was a taxi that just turned up to the entrance. He walked out and took a deep breath of fresh air.

*You can do this, Richard. This will work.*

# CHAPTER 3

# The Regus

He walked over to the vehicle. United Taxi was written in bright bold red lettering alongside of the luxury vehicle. He couldn't help but find humour in thinking about how luxurious the cab industry became after the legal battle in 2025 with Uber and other driver applications. The cab industry came out on top and won. They upped their ante after that to ensure their spot in the market by really investing in luxury vehicles.

Richard entered the taxi on the left-hand side, getting in behind the female driver.

"The Barrel Yards, please. The Regus building."

His taxi driver nodded her head, looking a little excited. She began to pull away from the hotel.

"Here for business?" she asked him.

"Yes and no, here to find a friend really."

"Your friend must be high up! The lofts there are some of the most high-end places in the city. But the Regus building??!" She let out a long whistle and nodded her head.

"My friend isn't there, but someone who knows where to find her is."

"I hope you know this friend well enough to get in. Security is really tight there."

"Oh, I have my ways. Don't you worry." He winked at her in the rearview while she glanced back at him.

She smiled back, and even blushed a little bit. And why shouldn't she? Richard was very good looking for his age. *Silver Fox.* A nickname Linda gave him years ago came to his mind. The story of his nickname came to mind. He remembered how he overheard it.

The first year their boys were off to college, Linda and her friends were talking about their husbands one evening. Earlier that night, he was "ordered to his man cave"—Linda's direct orders. She was having her girlfriends over for a wine night. Something they didn't do too often. But, when they did, Richard always woke the next day to find a least a few empty bottles in the wake of the night's festivities.

"I know Lou is handsome, and I love him, but I miss his full head of hair," said Linda's best friend, Shannon.

"Oh come now, bald is sexy—look at my Steve!" one of the other women exclaimed.

They all laughed in unison, definitely a few bottles deep at that point.

Richard didn't normally eavesdrop, but this subject he found to be hilarious, and they were talking about some of his friends.

"Yes, but Linda, we all agree your Richard is aging better than most."

*Who said that . . . not Shannon, maybe their other friend, Lindsay?* Whoever said it, Richard found himself blushing a little. He always knew he was better looking than most.

"He's my silver fox," Linda said out loud and proudly.

Richard felt so validated. It was nice to know Linda was still attracted to him after all these years.

Now in the taxi, he was glad to have full confidence in his appeal for moments just like this. Never cocky, he was too much of gentleman for that.

Minutes later, the taxi pulled up to the gated entrance and stopped at the security desk while the driver lowered both her window and the backseat window where Richard was sitting.

"Public transit ID please," asked the security officer in a very firm tone.

Melissa Burns was her name, written on the badge she handed to the officer. He scanned it and nodded in validation.

"Name of the guest expecting you, sir?" the officer then directed at Richard.

"I'm here to surprise an old friend at the Regus. She lives in 2D."

The security guard paused and looked shocked. Richard knew it was because of the particular resident he was there for. The guard then nodded and went over to his station to check the name in his computer. He looked even more shocked to read the level of security this resident had. He radioed over to the head of security at the Regus with the small state-of-the-art, two-way radio he kept in his belt along with weapons and a flashlight. The radios were very similar to what a police officer had at their disposal. They were designed to keep anything transmitted private. Hackers and those who scanned radios didn't have a chance. Richard heard every word he spoke despite being twenty feet away behind a glass wall.

"Hey, Scott, Matt here. Does Veronica Chastain have anyone on her visitor list?"

He heard the radio crystal clear.

"No, she never has visitors. There is nothing on the books on my end. He must be mistaken. Whoever it is, they do not have clearance."

The guard tensed a little and spoke back to the radio. "I understand, sir. I will not allow clearance."

He noticed the guard pat the weapon he carried on his right hip and look at him suspiciously in the back of the taxi.

The front gate guard leaned over his keyboard and pulled up the detailed clearance file on 2D and read further into it. Code R clearance. That was the strictest. The tightest security you could get. He left his station and walked back cautiously to the vehicle.

"Sir, you are not on the visitation clearance list. I'm going to have to ask you—"

"Matt, she is expecting me. I'm sure she just forgot to put me on the list," Richard said in a very strong tone.

"No name, no entry," replied the guard. He seemed a little dazed.

"I know she's expecting me and wants me to get clearance right away." Richard spoke in an even deeper voice.

"I, I guess you're probably right, just let me call over to the Regus one last time," the guard started to seem more and more out of it.

"I can speak with them over the radio. Don't you think that would clear up this whole confusion? Let me talk to Scott directly."

"Sir—yes, that would be helpful." The guard looked even more confused. *Did he hear him? How did he know Scott, or my name for that matter?*

The guard grabbed his radio from its holder on his pocket again and spoke to it while never breaking eye contact with Richard.

"Hey, Scott, it's me again," he spoke into his two-way. "The visitor here says—"

Then Richard grabbed the small device. He never let go of the guards' eye contact.

"Hi, Scott, my name is Richard. I know I am supposed to be on the list, and this is just a misunderstanding. Why don't you let me pass the gate, and we can clear this up in person." Richard spoke very firmly and assertively into the device. "I REALLY want to come talk with you."

Scott on the other end left a long silent pause of static. "Yes, you're right. Please come to the front desk and we can clear this up. It sounds reasonable."

Richard knew the guard on the other end was smiling. He couldn't see why.

He handed the two-way back to the guard.

"Thanks for your help, I'm sorry for the confusion."

"No problem, sir. I am the one who should be sorry. Have a nice day." He turned to Melissa quickly before her window was back up. "Miss, your car is marked for delivery only. I will notified all the officers on duty of your entry. You have to return in ten minutes or risk apprehension and possibly charges. Sir, you will exit the vehicle and wait for our head of security to approach you. Do not walk up to the doors on your own. Do you understand?"

"Yes."

"Ma'am, I have to inspect your vehicle first. Please open the trunk."

"Yes, sir."

The guard looked in the empty trunk and even lifted the cap over the spare tire. He closed the trunk and took out his flashlight. He inspected the vehicle on his hands and knees. He took out another device. Richard knew that he was looking for tracing signals, and any other signals that were not registered. It not only read signals, but could scan for any foreign substances that could be in a vehicle. Drugs, liquids used to make a bomb. Anything.

After about ten minutes, he knocked on the window and yelled to her, "Ok, you're clear! Please proceed down the lane and turn right after building 3!"

The gated then lifted, and Melissa nodded and slowly pressed the gas. They drove away from the entrance, and she could see the gates lower behind them.

"What was that?!" Melissa blurted out excitedly while looking in the rearview.

"Ms. Chastain is the mother of the friend I'm looking for. I know she wants to see me."

"I don't know any Chastain, but that, that was, that was just something." Melissa looked straight ahead, not sure what to make of what had just happened. "That was something off the *Gloria Stevens show*! You ever watch her?!"

"Not really my thing, but I've heard of her."

"You should look into it, maybe you—"

"I'm a doctor of medicine and still have disbeliefs in all that."

"How can you? It's been validated by your community, and the whole world!"

"Anyways," Richard spoke, trying to politely change the subject.

She drove the rest of the way in silence. Moments later, a huge sign made of pressed precious metals appeared on their right-hand side beside a gated driveway. *THE REGUS*. She pulled up the paved laneway and stopped in front of an imperial-sized set of multiple glass panes and doors.

"Good luck, and I hope you find your friend."

"Thanks Melissa."

He handed her some cash and saw the flush in her cheeks once again.

"Drive safe." Richard got out of the taxi.

Richard paused and waited in the laneway for the head of security as he was directed. He looked up in awe of the massive structure. After only seeing the pictures online, the Regus really lived up to its name. Centred in what was called the Barrel Yards, Richard really felt like he was in a part of Toronto again. He followed the building of the area a little online. He always thought if Linda and him ever wanted to leave Toronto for another city before they retired, this would be where they'd go. They built a few huge luxury buildings in the area back in the 2010s, but the Regus came in 2025, a few years after the recession when the economy got back on its feet.

It was built for the "who's who" left in the region. Only those who weren't affected by what happened in 2020–2022 were still able to afford such luxury. It was built to bring people with money back to the area to help invest in it. A gamble the city took—that really paid off. Even some celebrities lived here. Mostly in secret. This was all possible due to the compound around the building itself, and the added security around the Barrel Yards.

Richard watched as his taxi drove away. He glanced to his left and saw a man approach him. This wasn't the man on the radio. An ear piece was visible in his right ear, and it was easy to see he was security. To his surprise, he was greeted warmly by this man wearing a black tuxedo.

"Sir, please follow me to the security desk."

Richard followed the man inside the building through a smaller set of glass doors to the left of the grand entrance. A few feet away was a very plain glass table with two chairs. On the other side was another guard in a chic tuxedo.

*This must be Scott.*

"Good evening, Scott. My name is Richard. Thank you for your assistance. I have very important business to clear with Veronica."

Scott looked at him very smugly. Yet he was still smiling, just as Richard suspected. He stood up from his seat and took a long, interrogating look at Richard.

"Good afternoon, Richard. Thank you for your compliance. But, don't thank me yet. I needed to meet you in person to decide whether or not to let you into my building. A lot of residents here rely on me to keep them safe at all costs."

Richard, not sure where the conversation was going, spoke out to Scott once more in a firm controlled voice. "You will allow me to enter the building to—"

"Not so fast, sir." Scott laughed and shook his head. "Your little parlor tricks worked on Matt at the gates, but I have the higher position for a reason. I have my reasons for having let you get THIS close to this particular resident, as no one has ever tried in the years. Not even a family member."

Richard was always awe struck when he met others with abilities. He'd only met a handful of people able to sense his compulsion ability. This was surprising to him, especially given his age and strength. A look of worry came over his face. He was never able to immediately read into others with gifts. He never figured out why. It took a few spoken words for him to sense.

"What, you know you're not the only one, I hope?" Scott said, indicating their abilities.

Of course he knew he wasn't the only one. It just wasn't too common, and not that many people were as open about it so quickly.

"Scott, you seem like a reasonable man. If we could simply—"

"Save your flattery for someone else. I just need to shake your hand."

Startled, Richard shook his head. "You want to shake my hand?"

"Well, I have to make contact to be sure. I'm sure your abilities work in ways that you can't explain. Part of mine is physical contact. You know, anyone else would not have gotten this far. But, I knew someone was coming to see Veronica. Finally, after all these years. I just didn't know who or why. It's like my life, and not just mine, depends on it. And here you are."

"Ok..."

Richard wasn't sure what was about to happen. No one shook hands anymore. Not since 2020 and all the risks that came at that time. But, he was this close. Nothing would jeopardize all the work he'd done up till this point. Putting work aside, visiting Samantha in the hospital, and getting this far. The man in front of him put out his hand as if he wanted to shake his. So, in good faith, he did the same in a professional manor.

Scott stepped forwards and grabbed his hand right hand with a firm, strong grip. He folded his left hand over top of the grasp. Richard felt a warm flush run through his body from head to toe. A very strange sensation he'd never experienced before. What seemed to be a few minutes was merely ten seconds.

Nonetheless, a ten second firm handshake between two strangers in this day and age was extremely out of the ordinary. They released one another's grip on each other, and Scott took a step back.

"Ok, your cleared for entrance to suite 2D. I don't know what you're blocking from me, but I know you aren't here for any harm or malice. I also know it's vital to everyone, including myself, that I let you in. I don't understand it, but I'm never wrong about these things. I shall be sending an escort with you to announce you to Ms. Chastain, and your escort will wait outside the door to assist you in exiting the building. You are not allowed in any other area of the property for any reason, and you will check out with me when you are finished. I will have a taxi waiting for you."

Richard nodded his head and didn't say another word. He didn't want to press his luck, anyway.

Suddenly, another guard in a tuxedo was at their side, prompting Richard. "Please come with me, sir."

Richard looked straight forwards and followed the guard.

"See you soon," Scott spoke to Richard.

# CHAPTER 4

# Veronica

The new guard led Richard through the heavy glass doors after flashing his security badge in front of the door scanner. He could tell Scott was the only one with abilities. None of the other guards had any.

"Access Granted," an automotive voice said softly over the speaker system that was playing classical music. Tchaikovsky, if Richard was correct. "The Sleeping Beauty." One of his favourite pieces.

Walking in the building was everything he thought it would be. The double set of glass doors were clearly bulletproof. The marble floor looked like something he'd imagine would be inside Buckingham Palace.

A large waterfall stood in the centre of the lobby—a stunning sculpture that no doubt would have cost millions. No figures were in the fountains such as Greek Gods or angels, like those he'd seen and admired when touring parts of Europe. He loved being able to watch them be carved in his mind hundreds of years ago. This fountain was contemporary, yet sleek. Smooth round folds were carved out of the shiny marble-like substance.

The fountain had different facets of colour and different lights intricately placed within the art itself. It had five, or maybe six, directions in which the water flowed throughout each angle. The soothing sound of water relaxed you when you walked in, and the smell of the water hit your senses right away. Richard had visions of its construction. It was breathtaking, the amount of work that went into the piece.

There were no shops or stores in the building.

Dark smooth slabs of natural stone lined the walls from floor to ceiling behind the majestic water fountain. He couldn't read anything of the materials, meaning it had been mined from a source that mankind hadn't touched before its extraction.

The walls led to a wide corridor with only three elevators, one on each side of the hallway, and one at the end. The two on the sides were chrome, polished to perfection without a smudge or speck of dirt anywhere to be seen. The third, you could tell was special. It was platinum. Not shiny but smooth and regal. It was also behind another set of glass doors that required another security clearance. This time, a small laser placed at about shoulder level was used. There was also a plate with a hand shape on it at waist level.

*These must be for higher security levels*, he thought.

His chaperone walked sternly in front of him, leading him to the glass doors. He angled his head down toward the scanner, ensuring his eye was in line and his palm on the plate. They were to the right of the sliding glass doors. The glass door opened to the left, making a quiet swooshing sound, and they headed to the platinum elevator door. It opened immediately, seeming to be in sync with the security devices.

The two men entered the elevator where each floor was listed, only three to be exact. Each floor had a key hole to the left of the number sign. 2, 39, and 40. *Strange. Why did it have a lower floor and the other two were so high?* He said nothing of it while they rode the elevator to the second floor.

Richard waited for the guard to exit first and allowed for him to indicate the right direction. The guard went left off the elevator, heading down a rather long hallway. At the very end, he could see in bold lettering **2D**. Oddly enough, it was the only door in the hallway with numbers. The rest were blank.

They reached the suite, and the guard knocked softly on the door. The door was quickly opened by a young woman in a suit.

"Hello Sarah. Guest here to see Ms. Chastain."

The woman looked confused rather than concerned. "She is not expecting anyone. I know Scott called, but this is so—"

"He got clearance from the desk, Sarah. Scott scanned him personally."

Her eyes lit up with curiosity with that being said. "Alright. I will announce him. Please wait here." She then signaled to Richard to come inside the door.

"I will be waiting here until they are finished their business," spoke the guard to the young woman.

"Understood, thank you."

The door shut behind Richard.

The young woman walked down a hallway that was elegantly decorated to a large archway down the hall to the right. Richard didn't dare move. He'd come this close, nothing was going to wreck this chance.

Her high heels clicked down the hard surface of the halls, and Richard took in his surroundings. High ceilings with hidden lighting in the crown moldings. A few beautiful paintings hung on the perfectly painted walls. Nothing off-white like the walls of his home. No. Beautiful taupe and cream colours all over. Perfectly matched. No doubt a well sought after decorator was to thank for this space. Richard felt like he was in a home featured in interior design magazines. Maybe even a prizewinning space.

"Wow," Richard lightly said out loud.

He was so distracted that he hadn't heard Sarah come back down the hallway to him.

"She will see you now."

The young woman turned and walked down the hallway again, this time gesturing Richard to follow her. He kept pace behind the young woman, not too close yet not too far behind. Down the hall to the left was an even more impressive room. He took in more luxury and elegance—the room was simply stunning.

Richard felt his jaw drop as his eyes first landed on a painting that was no doubt meant to be the main focus of this room. He waited a few minutes and took in the sight of the valuable piece. He knew he was lucky to be seeing it in person, not just in a textbook or on a computer screen.

Richard felt overwhelmed with joy. He hadn't noticed he was speaking out loud. "It couldn't be—"

"Real?" Another woman's voice came from the side of the room.

She was sitting very comfortably on a large white sofa. A martini in hand. Richard was struck by seeing her after all these years. She had been out of the media's eye for some time now. No one had seen her. Age had been kind to Gloria's mother.

"Yes it is very real. A gift from a certain family member. I hate it. I look at it and see it for what it is."

"What's that?" asked Richard. "A historical masterpiece by Raphael?"

"Pfft. Raphael who. It's a bribe," said the woman sarcastically. "An offering to keep me held up here in privacy and keep to myself. If no one sees me, no one can bug HER about me." She took a big sip from her crystal martini glass. "Not that I needed it to keep to myself. I did always wonder what he could have been looking at."

Richard nodded, not sure how to reply.

"Mind telling me what you're doing here and how you got in? It's been four years since I moved up here, and you are sadly my first and only visitor."

"I was hoping to talk to you about—"

"Let me guess, Gloria?" She laughed while taking another big gulp from her elegant glassware.

"Yes, but it's not what you think."

"I've answered every question ever asked. Look at all the clips online. Dateline, 20/20. Even Walters came out of retirement to ask me questions in 2026. What else could you possibly want to know that I haven't already said?" Veronica was clearly annoyed.

"Well, I know I've kind of shown up here today, and I am at your mercy. You see, I want to talk to you about Gloria, but about her early years."

"How early . . ." she responded. Her eyes were becoming slits with venom spoken in each word.

"Kitchener, Southridge kind of early."

With that spoken, Veronica choked on her drink. She cleared her throat and looked at Richard. "So, how did you find me, anyways? I'd like to think Gloria covered all her tracks. I don't even know if you could find a photo from that time either. She had her minions see to that. No media, investigator or estranged fan has even seen me in over four years. I never leave the building."

"I ran into an old friend of yours."

A long, tense, silent minute followed.

"Let me guess, Samantha?" Veronica mustered while not seeming too impressed by the news.

"Yes. It wasn't easy to convince her to let me know where to find you. She even told me you refused to see her for the last few years. Something about an argument you had."

Veronica froze in place. "Well, no surprise here that she wanted to get back at me. I only told her where I was going as a courtesy. In case I died, I wanted someone to know where I was." The bitterness in her voice was even more apparent. "I think after you leave, I will have to have a little phone chat with Mrs. Kropf. Where is my old friend now, anyways?"

"I just saw her yesterday. She is at Grand River Hospital. It wasn't about getting back at you by any means. She is scared and wants to help. She is genuinely worried about you and misses you."

Veronica eased back into her seat and took a good look at Richard once more. "I see." She lost some hatred to her tone, but was not close to remorse. "So, tell me, I wouldn't even crack to Barbara all those years ago about those times, what makes you think I'm going to speak to you about those years?"

"Well, for starters, I want to say I am not a journalist. Anything you say to me will be said in the upmost confidence. If you'll allow me to, I can show you." Richard stood there, looking at her with the upmost respect and poise. "May I?" He pointed to a seat across from the sofa Veronica was on.

She nodded, looking at him cautiously.

Richard moved to the chair in front, and placed his briefcase on the coffee table that separated the two. As he got closer, he caught scent of her perfume. It reminded him of something he couldn't pin point. That didn't happened to him often. He clicked open the briefcase and pulled a file out. He opened the blue file folder and hander her one of three clipped stacks of paper.

"This is a legal document I had my lawyer prepare for you. It is a non-disclosure agreement. Anything said here today can never be documented or published in any way."

"You think I'd sign any of this nonsense without my lawyer reviewing it?"

"I expected nothing less from you, which I why I was pleased that Sarah is here today."

"How do you know she's my lawyer? How did you know my lawyer would be here?"

"I know someone of your stature would have your legal counsel be at your side at all times."

"Well done," she said while nodding very slightly. "Sarah!!" Veronica yelled.

Sarah came back into the room quickly. "Yes, Ms. Chastain?"

"Come read this document and tell me what you think. You aren't paid just to answer the door."

"Right away."

Sarah moved across the room and grabbed the documents to read over them quickly. Richard observed her as she did this. A very plain yet beautiful woman. She must have been about Richard's age. She did nothing to draw attention to herself. No makeup. Her hair in a neat and formal bun tied at the base of her neck. Her clothing was very simple. A tailored grey suit with a deep violet coloured shirt underneath. No jewelry to note of, and no wedding ring. She finished reading the document and looked up at Richard.

"It's precise and very well drafted. You must have a great law firm at your disposal," she spoke to Richard.

"One of the best in Toronto."

"Well ma'am, if you want to sign it, it's at your discretion. The dates mentioned in the agreement are what concern me. They are of a very sensitive nature. Just remember though that Gloria doesn't like when—"

"Well, she isn't here! And hasn't been for four years if I do say so!" Veronica took the last sip that remained in her crystal martini glass. "You're here to help ME, not her!" Veronica put down her empty glass and took a deep breath.

Sarah looked poised and not bothered by the sudden harshness from Veronica. Richard tried to read her, but he could not see anything out of the ordinary. He could see that she majored in law, and was very well educated. She clearly lived here with Veronica full-time and was simply a glorified assistant.

"Alright, I'll sign. But before I do, I want to know why you want to go down that road and I want an honest answer. A truthful answer. Many came before you and wanted to know about those years. Many dug, asked old classmates and teachers, but she always beat them. She had them all too scared to speak of what little they remembered. Those that were foolishly not afraid, were quickly made to be after a visit from her team and their deep pockets."

Richard made note of the tone she used on that.

"Anyone who couldn't be persuaded were paid off. So, it better be for a good reason. Not the trivial fluff I've heard before—she's so great, we just want to get to know her life better . . . blah blah blah. And just know, if I don't like what I hear, I'll have you thrown out of here so fast you won't know what happened!"

Richard meant business and this didn't scare him at all.

"I'm here because I need to know about her as deeply and as intimately as I can. I need knowledge of any private facts to get to her. We're in a lot of trouble here, and I don't mean maybe."

"We?"

"I think you know what I'm talking about. Every newscast, every news feed on every social media platform. It's all that the world is talking about. I'm scared, just as I'm sure you are. She's the only one who can find what they're all looking for. Many have tried, and no one is even close. It has to be her. There is no other way."

With that, Veronica arched her brows in curiosity. "I understand why you need her for that, but why do you need me to get to her?"

"You more than anyone should know how she is now. Surrounded at all times by security and sensors. They'd feel most people coming a mile away. But, there is a plan to get to her and when we do, we have to show her the past. Remind her of what she once was. No one has ever gone this deep into her past, and it will let her see times that she is suppressing. Maybe, just maybe when she reconnects with her old self, she'll agree to help. She was very different before the Coleman case, and you know it. It changed her, scared her of her own abilities. That's why she turned from a path of helping society to just being another piranha on TV. She accomplished so much, and then just stopped caring. If I'm going to have any shot to even get into the same room with her, I need to have ammunition to get there. And even when I get there, I need her to know how far I came, and I need her to be reminded of what she's blocking out."

"That is the most honest answer I've ever been given. But, I'm not sure it's going to get you what you want. She doesn't even come to see me, let alone allow some nobody in off the street to try and talk sense to her."

"She'll listen, she has to. She is our last hope if what the media is saying is true. How many lives could be lost if we don't at least try?"

"Do you want a drink Mr.—"

"Richard, please. Call me Richard. And, I'd love a drink."

"Sarah, please get me a fresh martini, and Richard here may have whatever he wants."

Sarah handed the document to Veronica and a pen she had in her jacket pocket. She grabbed her empty martini glass. She turned to Richard and asked what he would like to drink.

"Scotch, single malt. Neat. Don't be shy with it either."

Richard watched as Veronica signed the documents and handed him his copies back. Sarah returned with their drinks and collected her copy of the signed agreements.

"Will there be anything else, ma'am?"

"Call Scott downstairs and tell him everything is fine and to send the guard outside back down. I don't need him breaking in here to save the day when there is no issue."

"Yes, ma'am," Sarah said and proceeded to leave the room.

"And Sarah, keep the drinks coming. This is going to be a long day."

"Of course, Ms. Chastain." With that, Sarah nodded and left the room promptly.

"Ask away, Richard, ask away."

He leaned back in his chair with his scotch in hand, looked deeply at Veronica, and smiled a wicked smile.

"First off, tell me why the second floor in this building. And second, tell me about Gloria's father."

## CHAPTER 5

# The Beginning

A sinister laugh blurted from Veronica's mouth. "You don't waste any time, do you!"

"I don't have time to waste," replied Richard, sneering with content.

"Which is more important to you? Knowing why I live on the second floor or Gloria's father?"

"Curiosity killed the cat," Richard chuckled. He knew a joke would help Veronica to laugh and open up a little. He was also legitimately curious.

"Look, my daughter pays $25,000 a month just in fees for me to live in this fortress of solitude. To protect her privacy, she doesn't want me to see or be seen. If she was forcing me here, what was a $10,000,000 donation to the building owner's charity fund going to hurt her to make the VIP elevator have one more stop? Plus, I can't help it. I hate heights."

Richard's face must have shown his shock. *$25,000 month? That was seven times the amount of the average condo fees!*

She smirked like she had no cares in the world.

Richard took a sip of scotch and said, "Well played, Ms. Chastain." He let out a little laugh to have with her. "Very nice, by the way. What is this? I don't think I've had this scotch before."

"I'm not really sure. It has 63, or no. 64 is on the bottle. Whatever that is." She said as she waived her hands in the air.

"Damore 64 Trinitas??!!! Well . . . thank you! I've never had the pleasure of even trying it!"

"Did you come here to compliment my bar? No." Veronica sounded more annoyed than ever. "Well, now let's get to the other subject. It's the one thing I hoped you wouldn't ask, and it's the one I've been dreading. In all these years, I've never spoken to anyone, ANYONE about him."

Richard nodded and moved on. "Where did you meet him?"

"Are you sure you need to know this? There is so much more I could tell you about her years at Southridge that will make this story seem so irrelevant."

"Veronica, please. I need every bit of personal small details to put into her mind before she shuts me out. If one of her sensors pick up on a memory of her father, or her before the age of 10 they'll want to speak to me. To give me even five minutes to explain how much we need her help is going to take a LOT. And you know as well as I do, everyone depends on it. Look at the news. We need her gift. She will push it off until she can see clearly. I need personal deep facts to argue with her to give me those five minutes."

Veronica nodded and knew what he was saying was true. She avoided the news on purpose as it terrified her to see what was going on in the world. 2020 looked like child's play when you compared it to the news now.

Veronica got up from her seat. She walked over to a beautiful bay window that overlooked the meticulously kept grounds. She stared out blankly for a moment and then closed her eyes. She pressed her hand against the glass, and Richard noticed a sparkle from a stunning emerald ring adorned on her index finger. She paused a moment and then began to speak.

"Many secrets were hidden behind locked household doors in suburbia in the 60s and 70s. We just didn't understand, until much later, what monsters where lurking in the dark.

"Gloria was like a flashlight that could not only see behind doors, she could see through them. A lot of people weren't ready for what she would show us. Many couldn't accept things she had shown us. Not then, and that's still true today.

"I wish I could have comprehended the foreshadowing of what her dreams were telling her. What she tried to tell me. Warn me. It would have made the truth less earth-shattering when I realized what could have been saved. Who could have been saved! Had I just listened to her! And what upsets me most? There was no one else to listen to her then. No. It was me. Only me. Maybe Cathy. But, I truly didn't know, or especially understand, what I was hearing at the time."

She opened her eyes and stared out the window again. Richard looked at her and didn't speak. He could sense her emotions coming to the surface. Things she hadn't felt for years. He couldn't believe she was seventy-nine and looked as good as she did.

"I thank God all the time for who I met in those years. They were trivial to her becoming. I was not capable of sending her on that path. Not alone.

"There are things from those times I'm sure that I'm suppressing. Things the mind was never meant to live out once, let alone form a memory. I've learned that much. Your mind will block what you're not supposed to know. Things that are too painful to relive.

"What I went through, what I survived . . . I really don't know if I could have done it without her. She was, and always will be, an integral part of my life. While she grew up, so did I. And fast. I had to. For her. And, despite my age I remember things so vividly. They've been on replay in my head for so long."

"Knowing how important she was. The role she played for all of us up until this point. Thinking about what she might possibly do for everyone now. I'd like to think I would do every step the same again in a heartbeat. But, I can't say that without hesitation. No one could."

Veronica turned around and walked back over to her huge, perfectly white sofa. She sat directly in front of Richard again.

"Well, let me be perfectly clear. It's been years since this all happened. It all happened so quickly and in such a short period of time. Things like this didn't happen a lot back then. I was only fifteen at the time." Veronica paused and peered up at Richard with a grimacing face.

"I was fifteen years old. When I say it aloud, even I can believe it's been so long." She sat back into the plushness of her elegant sofa.

"I'll begin at the beginning as I knew it. As I lived it. There is no other way to tell my story. For some reason, I feel like I know you, I feel comfortable. Have we met?"

Richard shifted in his seat a little. "Me? No, I did not grow up around here. I am from Cambridge."

"Oh, well. My mistake."

"I appreciate anything you will share with me, Ms. Chastain." Richard nodded encouragingly.

"So, this is my story. Of how Gloria came to be my daughter, before she was the most validated psychic in history. The most sought after psychic in the world." She took a small pause. "I was born here in Kitchener. In 1947, my parents had moved here from out West, Victoria, BC. My father got a good job managing a leather factory called Tanners. He moved his young wife here, and shortly after getting settled, they decided to start a family. I came along in 1952, a younger sibling to my older brother, Harold. We grew up in small division of housing that was very suburban on Blucher Street. Rows of houses with lots of trees. On the outside, we seemed like a nice normal family. Living out the dream as some might say. But, illusions are easy to portray when people aren't looking. On the outside, we looked happy. Kept up the façade. I don't know if I could have survived my young life in today's world. Today's world scares me as much as the next person."

"I agree with you completely. The modern world is a scary place for young minds."

Richard meant what he said. Working in psychology for over thirty years, he'd seen a lot of minds. The memories of people who grew up in the 70s were very different compared to those who grew up in the 2010s. Technology made the world a different place. For better, and for worse.

Veronica nodded and took another sip of her martini. "I guess a good place to start is when I was fifteen. The year was 1967. Life up until that point was nothing worth noting, at least not as far as Gloria is concerned. I went to school, helped my mother around the house and didn't go out much. My father, was . . . if it wasn't for my mother . . ."

What flashed in Veronica's mind made Richard feel uneasy. Memories like that always did. He focused on her words to flush out the images that had just run through his head.

"Our family seemed typical to those living on our block. Dad went to work, mom stayed home with the kids. Pretty ordinary. But, behind the walls of that house was chaos. I lived on egg shells. Walking down a hallway was like walking on a patch of grass filled with landmines. There was only one certainty about my life as a very young woman, my father. My father never made it a secret that he didn't like his life. His patterns reflected the bitterness he held in his heart. His routine was always on schedule. It never occurred to him how it affected his family, especially my mother."

"I'd say his pattern of routine, if you will, began on Fridays. Friday, he'd come right home from work. His factory shift was weekdays until 2 p.m., and he'd always be home before my brother and I finished school. But, Fridays were special. You see, he didn't drink during the week. This made him a good father in his eyes. Despite the sober misery he all made us suffer through with him during the week, you can bet he let us know how hard his week was come Friday."

"On Fridays, he would stop on his way home for his usual. A case of beer, a bottle of whiskey . . . or three. Then, of course, his cigarettes. A carton of Canadas Finest French. I can still see the red box he'd set on the counter. Life at the Miller house on Fridays were exceptionally special. My mother would spend all day cleaning the house beyond anything normal. You could eat off the floors. Not that it mattered how clean or perfect she made it. My father would come home and surely make his presence known. Nitpicking the smallest thing, on edge like he was ready for an attack. Strange, as he did most of the attacking."

The dark memory formed in Richard's mind. He could see her father, clearly intoxicated, yelling at her mother. He was grabbing her by the arm and screaming so loud in her face that Richard could see the drops of spit.

*"Clare, what the fuck did you use to clean the floor? Turpentine?? Are you trying to wreck the house I pay for?! That I slave all day at my job for?!?!?"*

Richard had to mentally focus harder. Not to let in all her violent memory images in wasn't easy. They could be sharper in one's mind because of fear. Luckily the longer he spent with Veronica, the more control he had at images he would see in his head. The more time spent with an individual, the better. It usually only took a few hours with new patients. If he let in every image, he could be overwhelmed. The human mind was a busy place to look into if you weren't in control.

"I was usually in school Fridays, but the odd day home sick gave me the displeasure of witnessing firsthand how my father was before I'd normally be home from school. I only stayed home if I was sick on my death bed. Never missing for a common cold. I even went to school with the flu if I had a fever I could tolerate. I joined every school activity that kept me later, especially if it was on a Friday. I joined any social club that kept me from going home."

Richard sensed how vulnerable she felt sharing this. He needed to say something comforting.

"I'm sorry this is so painful. Please, take your time. Tell me what you can."

Veronica nodded her head and took a deep breath.

"I didn't hate my father, not at first. But I didn't love him the way a daughter should. So angry at the world. He didn't like his life. Married, two children. I never understood why. He made decent money at the factory. We never went without. We even had a summer cottage in northern Ontario."

"I didn't like our cottage. The cottage was where dad would really let loose. He'd get so drunk and take off roaming the wilderness for hours. The wait for him to return was so stressful. You never knew what his state of mind would be when he got back. Sometimes he was ok, he'd just come back and keep to himself and then go pass out. But more often, he'd come back enraged but still keep to himself. He'd be screaming gibberish that didn't make sense and throw and break his beer bottles. I never paid attention to what he was saying, but later I would learn to regret that."

"Is that what happened a lot?"

"A leopard can't change its spots, Richard." She paused for another sip of her martini. "Most girls learn love, respect and care from their fathers. Not me. Anger. Rage. Hatred. Sadly, all these things I learned from him. But what I learned most from him? Fear. The sense of pure terror."

Richard knew he needed to push her along. He didn't want to seem insensitive, but he tried to keep the conversation flowing. "What about your mother?"

"My mother?" Veronica's face lit up but was still washed in sadness. "She was a good mom. She did the best she could."

"Did she ever hurt you?"

"God no. Never!"

The sharpness in her voice and flash of memories let Richard understand. She was a good woman with a horrible husband.

"Did she condone what was going on? Why wouldn't she take you and your brother and leave?"

"My mom stayed. It was a long time ago. She didn't know how to get a job. She didn't know how to get a place on her own. Deep down, I know to this day that she stayed because she thought he would change. My father's rage grew as I grew, and he started showing his interest in violence toward me. But, my mom never stopped trying to take it for me. That was my mother's part in our usual Family Friday. Clean the house all day. She prepared everything. Tried to avoid anything that would give him a reason to go off. But it never mattered, he always went off on her. She truly thought she was doing the best thing for us. She tried to hide it. Cover it up. Sometimes with makeup, other times a hairstyle. Distract us. But I was old enough. I'd seen and heard my mother cry in pain and terror more than any young girl should ever have to witness."

Richard could feel the emotions getting so strong in Veronica. "You don't have to go on if you don't want to, Ms. Chastain. If it's too painful, let's move on."

"No. I can't. I think you need to understand where I was and what was happening in my world then. What's truly sad to me is that the diabolic things I witnessed from my father were just preparation for the things I would endure with Gloria. The things she would show us all scare me more than anything."

Richard opened up once more to let her memories in. He felt the hairs on his arm rise.

"One particular set of events happened right before the end of the school year in 1967. My father would get this way every year around this time, knowing that school was almost over for the year. That my brother and I would be home a lot more. He didn't like that. Especially on *his* Fridays. So it was late May. I remember that as it was the Victoria Day holiday. We went to our cottage that weekend every year and opened it up for the summer. There was always some minor winter damage that he wasn't too pleased about having to fix. A cottage then was a real cottage. No plumbing, barely electricity. We were able to get a phone line out which was rare. And we had a wood burning stove for cooking and keeping warm. Rustic is a good word to describe it."

"So after we got home on the holiday Monday, he went on about about all the work he had to do all week. By the time the following Friday came around, I knew things weren't going to be good. He was the same every year.

"That day after school, I stayed as late as I could. I finished class at 2:45 p.m., and I ended up finishing all my homework in the library. Unfortunately, I didn't have much as the school year was almost over. Around 4:30 p.m., I headed home. I took the long walk home and went as slow as possible. As I walked up to the driveway of my childhood home, I remember taking a moment to look at our house. It was quiet. So quiet. I hated it when it was quiet. I braced myself and walked up to the door. My father, who always sat at the dining room table, was in his usual seat. Our dining room was to the right from our front door in our home, through our living room. The kitchen was attached to the dining room. A common design in homes built around then. I walked in and saw my father's back. His room temperature case of beer at his feet. He drank it so fast that going to the refrigerator had become a chore."

"I tried as quietly as I could to shut the door and head to my room, but he heard the door close despite my best efforts."

*"Who's that?"* Veronica's father turned around abruptly in his chair. *"Oh, it's you."*

*"Hi, dad. I'm going to my room. I have a lot of homework to do."*

*"Not so fast. Come here."*

She could see him taking deep, laboured breaths. One of his putrid traits he portrayed when exceptionally drunk.

Her skin crawled as she took off her jacket and shoes in the front hallway closet and walked over to the dining table. As she came around the corner, I saw broken glass from a beer bottle that he had thrown at the wall."

*"Oh my God, dad. What happened?!"* Veronica looked down to make sure she hadn't stepped on any.

*"It's nothing. Your mother was just an idiot, that's all."* He grabbed Veronica's arm firmly and jerked her in closer. *"You're not an idiot, are you, Roni?"*

*"No, dad."* She always froze when he pulled her in like that.

Within seconds, her mother came running into the room. She had fresh bruises she had tried to cover with her usual makeup.

*"Roni, when did you get home? How was your day?"*

Veronica could see she was shaking. She grabbed her from her father and took her through their living room down the hall to the television set.

*"Sweetie, why don't you sit here and relax. Dinner will be ready in an hour."*

Her mother turned on the box television and put the volume to the highest possible setting.

*"I'd rather go to my room, mom."*

*"Honey, I have to clean that broken glass. It's not safe for you to walk around the house. Will you just sit her for a while? For me? Your brother will be home soon if I need a hand with it."*

"But I wasn't a fool. I knew what was going on. She wanted me here in front of the TV she had set to full volume so I wouldn't hear my parents argue."

*"What happened mom?"* Veronica reached out to her mother's face, worried about yet another bruise.
*"Oh, that's nothing dear. Just your mother being a klutz. You know how easily I bruise, Roni."*
*"Ok, mom."*
*"Thanks, dear. I owe you."*

"She left me in the TV room, but I could still hear everything. She cleaned up the glass my father smashed while he called her foul names. She'd be submissive and apologize for something HE did, and he'd still go after her. Whenever he mentioned coming to watch TV with me, she'd intervene and start another fight. She kept his attention and anger on her. It was all she knew how to do to keep us from him."

"How did that make you feel?"

"Me feel? At fifteen? I thought she was an idiot. For years, I partly resented her. But in the end, I loved her like a daughter should."

"That's seems normal." Richard had to remind himself she was not his patient and not to treat her that way.

"Did you feel safe?"

"Safe? I don't think I understood the word. I knew as well as my mother did that my father was a ticking time bomb. And the more things went on, the worse it got for my mother. We had locks on the outside of our bedroom doors when we were little. She put them in to keep us away when he got very violent. She didn't want a toddler wandering down the hall, curious to see what the noise was. As I got older, she stopped. She knew that I knew better than to come downstairs when he was in the middle of an episode. Anxiety was a feeling I was all too familiar with in my youth."

"More episodes like that happened every Friday until the end of the school year. My mother thought she was able to hide his known interest in not just hitting her but beating her down. I learned more than enough swear words and dirty degrading names to call someone. Enough for two lifetimes. All from my father. I don't know what was worse for her, getting hit—or what he'd say to her."

"Those few weeks passed, and summer break was finally upon us. It was time for our Canada Day week at the cottage. A few days leading up to it, my father's usual Friday night binge became a weeklong event. He had been off work for holidays for us to go away. He typically got six weeks off a year. I remember that because that's when he was a full-time drunk. Two weeks at Christmas, one week at spring break, and three weeks in the summer. We were set to leave for the cottage on Wednesday, and Canada Day was that Saturday. By Tuesday that week, he had drank a few cases of beer and was onto his second bottle of whiskey. I tried to keep out the house as much as possible."

"I kept busy with friends, and jumped at the chance for a sleepover any time I could. That Tuesday, I tried to sleep at my friend Martha's house. She and I had been friends since the 3rd grade. I didn't have her over to my house often, afraid of what could transpire. If she ever did come to the house, it was always a weekday night during the school year. My dad's usual night in front of the TV was very tame compared to how he got on weekends. That was only because, as you remember, he didn't drink on weekdays. I always thought it's what made him exceptionally angry on weekends. Like he saved it up. Anyways, my mother said I could go, but my father overheard."

Veronica was at the front door with an overnight bag in her hand.

*"Roni, just be home for 9 a.m. tomorrow. Your dad wants to get going to the cottage early. Love you, sweetie."*

*"Bye, mom. I love you too."* She reached around and gave her a bear hug. A sweet moment that didn't last long.

*"What the fuck? Where do you think she's going?"* Veronica's dad was right behind her mother. Neither of them noticed him sneak up.

*"Honey, please watch your language. It's fine. Roni is just going to Martha's for a sleepover. She's packed and all ready to go tomorrow."*

*"And you didn't ask me first?"*

He brushed past her mother and came right at Veronica. He grabbed her by both arms and pushed her against the door. She felt her head clock very hard in the back.

*"We're supposed to go away tomorrow. As a family. I don't work shifts at the plant so you can all run amuck and just come and go as you please. This is bullshit!!"*

*"Dad I'm just—"*

*"Don't you dad me."*

Veronica could remember the look on his face. She had never been that scared in her entire life. *At least, up until that point.* Her father was no small man. He stood 6'3" which was incredibly tall then.

Richard made a mental note on how she added *until that point*.

*"You—get your ass upstairs now. And as for you—"*

He turned to her mother Clare with uncontrollable rage. She tried to hide how terrified she was and tried to comfort Veronica.

*"Honey, just go upstairs."* She hugged Veronica again and whispered into her ear, *"I'll calm him down and get you out of here. Just give me a few minutes."*

"My mom had a look of fear I'd never seen before. It sent chills down my spine.

"I went upstairs. As I entered the room, I passed my older brother's room. I recall wishing I was him, older. Old enough to go out at night like he did. He knew staying out late was his best chance to avoid that drunken bastard. As I shut my door, I tried to not listen to what was going on downstairs. But, it was hard not to. My father knocked over some furniture, while my mother tried to calm him down. I'd hear her body hit the floor as he yelled at her some more. I just laid on my bed and cried. So scared and not sure what to do. I wish I could have helped her.

"After a few minutes, I noticed everything downstairs had gotten quiet. I hated quiet. I went into the fetal position on my bed and closed my eyes. What I wouldn't have given to be somewhere, anywhere but there. I felt hopeless and afraid. I knew my father was getting worse, but I just didn't know how much worse he would get. I must have zoned out because it startled me when my mom came into my room."

*"Roni? You ok?"*

*"Mom, what was that? Are you—"*

*"Baby, I'm fine. I'm fine. Your dad just had a bad day."*

*"Mom, why do you make excuses?"*

*"Roni, your father's not perfect, but he provides for us. You don't know how lucky we are."*

*"But—"*

*"Roni. Don't. I'm not in the mood. Anyways, I convinced your dad to let you go to Martha's."*

*"Mom, are you sure you don't want me to stay here? Stay with you?"*

*"Actually, that's another thing I wanted to talk to you about. I think you should stay back while we go to the cottage."*

Veronica was in shock. While deep inside she knew there was nothing she wanted more.

*"But mom—"*

*"Honey. Don't argue. I think it would be good for you to stay here and watch the house. It's supposed to storm this weekend, and you could bring in my plants and close the shutters. I will*

*have Martha's mom keep an eye on you of course. I'll call her in the morning."*

"Mom, are you sure? You sure you'll be alright?"

*"Oh, don't be silly. I'll be fine. But will you stay? For me?"*

"What about Harold?"

*"Oh, you know him. He'll come and take off in the boat to look for girls. So don't worry, he'll be around. And besides, I'm fine. I promise."*

"She looked so intensely at me. I know she did it for me. She saw my father come at me for the first time and it scared her. He was getting worse. My brother was big enough now to defend himself if that ever happened."

Richard agreed. Her father was getting worse. He could see the torment in her mother's eyes from what she showed him. Her mother wanted to protect her.

"So, I didn't say anything and I nodded. As I came down the stairs and saw the aftermath, the reality was very different than what my mother had made me believe. She didn't talk to my dad. He passed out. He was slumped over in some chair, his half-empty beer bottle dripping over the floor beneath him. I didn't say anything to my mother about it. I kissed her goodbye and left for Martha's. At Martha's that night, I didn't breathe a word about what had happened."

"The next morning, I laid awake next to Martha and couldn't help but wonder if my mother would change her mind. It was only 7:30 a.m. and we were supposed to leave no later than 9 a.m. I was honestly worried about her too. All of a sudden, I heard the phone ring. It was in the kitchen that was directly below Martha's bedroom."

"Hello? Oh hi, Clare, how are you?"

(silence)

"This weekend? Well, it's kind of short notice. Bill and I are going to his boss's house for a BBQ on Saturday. His house is at the edge of town where some fireworks are happening."

(silence)

"Well, I have no problem. She can stay here as much as she likes. But what about the weekend? Is Aaron ok with this?"

(silence)

"You're sure? Ok. Gosh. It's sad to think how big these girls are getting!"

(silence)

"Oh, hon. I've got the phone number. And I'm sure things will be fine. I'll let her know when the girls get up. Did you want her to come say goodbye?"

(silence)

"Okay, Clare. I'll see you on Monday, ok? We'll have a coffee."

(silence)

"Okay then, bye for now. Oh, and Clare, Happy Canada day."

# CHAPTER 6

# Canada Day

"I heard her hang up the phone and I drifted back to sleep. My body was awash with relief knowing I didn't have to be around my father."

"So your parents left you behind?"

"I'd more say my mother made me stay behind. I was really nervous but also a little excited. After all, I was fifteen and home alone for the first time. It would be the first real break I'd had from my abusive father's antics, and I was going to live every moment as best I could. And, like I said earlier, my father was on his best drunken behaviour while at the cottage, so I HOPED my mother would be safe.

"When I woke up and left Martha's, her mother made me promise to call after I checked on the house. I walked over to my house down the block and let myself in. It was strange yet exhilarating to be home alone. I looked over at where my father would sit at the dining room table and sighed a huge sigh of relief seeing it sit empty. I walked around to the kitchen and found a note. My mother's handwriting. No doubt she wrote something that my father would read over. It said—"

*Hi honey,*

*Betty phoned me this morning. I'm so sorry you're sick and will miss the cottage this weekend. She assured me you'll be there most of the time. Please make sure my plants are ok, and you shut the windows if it storms. Here is a little spending money for the weekend. There is some frozen leftovers in the freezer you can heat up if you get hungry. I hope you're feeling better, and we'll be home sometime on Monday.*

*Love, mom.*

"Were you upset they went without you?"

"Not at all. I was always pretty independent growing up. I had to be. My mom had her hands full, and dad was mentally checked out most of the time. In reality, being alone was a blessing. Martha's mother was so busy with the four children she had, she didn't notice I wasn't there most of the time. I was fifteen, not five."

Richard sat quietly across from Veronica. He focused on her memories she was looking through.

"As you can imagine, a teenager on their own tend to get restless. Martha and I went downtown to hang out and meet other friends. We met up at a coffee shop that was right by this appliance store, what was it? B something."

"Bullas?" Richard blurted out.

"Bullas. Bullas. Yes, that sounds right. How did you know that? Did you grow up around here? Actually, no. That doesn't even matter. You're too young to have known such a place."

Richard felt a rush of panic. He couldn't tell her that he could see it in her conscience. He rarely let anyone know about his abilities.

"Oh, I think I remember my parents telling me about that place. Anyways, go on?" He pressed a little compulsion on her. Not too much that she'd feel it later. Compulsion when used too heavily can leave a person confused when it clears.

"Yes. As I was saying. Martha and I got along just fine. We went to these lush gardens downtown that had some of the most stunning sculptures I'd seen at that point. Beautiful sea maidens entwined with elegant fish creatures. I remember them capturing my imagination as a young girl. I was sad when they tore up that part of downtown, but I was happy the city saved them. You can see them at the local art gallery in Centre in the Square now. That's Kitchener's biggest entertainment venue. I would love to visit them but, whatever."

"Now, I loved Martha and her family, but I was happy to spend time alone at home after a few days. The first night I stayed home was a hot summer night. June 30th, 1967. I remember the date as it was the last night of my old life."

"I woke up on July 1st around 9 a.m. I remember the silence, a rare moment of peace in my life. A sensation that was new to me. Usually, Saturday mornings were spent avoiding my father and trying to keep busy for my mother. Again, she always thought if we were distracted, we wouldn't let the reality of my father being a raging alcoholic set in. I went downstairs after brushing my teeth and getting dressed. I was eager to get out of the house that day. I decided to go for a walk after breakfast. I quickly ate some eggs and toast. After cleaning up, I headed to the front door to grab my shoes."

In the memory, Richard could see her walk through her childhood home. He always had a special fondness of memories of this era. The nostalgic perception he got of times past was truly unique. He could never describe how amazing it was to see the world and a time past from someone else's point of view. He always wondered if that was why he didn't like to tell people of his gifts. He never knew how to put into words what he could do. Being a man of medicine, he didn't like not being able to conclusively describe something.

Back in the memory, Veronica stopped at the front door to look into a beautiful antique mirror that was popular in those days. It was oval and hung on the wall to the right of her front door. There was sunbeam shaped plaster that spiked out all around the mirror, painted in a cheap gold paint. In the mirror, she glared at the reflection and didn't appreciate it. She was what he liked to call a classic beauty. Old Hollywood. Rich golden brown hair with soft tones of blond. It hung with natural waves and curls past her shoulders. Her big brown eyes were bright and catching.

"I grabbed my bag and keys and headed out of the house. I turned to lock the door and I started to walk toward downtown. My family lived a quick walk to the downtown core. Are you familiar with old downtown Kitchener, Richard?"

"I know some of the basics. I mostly grew up in Cambridge, but we came to downtown Kitchener often in my later teen years in the early 80s."

"Well, the 60s Kitchener was vastly different from what you might remember. By the 80s, this city grew a lot. In my time, your neighbourhood was like your own little world. You knew everyone in your area, and they knew you. You grew up together as small tight-knit community. I went to grade school with the same group of kids I went to high school with. While we never went without, we weren't super wealthy like the families that lived on old Margaret Avenue. Did you ever see the old homes there before the city tore them down?"

"Can't say that I did."

"That's too bad. They were stunning. They were some of the most majestic home built in the city. They really did live up to the title of Mansion. Had the city waited just a few years, I can't help but think they would still be standing today. No homes today in this area will ever compare. A few rumours had it over the years that they were torn down illegally. Such a waste."

Richard could see the houses she remembered. He had to agree, such a shame. They were monuments of craftsmanship and really would have added character to the city.

"I lived in a small area of houses near our train station. The area was very industrial once you left our neighbourhood. I lived on a small street named Blucher Street. Our house was large, but one thing I particularly loved about our house was our backyard. It was much bigger than most of the other houses' yards in our area. My dad once said that originally the city was going to put in a street, but the city planners decided against it. Only a few houses on our street were blessed with extra property. But who knows."

"I walked down a few side streets and through some shortcuts the local kids had made until I hit King Street. King was the main street of our downtown core since it was founded. I went left to head toward most of the shops. I wanted to go to a few book stores, check out this now long gone department store named Budds, and then make my way to this little coffee shop by Bullas store's gardens. I had completely forgotten that almost everything would be closed for the holiday."

"I went to enjoy my sculptures. Being there just made me happy. It was a favourite little spot of me and my girlfriends. This was my first time, however, being there alone. Sitting there with no one to talk to, I actually had a chance to watch people and their families as they walked by. Children with both their mothers and fathers strolled by. They made looking like a functioning family effortless. I always questioned if they were as happy as they seemed, or if their happy-go-lucky attitude in public was a bit of a façade, much like the one my own family put out when we did anything. None of my friends knew what life was really like at home. I have my mother to thank for that mostly.

"As I sat there and enjoyed a day of solitude and peace, I took in how quiet downtown was. It was after all a holiday weekend, and most people were busy having family get-togethers like BBQs, or were off to their summer homes, or to see family out of town. Kitchener had a lot to offer, but we weren't near a lake or any sort of summer attractions to keep local people here at that time of year. The sun was bright and hot that day. I watched bees feed from flowers, kids riding by on their bicycles, and people just out walking. I remember watching a few people sitting next to the road and saw all their heads turn at once. It took a moment to come into my view, but then I saw why. I could hear an engine coming down Charles Street that day and I'll never forget it. Once it passed some buildings and came into view, I saw a royal blue car. Not just any car. It sticks out so much in my memory as no one I knew in the city had a car like that. Most of the vehicles around here were not flashy. Simple beige or black colours. Family cars. This was not like that. Everyone within an eye's view shared my marvel. *Who was that?* I wondered, *and why are they here?* In my head, I just kept thinking to myself, *now if I had that car, I would be on a beach or something. Not in downtown Kitchener.* Just as quickly as it drove past the block, it was gone. I could overhear the few people around me talking."

*"Did you see that? Holy cow, that was incredible!"*

In the memory, Richard was able to pick up more details than Veronica's memory told her. Another kid by the road, must have been in his late teens, spoke up—

*"No way. I can't believe it. That was a Chevy Camero RS/SS. It must be right out of the factory!! Standard 5-speed transmission. They use those in the Grand Prix! I bet whoever owns that is going to race it at Mosport Park in August!!!"*

Richard was internally nodding his head. This kid knew his stuff. While Richard was a mild race car fanatic, another part of his gift was a photographic memory. If he saw a date or place, he could remember it as easily as snapping his fingers. That was the Grand Prix of '67 racing in Canada. He'd read about it in high school.

"I can see how unusual it would seem to see such a flashy car when you were so young."

"It was. Like I said, I knew everyone in my area, and no one who had a car had one like that. But, while Kitchener wasn't that big, you didn't really know anyone from other parts of town. If you went to a different high school then I did, you might as well be going to school in another province. And, being fifteen, I was even more just stuck in my little bubble."

"So, despite the holiday, my favourite coffee shop on that block was open, but I wanted to go for a walk before I went in. The coffee shop was on Charles Street, and it was only a block to our city park called Victoria Park. I sat up and headed toward the entrance just behind the appliance store. The gardens were just so beautiful then as they are now. What I miss is that it was little more unkempt then. More natural. You really felt like you could get lost, despite being surrounded by old houses that were built before the wars. I loved coming to the park just to escape my home sometimes, but I was usually with friends. Today, I got to relic in the solace of being alone. I walked from one end of the park to the far end, reaching a side street. I decided to turn around and head back to the coffee shop. Out of the corner of my eye, I saw the same royal blue car drive by me. At the time, I thought nothing of it."

"I arrived at the shop and got myself a drink. I sat down at a table with four chairs by the front window and grabbed an old magazine from the shelf at the front door. I read through the magazine, mostly looking at the pictures, and I was still looking out the window for people watching. The day was hot and muggy, and I was a little exhausted from the heat. After a few sips of my drink, I noticed how dry my lips where. I knew I had stashed a lip balm in my bag and realized how desperately I needed it. I reached into my bag which sat on the chair beside me. I fumbled around in my bag like I had a million times before and felt my hand grip one of my prized possessions at the time. My Bonne Belle lip gloss. I wasn't allowed to wear makeup yet, but this was a compromise I had with my mother. One of the first and only pieces of makeup I was allowed to wear. I started to pull it out of my bag and suddenly fumbled it to the ground. 'Clumsy, Roni,' I said out loud. I pushed my chair back and reached down for it, and when I came back up to the table, I almost fell out of my chair."

Richard could see it all, but wanted her to express things in her own words. "What did you see?"

"I sat up and saw the most gorgeous boy I'd ever seen. I stared into the brightest, blues eyes I'd ever look into. They looked like the ocean with flicks of green and gold. His hair was a rich dark brown, almost black. It was smooth and shiny, all neatly in place except a small piece that fell into his face. It took my breath away. I sat there in a state of shock and was certain he had the wrong table. Like a deer in headlights, I froze in terror, thinking that any move I'd make would scare this stunning creature before me."

"We sat in awkward silence for what was probably seconds, but felt like minutes. I didn't know what to say and had no idea why he was sitting with me. He was the first to break the tension with the most beautiful voice I'd ever heard."

*"Well, are you just going to sit there, or are you going to tell me your name?"*

"Me?" Veronica was in denial. No way was this person here to talk to her.

Richard looked at this boy in her mind and had to agree, he was the definition of attractive. Chiseled jaw, rather muscular, but still just a young kid like she was. He was staring at Veronica the way Richard noticed a lot of passersby looked at her. She was truly beautiful and had no idea how the outside world saw her.

*"Well, you are the only person at this table, aren't you?"*

She was still dumbstruck. Words would not come out. She literally felt like she forgot the English language. She tried to calm her nerves—she shifted in her seat and put on the lip gloss anyway.

He laughed again. She thought he was making fun of her and grabbed her bag. She was thinking about making a run for the door. She had little to no experience with the opposite sex.

*"Wait! Please!"* He reached his hand over the table and gestured for her to stop. *"I'm sorry I startled you. Here, let me go first. Hi, I'm Davian. What's your name?"*

*"Are you lost?"*

*"I don't think so. This is Kitchener, right? We're in an establishment that you can purchase a drink on such a hot day, right?"*

Still unsure of why he was talking to her, she stayed very reluctant. *"Well, ya. I guess."*

*"Perfect. Then no, I am not lost."*

They sat in awkward silence again.

*"Well, this is the part where usually you'd tell me your name..."*

"I remember looking around the shop, seeing the woman working the counter, and the few women in the shop having coffee with their husbands and families, all looking at him. When I looked around the room, they all looked away quickly, hoping I didn't notice."

*"Look, I am just here to have a drink before I walk home. What do you want?"*

*"Well, you aren't making this any easier, are you?"*

*"Making what easier?"*

*"Well, for starters, getting to know your name seems to be quite the task."*

He started to laugh again, and Veronica realized how dramatic she was being. It was broad daylight, in a public space, and an incredibly attractive guy wanted to speak to her. *Chill out, Roni*, she told herself.

*"I'm sorry. I'm not trying to be rude. You're not from around here, are you?"*

*"Me? No. I live a few counties outside of Waterloo. Not a long drive, but I wanted to get out of my town and check out some new surroundings."*

*"You're here with your parents? Where are they?"* She looked around the shop to see if she could find someone looking at him.

*"I never said I was here with my parents."*

*"But you said you drove to Kitchener?"*

*"Yes. I drove to Kitchener."*

*"You mean, you drove here?"*

*"Well, that's what's so funny about cars. They don't drive themselves! At least, not yet."*

Silence fell over the table again, and a fear that she was boring started to make her stir.

*"Have you ever been to Kitchener before?"*

*"No, I haven't. But I like it so far. Especially now."* He leaned in and gave Veronica the smile to end all smiles.

With that, her cheeks flushed crimson purple. *"Oh."*

*"So, how about it?"*

*"How about what?"*

*"Your name, beautiful. I'm sure I could start guessing down the alphabet, but there's just no fun in that."*

Veronica's face went even more purple.

*"Well, my name is Veronica, but some people call me Roni for short."*

*"What a beautiful name. So, Roni, what is there to do for fun around here?"*

*"Kitchener? It's not so bad. Usually a lot to do around here. We have lots of public pools, parks, places to shop. There is even a new mall built on the outside of town. I don't get there much. Only when my mother wants to go. We do most of our shopping here downtown."*

*"Well, that doesn't sound too bad. Why are you sitting here alone when there is so much to do in the city?"*

*"Well, it's a holiday. Most of the shops are closed, and people are out of town."*

*"Why aren't you then?"*

She wasn't about to tell this stranger she was by herself. No matter how beautiful she thought he was.

*"My family wanted to stay local this year. I just came downtown to get out of the house."*

Richard saw in the memory, Davian had a huge smirk. Richard knew all too well why; he knew she was lying. He thought it was cute. Richard knew Davian was no ordinary boy. He was gifted just like himself. But, Richard couldn't tell how. He could sense some inner thoughts, but his mind was like looking at a blur of colours. Most minds, whether gifted or not, were like square blocks of memories all tightly stacked together. He'd never seen a mind like this. It was more smooth round blobs than metrical shapes.

*"Well, that's lucky for me then, I guess. So, Roni, what are you up to right now?"*

*"Well, I have to get home for lunch. My mother is probably worried sick about me."*

*"Do you think I could meet you after lunch? As wonderful as it is to finally know your name, there is a lot more I'd love to know."*

*"Me? You want to meet me?"*

Davian gave a comical look around the coffee shop and the two empty seats at the table.

*"I would really like that. If you wanted to."*

Veronica didn't want to reveal how much she wanted that, and she was still so unsure of his intentions.

*"Well, I'm very busy today. My family will be having a BBQ."*

Davian's face looked crushed when she said this.

Richard knew why. He was genuine and really did want to see her later. He thought she was just blowing him off.

"*But, if you are still in town, I was thinking about going to sit at the park by my house. It isn't much, but maybe I'll see you there.*"

"*Sounds good to me. What time?*"

"*Well it's 11 now, I should be out and about by 1, I guess. If I see you there, then I see you there.*"

"*Veronica.*" Davian stood up at the table.

Veronica noticed all the women staring at him again in the coffee shop.

"*I mean, Roni. It will be my greatest pleasure to see you at the park. I am really looking forward to it.*"

"He got up and left the shop. I saw all the eyes on me disperse again, hoping I didn't see. I felt the warm flush over my cheeks again. I wasn't used to so much attention. I sat there stunned. Had that really just happened? Barely any of the boys at school had talked to me, let alone wanted to meet up with me."

Richard scanned the memories coming to her mind. He had to hide the smile. She really didn't have a clue. The boys at school didn't ignore her; she intimidated them. A Lot.

"After calming myself down, I got up from the table and headed out the door. The heat waved over me like a hot blanket. The humidity here in the summers can be brutal. That sunshine made me completely wake up from the daze of Davian's beautiful eyes, and it hit me."

"What did??"

"I never told him where the park was. While I was very upset, I thought it was for the better. I was so awkward around him, so I just figured I would probably have acted so weird that he would have gotten bored and left anyways. I just kept walking home and tried to push it out of my mind.

"I got home around noon and still loved my newfound freedom. No one home. I decided to heat up some of the leftovers my mother made for me. After using our oven to heat up the tray, the house was even hotter than outside. I ate and then went to our TV room that was down the hall from our kitchen. I laid down to relax and ended up falling asleep a little bit. I had opened the sliding window beside our couch, and an electric fan we had let a slightly cool breeze waft in. Sleep pulled me under quickly."

"About two hours later, I think the fan stopped working, and I woke up feeling smothered in heat. I gasped as I sat up quickly like someone had made a loud noise. Once I fully woke up, I realized I was alone. I went upstairs to have a cool bath. I pulled my sweaty hair up into a high ponytail, as I didn't want to wash my hair. I felt a lot better after a soak in the cool water, and I got out of the tub and went down the hall to my room. It was still so hot. I went to my closet and found I had nothing that was heat appropriate. Too much thick cottons and long shirts that covered my arms. My mother still dressed me like I was ten."

Richard saw a memory of Veronica and her mother shopping. Her mother wasn't naive. She noticed how people stared at her daughter, and she didn't like the attention Roni got at such a young age from boys and even men sometimes.

With her mother not there to question her wardrobe, and her father not there to reinforce the rules, she dug deep into her closet to a hidden part.

"Way in the back of my closet I hid some clothes I didn't want my mother to see. Nothing too scandalous, just more of what girls my age were wearing. My father didn't allow me to show my bare shoulders unless I was on the beach swimming."

*"Young women should cover up until they are mature enough to understand what showing off that kind of skin means to boys."*

"My father blurted that out one drunken supper. I never did pay too much attention to his opinions as I almost never got them without him either slurring or drooling."

"The temperature was 98°F on the thermometer outside our back sliding door, and that didn't include the humidity and sun. It was just too hot to be all covered up."

"I slipped into a spaghetti strapped tank top that I loved. It was one of my favourite colours, a peachy pink. It had some bohemian ruffles down the front. Then I grabbed some shorts that I had cut off from the summer before. That felt much better. It was now 3 p.m. and I wanted to head out to see if I could find anyone locals still home and perhaps go check out some fireworks."

"I ran down the stairs, locked up the back sliding door and headed for my front hall. I grabbed my bag and my keys and left, locking the door behind me. I don't know why I remember doing that, but I guess it's because I barely used my keys as someone was usually home."

"I went around a few blocks and saw that all the kids my age that I knew were gone. Their family cars were not in the driveway, and I knew a lot of them had plans to leave, so there was no surprise there. I kept mindlessly walking and came around a corner and saw the bright royal blue car again. I kept thinking how strange it was to see it again that day. I just figured one of my neighbours had bought it after school got out. I knew the whole school would know whose dad bought it on the first day back in September. A car like that boasted a lot of bragging rights. I kept going down a few more side streets and about ten minutes later, I came around the corner to our small neighbourhood park. The very one where I had planned to meet Davian, my handsome stranger. I was hot, so I found a bench in the shade and sat down."

"The park that day was dull as usual. I was too old to really play on the playground. When I went there with Martha, it was just a place to hang out. There was a nearby store that sold cold pop and snacks. It was such a hot day that I decided I should go get a popsicle and head home. It was too hot and too early to hang around and wait to see if someone set off fireworks. I stood up and stretched and was making a note of what I would get at the store to bring home. I wanted some Coke and a cherry popsicle. I finished my stretch and turned around to grab by bag. I flung it over my shoulder and headed out of the park. At least, that's what I planned to do. Within one step, I bumped right into someone."

*"Ooof. Oh my, I'm sorry. I didn't see you there."* Veronica shook her head in a daze and looked up and saw deep blue eyes with flecks of green and gold.

"While I was beyond ecstatic to see my handsome stranger again, I was a little timid. It was hours after we said we'd meet here, and to top it off, I had never told him where the park was. I was actually a little nervous. I took a few steps back, but at the same time, I enjoyed being so close to him."

*"Hi, Roni. Sorry to startle you. It's so hot out here I thought you might be thirsty. Here you go."* Out of a small bag, he produced an iced cold bottle of Coca-Cola.

*"What is going on? How did you find me?"*

"As soon as I said that out loud, the coincidence of meeting him here started to feel strange. Very strange. My nervousness turned to panic and I was again debating making a run for it. My body language must have gave it off as he took a step back and put his hand up again in a *wait* motion."

*"Wait, Roni. Please wait! Let me explain! Please! I won't sit near you. I'll stay here at the other end of the bench. If you don't understand when I'm finished talking, you can leave and walk away. I'll never bother you again!"*

She started looking around the park. Not a soul in sight. Of course. This park was usually infested with kids and parents. Her and Martha never did get so lucky to have it to themselves. She saw that the row of houses closest to the park had a car or two, and she knew the store around the corner she had planned to go to was just a block away.

"*Listen, take this.*" He stepped forwards just enough for her to grab the glass bottle. "*And if you think I'm being strange, you can hit me over the head with it and make a run for it. I know you can run fast.*"

She felt unsettled. She *could* run fast. She would have been on the school track team if her father had allowed it.

"*What makes you so sure I can run fast?*" She sneered at him like he was a lunatic.

"*Look, I'll sit here, you sit there, and let's just talk. Please? I promise I'll be a perfect gentleman, and you can leave at any time, ok?*"

He sat down on the bench and produced another bottle of Coke. He set the bag down and grabbed a small metal opener from his pocket and popped of the lid.

"*Here, take this one, and I'll open that one, ok?*" He held out the bottle, and moisture dripped down the side of it.

Roni was so thirsty and it was so hot. And, Coke was her favourite.

"*Ok, but if you do anything strange—*"

"*Got it, nothing strange. I'll be here, four feet away.*"

He took the open bottle and exchanged it for her unopened one. Veronica sat down and took a sip. She didn't realize just how thirsty she really was.

"*Thanks for the drink. Where did you get it?*"

"*I found a store around the corner. Only open a few hours for the holiday. They close up in about an hour. I was just happy to find somewhere that sold something cold. This heat is unreal.*"

"*I know, it's sticky.*"

*"Say, they had some popsicles too. Care for one? Here, you like cherry, right?"*

"What?" She was shaking her head in disbelief.

*"Cherry popsicles. Do you want one?"*

"I was hearing bells go off in my head. Was he following me? How did he know I'd be here? How did he bring exactly what I was going to get from the store right to me? I grabbed my bag and pulled it tight to my body and was looking at the glass bottle wondering where I should hit him. I looked around and to my relief, I saw a man mowing his lawn at one of the houses by the park. I nervously placed the bottle down on the bench and was ready to run. I grabbed the arm of the bench and was slowly shifting my body to take flight."

*"If you don't tell me what you're doing here and how you knew this is what I wanted, I swear to God I will scream my head off so loud that people in whatever county you said you came from will hear me."*

*"Ok, ok, wait. Ok? Geeze, I'm always going about this the wrong way. Shit."*

*"How did you find me and how did you know I wanted those?"*

*"Ok, look. I'm not everything I appear to be, ok? You have to trust me, I mean no harm. I really honestly just want to talk to you. I didn't follow you here. I knew you'd be here. I parked my car a block away, and I just trusted my instinct that you'd be here in this very spot."*

*"That makes zero sense."*

*"Look, I know it doesn't. If you let me try to explain, maybe you'll understand."*

Richard looked into Davian as best he could, and knew he was being truthful. Davian's powers were very different than anyone he'd studied. He meant no harm to Roni and was genuinely curious about her. What surprised him was that Veronica wasn't really scared. She was starting to feel comfortable around this stranger. She was just putting up a front of what she thought a normal girl would do. She didn't want to seem too eager. Her common sense was just questioning things regardless of how she felt.

*"Ok, so it's like, sometimes I just know things. I don't know why I know them, I just do. It's like a little voice inside me tells me what I want to know."*

*"So you hear voices in your head? They have doctors for that, you know."*

Davian paused. A sad look came over his face. What seemed like minutes later, he looked up at Veronica. Slowly and softly, he began to speak. *"Oh, I know... You'd better believe, I know. My father has sent me to more doctors than I care to think about."*

*"Your father did?"*

*"Yes. My dad is a massive devotee of our church. When I was kid, he sent me to see all the medicinal hospitals run by our church. He thought he needed to have me cured, or better yet, he called it 'being cleansed of what was inside me.' Like I was damaged."*

Richard tried to focus on Davian's memories. He couldn't make out much, but what he could make out he immediately regretted seeing. Memories of being tied to the bed, burnt, splashed with holy water. In short, torture. They tortured a helpless young boy, fearing what they could not explain. Doctors and priests surrounded him in rooms at time while he screamed for help. Richard held back a tear from falling down his cheek so Veronica wouldn't notice. Seeing children hurt irked him. It reminded him of his sons who he could never hurt. He could never comprehend how someone could hurt a child.

Veronica got up from the bench and moved closer to Davian. She leaned in and gave him a deep compassionate stare. *"For what it's worth, your dad and my dad sound like they have a lot in common."*

"*I know.*" His face shifted down and he looked sad and lost. *"So, after a few years of being a test subject and feared by my family both at home and at our church, I decided life would be easier if I wasn't so different."*

*"So, you hear voices. We all do. What makes yours so different?"*

*"Well, my voices aren't voices. It's like a feeling that explains things to me. They make me understand things that others can't."*

*"I have to be honest. That's simply not possible. It sounds like something I would have seen back on the* Twilight Zone *for crying out loud."*

Veronica laughed at bit, thinking he sounded ridiculous.

*"I'm telling you it's not."* Davian sat up straight and had a look across his face that said 'as matter of fact.'

*"Oh ya? Well, you're going to have to show me. Show me if you truly want me to understand."*

Davian sat there and stared at her with a smirk. She was dying to know what he was thinking. Was he just teasing her with all this nonsense?

Richard looked in his eyes in the memory. While still trying to peer into Davian's consciousness, he could feel Davian pulling memories from Veronica. Deep memories. Something Richard could do too. He could read a recent memory or one that was in conscious thought. But, he could also pull anything that had ever been thought or felt.

Davian smiled a crooked smile. *"Ok, got it. Ask me something. Ask me something personal about yourself I should not know."*

She gladly accepted the challenge. She thought he was just playing a joke on her, and it was mildly entertaining.

*"Ok. Let me think."* She looked around, having no idea what he was asking of her, so she started off easy. *"Ok, so I have a lip gloss in my purse. What kind is it?"*

*"Really? You can ask me anything deep and secret about yourself, or someone else for that matter, and you want to see if I know what makeup you have in your bag?"*

*"I guess you don't know?"*

*"Bonne Belle. Cherry."*

*"Hmmm. I thought it was easy. But, really you could have seen it when I dropped it at the coffee shop. What's my middle name?"*

*"Francis."*

Confusion and intrigue set in on Veronica.

*"You could have looked that up at the hospital."*

*"How would I have known where you were born?"*

*"You mean you don't know? You can't feel it?"*

*"Of course I can, but I don't want to scare you. Nobody has ever really accepted what I can do, they just fear it."*

When he said that, she felt bad. She still didn't know if he was just joking around, but for some reason, it felt truthful to her.

"*You're really being serious, aren't you?*"

"*Cross my heart!*" he said as he made the hand gesture over his chest.

"*Ok, how about this. Why don't you tell me three things that no one would know about me? Anything is on the table. Whatever you seem to 'feel', let it out. Let me see what you can do.*"

"*You promise me you won't run away?*"

"*Cross my heart.*"

She smiled at him and crossed her hand over her chest like he had done. They opened their cold treats and started to eat them.

"*Ok. I want this to be good, but I'm warning you. You could get . . .*"

Davian chewed his lip a little which she thought made him look even more dashing. She felt her heart speed up.

"*You could get uncomfortable. I'm going to tell you things that you don't even know about.*"

"*I can handle it.*" Veronica gave Davian a very serious look. If he was being truthful she wanted to know it.

"*Alright. Let me take you in. Really take you in.*"

She sat there watching him. Examining him on the park bench under the shade of a large maple tree. The warm wind moved around giving them little relief of the summer heat. They finished their popsicles quickly in silence. He sat there and looked out at the open space and then all around. Then he looked at her. But she knew he wasn't just looking at her. He was looking inside her.

He chewed the inside of his cheek a little and reached his right hand up behind his ear. She watched as his middle finger, and only his middle finger, began to rub up and down. Never down his neck, just right behind his ear. They sat in silence for a few minutes. Her anticipation and curiosity was growing every second. She was thinking, *what is he doing? Is he for real? What can he possibly tell me?*

"*Ok, there are a few things I can say that might make you believe me.*"

She sat back and crossed her arms. "*I'm waiting.*"

His right hand dropped down, and he shifted in his seat to look at her. He took a deep breath and began.

"*You and your best friend, Martha, met in Grade 3. She sat next to you on the first day. Your teacher, Mrs. Webb, assigned the seats. She became your partner in every school activity and your friendship really blossomed.*"

"*Wow! But how??*"

Davian shrugged his brows. "*I told you, I just know things when I concentrate.*"

"*Ok. Name my favourite band.*"

"*Hey, you said I got to pick what I want to tell you.*"

"*Ok, you're right. So, what else?*"

"*Your birthday. It was a Wednesday, no, wait. Tuesday. You were born Tuesday, February 12th, 1952. At the hospital here in town. The red one. St. something...*"

"*Oh my God. Yes. Yes! St. Mary's Hospital. You aren't kidding. This is incredible. How do you do that?*"

"*Like I said, I can't really explain it. I either hear or see something, and it comes to fruition when I speak, and it makes sense.*"

"*This is just fascinating. Say, how come you aren't like a millionaire or something? Can't you use it to get things from people? Like, did you have to pay for all this?"* Veronica pointed to the empty pop bottles and popsicle wrappers.

*"No, I don't like to do things like that. I mean I could, but it never works out. Karma is very real. What I put out comes back to me. And besides, that's the wrong thing to do. It isn't fair. And I like to think I'm better than that. Also, when you take things to a dark place, it can get bad. Really fast."*

*"How so?"*

*"Look. When you call a person out on something deep and secret for your gain, it can get ugly. People who feel exposed feel threatened. And, they act out accordingly. Even people you think you know well or trust. I know firsthand."*

*"What happened to you?"*

*"Well, when I was in treatment, on more than one occasion I could see which church figures had broken their vows. Thinking I could use it to save myself, I'd ask them privately. I'd say that if they'd help me, I would keep their secrets. It never worked in my favour. I have the scars to prove it."*

Richard blocked out the memory. He didn't want to see what he knew was true.

"So did that scare you? Him knowing things like that?"

"At first, I was a little scared. But, I can't explain it. Every minute with him felt like a year. But in a good way. I felt so at ease and safe around him. His energy was pure. Nothing like the immature boys at my school, and the exact opposite of my father. He was opening up to me. Really letting me get to know the person he was."

"So what else did he tell you about yourself?"

"One second, I'm going to need a drink for this. Sarah!!"

Richard was feeling a little groggy. He wasn't sure he should have more. He enjoyed alcohol, but it did dull his abilities. Yet the thought of passing up that expensive scotch won the best of him.

After Sarah brought the fresh drinks, Veronica settled back into the sofa.

"Well, what he opened up about next is what got me for sure. Before, a small part of me still had a feeling that maybe it was just for show. Like a parlor trick. But with what he told me next, I didn't doubt him whatsoever. He had a gift."

"What did he tell you?"

"Well, it was because I asked him to tell me something I wanted to know so badly. And, if he really could do what he said he could do, I would forever hate myself for not taking the chance . . ."

*"Davian, what can you tell me about my father? Why is he the way he is?"*

Davian stopped in mid motion. He turned into a cement statue. *"What do you mean, 'the way he is?'"*

She gave a look back full of grimace and frustration. If he was telling her the truth, he should know that she didn't want to say it out loud.

*"Ok, I'm sorry. I was just really hoping you wouldn't ask me about him. I just don't know if you want to open Pandora's box either . . ."*

*"Please,"* Veronica begged him. *"Why is he . . . you know. So angry?"*

Davian paused and took a deep gulp. He moved a little closer to Veronica and placed his hand over hers.

"Ok. Look. Your parents moved here from out west. Your father found good work here at one of the prominent factories. You live in a rather large nice house, not far from here. It's your childhood home. You have an older brother. Henry... no. Harold. Your mother stays home. She wants to work, but I don't think you know that. She wants to, but she can't."

Veronica looked a bit shocked at this point. She could feel it in her face. "*Why not?*"

She asked him because she had never thought her mother had any interest in working.

"*I know you know why. You just have never admitted it to yourself. She denies it as well.*"

"*What does that mean?*"

"*This is where things can get... uncomfortable, Roni.*"

"*Just tell me!*"

"*She already has a job. A full-time one. One she hates.*"

Once he said that, she was starting to understand.

"*You mean—*"

"*Your father. Looking after him takes so much out of her. But—I can tell you know that. It breaks your heart. I see what he does to her, and you. He's, he's a bad person, Roni. I think you should know that. Deep down, he really is. He isn't just unhappy. There is something deeply wrong with him. He blames your mom a lot. He fells trapped. He blames your mother for getting pregnant with your brother. Her father forced them into marriage. A life he never wanted.*"

"*But my parents were married before my brother came along.*"

"*Roni, please keep in mind I am just telling you what I see. Ok?*"

A long silence came about again. Roni didn't know what to think.

*"They lied about the year they got married. It's why they moved here before he was born. To protect their secret."*

Roni sat there stunned. She shook her head slightly.

*"He doesn't drink all week. He thinks it makes him better. It doesn't. It bottles up the rage. The rage you know all too well. It keeps him numb from his reality, but at the same time, awakens his anger. I think I already know, but what does he tell you he does for his work?"*

"My dad?" She shook her head at him, wondering what this had to do with her. *"Well, he's a sector manager at the plant. He's pretty high up."*

*"Hmmmm, well, I think you should ask him what he really does. Actually, you can ask your mother too. She knows. She didn't want you to know either."*

*"Know what? I know he works there, I've been to work BBQs and Christmas parties."*

*"He works there alright, but just ask your mother. It's not my place to say."*

*"Ok. Not that I have to, but I will. But why is he so mad?"*

*"Roni, I wish I could tell you. I really do. But some people, it's like their head is wired the wrong way from birth. They are made that way. Sadly, he was too. He was raised right. I know you've only met your grandparents a handful of times, but they are good people. They didn't do anything wrong. It's something within him. Thankfully, he can't pass it on to you. And your mom, she keeps you from it. She hides it, and what she has hidden I pray you never see or know."*

*"What is she hiding?? What don't I know!?"*

*"That is something I just can never tell you. I'm sorry, but I can't. Hate me if you want to. It's how these things work for people like me. We are only going to see what we're allowed to. We can't mess with fate too much. And, it's something I truly never hope you figure out."*

*"I don't understand what that means. And if anything it's making me more curious."*

*"Ok, think about it. First of all, if you care to believe it or not, I'm not the only person in the world who is like this. There are more. I've met a few. But we can't know everything. We can't stop everything. Only what we are allowed to."*

*"So you mean, if you knew someone was about to get killed, you couldn't warn them?"*

*"Sometimes, again. It's not an exact science. If I am supposed to be shown something, I will see it."*

*"I understand the what, but not the why,"* pleaded Veronica.

*"I'm sorry. Again, please don't hate me. I am not seeing certain details, but I can still sense things. Don't go looking in dark places. Do not dig up the past. Digging is bad, Roni."*

But the truth was, she didn't hate him. She couldn't. As mad as she was at him for leaving her hanging on his words like that, she had no ill will toward him. Only more toward her father.

*"Look, I hope I didn't upset you. I really like it better when you smile."* He looked at Roni and winked.

Her face immediately flushed a bright pink.

*"So, what time is your family BBQ? Shouldn't you be going home soon?"*

*"Oh, about that, there is no BBQ. I lied."* Her face went to a deep red.

Davian laughed and moved a little closer to Roni. *"Hey, it's ok. I already knew. Is there any chance you aren't sick of me yet and would like to try and catch some fireworks tonight?"*

*"I would love that. That's exactly what I wanted to do tonight! I just don't get how... Just... wow..."*

*"I'm so happy to hear that. Why don't we go get my car, and we'll try and find somewhere to eat?"*

*"Nowhere around here is really open. It's like they'll shut the city down for any reason. It's worse than a Sunday around here."*

*"Let me think. I know somewhere that's open. And, I know you'll like the food. Do you trust me?"*

While it felt strange to Veronica, she did. Despite having just met him, it felt right. He grabbed her hand and they started walking out of the park. As they were almost at the street, he looked over her shoulder. His face went cold.

*"What's wrong? You look upset? Did I do something?"*

*"You? No. Oh my, no. I just get sad when I see things like that."*

*"Things like what?"*

Richard could see in the memory what he saw. It was a missing pet poster attached to a phone line pole. It read:

Missing since May 15th: Porter
Reward Offered
Please come to 386 Ahrens street if found.

(There was a description of the dog in smaller writing.)

Friendly loving family pet ran away. We appreciate any help that the neighbourhood can give us.

Porter is a brown lab mix with brown eyes. He comes to his name. Porter was last seen wearing his blue collar with name tags on it. Please come see us if you have spotted Porter. Thank you.

*"Oh, that's one of my neighbours' dogs. He went missing a little over a month ago. A lot of dogs have been running away lately. It's sad."*

*"This happens a lot?"*

*"Recently, yeah. I think the first one was just around Christmas. It's sad, I hope they come back."*

*"Me too. Well, dogs will be dogs."*

*"Ya, I guess. So, where is your car?"*

*"I just parked it around the corner."*

They walked past the variety store that was now closed. They went around one more block, and Roni saw the royal blue car she had been seeing all day parked up ahead.

*"Hey, do you like cars?"*

*"I do. A lot. I work with cars actually. It's how I was able to get a car for today. I want to run my own car shop one day."*

*"Really? That's neat. Well, if you like cars, wait till you see what one of my neighbours just bought. It's out of this world. See that blue one up ahead?*

*"You mean the one on this side of the street? How could I miss it! It's a Chevy Camero RS/SS Standard 5-speed transmission."*

*"It's flashy, eh? My neighbour must be so proud of it and love showing it off. I've seen it around town all day."*

*"That isn't nice. I doubt they were showing it off."*

*"Well, they should be, it's like nothing I've ever seen. Not unless in a magazine."*

*"I think maybe, just maybe, it could have been someone from out of town looking around for something. Something they maybe didn't know they were looking for."*

Right then they were beside the car. Up close, Veronica looked in and saw the stereo and leather seats. Only in the movies had she ever seen something like this. She was blown away.

*"So, you like it?"*

*"Like it? I love it. Whoever owns it sure is lucky."*

Davian pulled a set of keys out of his pocket and dangled them for Roni. *"I think the guy driving it is the lucky one. He gets to take you out for dinner."*

*"Wait—you? You own THIS?? But, how?"*

*"Well, OWN is such a strong word."*

*"But, I know what those cars cost. How did you get it?"*

*"Well, it just so happened the guy who owned this wasn't so happily married. So unhappily, that even his mistress was getting tired of him. Do you know what I mean?"*

*"Davian! What did you do??"*

*"Like I said, I would never do anything dark to get something I wanted. To someone undeserving at least. I just let the owner of the car know if I am too busy driving this around all weekend, I'm too busy to have lunch with his wife to enlighten her on his extracurricular activities. His wife also happens to be my mother."*

*"No!"*

*"I think of it as a little retribution for all the prayer camps they both sent me to as a kid. Don't you?"*

In that moment, he unlocked the car door and held it open for her. The minute they made eye contact, they laughed. That moment was the first real memory she had of feeling grown-up. She felt truly free and safe.

# CHAPTER 7

# Fireworks

"He sounded charming. A real gentleman." Richard could see he really was. He also really cared about Veronica.

"Charming? That word doesn't do him justice. He was memorizing. I had no thoughts about anything other than myself and him when we were together that day. We drove around a while and even left the city limits. He knew of some tiny place out in the country that was still serving food, and we stopped. It was just a BBQ stand set up at the side of the road. But he was right, I really did like it."

*"You hungry?" Davian asked Veronica.*
*"Me? I'm famished. I can't believe you found a place that's open."*
*"It wasn't hard. Things just call to me when I think about it. That's why I love being able to drive. I just tune into my mind, and it takes me to where I want to go."*

"Is that what happened with me?" Veronica asked, half-flirting, half-curious.

"With you was different. I've had this before. One time I didn't take a usual route on the highway back home, and the next day, the papers showed a horrible accident with five cars. Someone died. Another time, I didn't go to a party, and the house burned down. A lot of people got hurt."

"Oh my, and you didn't warn anyone?"

"I couldn't. I didn't know what I was avoiding. I wish I did. And with you, something just drew me to this city. A city I've never been to before. I didn't know what was pulling me here until I saw you. I drove around a few blocks, sensing something was close. I parked and got out and walked around, then I saw you sitting by the window of the coffee shop. And I instantly knew it was you I was here for."

"That must have been hard for you to understand."

"It was, but look, I don't want to talk about that. I just want to enjoy my time with you now. Is that ok?"

He reached over the table and grabbed her hand. He caressed her fingers with his thumbs, and it made her delirious. They waited for their food and never broke eye contact.

Veronica blushed again, feeling over whelmed with joy and love in reliving such a happy moment.

Richard nodded and didn't pry ahead in her mind. While his abilities could easily let him, she was holding back. That and the alcohol would have made it tricky. Besides, he was enjoying reliving these moments with her.

"Everyone who drove by or stopped for a bite marveled over his car. If they found out it was his, they would come up to him and ask a million questions. I loved watching him talk to people. He seemed too kind and so genuine. After we finished eating, I asked him to drive around more as it was a new experience for me. I felt so free. The way any teenager does their first time in a car with no parents. We were driving so fast out on country roads. No one around. No one to stop us. We talked and talked and the more I got to know him, the more I liked him. We talked about anything and everything. He just wouldn't open up about where he was from. About his life. I would try and ask him what school he went to, where he worked, what his parents did, but he always managed to change the subject back to me. I didn't notice it at the time. Too high on lust. Looking back, I'll forever wished I pressed more."

"He drove around without a map. I asked him once if he'd ever driven around these parts, and he said no. It didn't matter. He'd always know what way to turn. Watching him tune into his instincts fascinated me. We started to head back to the city when he asked me about the fireworks."

Richard focused into Veronica's memory. As she was reliving that night in her mind, Richard could see her evolving. She was experiencing falling in love for the first time, and it changed her. Made her grow up even more. She was already very mature for her age. Richard could see that in the way she processed things in her conscience. Richard liked to call young people like this *old souls*.

"So did you end up seeing your fireworks?"

Veronica smiled a huge smile. She sat in silence across from Richard a moment. She leaned forwards, set down her martini, and started to blush.

Richard nodded but didn't say a thing. He already saw most of the night pan out.

"Have you ever been in a parade, Mr. Matheson?"

"Please, call me Richard. And no, I can't say that I have."

"Well, that night was the closest thing I ever came to being in one. We pulled into an area he knew would have fireworks. It was a large parking lot on the edge of the city. It was new, a part of this large complex built for playing hockey. Today it's called the Kitchener Auditorium. Anyone left in the city seemed to be there. A few kids my age too. Even some kids I went to school with. There wasn't a single head that didn't turn to look at his car. I even saw a few jaws drop. He parked on the outer edge of the lot, where we had a good view. Tons of people rushed over to see the car close up. He was so polite, so welcoming. He wasn't rude to a single soul. He even popped the hood at one point. I tried not to feel left out, but I couldn't help it. I knew I wanted all his attention on me so badly. Then all of a sudden, it was like no one else mattered to him. He turned all his focus back on me. The car no longer existed to him. It was overwhelming being the centre of his attention when all of Kitchener was in awe of him and his car. '*Who was he, where was he from?*' There were even a few girls there who I knew, and they were giving me the dirtiest looks."

As the memory became sharper to Richard, he knew what made Davian focus on her. He could sense she was feeling sad. He was trying to sweep her off her feet, not ignore her. He quickly changed his focus to swoon her. And, he knew it totally worked. He knew a lot of people she'd know would be at those particular fireworks. He also knew how many onlookers were staring at her just as much as his car. He felt lucky. He was really proud to be there with her.

"The fireworks ended and we left the complex. I felt like we were celebrities as everyone, and I mean EVERYONE, let us pass first. They just couldn't believe the car. I swear some kids actually believed we were famous."

Richard knew it to be true. He could see it in the imagination of some of the onlookers.

"With dusk having past more than an hour before, it was getting late. The city was shutting down and everyone was going home. I knew I didn't want the night to end, and I didn't know how to say it."

*"Thank you for being my date. I love fireworks. Say, this area is amazing. I wish we had one back in my town."*
*"And that town would be?"*
Davian laughed. *"Well, it's not here. Let's leave it at that."*
Veronica rolled her eyes in frustration.
*"This area is so nice, I feel bad for the people that live in homes over there."* Davian pointed to a field of farm land with a few houses.
*"Why? It's so nice here."*
*"Not that. Do you know what eminent domain means?"*

"No. What is it?"

"Well, they want to build a big road over there, and they will be forced to sell by the government so they can build the road. Strange, eh?"

"I'd say." Veronica didn't know the government could do that. "It's getting pretty late, how far is your drive home going to be, anyways?"

"It's going to take a while. But I'm in no rush . . . are you?" Davian looked at her quickly and smiled, then focused back on driving.

"No! No, not at all."

Trying to say what she wanted to say next was the most awkward moment of Veronica's life up to that point.

"Did . . . you . . . Did you want to come over?" Veronica nervously bit her bottom lip.

"*I thought you'd never ask.*" Davian gushed and smiled while looking onto the road ahead.

"Needless to say, I didn't have to tell him where to go. He just knew. After dropping me off at the bottom of my street, he parked around the block to not bring attention from any of my neighbours. Some were just getting home from the fireworks themselves."

*"Just head home, and I'll come around the back to your yard. I can already sense some of your neighbours are looking out at the sound of my engine."*

"I think I ran home." Veronica laughed and shook her head. "Seems silly, but I remember those feelings of lust and excitement. Nothing compares to those feelings and sensations you go through when you're young."

"I know exactly how that feels." Richard joined in on her laughter. He reminisced about the first few dates he had with Linda. He felt the same way and so had she.

"I rushed to unlock my back door and ran upstairs to freshen up. It was hot and sticky as the heat had not let up all night. I ran back downstairs in a matter of minutes, wondering if I'd ever been so quick in my whole life. I rushed to the back door, flicked on one of the lights, and saw Davian standing in the middle of our back concrete patio. He was just staring out into our yard."

*"Hey, you found the place ok?"* Veronica asked as she stepped out to stand beside Davian.

He smirked and looked at her. He slowly put his arm around her. *"Really?"*

*"Hey, I'm still getting used to you just knowing things, ok?"*

Davian looked back at the yard and was taken over by a blank expression.

*"Hey, what is it? See something?"*

*"Me? No, it's nothing. Just admiring how huge your backyard is."*

*"My dad told me that when this house was built, they were going to put another street behind it, then the planners changed their minds. There are only a few houses on this street that got lucky."*

Davian nodded his head. *"Yeah, I can see that now. It wasn't a decision, it was a mistake. Something at a city meeting was overlooked."*

*"Why don't we go inside? Our living room does cool down a bit, and we have a big electric fan that will help. It's sweltering out here."*

"He followed me inside and I got him situated in our TV room. I went down the hall to our kitchen and pulled out some juice. I poured us each a glass and found him standing at my father's record player. He had put on a record. I'll never forget the song. I didn't know it at the time, as my father didn't really listen to his records much anymore. He was usually too busy being drunk."

*Classic*, Richard thought. He adored old music. "I love Sam Cooke."

"Me too." Veronica paused and looked at Richard in confusion. "Wait, did I say what it was?" She took another moment. "I guess I must have. Boy, I think I need to take a break from these martinis. Ok, where was I?"

"Davian just put on some music." Richard felt a sense a relief and was thankful she blamed the drink.

"Right, he put on music and asked me to dance."

*"Roni, put down the drinks, I want you close to me."*

"Ok," she fumbled her word as she set the drinks down and turned on the electric fan on the floor. *"Davian."*

*"Yes."*

*"I'm not scared. Is that normal? Should I be?"*

*"Not with me, Roni, never."*

"That was the first kiss I ever had with a boy. I was floating on air. It was picture perfect. I never felt a rush like I did at that moment."

"That's beautiful."

"Thank you, Richard, it really was." Veronica smiled and looked so happy. As happy as she looked in the memory Richard was seeing.

"That night was a lot of firsts for me. I became a woman that night. Davian was slow, gentle and powerful. He made me feel safe and loved. Something every young woman should feel their first time making love."

Richard didn't peer into the memory. He had practice at leaving private moments private. They had spent a few hours together now, and he was in control of what he would let himself see. What she did that night was for her and her alone to remember.

"We fell sleep in the middle of my living room floor. The electric fan pulled us under with its light gentle hum. I woke up just before the sun came up. I was alone and immediately sought out Davian. His clothing and shoes were gone, so I thought I was alone. I felt panic come over me that maybe he just left and I slept through him leaving. I looked down the hall and saw him just sitting on the other side of my back door on a patio chair. He was just staring out into the dark."

*"Hey you."* Veronica came outside and pulled up a chair beside Davian.

*"Hey beautiful."* Davian kissed Veronica with pure passion. *"I have to leave soon, you neighbours will be up and*

*about soon. Some who still have their pets need to get them out for a walk."*

"I know. I wish you didn't have to."

*"I know. I wish I could stay too. Say, did your mom plant those flowers back there?"* Davian pointed out to a patch of bright wildflowers growing in the back corner. You could barely see them in the moonlight.

*"The bright ones? By the maple tree?"*

*"Yes, the ones in the corner there."*

*"No, they are just wildflowers."*

Richard recognized them from all the gardening Linda did. *Carrion* flowers he could see in one of her many books on the subject.

*"My mom said they just started growing on their own last summer. She couldn't explain it. She does do a little planting, but not that far down in the yard. It's too big to plant all over."*

*"Yes. Your yard is huge."*

Davian looked out at the flowers with a solemn face again.

*"What is it? You're making a face again."*

*"Oh, it's nothing. I'm just tired. Well, I can see your neighbours will be up any minute. I better get me and that car out of sight."*

*"Do you have to?"*

*"I do. Your neighbours will all talk, and I fear it getting around to your father."*

Panic struck Veronica. She had visions of what he'd do to her or her mother if he thought she had a boy at the house when they were gone.

*"Hey, don't think like that, ok?"* Davian grabbed Veronica by her shoulders and comforted her. Davian saw her

terrified visions of what she imagined her father doing. *"Listen, don't worry. I'm going to go before anyone sees me."*

In the memory, the sun had just cracked the sky. Richard saw beautiful hues of pink and orange trace their way from each corner of the skyline.

*"Veronica."*

*"Yes, Davian."*

*"I'm in love with you."*

*"I'm in love with you too."*

*"I know."*

Veronica smiled and let out a gentle laugh.

They kissed until the sun was almost up, and they both knew he had to get going.

*"Thank you for the most memorable night anyone could ever ask for. It was perfect. You're perfect."*

Veronica walked him to the edge of the yard.

*"When will I see you again?"*

*"Tonight. I'll come by after supper time, ok? I can't wait to be with you again."*

*"Davian, the girl is supposed to say that."*

*"I knew you wanted to and you were too shy to say it. I feel the same way. Don't you worry. Get some sleep, ok?"*

*"See you tonight."*

She gave him one last kiss and watched him disappear into the morning dew. That day was so long for her. She could barely sleep no matter how hard she tried. She tossed and turned in and out of sleep and was fully awake by noon. To keep busy, she put her father's records back. She didn't want him knowing she had even touched them. She cleaned and tidied everything to her mother's level of perfection. She knew she'd appreciate it after taking care of her father all week.

Finally, dusk came and she was pacing in the kitchen. She watched out the window until she saw movement come for the corner of the backyard. Quickly, she ran to the door and out into his arms. She didn't care if she seemed excited. She was well aware that he knew she was.

"*Hey you, ooof!!*" Davian caught his balance after Veronica jumped into his embrace.

"*Hey! How was your drive? How long is it to drive here from… ???*"

"*Long enough. I have bad news though.*" Davian was looking off into the yard. A blank expression came over his face.

When he let Veronica go, he brought his right hand up near his face and began to caress with his thumb behind his ear.

"*What? Did I do something?*"

"*You? No!! Never. Just a question, who's Betty?*"

"*Betty? Well that's my friend Martha's mom? Why?*"

"*Well, she'll be at your door in about fifteen minutes, to make you sleep at their house.*"

"*What?! No! No way. Well, I don't care. I'll tell her I'm staying here.*"

"*While I'd love nothing more than another night with you, she is not taking no for an answer. And, on another note, your parents had a huge fight tonight. One so bad your brother got in the mix.*"

"*What? He never does. Oh my God, is my mother ok?*"

*"She is fine. Harold actually calmed your dad down. A little. But, they will be on the road very early, around 4:30 in the morning. Your dad is out of alcohol."*

*"Of course he is."*

*"And your mom will be at Martha's door by 7:30 tomorrow. If you're home and not there, I can see your dad not being so understanding. He thinks you're really sick, but has his doubts. And, unfortunately, it's your mother he's questioning about the truth on the matter. I don't see things going well for her if you're not where she said you'd be."*

*"You're right."* Veronica let out a big sigh of disappointment.

*"Hey, don't stress. We'll have lots of other nights, ok?"*

*"Promise?"*

*"Always. Cross my heart."* Davian crossed his chest like he did in the park.

It made Veronica smile ear to ear.

Davian reached over and grabbed Veronica's chin and caressed it with his thumb. He lifted her sad face to have her eyes meet his.

*"I like it when you smile. It makes me happy. I'm sorry things didn't work out for us tonight. But, at least I did get to see you, even if only for a few minutes."*

*"When will I see you again?"*

*"I'll come back in a few days. My father's not impressed with me taking the Chevy this long. I have some retribution to pay. It will take me a few days to get him off my back so I can take off again. Why don't you meet me at our park on Saturday? Same time, same bench?"*

*"I can't wait."*

*"Neither can I."* Davian pulled Veronica deep into his embrace. He kissed her with the most passionate kiss.

The room in the beautiful loft grew cold and quiet. Richard was too busy watching the memory in his own mind to notice how still and withdrawn Veronica had become.

"Are you ok, Veronica?"

Silence followed for a few minutes. In those moments, Richard picked up on what was happening. Until now, she hadn't relived that moment for decades. Her heart was breaking all over again.

"I know I was so very young it seemed, but I know what I felt. It was real. What we had was real. More real than anything else I've experienced since when it comes to love. But, what happened the next few weeks made it that much harder to bare."

"What happened?" Richard felt out how she was feeling. She was fragile and vulnerable. He wasn't sure they should keep going. "Again, we can stop anytime you need to, Ms. Chastain."

"How many times do I have to tell you? It's Veronica!" With that, a bit of her sharp edge came back and helped her let go of some of the angst she'd just been feeling.

"Anyways, as he predicted, he was right about everything. A few minutes after watching him disappear into the night, a knock came at my door. Betty, Martha's mother, insisted I pack up and come over. We got back to their house, and she had a nice Norman Rockwell night ready for her family. Board games, snacks, the radio on in the background.

"I was in no mood to be social, I just wanted to be alone. Martha and I went up to her room and got ready for bed, and she started asking me what I did all weekend. I wanted to tell her everything, but being a gossipy girl was never my style. I didn't want to tell her about Davian just yet. He was like a secret I wanted to keep all to myself for the moment. I was in love and was just enjoying the power of it all. I told her some vague details about walking around and then seeing the fireworks. She started into me on how I got there and who I went with. I knew sooner or later I would have to tell her as a few kids from our school saw me there. And, as I knew how things like that could get around, I'd need to tell my best friend eventually. Luckily, we were out of school for the summer and things would cool off by fall.

"We shut off the lights. Now, while I'm sure Martha went right to sleep, sleep was nowhere in the cards for me that night. I was overwhelmed with emotions. Too much had happened that weekend to take in. I met and fell in love with someone. And not just anyone, someone who was gifted. He could tell me things that no one else could. He made me feel like a young woman, not a little girl. For the first time, I felt hopeful for the future. Like I would one day stand on my own two feet, and hopefully it would be beside him. Small trivial things didn't matter. School would be over one day and I'd move on. Maybe I'd have a family of my own, a husband."

"But what was bothering you so much at the same time?" Richard again blurted out.

He opted to slow down on the scotch for a while to clear his mind up. He set his glass down and prepared for the questions that were about to come.

"How do you know I was bothered?" Veronica looked at him again in a questioning manner.

"It's written all over your face." He paused and pressed a little again on Veronica. It was easier now given the amount of alcohol she'd had so far.

Veronica sighed and accepted his answer. "Yes, it was a troubling night to take everything in."

"So, what were you upset over after such a great weekend?"

"Well, I was happy. There is no doubt about that. But, you have to think. Davian didn't have all sunshine and roses to tell me. I had a lot to consider with my parents. I was really confused over some of the things he told me. He said a lot about my father that didn't just concern me—" She paused and looked Richard deep in his gaze. "It terrified me. I'd been overlooking so much of what happened in my family dynamic that I couldn't ignore things anymore. That night, I tried to suppress it, but some of what he said just kept going on replay in my head. And the more I thought about things, the more I worried for my mother's well-being. I knew he was getting worse, but I think I was in denial about how far things could go.

"Richard, I'm going to freshen up a moment. I'll be right back." With that, Veronica got up from her comfortable white sofa and left the room.

He was grateful for the moment alone. Richard could see what she didn't want to speak of. Not only that, he didn't want to have to sit through her talking and reliving what memories he already had seen. It scared him too. She was right to worry about her father, given what she had found out—what she was about to describe in great detail to him. The hairs on his arm stood up again.

A moment later, Veronica came back into the room, followed by Sarah and some fresh drinks. Richard was grateful as the visions in his head had sobered him up completely, and he knew it did the same for poor Veronica.

"Now. Where was I?"

"You were still at Martha's."

"Oh yes. Well, in the morning, my mother came to take me home and seemed off. She seemed rattled by something. No doubt it was the fight she had with my father. What was killing me at the time was that she didn't know that I knew about it. I couldn't ask her if she was ok. Plus, whenever I'd ask her about their fighting, she would never talk to me about it anyways."

"Veronica, just so you know, it's normal for a mother to act that way in that situation. I see it all the time in my medical practice."

"Is that what you do? Medicine?"

"Well, yes. I am a psychiatrist. My practice is in Toronto."

"Hmmm. I wonder if that's why I find it so easy to talk to you. Maybe Barbara Walters should have taken some classes and I would have told her about all this?"

The two began laughing. They both needed it to ease the tension in the air, given how serious of a talk they were having.

"But thank you, Richard. While I have heard that over the years in therapy, it's always nice to hear an affirmation about it."

"Of course."

# CHAPTER 8

# Don't Ask

"Well, my mother was not the only one in a mood when I got home. My father was still on his last week of holidays, so his sober routine during the week was out the window of course. He went and picked up a few cases of beer, some whiskey and a fresh carton of cigarettes as soon as the stores opened. I hadn't seen my older brother since they got home. That was his typical behaviour, so I thought nothing of it at the time. The day went on, and my father got drunker and drunker. Luckily, they had been up since before the sunrise and had a two hour drive, so he quietly passed out at the dining room table shortly after supper—a nicety he rarely bestowed upon my mother and I. I helped her clean up and we didn't dare disturb my father. We decided to go to the backyard and sit together. I have a few nice memories of doing this my mother. But this night was different."

*"So, mom, how was the cottage?"*

*"Oh, it was lovely. My flowers up there are in bloom and the water was not too chilly. I actually got out for a dip once or twice. How was your weekend, honey? Did you and Martha have fun?"*

*"I did, mom, but about that. What did you tell dad?"*

*"I told him the truth. You weren't up to going."*

*"Okay. But mom, in the letter you said I was sick. I just want to know what to tell dad in case he asks me. I don't want to get him upset."*

*"Don't stress, Roni. It's fine. He won't ask. He never does."*

*"Ok, mom."*

Her mother, Clare, went inside and made up some cold drinks and brought them out. She always did something to avoid more questioning. Veronica knew it was her way of dealing with things, but she was not about to let her off the hook so easily.

*"Mom, what does dad do for work?"*

*"Roni, honestly! What's going on with you? Your father Aaron works at the factory. You know that."*

*"I know that. But what does he do there?"*

*"Roni, I don't understand. You know your dad is in management there."*

*"Managing what?"*

Her mother was shocked. Her body language was enough to show that she wasn't ready to be asked that question."

*"Veronica Miller. What is the meaning of all this?! What are you getting at?!"*

*"Geez, mom, I'm sorry. I was just asking a simple question."*

*"Hardly. You're being very rude. Why are you trying to upset me like this?"*

*"Mom, I—"*

*"Enough! Now if you're through interrogating me, why don't you go inside?"*

*"Oh—ok, mom. I'm sorry if I upset you. Mom? I'm going to read in the living room then, ok?"*

*"Roni! You know your father is asleep in the next room. Just go to your room, ok?"*

*"Sure, mom."*

"What was throwing me off was that my mother never got upset with me. Not like that. I knew I hit a nerve and just didn't understand how. I was just asking my mother what my father did at his job. Why was that so bad?"

"I went into our TV room and turned on the fan and grabbed something to read. Over the buzz from the fan, I heard my father stumbling upstairs after waking up in our dining room. My mother came inside and finished cleaning up the dishes since she wouldn't do it earlier in fear of waking him up. Once she finished, she came and kissed me good night and went off to join my father. I waited awhile until I was pretty sure they were asleep, and I got to work."

"Got to work on what?" Richard hadn't seen this part of the memory. It was overshadowed by what was to come.

"I was looking for something, anything with information on my dad's work. It just didn't make sense for my mom to get so angry with me. Not unless she was hiding something. I looked all over. In our bookshelf, in piles of paper. My mom kept their checkbook in a small desk compartment in our living room that was just off the dining room. I had to be careful as this was closer to the stairway that led to my parent's room. I didn't want to wake them up. I found some pay stubs from my father, but it only said where he worked. Not what he did. We had some small night tables in our living room that had two drawers. They turned up empty with no luck. Just some paperwork on the house and other things that I found to have no relevance.

"As I was snooping, I didn't notice a set of headlights pull in and out of our driveway. My brother, Harold, was home after being out with his friends. He opened the front door so quickly I dropped all the papers in my hand. My heart started to pound. I wasn't close with my brother and didn't know if he'd tell on me for going through my parents' affairs."

*"Hey, Ronster. What the heck are you doing?"* Harold was laughing and looking at his little sister like she was a little crazed.

*"Nothing. I was just looking for something."*

*"Well, what would you be looking for in there? Hoping to find our inheritance papers, sis? Sorry to tell you, but I don't think we're secretly royalty."*

"Were you close with your brother?"

"Harold and I? Sadly no. I never really got to know him. He was only a few years older than me, but he kept as busy as possible to avoid my father. He played a lot of sports and was pretty popular. There was always somewhere for him to go. He was set to go off to university that fall, so his summer was pretty full of parties and girls. It was the 60s. Great time to be young.

"My brother was a sweet person though. Just because we weren't close didn't mean I didn't love him. He showed me love in his own way too."

*"Come here, Ronster. Tell me what's up. You're acting kinda crazy."*

Harold took off his coat and went and sat on the couch in their living room. He gestured at Veronica to come sit beside him.

*"Tell your big brother. What are you really looking for?"*

*"Harry, what does dad do?"*

*"Roni, he works at the factory, you know this."*

*"Come on, Harry. I'm not ten years old. I asked mom about it tonight and she freaked out on me. What's going on?"*

*"You asked mom?"*

*"Yes, and she completely shut down. Tell me the truth, Harold. I can handle it."*

*"Ok ok. But tell me, what brought this on?"*

*"Don't distract me. Just tell me!"*

Part of Veronica debated telling her brother about Davian. But when she played things out in her head about meeting someone who had special gifts, she decided not to.

*"Look. You were younger then, it happened a few years ago. Dad isn't father of the year by a long shot, but he does try. Unfortunately, some of his bad habits started following him to work. I was about eleven at the time, so I'm not surprised you don't remember."*

*"Remember what?! Come on!!"*

*"Would you calm down? I'm getting to it! So anyways, dad used to drink during the week too. Haven't you ever asked yourself why he only drinks on weekends?"*

*"Well sure, but he's just always done that."*

*"No. Not always. So his drinking was getting way out of hand. You know how dad can get on Fridays? Imagine that almost every night after work. Well, he started to get sick when he wouldn't drink. Sick so badly that he was drinking at work. His boss caught him, but his boss was a man's man. He knows dad is tough as nails and didn't want to let him go. Well, he almost fired dad, but he gave him a choice. I remember hearing him and mom talk about it. His boss said he could stay on staff, but he would no longer be a manager of production. They demoted him to janitor. He's a janitor, Roni. Do you have any idea how that makes him feel? How it makes mom feel?"*

Right then, Veronica knew why her mother didn't want to discuss it. She was ashamed. The only thing she could defend about their father about was that he was a provider. He had no other redeeming qualities about him.

*"But, how can we still live here on a janitor's income? That doesn't make sense?"*

*"Like I said, I heard them talk about it. His boss was also his buddy, so he cut him a deal. He'd still be paid the same wage as long as he never came to work drunk again. Dad really struggled with it, but he had no choice. Nowhere else was going to hire him. Not with his problems. It took him a few tries, because when he was there mopping the floors, no one noticed at first that his breath wreaked of booze. Finally, mom got him to stop. But hello, Roni! Doesn't it make sense to you now, why dad is so miserable? Well, at least one of the reasons?"*

Roni felt bad having never thought about it that way. But in the back of her mind, she also knew it didn't give him the right to be so awful.

"Now, mom and dad have no idea I know. Mom would die of embarrassment if she found out we know. You can't tell her or anyone about this."

"Well, I guess."

"Listen. Just cut dad some slack, ok? Just do what I did. Focus on school and stay the hell away from home as much as possible. Why do you think I am never home? My university scholarship wasn't handed to me, you know. My advice is just work your ass off and get out of here."

"I know. I do my best." Veronica waited and watched as her brother headed up to his room. "Harry, what happened last night with mom and dad? What did they fight about?"

"How do you know about that?!"

"Uh, mom might have mentioned something about it when she was upset. Never mind."

Harold turned around sternly and aggressively walked right up to Veronica.

"Listen . . . sister. I don't know what has gotten into you, but stop it. Stop snooping. Promise me."

"But I haven't done anything!"

"Look, just stop. Stop and I won't tell them I caught you meddling around down here, got it? What would mom say if I told her this?"

"Ok, I'm sorry, Harry. Just forget about the whole thing. Good night."

"Good night." Harold then stormed off upstairs.

## CHAPTER 9

# Moonlight and Discovery

"Had your brother ever talked to you that way?" Richard pressed with some concern.

"No. Never. And that's what made me more confused about everything. What were they hiding? I decided not to press my luck and went to my room. Truth be told, I didn't even know what to start looking for, but I knew they were keeping something from me, and I had to find out what it was."

"So, what did you think it could be?"

"I really had no idea. I was still so wrapped up in angst about seeing Davian again. It was now only Monday and I had days to go. My mind was going crazy with everything that had happened. I tried to keep busy, to make it seem like I was going about my usual days. I'd go see Martha during the day. We'd go downtown or to the movies."

"Remember my father was about routine. He only ever left the house for three things really. Alcohol, cigarettes, or to go to work. So it surprised me when one night after the cottage, he went for a walk. He must have been gone for hours. Up until that night he was unbearable. But, when he came back after being going one summer night, he came back and was a little more bearable. It was the strangest thing. This was really out of character for him and only ignited my drive even more."

"My mother and brother thought I'd moved on from snooping. But night after night that week, I'd stay up for hours, ripping apart the entire house. I eventually found some work papers validating what my brother told me. He was demoted alright. But I knew that was just a piece of the puzzle. Something else was being kept from me."

"I tried to keep as quiet as possible. I used a flashlight in case someone woke up. That someone being my father. I crept around the house with such stealth that I felt like a trained professional. By Thursday night, I was about to give up when I sitting in the dark in our TV room. I had just gone through every nook and cranny when I heard a door open upstairs. My brother had just gotten home a few hours before, so I knew it couldn't be him. I was so scared of being caught that I hid behind the couch. It was pitch black, so unless the lights were all turned on, no one would see me."

"At first, I feared I'd get caught because my heart was pounding so loud in my chest once I could tell from the sounds that it was my father. He was coming down the staircase. If he caught me sneaking around the house, I knew it would anger him. I heard his footsteps take him into the kitchen and open the fridge. A little relief came over me for a brief second when I figured he'd just woken up to grab a drink. But after closing the refrigerator, my worst fear was happening as he started turning on the lights."

Richard started to share in Veronica's sense of fear. She was crouching behind a sofa and her father was still half-intoxicated from what he drank the night before.

"Did he catch you?"

"I didn't realize how drunk he still was. I was paralyzed by fear nonetheless and didn't move a muscle. I heard him murmur his drunk grumble as he made his way down the hall. I was praying he wouldn't come into the TV room. But as he got closer, I felt my forehead break a sweat. I gasped with tension, however, that's when I noticed he turned the backyard light on. It quickly turned off, and I could see he'd turned it on by mistake. He quickly turned on the light beside the backdoor and started ruffling through a cupboard we had by the door. I heard him rustle through everything in there so loud, I was honestly just waiting for my mother to come downstairs to see what all the commotion was."

"He grabbed something and I heard a faint clicking sound. He then turned off the inside light and headed out the back door."

"What was he doing?"

"I had no idea. This was strange behaviour to me, and I'd never known my father to leave the house at night, let alone the middle of the night. I relaxed a little when I realized he was out of the house and I could escape to my room. A loud crash of our garbage bins at the side of the house caused me to almost have an aneurism. But I took a deep breath and I was about to make a run out of the TV room when I noticed a flashlight going off in our backyard. I was so baffled by what I was witnessing. I saw the light head right to the back maple tree. It was about twenty meters from our back door in the pitch black. I could only make out the light and where it had stopped. It was too far to see what he was doing. I watched in wonder, and my imagination couldn't come up with any reason for him to be out there. What was he doing? I didn't move until I saw the light moving back toward the house. I ran up to my room in the dark and got into my bed without making a decibel of noise. I heard him come in the back door and go back to bed."

"So you'd never heard him do that before?"

"Not that I could remember. Not once."

"Did he go back to bed or did he stay awake?"

"I heard him go back to my parents' bedroom and I didn't hear a sound the rest of the night. I know this because I couldn't sleep a wink. I was too confused over what had just happened. I laid awake in bed, trying to think of a way to figure out what he just did. I laid in bed until I saw the sun come up and heard my mother go downstairs and start breakfast. My dad usually slept in when he didn't have to work, so I knew it would be just me and my mom for a little while at least. I went down to the kitchen in my pajamas and joined my mother at our kitchen table."

*"Sleep good, dear?"* Veronica's mother asked, seemingly very chipper.

*"So so."*

*"What happened, bad dream?"* Her mother set down her coffee mug and reached out to Veronica.

*"Maybe, I think. Mom, I had a weird dream that dad went digging in your garden in the middle of the night. Isn't that strange?"*

Veronica sipped a big gulp from her martini. Richard noticed a slight tremor in her hands. The vodka in her glass was rippling at the top from her trembling.

"Are you ok, Veronica?! You're shaking."

"I'm sorry. I'm ok."

"Do you need to lay down?" Richard was worried she'd taken in too much. This was a lot for her to revisit.

"If you think this is hard, I've not even begun."

"As long as you're ok. I'll follow your lead."

"So I looked up at my mother who was staring at me with the widest eyes I've ever seen. She was so deep in her stare that she didn't notice the mug in her hand start to sag, spilling hot coffee all over the kitchen table."

*"MOM!"*

*"What!? Oh! Oh my. I'm sorry, dear. What were you saying? Oh right. I'm sorry you had a bad dream. Ron, can you go up to your room while I clean this up? Please, please just go. I've got to make breakfast. Just come back down in half hour and it will be ready ok?"*

"I sat there a moment and watched her scurry about the kitchen. Cleaning coffee and just mentally checking out. She didn't want to hear what I asked and she wasn't going to listen. I just excused myself from the table and went upstairs like she asked."

"Had she ever done that before?"

"Never. It was like I didn't even know her anymore. She was acting like someone I never met. And I only had myself to blame. The more I pressed her, the more she pushed away from me."

Richard could read what she was hiding in the memory. It gave him chills seeing in more detail what he already knew. "So what do you think your father was doing?"

"Something I wasn't ready to admit, even to myself—" Veronica paused and could not look Richard in the eye. She focused her sight off into the room, not really focusing on anything. "So I came back for breakfast a while later like my mother told me to. I ate in silence and didn't really interact with her. I said my please and thank yous, but our conversation was very dry. I just tried to focus on getting through the day so I could see Davian sooner. I was about to get up from the table when my father came into the kitchen. He was disoriented and still not fully awake. No doubt still suffering from how much he drank the night before. He sat down at his usual spot next to me at the table. I offered my usual 'good morning' and he gave me his usual grunt. I was staring at him, and neither he nor my mother noticed me examining him with my eyes. *What had he been doing the night before? WHAT ARE YOU UP TO??!!* I screamed inside my head. My mother poured him a cup of coffee and served him eggs she made for all of us. He started to eat, and when he grabbed for his cup of coffee, that's when I noticed it."

"Noticed what?"

"The dirt under his fingernails. It caught my eye right away. I sat there so still. My entire being focusing on my train of thought. Then it dawned on me . . . he was in the backyard . . . digging in the dirt or something."

"Did he ever help your mother garden?"

"My father? Help my mother? In ANY sense of the word? Never. His idea of helping her with anything plant related other than his fatherly duty of mowing the lawn? Well, that was to sit outside and drink his beer. Something he didn't really do as he didn't like how warm his beer would get out in the sun.

"I excused myself from the table and went to my room. I had that feeling again—everything I thought I knew about my father wasn't real, and somehow these things were connected. Why was my mother defending him? What did my brother not want me to find? What was my father doing in our backyard in the middle of the night? I had to sit and think. Clear my head. It didn't help that Davian was constantly on my mind in between thoughts. I must have been overly tired because I didn't know what time it was when I fell asleep. Do you dream often, Richard?"

"Me? Of course I do. Interesting enough, the year I graduated, a few of my colleagues wrote their thesis on dreaming and the theory of why we dream. Science wasn't able to figure it out. Even with studies posted with your daughter have produced very vague results. What procures most people in my field over anything related to dreams is why we can't remember them."

"Well, let me tell you. I fell asleep that day in a deep, but troubled sleep. I woke drenched in my own sweat and shaking uncontrollably."

Richard was fascinated how he saw her dream unfold and worked through the details. He enjoyed the process with most of his patience, except what Veronica dreamed was terrifying, and real.

*"Davian? Where are you? What's happening?"*
*"Don't dig into the past, Roni. Don't dig."*
*"Davian, why? What's going on? Where are you?"*
*"Don't dig, Roni. Promise me, don't dig."*
*"Davian, where did you go? What's happening?"*
*"Goodbye, I love you. I'll see you again. DON'T DIG."*

"I would have been screaming had it made sense to me at first. I woke up and cleared my throat. I took a sip of water from a glass beside my bed. *Don't dig. Don't dig… Why had he said that to me?* I couldn't get that thought from my mind. I dropped my glass of water the second I clued in. THE YARD. I had to see what my dad had done in our backyard. Whatever was back there was my answer. Even though he told me not to, I had to. I had to dig up whatever my father was trying to hide from me."

"How did you pull it off?" Richard asked, trying to keep her calm with his compulsion. He could sense her heart beat speeding up.

"I had to wait till dark. That day felt like years, and it seemed like the sun never went down. I paced in my room until the early evening. Martha had stopped in to see if I wanted to go to the movies. I thought it would be a good thing to do. It got me out of the house and distracted me, even if only for a while. We always walked to the movies, as the theater was just downtown. Right before she came, I hid a pair of shoes right beside our backdoor. One less thing to find in the dark later.

"At the movies, I remember Martha asking if I was mad at her more than once, and I just brushed it off. While she was my best friend, everything that was happening with me made it feel like she didn't really know me at all. I don't even remember what movie we saw that night. I watched the images on the big screen, but my mind was at home, in the backyard."

"We walked back to our neighbourhood and said our goodbyes. I came right home to find my father almost so inebriated he didn't know his name. I was never glad like I was that night to see him drunk. *Perfect*, I thought. The sooner he's out cold the better. What did he bury back there? Finally, I saw the sun setting, and I excused myself to bed. My brother was out with his friends for the night which made me grateful that I didn't have to worry about him coming home. Not too long after I shut my bedroom door, I heard my mother turning off the lights and coming up the stairs. I waited to hear my father come up but with no luck. I was certain he'd passed out at the dining room table. This was not good as the bay window in our dining room overlooked the yard. But, time was of the essence, and I had to do it that night. I don't know why, but it just could not wait."

Richard paused and really LOOKED into Veronica running her memories. Her anxiety was growing intense, and he didn't like how she was feeling. Her speed of speaking was getting faster and faster. "Veronica, do you need a moment?"

"No, I'm fine. Sorry. I'll slow down a little." She took a deep breath and continued.

"I think around 1 a.m. I decided to get things going. I slipped some shorts on over my nightgown and tucked it in. My plan was that if anyone woke up, I would pass them and say that I just got out of bed to get a snack. I could easily hide the shorts I was wearing. I wasn't sure what I'd say about wearing shoes and carrying a flashlight, but I hadn't thought that far ahead."

"I grabbed my flashlight and heading downstairs and to the back door. I passed by our living room and front door that had the perfect view of our dining room table. There, in the dark, I could hear my father snoring loudly. The smell of his cigarettes still wafting in the air. I knew he was out cold, and I didn't have to worry as long as I was quiet. I got to the back door and slipped on my shoes. Back then, we never locked the back door. I slowly opened it. Millimeter by millimeter, I turned the knob and pulled the door open. What I would normally do in seconds, I think must have taken me minutes. Once the door was open, I stepped outside and just as slowly shut it. I waited a moment, just to ensure I didn't wake anyone. I took a few steps in the dark, and not more than a few feet from the door, I fell. Not sure on what, but I went down quickly. My heart started pounding the second I did as my flashlight made a loud smash on our concrete patio. I was too panicked to notice if I was hurt and too focused on my flashlight. In the dark, I felt it and knew it was still in one piece, so I grabbed it and ran into the yard. It was awhile before I hit the tree line, and I focused on what little skyline I could make out at that time of night."

"Jesus, did anyone wake up?"

"No, they didn't, thank goodness. I sat in the pitch black for a long time, maybe fifteen minutes, ensuring I didn't wake my mother who was asleep upstairs, but especially my father who was drunk passed out only fifteen feet away in our dining room. At that point, I was worried the sound of my heart smashing in my chest would have woken them up. Finally, when my body allowed me to move, I turned on my flashlight. I was grateful it was still working, or I would have had to go find my father's. With the glow of the light, I let it lead me to the back of our yard. The huge maple tree was easy to find, and the flowers that grew there lit up brightly with the false light shining from the small gadget I held in my sweaty hand. Scanning the area, I saw a few patches of freshly earthed sections. I wondered to myself why I had never really looked by there, let alone noticed anything out of place. Now that it held my attention, I felt ignorant to my own surroundings. *How many times has this happened? Did it happen before? How had I not noticed my own father sneaking around in the night?*"

"I made my way over to the closest part and realized I didn't even bring a small shovel or tool. I didn't care either. I had to find out what he was hiding. I dropped to my knees and carefully placed my flashlight on the ground next to me. With the light as my guide, I just started digging with my bare hands. The earth was soft and dry, as it hadn't rained for a week. I dug maybe a few inches deep, not even sure there was anything there. I decided to keep going. There was no way he just came out here to move soil. Something was there, I could sense it."

"A few more sweeps of the soil with my hand and my finger felt something. I flashed the light down and saw the tiny bones of a squirrel or maybe a chipmunk. I figured it to be normal and went over to another freshly dug spot. I dug and it was the same thing, only this time a bird. But the third spot I dug was different. I dug with my hand and I once again felt something. Not only that, I heard something. A tiny bell sound came from the earth. The sound startled me and my body ceased moving. What the hell was that? Again, I started taking a few deep breaths and poised myself. I grabbed the flashlight. Instead of shining down on the tiny bones of an animal, something metal reflected back, and I knew whatever I was looking for, I just found it. I stared at the metal. I focused in and leaned closer to look."

"It was a bell. A tiny round bell. *What the hell is a bell doing back here? Did my dad hide this here?* I noticed the bell had a metal loop at the top. It was attached to something. I reached for the bell in what seemed like slow motion. It was light, and whatever was attached wasn't deeply imbedded with mud. I wiggled it a bit, and it slid out of its earthy encasement. It was attached to a blue piece of material, much like that of a rope. *What is this?* I stared at it in confusion and couldn't piece it together. As my eyes started to come into sharp focus, I noticed something that looked like black oil on it? *Oil?* I thought. *What is oil doing on this. What is . . ."*

Richard felt her emotion in the memory and his stomach flipped, almost making him sick. He set his drink down on the coffee table and embraced his chin with both hands and took some deep breaths. *What panic and terror she felt in that moment.*

"I dropped it when I realized what it was and let out a small scream. When I saw the metal tag that said Porter on it, I knew what it was. It wasn't oil, I had been fooled by the dark. It was blood. It was the collar of the latest missing neighbourhood pet. My father had killed that dog and buried him there. I didn't dig more, afraid of what I'd find. These animals didn't die of natural causes, they died at the hands of my father. My head rushed and I almost passed out, but instead of passing out, I threw up."

"My father. My father was a monster. I collected myself as best I could and grabbed my flashlight. The light was bouncing because my hands were shaking uncontrollably. I looked deep into the yard and saw more patches of freshly dug earth. How many animals had he killed? Why did he do this? When I sat there feeling the burning tears rush down my cheek onto my leg, I thought of all the missing pet posters I had seen in the last year. My brain wouldn't let me do the math at that point because if I had a number to put to the madness of it all, I think I would have lost my mind. My head and my heartbeat matched in intensity. My stomach joined in again and I threw up again. Luckily, I didn't get sick on the dry earth I just dug, and I pushed it back in place, covering the collar. What would I do now? When I zoned out in a daze of sadness and fear, I screamed out loud as I felt a firm set of hands on my shoulders."

"I felt my body being forced up and jerked around until I was looking into a set of eyes. These we're no ordinary eyes, they were eyes of pure rage."

*"What the hell are you doing back here, Roni!!?!?? What the hell do you think you're doing?"* Veronica's mother had her in her grasp and was whispering loudly, but not screaming. Veronica could feel traces of spit hitting her cheek. Her mother's hands were digging so hard into Veronica shoulders that she knew they'd leave bruises.

*"Mom... it's dad. He's... mom... it's awful."*

*"Why did you come out here?! You're not supposed to be out here. It's the middle of the night!"*

*"Mom, did you hear what I said?! Dad—"*

*"Nothing. Stop it. You shouldn't be back here."* Veronica's mother looked into the yard and out of her daughter's eyes. She looked blank and void of all emotion now.

*"You... you knew about this, didn't you?"*

She turned back to look Veronica deep in her eyes with anger and intensity. *"Get inside. There's nothing to know. You didn't find anything, you hear me? There is nothing back here. Do you understand me?"*

"But I didn't understand. She knew. I couldn't wrap my head around it. She knew, and did nothing."

"I think she was probably afraid. Killing animals is the first stage for some people in mental distress," Richard told her.

"Distress? My father wasn't distressed, he was sick. In every sense of the word."

"Did she tell your father anything?" Richard felt awkward still asking questions as he could SEE what he needed, but her reliving the memories in her mind let him SEE in more details.

"She knew better. Bringing something like that to his attention would only have put her in line for a massive blowup."

"So what did you do?" Richard asked.

"I was in shock. I just ran up to my room and hid. Hot tears streaming down my face, I looked out the window. The sun would be up soon. This meant only a few more hours until I'd see Davian again. I looked out the window, then at my closest full of clothes. I decided to ask him to take me with him. Runaway together. I didn't know what else to do because I knew living with my father was no longer an option. I packed a bag and found a piece of paper and wrote a note. I listened for my mother to come back upstairs and waited until I was sure she was asleep. I got dressed. I waited a few hours till dusk and grabbed my bag and headed downstairs. My father was still out cold as I tiptoed past him. I placed my note on the kitchen table and left."

*Morning mom,*

*I got up early to go for a walk and I'm meeting Martha later. I'll be home for dinner.*

*Love, Roni.*

"I went straight to the park to wait. I had no money and nowhere else to go. I sat on the same bench where just a week ago Davian had found me. I couldn't wait for the day to pass so he could find me again. I knew he'd take me with him. I knew that he'd already seen what I found and had tried to warn me about it. As minutes turned to hours, the day was long. I didn't eat or drink anything. I couldn't out of fear I'd just throw it up. My nerves were shot. Hour after hour, I watched families come and go, kids playing and laughing. I just sat on the bench alone. Waiting for him to come. It had been way too long. It had to be way past 1 when we were supposed to meet. My heart was pounding feverishly in my chest and wouldn't stop. I only spoke to one lady walking by."

*"Excuse me, do you know what time it is?"*
The lady looked at her watch. *"It's 3:30."*
*"Thank you."*

"I got dizzy. *3:30? It can't be. Where is he? Why didn't he show??* I got up and walked around the area for a while. I went to see if I could find his car. After an hour or so, I went back to the bench. *Maybe he got lost?* I waited and waited as the tears started dropping from my eyes with each blink. A dad and his kids walked by and he asked me if I was ok. I wasn't, but I just nodded my head. I couldn't speak anyways. I knew it was close to supper time, and I had no choice but to go home. The walk home was brutal. My heart broken and terrified to see my father. My emotions were all over the place. I walked up to our front door and my hand was shaking as I twisted the knob. I pushed in the door to see my father at his usual spot, drinking at the dining room table. I could hear my mother in the kitchen, and she shouted out to me."

*"Dinner will be ready in half hour! Go freshen up, hun!"*

"She was oblivious that her daughter tried to run away that day. I ran up the stair and flung myself on my bed. I needed to talk to someone. I needed a friend. I cleaned myself up and prepared to be near my father. I heard my brother come home and felt a bit a relief. At least I had one more person to separate me from my father at the table. I went down to our kitchen and called Martha. I asked her if I could stay over. I couldn't sleep a wink in that house. Never again. She got permission from her mom, and I quietly asked my mother if it was ok too. She looked over my shoulder and saw my father was distracted."

*"Look, hun, that's fine. Just don't mention it in front of your dad. He's really tired and probably will be asleep soon. No need to get him worked up."* Veronica's mother knelt down in front of her and embraced her a little. *"Hun, last night. I, I never. You shouldn't have ... Roni ... you can't tell anyone."*

"My body locked in place. Don't tell anyone? Was that all she had to say? Dinner was always awkward at our house, but that night was exceptional. It was so quiet you could hear everything. Clicking of cutlery on the dinnerware, chewing, my dad guzzling his beers. My dad noticed me cower away from him, but he didn't say anything. I have no idea why, but he let it be. Not one word was spoken by anyone at that dinner, so I figured he just wanted to keep that going."

# CHAPTER 10

# Looking for Answers

"After dinner, I got up and went to my room. I emptied my runaway bag and packed just what I needed for the night. I snuck out the front door so my father wouldn't notice and ran over to Martha's. I knocked on the door, and she opened it and took one look at me."

*"Oh my, you look awful. What's wrong?"* Martha rushed her in and shut the door.

"We sat in her room all night talking. I told her everything about Davian. Meeting him, the car, driving around. I didn't mention anything about his abilities; I was afraid she wouldn't understand. I tried to share her excitement and enthusiasm with her when I told her I lost my virginity."

*"Oh my god! I can't believe it! Did it hurt? Where you scared? Tell me EVERYTHING!"*

"I just couldn't fake it. She understood my melancholy when I got to the part about him not showing up that day."

*"Oh I'm so sorry, Roni. That's just awful. What are you going to do?"*

"That night I cried and confided in my friend about Davian. I wished more than anything she could have comforted me about all my problems. But out of fear, I didn't mention anything about my father. I was afraid of what my father would do if he found out I knew about his secret hobbies, let alone that I had told anyone. Martha was a good friend that night and I actually was able to get some sleep. I rested knowing I was safely away from my father's wrath, and I was exhausted from no sleep the night before."

"My peaceful sleep was short lived as I woke up to the room spinning. I sat up in the bed with Martha still asleep. I ran down the hall to her washroom and made it there in time. I threw up. I had never felt like this. I wasn't hot or sweaty like when I'd have the flu. This was different. A little while passed, and I started to feel better. I just wrote it off as a reaction to stress, and I was feeling a lot of that right now. I spent almost the entire day at her place, hiding from my reality back home with my father. After supper, I went home and immediately excused myself to my room. I blocked the door with my dresser and slept under my bed. I felt safer there. I woke up the next morning with the same dizziness I had at Martha's the night before. My mother must have woken when she heard me shove my dresser out of the way. She came to check on me."

*"Roni, are you ok?"*
*"Fine, mom."*
*"Are you getting sick in there? What's going on?"*
*"Fine, mom, must have been something I ate last night. I feel ok. I'll be out in a minute."*

"I brushed my teeth and splashed some water on my face when I was done throwing up and came out of the bathroom to see my mother staring. She didn't say anything; her face said it all. She looked angry and scared. She just stared at me for a good minute and then went back to bed. I will never forget that face."

"That week, I started going to the library where I looked in phone books of the surrounding area and called any car business I could think of. I barely had any money to begin with, so I would go downtown and ask anyone for change. I felt pathetic, but I didn't have a choice. The phone cost 10 cents and over the course of a week or two, I had called every possible place I could think of. Repair shops, sales centres, gas stations. For a course of two weeks, that was all I did. Leave home, beg for change, go to the library and make calls. Martha came with me at first, and I always appreciated her help. After a few days, however, she was starting to get annoyed with me. I could feel a bit of resentment coming from her. One day, she finally snapped."

*"Roni, are you sure about all this? Are you maybe just making it up? I won't judge you, but we should have found him by now. This all just doesn't make sense."*

*"Why would I make it up, Martha? What would I have to gain?"*

*"Well, for starters, it would have made you a little cooler, Roni. You aren't the most interesting person sometimes. Maybe you did it for attention."*

"My chest caved when she said that."

"Sure doesn't sound like a good friend there." Richard could see the jealousy in Martha's eyes. She was always a little jealous of Veronica's looks and the attention she got from the boys at school.

"She was young. It was what it was. Friends get close, some drift apart. She just became tired of my obsession over a boy she didn't believe existed."

"Another week or two passed, and I didn't hear from Martha at all. Before, I would have tried harder to reconnect with my friend, but I had way too much going on. After I stopped going to the daily to the library, I mostly hid in my room, pretending to read and study. My brother was a scholar who was off to university in the fall on his full scholarship, so I made my parents believe I was getting ahead for my school year. My father didn't care at all, but I'm sure my mother had her doubts. I would read whatever I could find in the house or go to the library and take new ones out. Anything I could do to distract me, the better. Whenever my mother gave me any money, I'd spend it at the coffee shop or go see a movie. Always alone. I had noticed my morning ritual of getting sick was ongoing. I didn't want to run into my mother, so I dealt with it in secret in my room and took care of the mess later when she was busy cooking or cleaning. She almost caught me once washing out my waste basket in the backyard with the hose, but I managed to get away with it, or so I thought.

"Summer vacation was ending soon, and it was then time for our last trip to the cottage. My brother was set to leave for university a few days before our planned trip. I was worried by the fact I'd be alone with my father the monster, and my mother would be in denial land in a car for two to three hours, when unbeknownst to me, my mother had another agenda.

"My mother was making dinner, my father sitting at the kitchen table waiting to be served. I heard them speaking while down the hall in our TV room."

*"Honey, I think Veronica should stay home this weekend."*

*"What? Like hell she is. Her brother gets to take off first, and now this? Check your fucking head. She is not staying here alone."*

*"Come on, Aaron. She'll be fine. She will just be at Betty's most of the time with Martha, anyways. She did it on Canada Day weekend, remember?"*

*"You said she was fucking sick. Is she sick again? Is this what you're telling me?"*

*"No, just . . . well, you've been working so hard lately. I just thought you'd love a little more peace and quiet at the cottage is all. I don't like seeing you that way."*

*"Ya, I do work hard. Really fucking hard."*

Veronica laughed to herself when she heard him. Sad thing, he really did believe himself. That he was some kind of martyr or something to his family. In reality, none of them could really stand him.

*"And I was thinking, why don't I pick you up some bottles of that special whiskey you like so much? I know it costs a little more, but with Harold off to school on scholarship, our budget can be reworked. Come on, honey, you deserve it, what do you say?"*

"I had never once heard my mother encourage my father's alcoholism. Sure, she would be the one to mostly go buy it for him, but she had never outright encouraged it before."

Richard could see in Veronica's memories that it was unusual. Extremely usual for her to enable him to that extent. She did what she had to in order to keep the peace. But, this was the first time she encouraged him. He took a moment and tried to look into her father's consciousness. Unfortunately, she avoided much interaction with him. If he met him in person, then it would be no problem, but seeing into someone's consciousness via someone else's had its limits.

"What did you make of it?" Richard had years of training with his patients to keep the conversation sounding normal.

"I'm getting to that part."

# CHAPTER 11

# Labour Day

"So my mother convinced my father to let me stay home. God only knows why he finally agreed to it, but he did. My brother took off for university a few days before they left. We had a small celebratory dinner, Miller style. My father grunted and barely spoke. No alcohol made him mute most days. He would sit there angry and fuel up for his weekend benders of having something to say about everything and anything. My mother cried and carried the conversation. My brother said a few words, and I mostly looked down at my plate. It had gotten worse since my episode of midnight gardening."

"A day or two later, my parents left. I was grateful as always for the time alone. I had spent a lot of time in my room reading and crying over Davian. Now, at least I could do so freely around the house. Martha didn't come around at all anymore, and I made peace with it. She really thought I was delusional about the entire thing and was convinced I made it up for attention."

"That day, I didn't amount to much, but lately I had noticed I never was up for much. The stress of everything was exhausting. After watching some television, and making something to eat, I felt my bed calling me around 8 p.m. The sun was still shining. I locked the house and turned off the lights. I went to my bedroom and was grateful the summer heat had broken. Compared to the day I met Davian, the air was cool at night and made it easy to fall asleep. *That night*. As soon as I let that thought come to mind, I found myself laying in my room as the sun was setting outside the window. I could hear kids playing and having fun. Cars were driving around and I could hear someone playing music at their house. Maybe they were having a party. They got to live and enjoy life while I didn't know which way was up in my world."

"I fell in love with a beautiful stranger whom I never saw again. My father was deeply disturbed and sick. And, he was getting worse. My best friend was no longer even a friend. And to top it off, my mother, who had always been the only stability in my life, was acting strange. The house was so silent, and I felt like she was watching me. No doubt making sure I was keeping our secret. I felt more alone during that time than I have in my entire life."

"I fell asleep finally, exhausted from crying. I must have fallen deep asleep as I could remember my dreams..."

"I was walking in the park, our park. It was a beautiful day. I was alone at first, no one in sight but the dewy haze in the park at sunrise. The blades of grass still had beads of moisture that I could feel as I walked through the lush lawn, and it felt cold at my feet. I was happy, I felt safe. No one but me and the beauty of a perfect sunrise. I heard my name. I turned around. Still at peace and full of joy, I saw the bench. Our bench. It made me think of popsicles and cold Coke. I smiled as the memory came to me in the dream, just happy to cherish the moment. I heard my name again, and this time the rising sun was overshadowed by clouds. The morning grew dark and a cold breeze came in. I was shivering, only dressed in my night gown. I no longer felt safe. My heart was racing and I embraced myself. I heard my name again, getting louder. I didn't know who it was. I headed toward our bench as I thought that's where it was coming from. It grew louder, but I still didn't know the voice."

*"Veronica, you have to wake up. Veronica, get up."*

"This time, I could clearly hear the voice."

*"Veronica, get up now! We have to hurry."*

"As I made out the voice, I felt hands on my face that quickly covered my screams."

*"Veronica, Veronica!! It's me! It's mom. See?"* Her mother had turned on her bedside lamp before waking her. *"Calm down, it's just me. You're safe."*
*"Mom?? What? What time is it?"*
*"Veronica, get dressed. I already had your bags packed before we left. There isn't much time. We have to move. Now."*

*"Mom? What time is it?"* Veronica was so dazed and still half-asleep.

*"Honey, time is of the essence. We have to move. Get dressed. Don't turn on any lights and come downstairs to the front door. Turn off your lamp as soon as you can."*

Veronica didn't question it. She knew that tone of voice. Her mother was pleading with her, and she meant it. She was serious. Veronica got dressed, turned off her lamp, and headed to the front door where she could faintly see her mother's silhouette.

*"Mom, I'm scared. What's happening?"*

*"I'll explain on the drive. Look, I parked down the road around the corner. I don't want the neighbours to see us. They can't know I was here tonight. Be quiet, move quickly, and get in the car and don't slam the door. Do you understand me?"*

She shook her head. Too scared to even speak. There was so many questions she needed answered. But, when she said move, Veronica listened. In seconds, they were outside the house and her mother was locking the door behind them.

*"Go. Quickly and quietly."*

Veronica didn't know if they ran or flew, but in what felt like seconds, they were in the car. She shut her car door as gently as possible and her mother got in the driver's seat and did the same. She started the car and pulled down a few more streets before turning on the lights. A few more minutes passed and she couldn't wait any longer.

*"Mom! What is going on?! Where are you taking me? Aren't you supposed to be at the cottage with dad? How did you get here? It's... the middle of the night!!"*

*"Honey, look. I know we haven't had a chance to talk. But, I was hoping this would have blown over."*

*"Are you talking about dad? Mom, you don't have to worry, I'll never tell. I'm worried more about you, mom. How could you hide this? What were you thinking!?"*

*"Listen, Veronica, you're young. You have your whole life ahead of you. One day, you'll be married and have kids of your own, at least I hope you will. But until then, you have to trust me. Your dad, look. I'm not naive. He's sick. He needs help. But it's too late for me. I made my bed, now I have to sleep in it."*

*"Mom, that's ridiculous. You always have a choice. This is the 60s, mom. Women are able to make it on their own."*

*"You don't think I know that? You don't think I want that? Of course I do. But most of the women out there doing their own thing don't have two kids to watch over."*

*"Mom, we're grown. We can handle ourselves."*

*"Roni, listen to me, ok?"*

Suddenly, her mother pulled over the car. They were well out of Kitchener City limits, but Veronica still had no clue where they were going yet.

Richard knew. He had no idea how her mother pulled it off, but he was impressed by her determination and skill at planning everything.

*"Veronica Miller. I'm no fool. But, I had a plan. A good plan. A safe plan for us all to get out. Your brother made his part easy by getting into university. His scholarship was a blessing in more ways than that school will ever know. I really thought you'd be the same. You're always studying and staying after school."*

Veronica envied her brother so much at that moment. He really did get his ticket out of there.

"Harold is gone, he is safe. I'm grateful for that. I love your brother, and I love you too. But, Veronica, your dad's sickness is getting worse. The animals, that hasn't been going on long, thank God. But, it's just the first step."

"First step, mom? What the hell are you talking about? What's dad going to do?!"

"Honey, I'm taking you somewhere to see someone who will explain everything to you. He helped me, and he's the reason why I came tonight. See, your father's rage... it's almost at capacity, so to speak. He is more violent and angry than ever."

"I know, mom. I've noticed it too."

"No, you don't get it. He is one incident, one tiny little 'event' away from going over the edge."

"My mom stared at me in the car. While it wasn't that bright, I could see her facial expression in the glow of the moon. She was staring at me like she had in the hallway a few weeks ago. Not just fear and judgment. She was looking at me like a woman, not a little girl."

"Veronica, when he finds out you're pregnant, I don't know what he'll do. To either of us..."

# CHAPTER 12

# Secret Allies

"I didn't speak after that. I didn't know what to say. My mother started driving again. Thoughts were racing in my mind. My biggest question was *who were we going to see at this hour?* I was scared and confused, but I trusted my mother."

"What could have been minutes or hours later, we were suddenly pulling into a country home in the middle of nowhere. We stopped the car and my mother said to follow her. As soon as I stepped out of the car, I knew we were up north. I could feel it in the air and was certain I could smell a lake. The house was huge. A grand veranda porch wrapped around the white painted wood panels above a few layers of old brick rock. This house had been there a long time. I didn't see any farming equipment or barns and wondered what a home like this was doing out here in the fields. We followed a perfectly landscaped garden path to the back of the house, and there was my answer lit up on a bold sign."

DR. WAGNER. Private Practice.

*"Mom, what are we doing here?"*

*"Just come inside, we'll explain everything."*

"We?" commented Richard.

"I know. It was overwhelming."

"So she led me inside this small office in the smaller home behind the massive white house. I believe it was probably a guest house at some point. I walked into the front room that had chairs lined around and a glass window directly ahead with a door to the right. Behind the locked glass, I saw many filing cabinets and a desk. It looked very similar to my family doctor's office back in Kitchener. We walked through an unlocked door and down a small hallway. We passed the desk area which I could more clearly see on my left. To my right was a washroom and down the hallway were three more doors. Two were examining rooms fully equipped. And the third door on the right was a small office with a large desk and some chairs. This room was lined with textbooks and a few photos. I could tell it was the doctor's personal office. We went down the hall toward the examining rooms, and I heard a voice call out."

*"I'm in here, Clare, to the left."*

"We entered the small yet very nice examining room and beside the medical table sat a small man with salt and pepper hair. He had deep brown eyes, a mustache, and pale skin. He looked about forty, and I remember his face so well as he seemed very calming. His energy made me relax instantly."

The man Veronica took her to see was a medical doctor, but he was also a healer and didn't know anything about his abilities. Richard always found it fascinating when seeing others like him from years before they understood what they were. Davian was not like this in Veronica's memories. He knew what he was and what he could do. This man was of old medicine. Such ideas were never discussed. He never knew why he could always find out what was ailing someone back then with little technologies available. X-rays would have been widely used, but such advancement like a CT scan were still a few years away. Dr. Wagner always seemed to know where a nerve was being pinched, or deep tissue issues like inner tumors he always could find, or if there was distress during child birth. *Fascinating*, Richard thought. He would have loved to have seen in the mind of the first medicine healer's centuries ago. First known doctors or even 'witch doctors.'

"*Hello, Veronica. I'm Dr. Wagner. Your mother, Clare, has told me a lot about you.*"

"*Well, I know nothing about you. Can you please tell me what is going on?*"

"*Yes, please come up on the table and have a seat, won't you?*"

Veronica nervously went and sat at the table beside the doctor. Her mom grabbed a seat at the door.

"*Veronica, your mother and I are old friends, I guess you could say. You see, I have a cottage not that far from your family cottage down the beach on the lake.*"

"*Then why haven't I seen you before?*"

"*It's not exactly close by. It's a good hike away, but on the same lake.*"

"*So, how did you meet my mom?*"

"Well...ugh..." Dr. Wagner looked over at Clare to see if he was ok to give more detail.

*"Go ahead, Don, she needs to know everything."*

Veronica looked at both her mother and the doctor. She was more confused than ever.

"Ok, where do I start?" He poised himself in the seat and rested his chin in his hand. *"So sometime last season, I was out on my property doing some work on the landscape. Pulling weeds, watering flowers, typical maintenance. I was minding my own business when I heard something in the far off bush. I went to check it out and found your mother crying. She was sitting on a large boulder in the bush with her back to me. I approached her and asked her if she was ok? Clare ... are you sure about this?"*

*"It's ok, Don. Really, it's easier for me if you tell her."*

*"As long as you're sure?"*

Clare nodded at Dr. Wagner in reassurance.

*"Well, your mom seemed to be paralyzed by fear. I got closer, letting her know I was a doctor and that I meant no harm, I just wanted to help. As I got closer, she was still sobbing, and that's when I saw the blood."*

"My father," Veronica piped up immediately.

*"Sadly, yes. She explained to me that they had an altercation."* He looked up at Clare, whose eyes were starting to welt. *"Apparently, this is a normal interaction with Aaron, your father."*

"Not sure if normal is the word I'd use," Veronica added.

*"No, you're right. Definitely nothing normal about it, dear."* He looked up a Clare with great concern in his eyes. *"You were so scared, so frail, and so empty. It was like finding a bird that fell out of its nest and was lost."*

*"You have no idea how alone I felt, Veronica. You were swimming in the lake with your brother at the time. I was so glad you were too preoccupied to have witnessed our fight."*

*"What happened, mom?"* Veronica looked over at her mother, tears also forming in her eyes.

*"Don, you have to, I can't."* Veronica's mother left the room. Her eyes were no longer just welting. Fresh tears were now streaming down her face. *"I'll give you two some time."*

*"Ok, Veronica, you need to listen carefully. This is very serious. My medical practice here is very lucrative. I see local patients and take care of their daily health and well-being. Any major concerns, I send them to the city to be checked on at the hospital, if it's something I can't handle here. But Veronica, the country life isn't so different from your more suburban upbringing. Over the years, it's sad to say, but I've met many woman like your mother. She tells me you're not oblivious to how your father treats her?"*

*"Dr. Wager, I'd have to be blind and naive to not see what's happening."*

*"Yes. Well then, you must understand your mother notices his attention is starting to turn to you?"*

Veronica sat there and felt every drop of moisture leave her mouth. Her voice, barely a crackle, mustered out one word as the hairs on her arms stood straight up. *"Y-Y-Yes."* She took a deep swallow. *"May I have a glass of water, please?"*

*"Of course, dear."* Dr. Wagner got up and grabbed a small paper cup out of a dispenser by the sink in the examination room. *"Here you go, sweetie. Drink up. I'm not done yet. It gets worse. A lot worse."*

Veronica sat straight, embracing the examination bed she was still sitting on.

"So I treated your mother a few times in my office at my cottage. I keep some minor surgical tools there for emergencies. Fluids for sterilizing tools, things I'd need for stiches, some painkillers. Just very basic things. Thankfully, I didn't see her too often. She said to me your father tends to be a bit more relaxed when you guys are up there, is that true?"

"Usually he is. But, when he goes off, it's over the top."

"See that's what got my attention. In med school, I dabbled a little in psychology before finalizing my path as a general practitioner. I knew I wanted a private practice here at my home, but at first I couldn't decide if I wanted that as a psychiatrist. Eventually, my fascination with biology made the decision for me. But, I still do have training in the other fields, and made some friends who made a name for themselves in psychology. One, in particular, decided to write his thesis on sociopaths."

Veronica looked at him in wonder. "Sociopaths? What is that?"

"Allow me to explain. While I do believe your father exhibits some very strong traits of the disorder, I don't think we can classify him in one category. A sociopath is a person with zero emotions. No happiness, no joy, no sympathy or empathy."

"That sure does sound like one Aaron Miller."

"Yes, I know. However, the other traits one would display is no fear, no rage, no anger. Your father has a lot of that troubling him emotionally."

"So, what is he then? What's wrong with him?" Veronica looked at the doctor with so much worry on her face.

"Well, unless he would agree to speak with someone, we'll never be able to give him a proper diagnosis. But some of what your mothers told me is sending up major signs of deeper problems."

"Deeper? You mean he could be worse?"

"Veronica, I hate to bring this up as it disturbs me greatly. Your mother told me you found something in the backyard. Something so awful, I can't even wrap my head around it."

"The animals? Are you talking about the pets he killed?" Tears were slowly streaming down Veronica's face now, and her hands began to tremble.

"Yes. I'm sorry. I know this is hard. Just take a deep breath. So, in studies, people with certain disorders start by abusing animals because they're easy to control and manipulate."

"First? What do you mean first? There's a second?!"

"Veronica, calm yourself. Please. Gosh, this was just as hard as it was when I explained this to your mother. Be strong, she was and you can be too."

With that, Veronica focused on her breathing and told the Dr. to continue.

"Ok, well, your mother at first wanted to run. Just leave and never come back, but she knew she had to stay and protect you. Your mom has no savings, no support. If she left to go back west, you know as well as she does your father would come for you. I at first suggested to your mother to take you to her parents' house in Alberta. But, like many family lineages, she lived the same truth."

"Grandma? Grandpa beat grandma?"

"Not to the extent of what you and your family are dealing with. Abuse comes in many forms. I hate to have to tell you this, but your grandmother got mad. She told your mom to deal with it and wouldn't listen to her cries. I let her make the call in this very building. Just a few months ago."

*"Grandma won't help us?"*

*"No, Veronica, we're on our own."* Veronica's mother came back to the exam room. No longer crying, she collected herself to be there for her daughter. *"Tell her what else you told me, Don."*

Dr. Wagner took a deep breath. *"Well, Veronica, you see, animals are step one. But the rage in him is growing. He's hunting, Veronica. Do you remember when you mother and father came home early on the Canada weekend?"*

Veronica couldn't get the breath to speak louder than a whisper. *"Yes."*

*"Well, your mother and I went for a walk. I've been counselling her the best I can. We've been trying to come up with a plan to get you out, but it's very hard. I'd take you all in if I could."*

*"Don't be silly, Don. You've done so much for me already. Words can't even express my gratitude."* Clare walked over and placed her hand on Dr Wagner's shoulder.

He clasped his hand over top of hers in return.

*"Go on, it's ok. She can handle it."*

They both looked at Veronica.

*"Ok, well, we got lost in our conversation. I have no idea how long we were out when your mother grabbed my arm and stopped dead in her tracks. 'It's Aaron, we have to hide. If he sees me with you ... oh God.' She pulled me over and we ducked behind some brush. I could hear a man's voice, but I had never met your father. Your mother and I followed the voice until we spotted him. He was talking to someone. I could hear him say ... 'Come with me—it's just over there, you have to see this.' We heard another voice then. The other voice was hesitant. It was a young voice, we couldn't make out if it was a boy or a girl. They kept saying they had to go back, that their parents would be worried. Your father ..."* Dr

Wagner paused and took a deep breath again. "*I can't give more detail without getting really upset myself. You seem bright, do you understand what I'm trying to explain?*"

"*I'm going to be sick.*" Veronica braced her body for convulsion and tried to keep it together.

"*Veronica, he didn't do it. I stopped him. I ran out of the bushes and stopped him. The kid ran off into the trees and we went back to house. I don't want to tell you what happened to me.*" Clare embraced herself. "*But, I stopped him.*"

"*Mom? Why is this happening to us?*" Veronica was fully crying now. Her face was purple with the force of her tears.

"*Honey.*" Veronica's mom came and sat beside her on the examination bed. "*I don't know. You didn't do anything wrong.*"

"*Let's leave, mom, and never go back. Harold is safe at school. Let's just go. We'll be safe together.*"

"*Honey, I would love nothing more than that. But, I can't. I can't leave your father to potentially hurt, let alone kill, an innocent person. If we both left, I don't know what he'd do.*"

"*But mom!*"

"*Veronica, it has to be this way. I'm sorry. But there is too much at stake now. We can't only think of ourselves anymore.*" Her mother reached over and gently placed her hand on Veronica's stomach. "*I want you both to be safe.*"

"*Both?*" Veronica stood up off the medical table in shock. "*Mom, what is wrong with you! I'm not pregnant!*" In her hysteria, she took a few steps around and gripped the table. She looked around the room and felt dizzy and sat back down. "*Am I?*" she asked as she looked at both of them.

"Veronica, I've had two babies, I think I know the signs. And, that's another reason you're here. Dr?" Clare looked at Dr. Wagner and nodded.

"*Veronica,*" said the doctor. "*I need you to go collect me a urine sample.*" He handed her a small glass cup. "*You know where it is? The door in the hallway on the left?*"

With Veronica silent again, he knew this was a good time to speak up and encourage her. "How did you feel in that moment?"

"I don't know if I could ever make anyone understand the pure sense of shock I was in. I was numb. On autopilot. I just . . . can't tell you how I was feeling."

Richard could feel the emotions coming through her memories. She was in a textbook state of shock. Yet, he was impressed by her composure at such a time. She was still able to go through the motions and not disassociate herself. He'd seen this before, and he had learned that some people's minds cope in different ways than others.

Veronica brought back the small glass cup in the room and placed it on a silver tray that Dr. Wagner held out to her.

"*Ladies, I'll be back shortly.*" He left the room and shut the door behind him.

"*Are you ok, Roni? I'm sorry all this is happening. I have a plan, I promise. This is all going to be ok.*"

"Mom..." But she was crying too hard to speak.

Her mother embraced her and coddled her the best she could. "*Baby, can I ask you one thing? And I promise I will never bring it up again.*"

"What, mom?"

*"Who's the father, Veronica?"*

Every muscle in Veronica's body tensed with the question. *"Mom, I can't tell you that."*

Her mother looked annoyed and frustrated with that answer.

*"Mom, please. It's not that I won't tell you, it's that I can't. I knew him so well and trusted him, but I don't know who he is. Well, I do, but not really."*

*"You're not making any sense, Veronica Miller."* Her mother was scolding Veronica through her expressions and body language.

*"Mom—look. I've always been a good daughter. I've never talked back, been grounded, or gotten into trouble at school, right?"*

Her mother nodded but was still clearly upset.

*"Well, you're going to have to trust that I knew what I was doing, and I don't regret it. And for what it's worth—I loved him, mom. So deeply, I really did."*

*"Why are you saying this in past tense? You DID love him?"*

*"Mom, I can't explain that. I can't get into it, not right now. Please."*

Richard could sense her mother accepting what her daughter was saying. She had no choice. The night wasn't over, and from what he could read in her mind of things to come, he understood why she left the subject alone. She wanted this time with her daughter and didn't want to spoil it.

*"Veronica. No matter what happens tonight, I want you to know something. I am so proud of you. The way you are, your poise and personality. I am proud of the young woman you've become. And most of all, I love you."*

Hot tears streamed down both their faces and they hugged each other as tight as they could.

Doctor Wagner came back into the room and the expression on his face said it all.

*"How far along is she, doctor?"*

*"Canada Day."* Veronica said and both her mother and the doctor looked at her. *"There is no other time this could have happened. I only… one time. There was only one time."*

*"You're sure?"* the doctor asked Veronica.

*"There is not a shred of doubt."* Veronica said, looking straight into the doctor's eyes.

*"Ok, well then. That is helpful information. Clare, the home staff are ready and waiting with a bed for her. I can take her there first thing in the morning."*

Veronica heard the term 'take her' and immediately embraced her stomach with her right hand. She hadn't fully accepted the fact she was really pregnant, but the motion of feeling her own abdomen helped to make it more real.

*"Take me?"* She looked up at both of them with wide eyes. *"Take me where exactly? What's going to happen to me?!"* A bit of panic was starting to bubble in her throat that made her voice crackle.

Richard felt for Veronica in that moment. She had no idea what was going to happen to her. And, as far as Richard could see, it was going to be a long road ahead. There are times while peering into someone's memories that Richard empathized certain memories more than others. He really wished Veronica was a patient at the moment so he could help her sort through the emotions she carried from her past.

"You must have been terrified."

"That doesn't even come close to how I would describe it. But, I was with my mother, whom I trusted. And, for all matter's sake, a doctor whom she trusted. I had to have a little faith in the situation that everything would work out like it was supposed to."

Veronica's mother grabbed her hands and sat close to her. She knew what she was about to say would not come lightly. *"Honey, you have to listen to me. I don't have much time. Your father will be up in a while and can't know that I left. I have to get back before the sun is up. Veronica, the doctor has arranged a bed for you at a home."*

"A home? What kind of home?!"

*"It's a home for girls, or young woman I should say, that are in your particular situation."*

"I don't understand." Veronica looked at her mother, helpless and sad.

*"Veronica, if I may,"* the doctor added in, *"this home is just a few hours from here. It's one I've had to send other young ladies just like yourself to come to term with their pregnancies."*

*"Come to term? I'm not giving this baby up if that's what you mean. This is my baby."*

*"No, dear, of course not. I mean come to full term in your pregnancy. You're only in your first trimester. Look, all this is a part of your senior year curriculum at school, I'm not surprised you don't understand that yet."*

"What's going to happen to me at this home?"

The doctor was calm and collected. He knew Veronica was in a delicate state and clearly exhausted. *"Well, that's entirely your choice. When you go, you're going to learn everything that is going on in your body. You will see a doctor when needed, and the midwives will be there to help you with anything that may or may not happen along the way. And, in a few months, you will decide what you want to do. You can give your new baby to a family who isn't as fortunate as you or..."*

"No!! No!!! If it is true, and I am really having a child, I am not giving up on them. Never. I just couldn't do that." She looked over at her mother, Clare. "Mom, don't think that could even be an option for me."

"Well, dear, that's for you to decide. You say that now, but a few months from now, you might feel differently. Raising a baby is hard enough, let alone doing it on your own. The midwives will prepare you and teach you things you'll need to know. A baby is a lot of work. Changing diapers, feedings, doctor appointments. For a girl your age, quite frankly, it will be overwhelming. Veronica, I am only asking this one more time to be sure. You sure the father won't be around?"

"Mom, I'm not sure of anything anymore. I just know that he's gone. Something happened and I can't explain it to you, but he is gone."

"The weirdest part about that night, was I knew in my soul he was gone. He wasn't just far away and not coming back. I knew that I'd never see him again."

Richard peered into the emotions and instincts of her memory. She was right. Her insight was giving her strong intuitions she'd never felt before. *Gloria*. It must have been her communicating with her mother while she was still pregnant with her.

"Sometimes our instinct will speak to us at just the right time. Things we can't explain, but we are sure of them."

"You sound like Gloria used to. Or Davian for that matter."

Both of them said nothing after she spoke his name again. The tension in the air hung heavy.

*"Ok, honey, I'm sorry I brought it up again."*

*"When do I leave?"*

*"Now."* Veronica's mother didn't hesitate one second to answer. She was looking at her dead in the eye.

The look of shock took over Veronica's face once again. Her mother was still tightly holding her hands.

*"Roni, listen. I am going back to your father now. If he finds out I left, I don't want to think of what he'll do. He's way out of control and has been getting more violent by the minute. The doctor is going to take you to the home, and you'll be there by morning."*

*"Mom, what about you? Are you sure you'll be ok? When can I call you? When will you come and see me?"*

Veronica's mother Clare and Don the doctor looked up at each other immediately.

Fresh tears welted in Clare's eyes. *"Honey, you don't, I won't, we can't."*

*"What? You mean I'll never see you again? But why, mom? Why is this happening? Do you hate me?"*

*"Oh my gosh, no!! I could never and I will never hate you. You are so precious to me, I don't think you understand. Veronica, it has to be this way. It has to. It's the only way I know how to save you."* Clare hugged her daughter tight.

*"Mom, you need to be saved too."* When Veronica said that, Doctor Wagner stood up.

*"I'll go start the car, Clare. Where is her bag?"*

*"It's in the back seat, Don. We'll just be a minute."*

*"Ok, the door will lock when you leave, so don't forget anything. I'll see you outside, ok?"* Veronica nodded faintly. She was losing her energy by the second, drained by emotions.

*"Honey, look. I made vows. Vows to stand by your father no matter what. I can handle this. But, you coming home unmarried and pregnant? That is a reality neither of us can stand to face. Ballistic, enraged, beside himself with anger—that would just be the tip of the iceberg. If he thinks you ran away, he won't know anything. He won't understand. Sadly, after a while, honey ... he won't care. He's got problems, Veronica, but I'm his wife. They're my problems too."*

"But you're also my mom."

*"Please baby, please. This is so hard on me too. You'll understand. You're going to be a mom soon."*

*"I'd never desert my child."*

A look of pain set into her mother's face. The words were harsh, and Veronica immediately regretted them.

*"Veronica, we have only a few minutes left together. Please try and understand. I'm only doing what I think is best. This pains me to ask, but I need one more thing from you."*

Veronica looked up at her mother who was reaching into her purse. She grabbed a pen and paper. *"You have to write your runaway note. And it has to sound mean. And not just to your father, but more importantly, to me. I know you won't mean it, but it has to sound like you hate everything. School, Kitchener, but especially, me. And your father."*

"I don't know if I can do that. I'm scared, mom. So I'll never see you or Harold again?"

*"It has to be this way, Veronica. I want you and my grandchild to live a healthy, safe, and happy life. This is just something that*

*won't happen if you don't do this. You have to disappear. I can only live with myself if I know you're safe and away from him. Please. Please."*

"I did it for her, you know. No one else. It hadn't fully sunk in that I was having a child. But, she was my mom since the day I was born. And, I knew she was right. He'd kill me. That much I knew."

Richard felt her strong intuition again come through her memory. *Amazing Gloria could do that while still not even fully developed. What raw power.*

"What did your note say?"

"Things I don't care to repeat. Things I don't remember and I'm happy it's that way. I said awful things. Mean things. Things I didn't mean, and some that I did. Each printed word broke my heart even deeper. To a level I hope no one else has ever had to endure. When I was done, she took the note and put it in her purse. She got up from the table and pulled me into her again. That was the deepest embrace my mother ever gave me. She didn't always show me how much she loved me, but I felt it in that moment. She walked me outside while I shifted back into my blank state of mind. Still numb and back into autopilot."

*"I love you, honey. Be safe. And here, take this."*

"What did she give you?" Richard asked while already knowing, staring at Veronica's hand while she held her martini.

"A family ring. My Ring." Veronica held up her hand to admire it in the light. "One that her mother gave to her, and I knew one day she would give to me. It was soft gold with a small diamond encrusted with green emeralds all around it. I'd admired it as a kid. I couldn't wait to get it, as I knew that day would probably be my wedding day. But, not that day. Not a day that ended like this. It's how I really knew she was saying goodbye. And, goodbye forever."

Veronica started crying harder, clasping the ring in her hand.

*"Mom, please promise me if it is ever safe, you'll come find me."*

Veronica's mother didn't say anything as she watched her daughter get into the doctor's car. He pulled the car onto the country road. His house got smaller and smaller as Veronica watched while looking out the back window. Her mother's figure slowly blurred in the distance. After a few minutes, the light from the house vanished and all she could see was darkness. She turned around and looked at the doctor in the rearview mirror. She could just make out his eyes that were staring straight ahead.

Veronica spoke up. *"Why are you doing this?"*

In a bit of shock, the doctor shook his head. *"Excuse me, dear? I'm a doctor, I want to help."*

*"No, this is more than your call of duty as a doctor. Why me? Why my mother? Why are you helping us?"*

Silence fell over the doctor.

*"Look, I'll tell you, but I must warn you, it's a painful place I don't like to go to. A dark, painful place."*

Veronica sat in silence and gave the doctor some time.

*"Your mother isn't the first woman to come to me for help. Well, your mother didn't come to me for help, I just happened to find her. And if I may say so, I'm glad I did. Your father…"*

Veronica could see him shake his head.

*"Look, I see a lot in my practice. A LOT. I'd like to say I don't see bruises on women and children, but from time to time, it does happen. More often than not, it's accidents. Young boys playing baseball or wrestling. Little girls playing hopscotch or dancing, and they fall. Mothers have all kinds of things happen while looking after a house and home. But, a few years ago, a mother and her three children became new patients of mine. She was a beautiful young girl, around your mother's age, I think. Her children were all a lot younger than you, under ten if I remember correctly. I first became concerned when I noticed how often I'd see them. I'd ask the mother, 'What happened? You were just here?' She always had an excuse. Her stories all made sense. When I'd ask the children, they always had the same stories. Kids are usually terrible liars, and true to form, I could tell they were lying. But they had been so rehearsed in what to say to me, I couldn't get them to crack. Then, she started to repeat stories. 'Keith broke his arm again in baseball? Jenny fell out of her bunk beds again?' I would ask her. Then the injuries got worse. I knew deep down she was lying. It was driving me crazy as I always knew what was wrong with them before a full exam. I thought, if I can sense what their injuries are, why can't I tell why they're hurt? Then one night while looking at my notes, something else dawned on me. Why does the father never come to these appointments? That was highly unusual. I knew all the families of all my patients. That's just how I like to run my practice."*

*"So what happened?"*

"Well, I confronted the mother about it. I was concerned. I wanted call the police, but I had no proof. When I finally asked her about it, she broke down. She confided in me. She told me she was scared and wanted to leave him but didn't know how. I told her I'd help her. But, I also told her she needed proof. Either she'd need some kind of witness, or she'd need to get the children to speak up."

The doctor stopped speaking. A few minutes passed.

"And then what happened?" Veronica asked.

A few more minutes in silence went by, and she could see a tear form in his eye.

"I asked for too much and didn't act when I had the chance. A few weeks later, I attended a funeral. A funeral for four. I never want to attend a funeral like that again. Ever. When I met your mom, she reminded me of that poor woman I didn't help. I promised myself I would do anything in my power to help her and her children. This is me keeping that promise."

Veronica didn't know what else to say. She understood, but no words came to her. In the darkness and silence, she let sleep pull her under. The stress of the night was intense, and her mind was all over the place. A few hours later, she woke up to sunlight and the sound of traffic.

## CHAPTER 13

# A New Beginning

She looked up at Doctor Wagner and looked out the windows. She didn't recognize anything. *"Where are we? What time is it?"*

*"Morning. It's only about 7. You've been asleep a little over three hours. Were almost at the home now."*

Veronica was scared and stayed silent. But, through the fear, she was somehow comforted by a sense of knowing she was safe and that the worst part was over. She didn't understand the feeling, but she trusted it. A few minutes later, the car stopped and she was in front of a large old home with red bricks and dark grey and white trim. White shudders sided each long window on all three stories of the home. There was no sign on the lawn or the front door like she was expecting.

*"This is it? Where are the signs?"*

*"There are no signs. They like to keep the patients—or I guess I should say residents—they like them to have privacy. While they don't advertise what goes on here, I'm sure people in the area have figured it out."*

"So, what do I do now?" Veronica started to feel stressed and anxious again. Seeing the house made it more believable. She was pregnant, she was alone, and would never see her family again.

*"Well, dear, I'm going to get you registered in the home. But, we can't use your real name, in fear that your father or other family members could find you."*

"But I like my name. I have always loved the name Veronica."

*"Well, I had to register you under a different name for now. Tell everyone you have a nickname or something. I just don't want to risk you being found by anyone. Only one person will know your whereabouts and that's me. Your mother doesn't even know, just in case."*

"In case? In case what?" Veronica looked at the face of the doctor and understood. "Oh."

*"When you leave and relocate, you can use whatever name you want. I will contact you before your due date, and I can arrange all the paperwork you'll need. There is a new government program that is coming that is designed to help single mothers such as yourself. It will help you get by until you have a job, and it will also help you to find a place to live. We'll discuss this further then. I can tell by looking at you that you need your rest."*

The doctor was blunt, but it was true. Veronica looked like she'd been through hell.

"That must have been a lot to go through at that age, let alone during those times." Richard knew she needed some comforting. He could feel her emotions about that memory.

"To say the least." Veronica said matter-of-factly.

"The first day, Doctor Wagner had me registered. We went with Barbara Smith. No importance that I knew of, he just said he had some forms already filled out in that name."

Richard found it interesting he went with that name. He looked into him and knew that was the name of the mother who he tried to help before Veronica's mother, Clare.

"Doctor Wagner showed me to my room. He said goodbye and gave me a hug. I found that very sincere and genuine. He really did care that I was ok, and he went to all this trouble to arrange getting me into this home. I never did really have a father figure in my life, but in that moment, that was the closest I ever felt to what I imagined it to be like."

After the hug, Doctor Wagner grabbed both of Veronica's hands in his. *"I have to go now. Be safe, Veronica. Don't tell anyone your name or where you're from. Just keeping distance is best really. This time is going to go by fast. You'll see. In a few months, you'll be on your own, and this can all stay behind you if you choose. But know you have a choice. Take this time to learn what you need to should you decide to keep the baby, and prepare for either outcome. You're very brave, I can tell. You can do this."*

"He left the room; the reality fully set in, and I knew I needed to sleep. I slept for almost two days, only woken by the night nurse to make sure I was hydrated and had something to eat."

"So what happened in the home? What was it like?"

"It was an adjustment. As I went along with my pregnancy, my body started changing. I was growing both up and out. I felt alien. The morning sickness eventually started to lessen, but certain foods just didn't appeal to me anymore."

"Different stages of depression can go hand in hand in pregnancy. I see that in practice a lot."

"I wasn't exactly depressed, I was bored. Daily life was drab. It was like going to school at home. We'd wake up, go to a part of the old house and set up with rows of chairs. A chalkboard and table in front. We learned about what was going on in our pregnant bodies during each trimester. We prepared for the baby's care, and what to expect with the delivery. I kept mostly to myself, and most of the girls did the same. We weren't on vacation, and most of them were there because their families were forcing them to be there. That was a dark time for me. But nothing in particular happened. At least, as far as Gloria's past is concerned."

"How long were you in the home?"

"Right up until birth. Doctor Wagner was true to his word and came to see me before my due date. He asked me about my name and I wanted to be Veronica again. Barbara never stuck. We had to change my last name and birthdate on documents to hide my identity. My name after that was Veronica Chastain."

Richard laughed and so did Veronica. He understood the joke. Due to the martinis she'd had, she luckily didn't clue into the fact that he was laughing because her new last name was a play on her chastity, or lack thereof.

"What was your child birth like?"

"You know, most people, well woman especially, hated when I told them this. For me, it was calm. Safe. Comfortable."

"You mean no labour pain?" Richard knew she was telling the truth.

"None. None whatsoever. I know, very anti-climactic for someone of Gloria's stature, right?"

"Actually, quite the opposite. And even more so that you opted out of the twilight sleep. How did you convince the doctors to allow that?"

"My heart rate was steady, I wasn't perspiring, nothing. It was like it wasn't even happening. I just knew I was going to give birth when I was ready."

Veronica woke up that day, went to the desk at the home and said, *"Today is the day."*

They laughed. *"Oh honey, you'll know when it's really time. Your body will be loud and clear that the baby is coming."*

She had to argue back, *"I'm not kidding, the baby is coming soon."*

One of the midwives took her to the exam room, thinking she was mistaken. She more or less did it to shut her up. When she was done, she brought Veronica back out.

*"No, she's right. She's almost fully dilated!"*

They all scrambled around, called the doctor and got Veronica set up in the medical room in the house. The town they were in was too small for a hospital of its own, and the closest city was a forty minute drive. They also used the room for other emergencies.

"Say—how did you know I didn't take twilight?"

Richard used just a little compulsion again. "Oh, you mentioned it a moment ago."

"Oh right. Well, like I said before. My calm happy demeanor made the other pregnant moms uncomfortable. My lack of labour in general made the midwives concerned. Not so much in a mean way, but more in marvel. They kept telling me that they couldn't believe how well I was doing. That it was a miracle."

"Do you think that maybe it was the fact that Gloria—"

"That I was pregnant with Gloria? Pfft, of course I do. I know now it was her keeping me calm. Controlling my nerve senses for pain. I didn't fully understand it then. Sorry, I know I sound like a broken record saying that."

"You know, Veronica, Gloria headed a lot of studies on mothers carrying children with abilities and how it can influence them till they come to full term. It's very fascinating, you should read up on it."

"Her career was remarkable, wasn't it? I think I remember reading something about that. It impresses me yet saddens me that there is so much about her I don't even know. I feel like I've lost so much time with her by being stuck here in isolation."

"Can I say something to that? And not come across as judgmental?"

Veronica looked at Richard cautiously. "Ok . . ."

"Well, given why she has you here. After what happened and all, do you really think she could have done anything else to help you? I mean, think about the risk you were under. They were coming for you, to get to her."

"I know that, but they're locked away now. They threw away the key. They'll never see the light of day again. I would think maybe a visit? I mean we went through 2020–2023 and all that hardship. Then a few years later, she puts me here. I have spent too much time alone."

"I see your point on that. But, hopefully, when I get to her—if I am able to get her to use her gifts again—I am confident she will be back in your life."

"And that is the main reason I am helping you. Not only does the world need Gloria back, I do too. I miss my daughter." A small grin came over Veronica. She truly did miss her daughter, and knew this could help to bring her back into her life.

"March 3rd, 1968. That was one of the best days of my life. Do you have any children, Mr. Matheson?"

"Me? I have two boys. The best gifts in my life are them. Children can really be a blessing." Richard leaned in and took the last sip of his scotch.

Veronica took a big sip of her martini. "Sarah! We need refills!" Sarah rushed into the room as if she had been just sitting and waiting for an order. She refreshed their drinks in no time.

"May I ask, why did you choose the name Gloria?"

Veronica's face lit up with joy at this question. "That's simple. The day I gave birth was one of most important days of my life. March 3rd, 1968. While I was happy, I was so young. Alone. I was alone. Except—I had my little girl. The doctor stitched me up while the midwives cleaned up my baby. The doctor couldn't believe how easy my birth was either. He said it was the easiest birth he'd ever had to deliver. When he was finished, one of the midwives came back into the room with my little gift in her arms. She handed me this little bundle tightly wrapped with this new being that I'd brought into this world. Her eyes were piercing green. The doctor and the midwives told me that was extremely rare. Odds are one in millions. Most babies are born with blue eyes."

"Yes, that is something you learn in medical school. It's rare, but it does happen."

*Excellent*, Richard thought. *Another personal detail*, he made a mental note.

"Her eyes were green emeralds. As I held her, I looked down at my ring and found it strange how much her eyes resembled the only family heirloom I'd ever been given. She looked at me, and I looked into her eyes and fell so deeply in love with her. A love like only a mother could understand. She gave me hope. She comforted me that I had made the right decision. She was like a ray of sunshine. She was glorious. Before I could put that together in my head, my body reacted and I said 'Gloria' out loud. The midwives all smiled and one of them said, 'That's the perfect name, she really is glorious!' I smiled and kissed her on her forehead and promised to take care of her forever."

Veronica paused and looked away for a moment. "In that moment, I did think of my mother and understood why she did what she did. She protected me the best way she knew how, and only then did I truly understand what a sacrifice she had made. Not just for me but for the granddaughter she'd never get to meet."

"So where did you go after you gave birth?"

"Well, the doctor gave me a little bit of money, and got me into a new program that started that year. Today, we know it as welfare. The system got me set up in a small apartment, and the first few years were really tough, but we were happy. At first, I was living in a small area in downtown Toronto. The doctor wanted me there where all the government offices I might need were close by, and since the early 1950s, Toronto had one of the most advanced public transportation systems in the country. I didn't hear from the doctor much after I settled in Toronto. He kept in touch and made sure I'd always know how to reach him. But, I really didn't mind as it just reminded me of my past."

"So what about Gloria? As a baby, did she show any advanced development?"

"As a baby, the only thing that was unique was how drawn people were to her. I only noticed this as it would happen even as she slept in her carriage. Mothers today will never know how well a baby can sleep on a walk if they are in a proper carriage. I got hers used at a secondhand shop in Toronto when she was very young. It was a beautiful navy blue with white trim and stainless steel. I lined it with pillows and blankets and she would just sleep. But even as she slept with the shade canopy up, people would come up to me. At first, it made me nervous, but then it just became so normal. People would come ask me how old she was, and tell me she was stunning. On the odd time she would wake up from the talking, onlookers would gasp at her emerald green eyes. Then, they would make even more of a big deal about her."

Seeing Gloria in her mother's memories was truly a gift to Richard. There were no known photos of her at this age. She was a very beautiful baby. But her eyes were one of a kind. Then as a baby, and they still were just as piercing now when you saw her in photos or on TV.

"So, we lived in Toronto until 1972. Either that year or the year after our government started to give single mothers a little more each month. It made things easier being back in a smaller city. I just missed Kitchener so much."

"But, what about your family? Were you not scared they would still be here?"

"A little bit, yes. But, the population had grown so much I wasn't too concerned. Anyone my age would either be off to college or moved on. Plus, I had done so much growing that I wasn't concerned about people recognizing me. My body and appearance had changed so much as well. I sometimes didn't even recognize myself in the mirror."

Richard could see her in his mind. The surge in hormones from pregnancy had changed so much about her appearance. This was somewhat normal after giving birth. But Veronica's hair had turned to a dark rich brown, no longer light with curls. It hung straight and heavy, and through maturity, her facial features had really set it. While a beautiful young girl, she had become a stunning young woman.

## CHAPTER 14

# Back to Kitchener

"So we got settled back into Kitchener. We got a small apartment on Charles Street. I found it ironic as right across the street was where I met Davian the first time. It brought me peace of mind knowing I was that close. Sometimes, I'd wonder if he was real. Of course, I have Gloria to prove that, but moreover that he was real inside—his heart, his abilities. But I never doubted it too much. Just seeing the area gave me great comfort."

"Did you run into anyone that you knew?"

"Gladly, no. It had been years and I grew up a lot. My hair was different, and I was different. Now that we are getting to her place in my story, understand I am only telling things that stood out for me as I saw her get stronger."

"Veronica, any details you tell me are appreciated."

"Small details are minute. If I tell tales of every time she guessed a gift, knew someone's name, we could be here for hours. These are what stands out in my mind."

"Did she do that a lot?"

"When she was younger? All the time. But let's not waste time on that unless it's relevant."

"Good idea." Richard followed the flow of memories that were coursing through Veronica's memories. She wasn't kidding. It could take years to go over every psychic blip in her existence.

"So we moved back to Kitchener. Oh yes, sorry. I already mentioned that. I think I should slow down on my martinis. But then again, I'm not paying for the Billionaire Vodka."

With that, Richard spit out his drink in its entirety.

"Excuse me? You're saying you drink Billionaire Vodka? Like every day?"

"Sure am. My daughter's only affiliation with me anymore is paying the bills. Might as well make the most out of it."

"I think for my next drink, I'll have to try some of that," he said while deeply laughing.

"Why don't you just take a bottle when you're done here?"

"You're going to give me a $5.8 million dollar bottle of vodka??!"

"Why not? I have six on hand. And I'll just demand two more next month. She can afford it."

Richard just stared in disbelief. She was being serious.

"Anyways, I was grateful to be home. Toronto was much too busy of a life than I wanted for myself. Kitchener was familiar and felt safe. The only place I wanted to raise my Gloria."

"The region in that time truly was unique." Richard agreed, having fond memories of it himself.

"So when was the first time you started to see Gloria's abilities?"

"My first memory of them was around the time Gloria was four. We were settled into our new home. It was springtime, and I wanted to get to know the city again. Much had changed in the five years since I left. She would be starting school in the fall, and I was planning on finding work. I wanted to enjoy that summer as much as we could. I took her downtown to a movie when I could afford it. While we kept mostly to ourselves, I could see the need for her to be around other kids. I started taking her to Victoria Park often.

"They had a huge playground there that she just loved to play on, and it was very beautiful in the summer. After a few weeks, I got to know a few of the other moms there, and Gloria started to make friends too. It came easily to her. She got along with all the kids. Again, her ability to draw people to her started to flourish. I even befriended two other moms. One was Shareen who had a daughter named Crystal, and the other was Kimberly who had a son named Steve. A few times, they had us over to one of their homes for a daytime playdate. It was nice, except I always felt bad I couldn't have them over to our home. Their husbands worked, and both of these women had lovely homes with a yard and nearby to the park too. We lived in a tiny two-bedroom apartment with no balcony. I was always too embarrassed. They knew our situation and never seemed to really judge me. At first, at least."

"So things didn't stay very amicable, I take it?"

Richard was sad to have already seen what happened in his head. Back then, it's understandable why the women reacted the way they did. People didn't understand Gloria.

"No. Not. At. All. The catalyst to that was sadly harmless. Gloria didn't know or understand what was happening. Neither did I. She was only four."

"Do tell."

"Well, again. She meant well. We went to the park on a beautiful afternoon. It was summer, but not a sticky hot summer day. The humidity was very mild, and it was just perfect. I sat on a bench with Kim and Shareen, and the kids were on the jungle gym in front of us having what seemed to be the time of their lives. There were a ton of kids running around playing and carrying on. It was really nice to see. The playground the kids had at the park in the early 70s looked so fun, I think even the adults wished they could play on it. Not the plastic nightmares they build nowadays."

"So, the three of us chatted about what we did the night before. We all kept a close eye on the kids, but they still managed to run around and get into trouble from time to time. As we sat there talking, we heard the kids start to yell. Crystal and Steven were fighting over something, so their moms got up to intervene. I went to see what was going on when Gloria came running up to me. She seemed excited about something..."

*"Hey, honey, what's all the fuss about?"*

"I dunno, mommy. I don't like when they fight. I'm gonna go play with Toby on the swings, ok?"

Veronica watched as Gloria walked over to a separate swing set, away from the rest of the park.

Shareen came back to the bench first. "*My, those kids fight like cats and dogs.*" She let out a light laugh.

"*What on earth was that about?*" Veronica asked her.

"*Who knows with these kids. I think it was over who got to go down the slide next. I forget we were that age too once. Kim is still trying to calm down Steve. Who knew a slide could be such a big deal!*"

Both women started to laugh a bit.

"*Say, where did Gloria go, Veronica?*"

"*Oh, she went over to the tire swings there, said she wanted to play with Tobi.*" Veronica pointed to Gloria who was on the tire swing with a huge smile and giggling.

Shareen stopped in her tracks. "*What did you say?*"

"*Oh, it's nothing. Gloria just said she didn't like the fighting and went to play with Tobi. Hey, do you know who Tobi is? And who is Tobi's mother? I don't think I've met her.*"

"Is this some kind of sick joke?" Shareen harshly said to Veronica.

"*What, what did I say?*"

"*Your daughter is on the swing set alone. Who could she be playing with??!!*"

Veronica looked at Gloria on the tire swings. She then realized Gloria wasn't giggling on the swings, she was talking. Talking to herself.

"*I don't understand. She just said she was going to play with a kid named Tobi. What did I do?!*"

"Look, I don't know if someone put you up to this. But it's not right, Veronica. You know, a lot of the mothers here have made comments about you and your daughter. Kim and I always tried to look past the gossip and give you the benefit of the doubt. Now I finally see what they've all seen, and I've just been too stupid to realize for myself."

"Wha—what?? What's happening?! I don't understand!"

Shareen got up in Veronica's face with rage and anger. "You're sick, Veronica, sick. To think you'd find this funny. Well, it's not! You crossed a line, Veronica. A big one. Stay away from me, and keep your daughter away from my daughter Crystal!!!"

Shareen walked away and went up to Kim, who was still trying to calm the kids down. Veronica could see them talk intensely. Kim seemed to appear to try and calm down Shareen, but it wasn't working. Shareen said something to Kim, and she looked back over her shoulder with a cold look full of hatred. Both mothers grabbed their kids and left the park, not saying a word to Veronica.

Richard already seen the whole fight play out in his mind. *What awful women, to think Veronica would do that.* He thought to himself.

"Wow, that's awful."

"Worst part was that I truly didn't understand what I did that was so awful. After the incident at the park, Gloria was talking to herself more and more. I heard her in her room mentioning other names, but Tobi seemed to be around the most. I was in fear that Gloria would be seen talking to herself and people would think she was strange, so I avoided the park completely. After a week or two, Gloria started to ask me why we never went to parks to play anymore. She kept saying she wanted to play with other kids. I just kept us busy doing other things and told her that when she went to school in a few weeks, she'd make lots of friends. This was the first time she was able to use her gifts to help me navigate in my life."

Days later, back at their apartment, Veronica was preparing lunch for them. With her back to Gloria while stirring a pot on the stove, Gloria spoke up from her booster seat at the kitchen table.

*"Mommy, why do we never go back to the big park? I like it there."*

*"Honey, we will, I just want you to try other things too. There is a lot of fun to be had still while doing other activities."*

*"The others aren't like that one. I like to play and run around at the park. And big park has my favourite slide."* Gloria smiled ear to ear, her emerald green eyes wide and bright.

*"Baby, we will go back, just not yet. Give it some time, ok?"*

*"Are the other mommies mad at you because I like to play with Toby?"*

Veronica stopped stirring and turned around to look at Gloria. She walked over the table and knelt down to look at Gloria at eye level.

*"How do you know about that, honey?"*

*"Mommy, I feel bad. I don't want the other mommies to be mad. Toby told me not to tell. I just like playing with him, and I only meet him when I get to play with Steve. He said he likes being*

*around Steve as they were best friends. Only Steve can't play with him, but I can—"*

"Baby, you don't make sense. What do you mean?"

*"No one can see Toby but me. He says I'm special. So we like to play together and have a lot of fun. He told me not to tell as I might scare people. That's what makes me special, but other mommies might not understand. I'm sorry, mommy."*

"Did your friend say I wouldn't be scared?"

Gloria laughed and kicked her feet, swinging from her booster seat. *"Of course not. You're my mommy. He said you are ok with secrets like this."* Still giggling, she reached out to Veronica and gave her a big hug.

Richard understood too well. He just wished his abilities could see into Gloria's mind in the memory. But, even at four years old, she was much too powerful, even for him.

"Did you make sense of what she was saying?"

"At first only a little, but a few days later, we were grocery shopping downtown. I ran into Shareen at the store we both shopped at, this grocery store called Dutchboy that was right on King Street. It's long gone now, but it once stood where Kitchener City Hall is today."

"Uh oh," Richard said. He was seeing the awful confrontation in his head while Veronica described it.

Veronica was walking with a grocery cart down an aisle filled with canned goods. While browsing for some soup that she could afford, she looked over and saw Shareen coming down the aisle. Her head was down as she was going over the grocery list she had placed on top of her purse in the cart. Veronica noticed her daughter Crystal wasn't with her. No doubt she was home with her father. A source of support Veronica did not have being a young single mom. Gloria was in tow in the child's seat in the cart.

"*Shareen—hey! Shareen! How are you?*" Veronica yelled down the aisle and headed toward the woman pushing her cart.

Shareen looked up from her list. As soon as she saw it was Veronica, her facial expression went dark. "*Oh, it's you.*" She started to turn her cart around to leave the aisle when Veronica reached her.

She let go of her cart and walked toward Shareen. She reached out and grasped Shareen's arm. "*Hey, what did I do? Why are you so mad at me?*"

Shareen sneered down at her arm.

"*Do not touch me!!*" she said not too loudly. "*Don't make me lose it in front of your little freak!!*"

"*Pardon me?*" Veronica let go of Shareen and stepped back in shock. She couldn't believe what she just heard. "*Baby,*" Veronica said while lifting Gloria out of the cart. "*Mommy forgot a loaf of bread at the front, can you be a big girl and go get the bread I know you like? You know the one?*"

"*Yes, mommy!!*" Gloria seemed eager and excited to be given such a task. She ran down the aisle and out of sight.

"*Ok, seriously, Shareen. This is me. You know me, at least I like to think you do. What is this all about?*"

"*Oh, don't act like you don't know.*"

*"I don't. I really don't. Now, could you please give me the benefit of the doubt and fill me in on what I did?!"*

*"Look, it's not just you. Your daughter. She's weird. Always smiling, always laughing. She never gets mad. Look at the other day, our kids start fighting and your daughter acts like a maniac and leaves to go play alone. Who does that? What four year old does that? They don't! At least not normal kids. Your daughter gives me, and all the other mothers, the creeps. She's too—happy! And then there is you."*

*"Me!?!"*

*"Ya. Don't think Kim and I aren't on to your little games. You come to the park, act like you are better than all of us. You come down, show off to our husbands—"*

*"What are you talking about??!! I don't—"*

Richard wished more than ever he could explain to Veronica what he saw that she didn't. The mothers were jealous. She was so striking that all their husbands noticed on the odd time they came to the park. The wives didn't like it. Not at all. Even mothers who never spoke to Veronica held her in their minds in contempt. Gloria was the star of the park whenever they came, and she shined bright with laughter and joy. All the other kids flocked to her, and the other moms wanted their kids to be as popular. Then when the whole Toby thing came up . . .

*"Look, it's just sick. We don't even know how you found out about Toby, but it's sick. You probably took time to go to the library and look up old newspapers. Well, frankly, that's just sad. But, at least we see you for what you are now. A psycho with a freak for a daughter."*

Veronica stood in the grocery aisle in shock. No one had ever spoken to her like that, not since her father.

"Look, Shareen, I'm sorry if I did something to upset Kim, or you! I really didn't—"

"Didn't what! Think bringing up Kim's dead son would upset her? Upset me? Well you did, all the mothers at the park know. They are disgusted by you. To think you'd bring up someone else's misfortune for even more attention. Haven't you got enough?! So if we're done now—I'm going to be going. I have nothing else to say to you, neither does anyone from the park."

Shareen started to walk away past Veronica who was speechless.

"Oh, and do yourself a favour, there is nothing and no one that's in any rush to see you or that thing back at the park, ever!!"

Veronica was motionless. She understood that her daughter was speaking to something she couldn't understand or wrap her head around. But she knew it wasn't Gloria's fault either. She would have spent all day standing there had Gloria not come up to her calmly and grabbed her hand.

"Mommy, I'm sorry about that. Toby told me not to tell. I know now I can't tell anyone ever again."

Veronica knelt down to hug her daughter. "Baby, don't you worry. Just promise me from now on, you'll only talk to me about these things, no one else, ok? It's scary for people. You are special, do you understand me?"

"What does freak mean?"

"I'll tell you when you're older, you don't have to worry about that now."

"I hear a lot of people say that about me, mommy."

Veronica pushed Gloria away to be face to face. "*You do? When?!*"

"*Mommy, don't worry. One day, you'll understand. Can we go home soon? I'm tired.*"

"Well that would have been upsetting for anyone!" Richard could see in the memory how distraught Veronica was after the altercation.

He really found Gloria's behaviour to be interesting, rather than disturbing, given her age.

While Veronica replayed the moment in her consciousness, Richard peered into Shareen's visions of her memories of Gloria at the park. How it must have seemed to a housewife in the early 70s. As rude as she was to Veronica, she was a victim of her circumstance. She didn't know any better. By standards of that era, Gloria was acting odd.

But, to someone of this millennia, she was an amazement. She held entire conversations with what must have been entities or transgressions, at a park, on her own, at four years old. There were those with abilities whom could not do that at the age of forty, let alone four. What he wouldn't have given to have met her at that age, while at his age with his training. What he thought he could have learned!

"Upsetting indeed. But afterwards, Gloria assured me she wouldn't tell anyone about things she saw or heard. I was only beginning to scratch the surface of what was to come with her in the following few years at Southridge, but none of this prepared me for it."

"I can't wait to learn more." Richard shifted in his seat. He took the last sip of his current scotch and leaned into Veronica over the coffee table. "So tell me, what was her first day of school like?"

## CHAPTER 15

# Off to School We Go

"Well, with only a week or so until school after the run in with Shareen, I avoided the park and kept Gloria and I as busy as I could. I didn't have too much money at the time, so I bought her what I could afford and found most of what I needed at the secondhand stores. She got some cute little dresses, and new shoes—well, new to us at least. At the rate she'd been growing, I knew what little I got her wouldn't hold up long anyways."

"Crazy how fast they grow, eh?"

"Like weeds. Beautiful little weeds. My little Gloria. On her first day of kindergarten, I remember looking at her while I brushed her hair out that morning. I was so excited yet so nervous at the same time. It would be the first time in her life I wouldn't be at her side all day. If anything happened, I didn't know what I would do."

"You were worried about her abilities while around strangers, weren't you?"

"Like nothing I'd ever worried about before. If a woman I barely knew could react like that about her, what would a teacher or the other kids think? She'd be around them all day. I was super anxious to get her to school and meet her teachers and some of the other kids."

Richard looked in the memory and saw a sweet moment between the two of them. She had dressed Gloria up in a coverall dress made out of a mustard-coloured corduroy material. It had brass buckles and a big front pocket across her chest. She was wearing brown little loafer style shoes and Veronica was brushing her hair out with her favourite brush. It was plastic and had bumble bees on it. Veronica loved brushing her hair with it, as it was her baby brush. She was feeling sad at the moment, knowing Gloria soon would need a proper comb as her hair was getting quite thick. No longer the soft golden mane of baby hair she was currently styling. A bittersweet moment all good parents sooner or later face.

"So we got on the 1 Queen Street South bus that took us from downtown to her new school, Southridge Public School."

"Now, I am not familiar with the school districts of Kitchener in the 70s. But, if you lived downtown on Charles Street, why would you not have just had her go to Victoria Public school which would have been a two minute walk and saved the trouble of the bus?"

"You caught that? Well, you certainly do know some of Kitchener."

Richard pulled his hand up over his mouth in a gesture of concentration. "Thank you," Richard replied while shifting up his eyebrows. He was secretly smiling, knowing he did not know Kitchener and that he was reading her mind. A private joke he had with himself from time to time.

"Originally, I did have Gloria signed up at that school. However, a building that was built over sixty years ago, I worried about what she might sense on a daily basis. Especially given the history of that school."

"That was very innovative!"

"Well, what made my mind up was when we were in certain parts of downtown, she kept telling me about stories of it being called Berlin. Which Kitchener hadn't been called for over fifty years, and the small street we would walk down would one day change its name from Foundry Street to Ontario Street. She knew too many exact details to take a chance in a sixty-year-old building. Southridge was brand new, and I wanted her to have the best shot at fitting in and making friends."

"How did you make the change?"

"I made up a fake new address. It wasn't like they had a way to check up on where I actually lived."

"Cheeky, Veronica, I like it."

They both laughed in unison.

"It was one of the newest schools in town with a great reputation. I was so happy I was able to get her in. We got off the bus on Queen Street and walked up a long concrete path on the school's property. On the left was just fencing, backyards to houses that weren't that old. I looked at them and thought, *'One day, Gloria, you will live in a house like that, I promise.'*"

"We continued up the path to a small playground which I knew was for smaller children. It was very tiny, most play obstacles only a few feet high. Luckily, we took a bus trip a few days before to familiarize myself so I'd know where to go. In front of a set of large stainless steel doors stood groups of moms with their kids. And to make matters worse, it wasn't just the mothers, they were with their husbands as well. They were all deep in conversation, talking about parties and BBQs they'd all been to as a family over the summer. They all looked so in sync. When I rolled up, everyone stopped and stared. It was like I'd missed a secret meeting and could never be a part of the exclusive club. I scanned around at every left hand I could see and saw a big diamond on all the women and a thick gold band on any man within eyesight. I had a lot of comfort knowing that day I wore the ring my mother gave me.

"I then suddenly realized how poorly I dressed when compared to these new moms. Beautifully tailored blouses, colourful leather purses on hand, new shiny high heels. No doubt these women could afford to shop at Eaton's or Budds downtown. Some of them definitely shopped at Simpsons in the new mall. Those were the big department stores that were all the rage," Veronica spoke to Richard.

He remembered going to Eaton's in Kitchener as a young man. It was part of the mall he loved to visit as a young man called Market Square.

Veronica went on.

"I usually found items to wear from the hand-me-downs from people who lived in my building. The only one who got new clothes was Gloria. I loved to spoil her in what little ways I could."

"We were all standing around waiting like cattle, then finally a lady in a blue dress with white lace trim came out of the building. All the other parents swooned to her in drones. It was like they all wanted her attention. She seemed like the prom queen meeting everyone after just receiving her crown. From a distance, I could tell she politely said hello, but was eager to walk over in my direction. She shook a few hands and said a few good morning's, and walked right up to us."

*"Hello, I'm Miss Stevens. You must be Veronica."* She held out her hand and gave a gentle dainty handshake.

*"Hi, yes, I am. But please, call me Roni."*

She seemed so nice and sweet that Veronica instantly liked her. Just then, Gloria started to pull on her clothes to pull the attention down to herself.

*"Well, now. This must be the infamous Gloria,"* the teacher directed at Gloria.

Gloria held out her hand and said, *"How do you do?"* She gave her one of her infectious smiles.

*"Well, aren't you just the image of good manners!"* Miss Stevens seemed delighted at the gesture.

The other mothers watching rolled their eyes, and one could sense the jealousy over the attention Veronica and Gloria were getting.

*"Look, I am so pleased to finally meet the both of you. This year is going to be so wonderful. I understand we are meeting tomorrow for our introductions?"*

*"Yes, I will see you at 3:15 p.m., Miss Stevens."*

*"Please, Miss Stevens is for my students. But parents I like call me Cathy, ok?"*

*"Ok thanks, Cathy."*

Richard tried to read into Cathy Stevens in Veronica's memories, but they were too brief. Veronica had a lot of anxiety that day with Gloria going to school, and that often clouded how well he could read someone just from memory.

The bell rang and she said goodbye to her little girl. Though she was no longer a baby, she always would be in her eyes. She held her tight and kissed her softly on top of her head and knelt down in front of her.

*"Now you be a good girl for mommy?"*

Gloria nodded, exaggeratedly swaying her head back and forth.

Veronica laughed out loud, not caring about the dirty looks from the other moms.

*"You be nice and all the other kids will love you, ok? I will be right here waiting for you after school, do you understand? You wait for me right here, ok?"*

Gloria nodded again. Veronica watched her run into the doors with the kind of excitement only a young child could have.

Veronica took a deep breath and started to walk away. She could feel the stares from the other parents. No doubt the special attention from Ms. Stevens . . . or Cathy, would have cost her. But, she was just relieved the morning send-off on her first day of school was over.

"So that day I knew was going to be a long one for me. It was my first day with no Gloria on my hands. While I wanted nothing more than to sit around and feel sorry for myself, I was in for no such luck. After seeing the other mothers, I had made up my mind once and for all that it was time. I needed to find a job and get us to a better place in life. I was heart sick over the 'what ifs' that day while she was in school, but I also knew keeping busy would be my best friend.

"I took the bus home and walked up to our brown apartment building. I'd never stopped to really look at it, and I understood why. We were poor, living in a poor neighbourhood. I wanted to change this and get us into a place we could call home for a long time, or at least until Gloria was old enough to walk to school or take the bus on her own. As soon as I got back into our apartment, I changed into my best outfit and prepared to go look for a job. I was assigned a case worker for the last few years who had helped me type out a resume, seeing as I couldn't afford my own typewriter. I had about fifteen copies of my resume on me, and I decided working close to home would be best for me. I headed out on the sunny morning and set foot. I managed to drop off all my resumes that day. I applied to Budds, Simpson's, and quite a few shops downtown along King Street. My last stop was the newly renovated mall, Market Square. I was always in awe when I went to shop there. Originally, it was more of an outdoor mall, but some developers renovated the mall by enclosing it with this beautiful green glass. As far as I know, it is still standing today."

"It is, actually, but sadly, it is very run down from how you remember it. I'm staying at the Crowne Plaza next door to it. It sits practically vacant. All the offices that took over are long gone, and I imagine they will just tear it down sooner or later."

"That's such a shame. It used to be the best mall in town, in my opinion. I also loved visiting the hotel next to it, but long ago, it used to be call the Valhalla. It's changed hands many times over the last few decades."

Richard loved focusing in on her memory. The mall really was breathtaking when it stood shiny and new. And the old Valhalla hotel had such unique charm.

"So I entered the mall and handed out a resume to a few clothing stores. I held onto my last resume and went upstairs to enter Eaton's. They were the largest store in the three-level mall. When you walked into Eaton's on the third floor, you were right at the beauty counters. Women loved that part of Eaton's. I passed by a few counters. I was so nervous that day when I got there. I didn't usually get so unnerved, but I was about to try and talk to the women there, and I had never talked to them before. I couldn't afford makeup at all, let alone the good stuff."

Richard wanted to tell her it wasn't nerves. It was the vibrations that some of the women working in that area were giving off. Veronica was simply stunning, makeup or not. She was getting dirty looks and cold body language as she walked in. She walked past signs that read Clinique, Estée Lauder, Elizabeth Arden and others. All the counters were clear glass, showcasing the beauty products below. They were all well-lit and made all the items inside look like little treasures. But as she approached the Lancôme counter, she was greeted much differently.

*"Well hello, sunshine. Beautiful day out there, don't you think?"* a voice said with a thick Russian accent.

*"Who, me?"* Veronica asked, shocked.

*"Well yes, you! I don't see anyone else around you,"* the lady laughed.

She looked about thirty years old. She wore a beautiful ocean blue jacket with a matching knee length skirt. Under it, she had on a white blouse, and she had a beautiful silk scarf of bright blue with matching blue trim. She was a very petite woman with pretty blonde hair cut into a very short, elegant bob. Every last detail about her was polished. Elegant makeup, painted fingernails, and she smelled beautiful too. Her name tag read **Ursula—Lancôme Cosmetics**. Veronica admired the name as she'd never hear it before.

*"So what brings you to the mall?"* Ursula asked, genuinely wanting to know. *"Are you shopping for something I could help you find? Maybe a nice lipstick or something?"*

*"Me? Oh I don't have the tiniest idea of what to do when it comes to putting on makeup,"* Veronica said. Her cheeks flushing a little.

Ursula noticed and took it lightheartedly. *"Honey, all women need to know their signature colour. My name is Ursula. Now, I don't see a wedding ring on your finger, Miss...?"*

*"I'm sorry, how rude of me. I'm Veronica. Nice to meet you, Ursula."*

*"Veronica, darling. Are you always this nervous? Please, sweetie, I don't bite."*

She shot Veronica a little wink. It made her feel a lot more comfortable.

*"Well, like I was saying, no ring on your finger, and you're this stunning? Trust me, a little lipstick goes a long way."*

*"I am actually more or less looking for a job, not lipstick. Is there a personnel office here? I'd like to drop off my resume."*

*"You're looking for a job here at Eaton's? May I see your resume?"*

*"Oh, uh. Sure. Here you go."*

Veronica nervously passed over her resume. She didn't have a lot of skills and didn't have her high school diploma either. He case worker helped word it well with tasking she did on her own around the house and with her finances.

*"So you have no experience in much. What part of the store are you looking to be hired in?"*

*"I'd take anything. Sweeping floors, washing toilets, or stocking shelves. I just need a job. Any job."*

*"Oh, honey. Someone as cute and pretty as you could do more than just sweep or stock. Have you looked in the mirror? You're a knockout! We just have to tweak a few things."*

*"Thank you. I think."* Veronica let out a little nervous laugh.

*"Now you're going to have to learn to relax a little if you want to sell. I think you'd be great up here in cosmetics. You look exactly how most of our customers strive to look. What moisturizer do you use?"*

*"Um, Vaseline? I don't know, I've never really paid attention."*

*"Oh my goodness, I could fall over! Let me just tell you, when you're older, you will thank your lucky stars you met me when you did! Please come sit. I just want to check something out."*

*"Ok."*

Veronica looked around. She was not used to being treated so nicely. She wanted to be sure Ursula was in fact talking to her. She walked to the end of the counter and sat in a cream coloured chair. It had a handheld mirror beside it on the glass display.

*"Listen, dear, I've been doing this many years. I just have a knack for knowing when someone will make a great sales person. If we just gave you some help to spice up your look, our clients will take it much more seriously that one, you use our products. And two, that you love them!"* Ursula approached Veronica and brought a small tray with a few products on them. *"Now, close your eyes and trust me. You're going to love it."*

A few minutes passed, and Veronica felt this nice stranger apply some makeup. Having only wore some lip gloss years ago, she hadn't taken any time for self-care since becoming a mother. While she did feel guilty, she also reveled in the experience. It felt really nice for a change.

*"And, voila!!! My god, I'd kill for your skin. Your pores!! Flawless. You look the part now."*

Veronica opened her eyes and looked around. She saw the other sales clerks staring at her. They were impressed with the change and how it made her look.

*"Here's a mirror, dear. Tell me, what you think?!"* Ursula passed the mirror to Veronica.

She looked in the mirror and didn't recognize herself. Ursula had done a great job. It wasn't too heavy, but Veronica felt it made her look more mature and more pieced together.

*"Wow... I don't know what to say!"*

*"Don't thank me, honey, it's easy to work on someone as gorgeous as you. Now, what do you say?"*

"*Thank you, I mean it. I have never looked like this and I love it.*"

"*No no, not about the makeover, the job?*"

"*You, want to hire... me?*"

"*Yes, you! I know I can train you and help you become a great seller. You just needed a small push in my direction. I'm so lucky I was in today. If I had the day off, I bet one of the other counter girls would have snatched you right up!*"

Veronica laughed, and gasped at the same time. "*Well, of course I would love to work with you here. But, I have to tell you. I have a little girl, and I'd need to be able to get her to and from school.*"

"*Oh, honey, that's perfect. I just need someone to help out a bit on my days off and on the weekends too. Sound good?*"

Veronica knew a few people in the building that could help out with Gloria if needed. Most of the people in her building were not employed and were home all the time. "*Uh, that sounds better than good. This is amazing! Thank you so much, Ursula!*"

"*Well, dear, tell you what. I'm about to go on my lunch. Can you come tomorrow? We'll get some paperwork signed and I'll show you around? My other employee, Janet, will be here tomorrow, so it will be easier for us to chat.*"

"*Sounds great! 9 a.m.? Or...*"

"*Come at 10, honey. I'll see you tomorrow, Veronica. This is going to be great! I can just feel it.*"

"So she hired you on the spot? That must have felt great."

Richard could sense her pride in her memory. He also had to admit how amazing she looked. She really did have a look that would have customers eating out of the palm of her hand.

"I left there on cloud nine. Having income would greatly change our lives for the better. I also knew I really needed some straight adult time. I mean, I loved my Gloria. But the few weeks of not even going to the park to talk to other moms made me realize how much I depended on those adult conversations."

"It sounds like you were a typical new mom," Richard said.

"So I went home and changed and went to grab the bus to get Gloria after school. She was only in class from 8:45 in the morning until 1 in the afternoon. I was smiling from ear to ear on the bus and noticed a lot of strangers staring at me. But I really noticed when I got to the school yard and the other mothers were REALLY staring at me. I wasn't sure what was going on. The bell rang and the kids came running out to greet their parents. I stood and waited as Gloria was one of the last kids to come out. She came running out to me, and her new teacher, Miss Stevens, or Cathy, was right behind her, holding her hand. I saw lots of the mothers run up to her like they did in the morning. No doubt looking for information on how their kids behaved in her class. I couldn't have cared less, I just wanted to see Gloria."

Gloria got impatient with waiting. She let go of Miss Stevens' hand and ran to Veronica.

"*Mommy!!*" Gloria said while running and jumping into her arms.

*"Hi, honey, so how was your first day?!"* Veronica let go of her in her arms and noticed Gloria looked at her strangely.

*"Mommy, what happened?? You look so pretty!!!"* Gloria chirped and giggled.

*"Oh!!!"* Veronica realized now why people were staring. She really did looked glammed up to be picking up her daughter from grade school. *"Mommy had a makeover, do you like it?"*

*"I love it, mommy!"*

*"Well thanks, baby, but enough about that. How was your first day of school?"*

*"Mommy, I love school! All the kids are just great. We played all sorts of games, and tomorrow we're going to start learning about colours and numbers one to five."*

*"That is just great, babe."* Veronica looked to make sure no one was standing too close. *"Did you see anything today? Or did anyone talk to you? Like anyone like Toby from the park?"*

*"Don't worry, mom. Once this place was a farm and close by is where they took garbage. If I try and see things, it smells so stinky. But I was trying to focus on my teacher. She's so nice, mommy. So nice that it made it easy for me to feel relaxed and ignore other stuff."*

*"That's great news."* Veronica looked over Gloria and saw Ms. Stevens approaching them.

*"Hi, Veronica. Gloria did really well today."*

*"Hi, Cathy. That's great. She seems really happy. I have to thank you."*

*"Gloria is an absolute peach. The pleasure is mine, really. Say, I was wondering. Do you think you could get a sitter for Gloria tomorrow night and come at 6 p.m. to meet me? I know it's*

*parent-teacher meetings tomorrow and you're scheduled for 2 p.m. However, I have another mother who can't take that time, and she said 2 p.m. works best for her."*

"*Um. Sure, I don't see why not. I can ask our neighbour to tuck Gloria in and watch her.*"

"*Yay! I love seeing Mrs. Thompson down the hall,*" Gloria said ecstatically. "*She lets me play with her kitty!!!*"

"*Ok, well it should be just fine with my neighbour. I'll let you know tomorrow if it won't work.*"

"*Great, see you tomorrow, Veronica! Bye, Gloria! And I'll see you in the morning!*" Miss Stevens turned around and spoke to a few more parents before going back into the school.

Richard was trying to focus in on Miss Stevens mind, but he couldn't. He could make out some images in her mind, but they moved much too fast for him to line up what he was seeing. The alcohol was really getting to him.

"Well, I wouldn't find that out till the next day. In the meantime, Gloria was over stimulated on the bus ride home. She went on and on about every detail of the new toys, her new classmates and how big the school was. They went on a tour. She saw where she'd be going to classes all the way up to Grade 6, and it made her feel like a big girl. Despite having a nap, she still went out like a light at bed time. I was really tired too, but I quickly went and asked my neighbour if she could watch Gloria for me and put her to bed the following evening. She had no problem with it like I knew she wouldn't. She found Gloria charming and loved the attention Gloria gave to her cat. The cat loved her. He would just curl up on her lap and purr. She had lost her husband seven years prior, and I think she really did love the company."

Richard could see the memories. The cat was a big orange tabby named Marcus. Mrs. Thompson named the cat after her late husband. He brought a lot of joy to the lonely elderly lady. He loved the studies of how animals can sense psychic vibrations while humans often cannot. He found it so fascinating. These studies were only made possible because of Gloria. It was like watching history in the making. He could see the bond the cat had with the young Gloria. Animals were always drawn to those with gifts.

"So the next day, I got Gloria to school and told Cathy I would see her that night at 6. I went back downtown on the bus and walked over to Eaton's. I was so nervous. I was worried I wasn't dressed right or that I looked like a slob. I had no makeup at home to try and look made-up. But I wore as nice an outfit as I could. Part of me thought Ursula might change her mind and not want me to come work for her."

Richard saw her look in the mirror before leaving. She had on a nicely pressed white dress shirt and a pleated black skirt with black penny loafers to match. He noticed Veronica looking down on herself in the mirror as everything she was wearing was secondhand. She looked great nonetheless.

"I was so excited and when I walked into the store and saw Ursula again, I knew it was for real. She smiled and greeted me just like she had the day before."

*"Hey, you! 9:45 sharp. I love a young woman who's early."* She smiled at Veronica.

*"I'm ready to work! What should I do?"*

*"Slow down, honey. First, I'm going to take you to personnel. You'll have to sign some papers, and I'll show you where you can pick up your paycheque. We have a staff room where you can keep your things, and it's where you'll go for a break and eat lunch. Come with me. Janet will be in soon, and she can't wait to meet you. She's great, you two will get along swimmingly."*

*"Great, can't wait!"*

Ursula took Veronica around the entire store, showing her all the levels and every department. She took her to personnel and got her all ready to start work. Veronica was so excited. A real job! She had never worked before and couldn't wait to buy nice things for her and Gloria. She was overjoyed by how welcome she felt. Everyone was so nice, and the store was just beautiful. Ursula took her back to the cosmetics area on the third floor and gave her a schedule and a uniform.

*"Well, that's it for today, honey. I will start training you, and we'll get you familiar with the cash register. Let's head back to the counter and you can meet Janet. I'll quickly show you around our counter and send you home with some reading."*

*"Amazing! And Ursula, thank you so much for the chance. You will not regret this, I promise you!"*

*"Thanks, dear. But you'll do great. You'll love working here. I can just tell."* Ursula grabbed Veronica's arm and gave her a reassuring squeeze.

"Department stores like that were amazing. I miss them so much," Richard added.

"I know, sadly very few are left. And I don't think any will really stand the test of time. We lost Simpson's, Budds, Eaton's, Sears. Too many to really go on about."

"So you were happy?"

"I was. But I was even more happy when she let me tour around the counter. I met Janet that day, and we did end up getting along quite fabulously. She was warm and welcoming. I noticed there wasn't as much camaraderie with women who worked other counters. It made sense when I learned about the commissions you would earn selling. But I felt something special about working for Lancôme. I think it had to do with Ursula and how she made me feel worthy. As years went on, I fell in love with the line more and more, but to start, I was so proud to tell people where I worked and for what brand."

Richard could see the admiration in Veronica's eyes in her memory, and now even as she told this part of her story.

"Well, that's how I got my first job in the early 70s to help me and Gloria. I won't bore you with the details—how I could go on about makeup and skin care. I'll leave that up to Sarah to have to endure." She laughed out loud. "Speaking of Sarah . . ."

About five seconds after speaking her name, Richard heard high heels click on the marble floors as Sarah walked into the living area they were sitting in. Two fresh drinks on hand, this time, two martinis.

# CHAPTER 16

# The Martini and The Memory

"So, Richard, I know we should slowed down on the refreshments, but it's 4 p.m. It's my afternoon cap. Would you care to join me?"

"Your afternoon cap?"

"Yes, it's a phrase I've coined. It's like a night cap, but in the midafternoon."

Richard laughed.

"Hey, I'm an old lady about to turn 80 with nothing better to do." She smiled.

Richard thought Sarah must have been waiting around the corner. Unless . . . unless she sensed this was coming. Sarah handed Veronica her martini and walked right over to Richard.

"Wow, it's like you knew we would want these or something, isn't it?" He stared into Sarah's brown eyes and scanned her consciousness. He picked up on absolutely no sense of intuition. To his surprise.

Sarah let out a dry, vague laugh. "Hardly, it's 4 p.m. Ms. Chastain always has a martini at 4 p.m. I just figured you'd like to try one after hearing the uproar and commotion you let out when you found out she drinks Billionaire Vodka."

Richard immediately blushed. He really did make a ruckus when she told him.

"Oh sorry, I wasn't trying to be disruptive."

"No need to apologize. Simply making an observation, sir."

Richard nodded, still feeling embarrassed. "Thank you, Sarah."

The sun was casting into the room at this time of day and finally made it to where they were sitting. The bay window at the end of the long room made sense. The priceless art work was at this end of the room. Richard then noticed how it had been designed that way to keep sunlight off the rare paintings. Even though they were enclosed in a class covering that had a digital moisture regulator and light activated tinting, he realized every last detail in the loft, let alone the entire building, had been precisely designed.

In the light, the sun shone through Veronica's martini glass, making it apparent it was made from the finest crystal. She took a sip and placed her glass on the coffee table. The intricately shaped glass twinkled beams of colours all over the table. It was so beautiful. Richard looked down to his hand to appreciate the craftsmanship he possessed. It was not heavy, but just the right weight. He wondered what a glass like this would cost? Must be expensive, seeing as the drink it held was literally worth tens of thousands of dollars in vodka. The complexity at the bottom of the bowl of the glass carried down the stem to a single blue gemstone of some sorts. *Sapphire*, he thought. *Wow, I am drinking a drink worth the cost of some homes in the area with a jewel encrusted glass.*

He took a deep inhale of the drink to appreciate its aroma. He'd never smelled something so smooth and crisp in his life. This vodka was normally for royalty and the superrich and famous. He understood why.

"So, are you going to drink it or just stare at it, Rich?"

"Oh, sorry, Veronica." He laughed a gentle laugh to ensure he didn't come across as offensive. "It's just that this is a first for me, and I am trying to savour the experience."

"That's ok. But remember, you have to drink it to really appreciate it. Let's have a toast before you have another staring competition with your glass, shall we?"

"Sure."

Veronica grabbed her glass off the table, and the two raised their glasses in the air.

Veronica looked Richard in the eye. "Here to hoping you learn what you need today. Cheers."

"Cheers, Veronica, and thank you."

Richard put the glass to his lips. He'd never felt a glass so smooth and naturally at the perfect temperature. He took a sip and let heavenly fluid coast over his palette the way he would an aged single malt scotch or a vintage prestige wine. *Wow.* He shook his head in disbelief. *Just wow.* He didn't know whether to give a standing ovation or a round of applause.

"This is truly a treat for me, Veronica. Thank you so much. Say, is this a sapphire on the stem? It's really quite beautiful." He took the glass to his lips and took another sip.

"Sapphire? Huh. No nothing like that would cross the threshold of this little palace of solitude."

Richard was puzzled as to why and how she could hate her beautifully stunning home so much.

"No sorry, those are blue diamonds."

With that, Richard choked on his drink and spit some out with quite a bit of force.

"Richard!"

"I'm so sorry, Ms. Chastain, I'm so sorry." He felt truly out of place. He didn't want to think of the cost of the vodka he'd just wasted. "It's just, a blue diamond? One that size? It looks like a medium sized pea, and on stemware? You'll have to excuse my ignorance, I'm just in awe."

"Well, my daughter can afford it. So why not? She does after all own land all over the world where she does fair trade. Now that mining is almost purely ethical thanks to her endeavors, she has first access to the finest. And she still pays face value. Even though she is a shell of what she once was psychically, she would never sacrifice some her values." Veronica's face seemed to dim.

Richard could see a memory he knew she didn't want to share coming to light and sat back in silence to observe it. It was an important memory and one to take mental note of in all its detail.

\* \* \*

*"Come on, mother, stop being so difficult."*

*"Stop calling me mother, you know I hate that!"*

Richard explored the memory, looking around in detail. Looking at Gloria through Veronica's gaze, she must have been in her mid to late 50s by then. Probably 2024 or so? The two woman were in the most luxurious limo he'd ever seen. Not quite as large as a bus but still huge. It was classy all the way to the last detail. He noticed the brand logo Brentwood Livery on the back wall lit in diamonds on shiny smooth mahogany. Real wood too. Not the plastic look-alike. The seats were all the finest vegan leather you could buy. It even smelled like a real hide.

Gloria was an avid animal rights activist and almost vegan. She would never travel in a car with real leather at that point. The limo had a small washroom in the far end and a bar filled with crystal glasses (probably like the one he was currently drinking from) and no expense was spared on the selection of liquor either. Gloria got up in what looked like sheer frustration and made them a drink and sat back down.

The windows were tinted inward for pure privacy looking, but to look out, you could see as clear as if there was no glass at all. Looking above was clear too. It was a foggy day, so the tints had not been activated.

Surrounding the limo were four armed SUVs parked at each corner of the vehicle. Glancing down the other end of the limo was an armed body guard standing at the entrance. He stood in perfect stillness with a seriousness on his face that only a professional could have.

"Mom, come on! Don't be so difficult. It's like you enjoy being combative with me. This is the best thing for you and for me. After the Coleman case, you know I wasn't the only one who got threats. He had devotees, followers. Some are even more loyal to him now than ever before because he is where he is. They'll never get to him or hear from him again, but still, they have hope. And hope can be dangerous. They'll use you to hurt me. I can sense it. This place, this place would change all of that for us. Look around you!"

"Look at what? The waste land of what's left of this part of Waterloo? Maybe all the booze you've been drinking lately is clouding what you see. I see dirt and abandoned buildings."

"Mom, 2020 destroyed a vast part of the world and its economy. It may have taken years to catch up to show the damage, but the pandemic of 2020 took its toll on the world. Nothing could shelter Waterloo from that. Not even after the surge in real estate here. No corner of the world was left untouched."

"But the Barrel Yards? Gloria, this place looks like ruins now. How many of these condos were abandoned and foreclosed? Yes it's only been three years since most of them were left deserted, but that many years just sitting here? Father Time can do a number."

"Mom, please. I know right now it doesn't look like much, but you have to envision it. If you could see what I see—what this place will become in just five or six years? You'd gasp at the revelation. It's why I bought it. Mom, look: They are digging up Erb Street sixty meters down. They are inputting sonar radar technology with other safety measures. No one is coming from the ground up—it's impossible. The radars reach far beyond depths which mankind will reach for a few hundred more years. They are building a fortress wall around all the buildings, and this is the hope for the future of the city. The vision is to gain celebrity and wealth to help rebuild the economy. Look how Toronto destroyed *itself after the pandemic. It's a shadow of its former glory. The market crashed there too, and those with wealth moved on. This is one of the places they hope to attract them to!"*

"I'm still not impressed."

*"Did I tell you about how environmentally correct this building will be? All state-of-the-art recycling and waste disposal. It will have its own water filtration system that will clean most of the water used, and the water will be the cleanest and purest water in the city. Part of the filtration system will have a grand display in the lobby when you come in. It will be a one of a kind fountain filtration, and the project is being designed by Frank Gehry. I sense you don't know who he is, but he is the most sought after architect in the world. He was semi-retired and did this as a personal favour to me. To design this building."*

"And I care about that because?"

*"You know how I feel about pollution. We haven't even begun to scratch the surface of the damage the pandemic of 2020 caused. I can't fully see the outcome yet as all the plastic garbage and waste is still circulating the globe. When it settles, I will have a better vision of what's to come of it. But I know it won't be good. Not at all. I just can't see it clearly, not yet. It's still moving too fast."*

"How about another drink, dear, would that help!?"

"You're one to talk!" Gloria shook her head in frustration.

Richard could see a vein in her forehead start to throb.

"Look, mother, I'm sorry. This is going to be the most amazing space ever."

Richard could see Veronica shake her head and cross her arms in the limo. *My, she really was being so stubborn.*

*"Well and then there's the air space. This is the first civilian compound where the inhabitants own the space above. No planes can fly over you, no unauthorized helicopters. No drones can enter the air space. They have security measures in place that will take care of any attempts to enter. Even aerial view. No cameras will see past the invisible sonic waves that are above all the buildings. No pictures can be taken on the grounds or from above. Even NASA can't take a picture, record infrared movements, nothing. This is the first and only place this safe in North America, let alone Canada. We own the technology and it will be years until they negotiate the sale of it to anywhere in the world. I know this. In fifteen years, we will strike a deal with Sweden and a few other allies. While this is civilian space, it's military grade. And they all want a piece. But with myself on the executive committee, I see what's safe and what's not."*

Veronica wouldn't admit it, but it did sound impressive. She looked out the window, and Richard could see the sign she was seeing:

The Regus, coming soon!

*"Well what about me? You know I'm not a fan of high up apartments! I don't want to live on the top floor. I want to live on the ground floor."*

*"Mom, for safety reasons, you can't. Why wouldn't you want the top floor? You'd have the rooftop to yourself. I could have them put a pool in and a garden just for you?"*

*"No. I want to be close to the ground. Put a pool on my floor. A private pool. And, I want the entire level. And a private elevator."*

*"Mom—"*

*"What, you can afford it! Am I not worth it?"*

Gloria sighed. She must have not wanted the fight.

"Mom, whatever you want. The TV show deal went through, so I'll have even more net worth. Thank you for doing this. I'll feel so much better. You'll be safe. If something ever happened—if somehow someone got by me. If I didn't see it coming. I don't know what I'd do."

"Whatever."

"You know I'll entrust someone to watch over the building, someone with insight. To sense threats and make sure no one can even get close."

\* \* \*

Richard thought of Scott at the entrance downstairs. *Smart, Gloria,* he thought. The psychic to sense a psychic.

Richard brought his attention back to Veronica in present day. While the end of the memory came, he knew why Veronica hated this place. It was like solitary confinement. She really wasn't safe to leave. Not while Gloria wasn't in full tune of her powers. Gloria could only sense what was coming to herself in her state of mind right now. She was so deep in despair while her mother sat in this prison of luxury waiting. Waiting for her daughter to come visit. Waiting for her to wake up. Wake up and take over the power she was given and end all the madness in the world. Powers she hadn't used since the Coleman case.

# CHAPTER 17

# First Parent-Teacher Night

"So my first day on the job was just wonderful. I was excited about where this opportunity would lead me. Our future looked bright. I was working and Gloria was in school. I was actually looking forward to the days ahead. Hopefully, our lives of struggling would soon be over. I picked up Gloria after her second day of school and she was even more excited. She told me all about what she learned, the games she played, and how much she loved the other kids. She went on and on, mostly about her teacher, Miss Stevens."

Richard saw her beaming on the bus ride home. She was ecstatic and so hyper. Veronica was so happy in the memory.

"I made Gloria and I a light supper and Mrs. Thompson showed up on time for me to take the bus back to Southridge school and make it by 5:45. I was sitting in the hallway, and the school seemed so quite. The only people still in the building were janitorial staff and some teachers who were finishing their parent-teacher interviews. The school held them over the first week of classes to meet every parent quickly after classes finished.

"I sat in the hall and looked around at the bare walls. Outside each classroom was a blank board I knew was for hanging announcements and to display student work. I couldn't wait to come get Gloria from school and see something she made on one of those boards.

"I was lost in daydreams when I heard some voices coming closer to the door of the kindergarten classroom, and then the door popped open."

*"Goodbye, Shelly, and it was nice to meet you, Mike. Jesse is a great kid, and I'm happy to have him in my class."* Miss Stevens said to the parents leaving.

Veronica watched the happy couple leave the school hand in hand. She didn't like how sad she felt that she didn't have Davian there with her on their daughter's first day of school. She felt guilty she hadn't thought of him that day until just then. *Let it go, Roni, let it go,* she told herself.

The door closed behind the couple, and Veronica didn't notice how she drifted off in thought again. When Ms. Stevens approached her, it startled her.

*"Hi, Veronica."*

Veronica jumped a little in her seat. *"Oh my, oh, I'm sorry. I was not paying attention."*

*"Don't be silly, I tend to sneak up on people and they don't even notice. I'm quiet like that."*

The two women laughed.

"*Come in, please.*" Cathy held the door open and let Veronica in. She shut the door and Veronica heard her lock it behind her.

"*I've set up some adult chairs over in the far corner by the window. It will give us a nice breeze after it being so warm in here today.*" Cathy pointed to the far side of the room.

The room was sectioned off in four ways. There was a big open space on thin carpet with a sign that read *Story Time*, the craft section, the desk for Ms. Stevens and some larger chairs, and the coat area where the kids left their boots and coats in the winter months.

The two women crossed the room and sat down across from each other.

"*First off, thank you so much for coming in later, I appreciate that. I hope it's ok I locked the door. I don't want the janitor to come in and disturb us.*"

"*I noticed that. So, what's going on? I feel like we're meeting in secret or something.*"

"*Well, that's not far off. I just really needed to speak with you.*"

In the memory, Richard pieced together what was going on with Cathy. *What a small world*, he thought to himself.

"*So this is a bit awkward, and I'm not exactly sure how to broach this subject. So bear with me.*"

"*Ok…*" Veronica said very unsurely.

"*You know Gloria is special, right?*"

"*Of course. She's great. I'm lucky to be her mom.*"

"*Yes, she is a delight. But I mean she's special… really special. You know this, right?*"

"*What do you mean?*"

*"Ok, I can see she's told you about this before. And to be clear, before I try and help her, I wanted your permission."*

*"Permission? Permission for what?"*

*"Urg, ok. I just can't sugar coat this. I'm talking about her abilities. Her gifts. I know you know what I'm talking about."*

Veronica panicked inside. *What did Gloria see? What did she say?*

*"Look, Gloria is just fine. I don't know what you think she said or did but—"* Veronica stood up out of her seat.

*"It's not a bad thing. Calm down please!! Please sit!! I'm trying to talk with you about how special she is, and I think I can help."*

*"Help? Help how? There is nothing wrong with my little girl. She has an active imagination and that's all."*

*"Oh, that is certainly not all. Not by far."* Cathy laughed and gestured to Veronica to sit and calm down. *"Look. Please sit. I know you know what's going on. See, I was just like Gloria growing up. It can be scary and overwhelming as her senses get stronger. Trust me, I've been there."*

Veronica sat back down. *"Really? So you—"*

*"Yes. I am. But, nothing as powerful as your daughter. Ms. Chastain, I have insight. I'm what some would call slightly clairvoyant. I can sense things before they happen, or I can sometimes find things that are lost. I have more ability in reading ones past over anything. I grew up thinking something was wrong with me. No one in my family had the sense. None. I NEVER brought it up to my parents. The 1950s were not a time to be out in the open with things like this. Sadly, not much has changed now in the 70s. But, I don't want Gloria to grow up afraid of her own gifts. Every day she gets more mature, more aware of what she can see and do. It's going to scare her. And, Veronica, it's going to get hard on you. Trust me."*

Veronica sat there for a minute. She wasn't sure if she could trust this woman yet.

*"How can I believe you? How do I know you're like Gloria? How am I to trust you—and the fact you say you want to help her. Help her, and not just punish her for this somehow?"*

"I understand your hesitation. Here, give me a minute." Cathy sat and stared at Veronica with intensity. "May I?" And she held out her hand for Veronica to grab it.

*"Are you sure about this? This seems so strange. How can I be sure you're telling me the truth? That you aren't setting me up to somehow hurt Gloria or something?"*

"You'll never know until you give me a chance. Please?" She urged her hand forwards again.

*"Ok."* Veronica nervously passed her hand over to Cathy.

Cathy grabbed Veronica's hand and clasped it with the other. She closed her eyes, and Veronica could see them shift under her eyelids. The two sat there in silence for just a few minutes. To Veronica, it felt much longer.

*"Ok, I have some things."* With that, Cathy opened her eyes.

*"You have things?"*

Cathy laughed and let go of Veronica's hand. She sat back and grabbed her purse. She pulled out a pack of cigarettes and went to the window beside them and sat up on the ledge. *"Do you mind?"*

*"I don't care, but won't you get in trouble?"*

*"Trouble? Ha! You should see how much we smoke in the teachers' lounge. Besides, the smell will be gone before the first bell rings in the morning."*

Veronica never minded the smoke, though she never smoked herself. *"No worries here."*

*"Thanks, reading is always nerve-rattling to me. I don't get to do it much, though my mentor tells me the more I do it, the less it will bother me."*

*"You have a mentor?"*

*"Oh yes. She is leagues beyond me with what she can do. Unfortunately, she lives far away in the States, but everyone who has a gift should have someone help them."*

Veronica felt Cathy was stalling and not being forthcoming with whether she had abilities or not.

*"So… you were going to tell me about…"*

*"Oh yes! I'm sorry. I really need this cigarette. Where was I."* Cathy put a cigarette in her mouth, and set her purse aside. She lit the cigarette and took a drag. *"Ok, you."*

Veronica sat there in complete distrust, yet to her surprise, she also had a little curiosity.

*"While I could dig into your past, I see great hesitation about you wanting to talk about it. It's very jaded, and so I didn't dig too deep."*

Veronica rolled her eyes. *"That doesn't prove anything. A lot of people hate their past."*

*"True!"* Cathy said, then sat up straight, pointing her hand with a lit cigarette at Veronica. *"But you! Oh, that's not just jaded. I don't have the ability to dig too deep like others could, but I could tell it would upset you. There is a wall in your own personal charisma if I feel back to before Gloria was born. There is stuff buried there that you want no one to know about."*

Veronica tensed in her seat. *Maybe this girl is the real deal,* she thought.

"Yes, everything before Gloria is off limits. At least for now. You aren't ready to talk about whatever it is, and I don't see you opening up about that anytime soon."

"To say the least."

"Yes." Cathy took another drag of her cigarette. "And that ring. It was given to you by your mother. A family heirloom of some sorts. It's very beautiful. Reminds me of Gloria's eyes."

Veronica was still in a bit of shock. This woman was telling the truth. "Yes. Yes it is. And, everyone tells me that."

"I know. I could see a nurse telling you that after you gave birth."

"You can see when I gave birth?"

"Not clearly, like a picture. I can't explain—I see or sense things. They just become clear to me in my mind, and I know it's right."

"Well, that's impressive. I'm sorry I didn't believe you. Is—is Gloria ok? I mean—"

"Ok? She is more than ok. Look, I am not an expert. I just know what I know and what I've been taught. But Gloria? To someone like me, she is like a wave of energy when she comes into a room. I have no control over her, as she has little control over herself. In class the last two days, I couldn't stop things from coming to her, but I was able to get her to focus on me. Veronica, I won't be able to do that for long. A few weeks maybe. She will get out of control like a wild fire if we don't help her to learn how to focus. It will consume her. I've seen it before."

"What does that mean?!" Veronica's voice cracked with panic. She knew Gloria was special, she just didn't realize how special until then.

"Veronica, please. I am not trying to scare you. I just want you to know how serious this can be. I can help her focus on me for *what, a few weeks? What happens when she has another teacher? Or she's in another classroom and starts seeing or hearing things? Things no one else can?"*

Of course Veronica had thought of that; it was her worst fear.

*"What could happen to her? If we don't help her? Can't this go away?"*

*"Happen? Well, not all the time, but sometimes people like us get mislabeled. We get called crazy and get locked up in a facility somewhere. There are legitimately mentally ill people who need places like that, but I know of cases here in Canada and all over the world, of that happening to people like us. Things like this—insight, clairvoyance, intuition. These things don't just 'go away', we're born with them. It would be like—"* Cathy swirled her cigarette around in the air and looked past Veronica. She looked down at her and scanned her body up and down. *"It would be like—hoping your left arm just goes away. It's a part of us, who we are. And for someone like Gloria? I think they would lock her up and throw away the key."*

Veronica couldn't believe what she was hearing. An asylum? She would never let that happen. *"So you really think you can help ... guide her in some way?"*

*"Oh, most definitely. I can help prepare her for things to come and help her deal with things she is seeing now. She'll need to learn boundaries on listening to others thoughts too. Trust me, that was a lesson I learned in a very hard way. She is going to need someone to talk to that understands what she's going through. It shouldn't burden you, and I wish I had this when I was her age."*

Veronica sat back in her chair. *"I see. So how do we do this? What's next?"*

"That must have been a shock to your system. You were what, twenty or twenty-one? With a toddler being told is too psychic for their own good?" Richard read Veronica's emotions to her. He found it helped calmed people down when they were getting worked up talking about something that had passed.

"While I think shock is a word used by most parents to describe new discoveries in parenthood, I was past that. I somehow knew this was just the beginning and the sooner I accepted it, the better off we'd both be."

"That is such a healthy attitude. Gloria was so lucky to have a mother like you."

"Thank you." Veronica smiled.

Richard could sense how much she took that as a compliment, and that's exactly how he meant it. He tried looking further into her memories, but he'd had too much alcohol by that point. He could vividly see her memories as she went into detail, but until he sobered up, he couldn't foresee anything like he normally would.

"So, how did her lessons work?"

"Well, Cathy started immediately. Given what she told me could happen to Gloria if we didn't, I didn't want to wait either. So, every day after school, she stayed behind with Miss Stevens. The kindergarten class was only a half day, and lucky for us, Cathy didn't have an afternoon group. It worked out so well for me too, as then I was able to work more hours if I needed to. Gloria would stay with Miss Stevens after the other kids went home. She would have Gloria take a nap in the classroom on some mats and pillows she had ready for when any of her students needed it. They were only five after all.

"I remember my boys at that age; naps were a must."

"It was better for Gloria too. Cathy told me that she would take a nap and wake up refreshed and ready to focus. She said they got a lot more work done that way."

"What I wouldn't give to have seen THAT lesson plan."

"Yes, you and the rest of the world."

The two laughed in unison.

"So how did you know what she was learning? What she was accomplishing?"

"Well, like any parent, the teacher kept me informed. While Gloria had all the same lessons in the daytime as all the other kids, but then she had a second set of homework."

"How did that work?" Richard leaned forwards in his seat to rest his drink down. He wanted to slow down so he didn't dull his abilities any more than they were.

"Well, I would come a little early every few weeks, and Cathy would go over things she'd learned. She'd keep me up to date on how she was coping with things, and she would tell me more of what I needed to know about her ever-growing power."

"Needed to know?" Richard asked and shrugged his brow.

"Well, as we got to know one other better, I realized she didn't tell me everything at first. It was the right idea as she had told me that she didn't want to scare me anymore than I already was. She slowly told me more changes were coming. I knew Gloria could communicate with those around her, those only she or Cathy could see or hear."

"I'm aware of everything that she is capable of now, but what came to her at such a young age?"

"Well, at only four, she could see things, hear things. But she could smell and taste the past too."

"At four???!! Wow. Do you know what some of her fan clubs and study groups would do to learn that information? The gift of smell associated with the past— at four YEARS OLD!!! That usually takes someone who is awakened to their gifts – or at very least excepted them into their late teens to early twenties. Some- that come even later for a late developer. You have no idea."

"I didn't at that time. Now I understand a lot more with all the published studies. I learned so much from Cathy on what things were for Gloria. On how to talk to things with her and comfort her when she got scared."

"Did she get scared often?"

"Richard, she was four seeing things that most people with abilities don't experience until puberty. Cathy explained to me it was going to be a lot of work for her to be able to control what she let in. For now, given her age in 1972, at least knowing what was real and what was what some people label a vision would help her stay calm. She would be able to ignore it. Most of the time at least."

"Most of the time? What happened?"

"Nothing happened—yet. That would be a few years later. But Cathy was preparing me for other things to come."

"Like what?" Richard was so angry at himself for drinking as much as he did. He need to sober up to have better insight on her memories.

Veronica must have seen him look down at his glass and give it a look.

"Sarah!"

"Oh gosh no, Ms. Chastain, I can't."

Sarah came running into the room immediately.

"Yes?"

"Sarah, thank you. I was just hoping you could get me a coffee if it's not too much trouble?"

"No trouble at all, sir." She looked at Veronica. Before she could speak—

"Just put ice in my martini. That's good enough for me." She looked at Richard and they both laughed again.

The two both noticed how much they felt at ease around each other, and it made the situation less and less awkward.

## CHAPTER 18

# The Real Lesson Plan

"Do you know what a lesson looked like? Did Cathy ever let you sit in on one?"

"Well, I did once, but I didn't understand it. While Gloria was busy learning her abilities, I was busy learning to accept and make sense of everything Cathy was telling me."

A troubled look immediately washed over her face. Richard—psychic or not—knew it was something related that she was hesitant to share.

"What happened? Why only once?"

Silence fell in the air and Veronica slowly started to speak as the image became sharper and sharper in Richard's mind . . .

It was just after Christmas time and the beginning of a new year, 1973. They had a wonderful Christmas, seeing as Veronica finally had money that year for a small tree and gifts. It was nothing too lavish compared to all the other kids, but Gloria never seemed to mind.

She was content as long as she was with her mother. The two spent Christmas dinner with Cathy, as she was unmarried with no children. She invited them to her parents' home for turkey dinner and the two had the best time in their beautiful home. Richard noticed neither of them ate the turkey, and made note to ask about that later.

One weekday in January, Veronica got finished work an hour earlier than expected. Something that didn't happen too often. She had been eyeing a few little items around the department store that went on sale after the holiday, and she grabbed them for Gloria. Nothing too big, just some candies and small toys. She just loved the chance to spoil Gloria when she could afford to.

She paid for her items and left the mall to directly catch the bus. Normally, she went home to change out of her bright blue uniform. She wore it at first to pick up Gloria, to show off to some of the mothers that she was working. A few of them even recognized the uniform and were impressed. After a few weeks, the novelty grew old and since she was finally able to buy some new clothes when she could, she opted to wear those instead.

Blue uniform in tow, she rode the bus up Queen Street from the downtown area and got dropped off at the Southridge school stop. She made her way through the snow and let herself into the school building. School was still in session for the full day. Cathy's classroom was still the first door on the right, and no other teachers noticed her enter. Neither did Cathy . . .

Veronica snuck in quietly as she heard Cathy speak very sternly to her daughter.

*"You can't be scared, Gloria. I know this is hard, but believe me, it's going to be harder. You are such a brave girl, you know this, right?"*

Veronica stopped when she heard Gloria sobbing a little.

*"I know, Miss Stevens, but I'm scared."*

*"It's ok, honey, here. Give me a hug."*

Veronica could hear Gloria calm down instantly. She took a few more steps so she could see them interacting.

*"Gloria, remember. Nothing can hurt you. And the sooner you realize you're in control, the better. I know you're only four, but you're turning five soon. The more we do this, the less scary things will be. You're a big girl, right?"*

Veronica could see Gloria nod her head. Miss Stevens still had her hands on her shoulders, comforting her.

*"Ok, You can do this. Just go stare out the window. And remember, look at the fence first and touch the wall. The wall is real. The wall is now. What you see out the window is just like shadows. Nothing more, nothing less."*

Veronica watched as her little girl wiped her tears and headed to the window. She was too short to see out the regular window, but there was a long window by an emergency exit in the room. Gloria went to it, put her hand on the wall beside it, and focused out the window. Veronica took that moment to enter to room and be heard.

*"Eh-hem,"* She cleared her throat as she approached Cathy.

*"Oh, Veronica, hello! You're early, this is fantastic!"*

"Is it? Things seemed pretty intense just now."

"I know what you heard, and I just wanted to avoid this conversation today. It's been a little intense for our lesson."

"How so?"

"Well..." A concerned expression came over Cathy. "Well, I'm sure you didn't know this, but this was a farm a long time ago."

"A farm?"

"Ya, a few decades ago."

"What does that have to do with Gloria?"

"Well, on farms they had animals. Sometimes, that was animals we grew to eat. Sometimes—"

"Oh. Got it. Got it." Veronica held her hands up at Cathy to say stop.

"So, not the best lesson, but an important one. She took it rather well. I calmed her down a bit, and she's going to be fine. I'm just thankful that for her first time seeing something so horrific, she was with me so I could help her through it."

"Me too. I hope she's with you for a lot of firsts like that. I wouldn't know what to say."

"Speaking of firsts, mind if we chat a bit?"

"Oh no. Whenever you want to just 'chat' with me, it's never good."

"I'm sorry. Like I've told you many, many times. I am easing you BOTH into this. There is a lot to take in. Gloria?"

Gloria was in a trance-like state, looking out the window.

"Keep focusing, I'm just outside the door, ok?"

Veronica was shocked Gloria didn't acknowledge the fact she was there. "Is she ok? She didn't even say hello."

*"Oh, I have her intensely focusing so she is hearing and seeing mostly something you can't. It's on another realm."*

"Realm?" Veronica said, raising her brows.

Cathy looked at her with an expression of recognition.

*"Let me guess—that's for another lesson?"*

Cathy smiled and nodded. *"Are you sure you're not a little psychic too?"* She softly grabbed Veronica by the arm and took her close to the door.

*"Ok, well she is just, just. Words cannot describe this. What she is going to be capable of, what she can ALREADY do, blows my mind. She is magnificent."*

Veronica shook her head a little at the use of such an extravagant word. "Magnificent? What does that mean?"

*"It's a huge compliment. Believe me. She is going to outgrow me and what I can show her. She already has a deeper sense of sight then me, ten-fold and she's just getting stronger. By the time she hits high school, I won't be able to help her. I am simply helping her to learn and navigate through what she is able to see, but someone more skilled and developed than me can help her get stronger. See more. Feel more."*

"Is that something good?"

*"Good?!! It's—"*

"Magnificent, right?" Veronica said with a little attitude. She felt a little overwhelmed and wasn't following Cathy and what she was trying to say.

*"Ok ok. So—"* Cathy looked at Veronica up and down as if looking for something. *"Oh, thank God you wore it. Look—the first day we met, I was a little vague on what I saw."*

Veronica's body language immediately shifted into distress.

"Wait wait! Nothing before Gloria was born. Listen, I respect boundaries."

Veronica visibly relaxed a bit. Cathy reached out and grabbed her hand with her mother's ring on it.

"*Tonight I want to let this settle with you. Just what she will be able to do compared to someone like myself.*" Cathy clasped Veronica's hand with both of hers. "*So this ring, it was your mother's, Clare. She was a sweet, lovely lady. She had wavy brown hair to her shoulders. She was a stay-at-home mother and she only wore this ring at Christmas. You adored it as a child. Seeing as your only sibling was your brother, you knew it would be yours one day. Her mother, Pearl, gave it to her on her wedding, and you hoped she would give it to you on yours. I am only channeling the ring and its history, not yours. You made it clear that was private, and I will always respect that. Then, and especially now as we are friends.*"

"*Wow, you really did hold back. And, for what's it's worth, thank you. My past is not something I'm ready to share.*"

"*Absolutely, Veronica. I promise. But what I did was nothing impressive. Your daughter over there?*" Cathy pointed to Gloria still focusing on the window. "*What she will be able to see one day will make what I just did look like a grain of sand in the desert. She will be able to tell you when the gold was mined, where, by who—she could tell you anything about that individual. Not just that, but go into tiny details about any person who had contact with that ring. Even if, let's say, it was on a delivery truck. Maybe the driver never touched the ring, or the box it was in, or the materials it was made of. But, their conscience was near it. So, she will be able to obtain information on that person too. Not as much detail as those who made it or touched it. But still pick up on some sense of them. Do you get it?*" Cathy let go of Veronica's hand.

Veronica just stared at her ring and took in all the information. It was overwhelming.

*"Look. Go home. Gloria loves the surprises by the way. I can see it already. I put a lot on you, so please. Go home, have a bath, and let it all sink in."*

Veronica just shook her head and went over to Gloria who was still in deep concentration. Veronica didn't like how serious her four year old looked at the time, but knew she'd never be an ordinary little girl.

*"Mommy! I'm so happy! Can I go home early?"*

*"Of course, honey, I have some goodies for you."*

*"I know, mommy, I saw you pick them out. You always know what to get me!!"*

*"Gloria, you know you're not supposed to peek in at me. Remember the rule—no reading someone unless you have permission. Now let's go home."* She hugged her little girl with all her might.

*"I know, mom, just having a little fun sometimes."*

"You poor thing. I don't know how you were able to take that with a straight face."

"How do you know that I did?" Veronica shot back quickly.

It caught Richard off guard. "Well, just for you to be able to tell me such an event with such poise, I know you did."

*Way to go, Richard,* he thought. *She'll sense you in no time if you keep this up.*

"Veronica, parents of gifted children who are not themselves gifted have a hard time understanding the process some prodigies experience when learning.

Developing these skills is like strengthening a muscle. It takes patience and time. I'm just blown away knowing you did this for her."

"Thank you, but really the thanks goes to Ms. Stevens."

"Well, I guess it explains why Gloria chose to become Gloria Stevens as we know her today."

"Yes. She owes a lot to that woman. Come to think of it, so do I. I'm so sad we lost touch over the years, but being a shut-in has that effect on any relationship. I read she passed away not long ago which makes me sad."

"Well, she was living in BC with her family. That's not your fault," Richard added.

"How did you know that?"

"I told you, I did my research." Richard grinned at Veronica.

"So you did . . ." Veronica replied, smirking back.

## CHAPTER 19

# The New Teacher

"A few years passed like that. My job at Eaton's was going very well, and Gloria was excelling at school. Not just in the normal classroom, but in her private lessons after school with Cathy—or Miss Stevens as you will. By Grade 1, Gloria's half days turned to full days. Cathy simply brought her home after school which helped me immensely, and a few Saturdays a month, she spent the day with her. This was great as it allowed me to work more. I simply did not need to be there with them, nor did I really like to. Gloria's intuition became sharper and much more controlled. In her new classroom, she was able to block out things from coming to her and pick and choose when she would allow such information to come to her."

"Grade 1 and 2 just flew by."

"When she was finishing Grade 3, the school announced some new teachers who were coming to Southridge for the following year. Lucky for us, Cathy was still remaining at the school. She had no reason to leave, and she was really bonded to Gloria. The two were very close."

"Did that bother you at all?" Richard asked.

"Not at all. I was so lucky that Miss Stevens came into our lives. She was a blessing to Gloria. I can't imagine what could have happened without her help."

"You are right there. In my practice, it's common to have those with abilities misdiagnosed. The team of trained experts now can help spot those suffering with psychic diagnosis dementia. But again, none of them would have a job without Gloria."

"So, the summer before Grade 4 wasn't too eventful. The only thing that we really noticed was Cathy had slightly less of a presence in our lives. She had gone to a teacher-only event weeks before school to meet the new staff and say goodbye to those moving on. She met a young new teacher who happened to be Gloria's teacher in the upcoming school year. The two had gotten close and started dating. She still helped train Gloria when she could, but a budding new romance was her primary beck and call. I understood, and it gave me more time with my daughter to take her out in the summer. We went swimming, saw movies, and furthermore went shopping. We went all over downtown. A favourite spot of both of ours was the farmers market. Since the city had torn down out City Hall and built the mall where I now worked, they eventually relocated the farmers market to a section in the mall built specifically for it. It had wonderful baking and arts and crafts on the first floor, and an outside section with lots of local vendors selling fresh fruits and vegetables."

Richard was slowly starting to sober up; the coffee was helping. He still needed Veronica to go into certain detail to see full memories. "So what did Grade 4 bring for you both?"

"A monumental thing that stands out in her history was the first day of Grade 4. That's when she met Mr. West for the first time. I know there are many speculations about what happened to him on her Grade 6 field trip. Nothing was ever verified though."

"I've heard various versions of the ice skating trip. Mostly stories I've read on the dark web."

"Well, the dark web is the type of place you'd find some of these stories to be true in deed," Veronica sneered.

"When the first day of Grade 4 came, she was still too young to take the bus alone. I would take the bus with her before work, and I had a lot of help from Cathy after school and on weekends. It was a good system; it got Gloria to school safely and allowed me to work as much as possible so we could move to a better neighbourhood. Downtown Kitchener was developing so fast, and I wanted to be in an area that had more small children. I was looking for something near the school so Gloria could eventually walk there."

"Grade 4. I was marveling at how much my baby was growing up."

"So, Grade 4 was a big year for her. At school, kindergarten to Grade 3 students had one section of the school, and Grade 4 had a separate section from students in Grade 5 and 6. It was like its own private school with fun classrooms that even had a small science section. I could imagine how big a deal that would have been for a small girl. But trust me, she let me know how excited and happy she was all summer long.

"Her first day I was sure to book off work. I was still a new mom and these events were as big to me as they were for her in some ways. We got on our bus down Queen Street. We started to head to the different section of the school, and it was another new beginning for her. 'She's growing up too fast,' I thought. We did our usual routine, and I walked her to the door and bent over to kiss her. Some new parents greeted me, while the usual group of parents ignored me."

After arriving at the Grade 4 class doors, Veronica bent down to hug and kiss Gloria.

"*Bye, baby, you have a great day. I'll be right here when you get finished class. I want to hear all about your big day.*"

"*Mommy, I love you! I hope Mr. West likes me. Miss Stevens told me a little bit about him. She said he's super nice.*"

"*You'll do great, babe. You know where you're going?*"

"*Mom, of course I do.*" Gloria smiled and laughed.

"*Silly me. Have fun, sweetie.*" Veronica squeezed her tight, then watched her head into school.

The school day flew by for Veronica. She cleaned their small apartment and started a special dinner. She left to get the bus to pick up Gloria. She enjoyed the first day of school with her daughter; it was a little tradition they had.

Veronica laughed and took a sip of her freshest martini.

"What's so funny?" Richard asked, a big smile forming on his face.

"Oh nothing, sorry, where was I?"

Richard had to hold back his laugh. He knew exactly what she was just thinking. She told herself it was a good thing she didn't drink Billionaire Vodka martinis back then; she wouldn't have gotten anything done.

"So I got off the bus and headed to the Grade 4 wing. The bell rang and many children burst through the door. Gloria was often the first. This year however, she didn't come running out with excitement. What I saw instead was worse. So much worse."

Richard could see it before she spoke it. Thankfully, his coffee was starting to kick in.

Gloria walked out the door and looked exhausted. Just defeated. Sad even.

*"Hey, sunshine, what's the matter?"* Veronica asked her while bending down to take her into her arms.

*"I want to go home, mommy."*

*"Why, are you sick? Did something happen? Talk to me, honey."*

*"No, mom, school is fun. I'm just tired."*

"I am definitely not gifted in any manner. But I was not a fool. She was hiding something. She didn't mention any of the things that she usually went on and on about. Nothing about her old friends, who she sat beside, and most of all, nothing about her new teacher. I let well enough alone and took her home and put her down for a nap. She never took naps much anymore, which was another red flag that she wanted a nap on her first day of the year."

"She had her nap and woke up still in a daze. She came down the small hallway of our place, and I could tell she needed to talk. I went to grab the phone to call Cathy, assuming it was about something I couldn't help her much with."

*"Mom, please. Don't call Miss Stevens. Actually, I wanted to talk to you."*

Veronica seemed in awe over the statement. She didn't get a lot of mother-daughter talks in, as Gloria was too young for "woman stuff," and most of what seemed to trouble her was her work with Cathy, not school.

*"Oh! Well, isn't this nice. Would you like me to make tea or anything? Some milk perhaps?"*

*"Milk will do, mom."*

*"Honey, come sit at the table. I'll make you some chocolate milk, your favourite."*

Gloria pulled up a chair to their kitchen table. The table was in the apartment when they moved in and was clearly from the 50s. It has white laminate with gold and black flecks in it. The trim was stainless steel. At one point, it had a leaf you could put in it to extent the table, but that was not left behind when Veronica and Gloria moved in years ago.

*"Mom, I don't know what to do."*

*"About what?"* Veronica asked while stirring the chocolate powder into the milk.

*"Well, Cathy is our friend, right? Yours too, not just mine?"*

*"Of course, Cathy is great. She's more like a family member at this point, don't you think?"*

*"I do. She is like what I imagine having an aunt would be like. That's what makes this so much harder for me."*

*"What's harder? What's wrong, Gloria?"* She handed her a glass of milk and sat down at the table beside her.

*"Mom, I know you don't understand what I see and how I see it. I can't explain it very well to you sometimes."*

*"It's ok, honey. Slow down. What are you getting at?"*

*"Well, I know Miss Stevens has told you I have a little more intensity to my visions. That mine have more detail, does that make sense?"*

*"Yes, dear, I follow. Are you upset with Cathy—or, Miss Stevens, for some reason?"*

*"No, that's just it. I know she can see things too, just not like me. And she really likes this Mr. West. My new teacher."*

*"Ok."* Veronica was nodding, waiting for Gloria to make her point.

*"So at first I was a little nervous I didn't pick up on anything about him before today. Mom, I can't explain it. He's so nice to me. Polite. I can even see how Miss Stevens might think he's cute. But mom, he's not."*

*"Oh? He really ugly?"* she said and jokingly nudged her arm.

*"Mom, you aren't listening! This is serious!"*

*"Oh, sorry. I didn't realize."*

*"Mom, he's dark inside. Something is off. Very off. I can feel it. I don't know how to tell her."*

*"Well, maybe you just have to get to know him a little more? He is your teacher after all. For the whole school year too."*

*"That's my point too, mom. I have to spend this entire school year with him, and he is wrong. Very, very wrong, mom."*

*"Tell you what, you know I have parent-teacher night with him tomorrow. Don't tell Cathy anything just yet. Or—will she sense you're keeping it from her?"*

Gloria laughed a little. *"No, mom, she hasn't been able to read into me since the second grade. Even IF she tried."*

*"Gloria, what did she teach you about being humble?"*

*"Mom, she is always teaching me about being humble. And not using my insight for cheating at school or hurting others."*

Veronica never got tired about hearing about that.

*"I think what's bugging me the most is that's all I can pick up from him. It's like his thoughts are a black canvas. No memories come to light. No sense of joy. Just darkness and nothing. He even has a scar on his face that no one really notices. I should be able to pick up on the scar at very least. But, nothing. Not even a hunch."*

Not sure what to say, Veronica tried to comfort her daughter. *"Well, maybe he just has a strong sense of self, and you've never met anyone like him before. That's possible, isn't it?"*

*"I never thought of it that way."* Gloria sounded a little more assured.

*"And Miss Stevens said there is a lot of lessons you have yet to get to, right?"*

*"I know, but I'm not sure that's what this is. My tummy says it's not anything like that."*

*"Ok well, just get through your day at school tomorrow, and let me see if I find anything out about him at parent teacher night."*

Gloria finished her glass of milk and headed to her room.

*"Honey, supper will be done in a bit. I'll come get you when it's ready, ok?"*

"Yes, mom." Gloria shut her bedroom door behind her.

Richard, able to analyze the memory a little more, couldn't pick up on any vibrations yet. Knowing what he knew would happen with Mr. West years later made him uneasy to hear how oblivious Veronica and even Cathy had been. He was eager to see if he would have sensed the same 'dark canvas' as she had put it.

"I didn't sleep well that night. I tossed and turned, feeling a little uneasy about how my daughter was feeling. I eventually fell asleep with a little comfort in knowing that Cathy didn't pick up on anything wrong. She may not have been as powerful as my Gloria, but that had to count for something."

"The next day, I watched her get ready for school with as little joy as I'd ever seen. She barely spoke on the bus to school. She was old enough that I didn't have to walk her to the door anymore. As the bus drove away, I could see the world was on her shoulders as she walked the path and through the school yard."

"That day at work, I kept myself busy. I remember Janet going on about a launch party they had to go to in Toronto. I never went, as Gloria never had a sitter in the evening. While Cathy was a great help, I didn't feel comfortable asking her to take Gloria for a late night."

"What was a launch?" Richard asked. He could see Veronica's excitement when she recalled those.

"Launches- or launch parties were the best perk of my job. I didn't go to many until Gloria was a little older, but they were amazing. If the company I worked for, Lancôme, launched a new perfume or something, they would host these awesome parties. Usually in Toronto. They would serve wine, have hors d'oeuvres, and you would get a bunch of free products at the end."

"Wow, I am in the wrong business." Richard laughed.

"They are very uncommon now. After 2020, most things moved online. But I'm happy I experienced them. Even more so with Janet and Ursula over the years—they were both so passionate about their work that it wasn't hard for me to feel the same."

Richard explored her memories of herself in that time. He watched her start to take more and better care of herself and her appearance. She was much more polished. He was amazed at how time made her much more beautiful. He couldn't help but notice how clueless she still was then to her beauty. She never noticed how much men stared at her and women admired her.

"When my shift was over, I took the bus right to Southridge. Our neighbour Mrs. Thompson was picking up Gloria after school since I had parent-teacher night. Cathy was meeting the parents of her students, so she couldn't help me that day."

"I arrived back at Southridge at 4:15 p.m. with a few minutes to spare. The school had set up extra chairs outside each classroom for parents to sit and wait for their time slot with their children's teacher. No one was in the hallway waiting when I got there, and I took the time to look at current class projects that were hung up outside the classrooms. Same as every year, they were black. I looked at them and imagined how much of Gloria's work I would see on here like her other class boards over the years. Suddenly, the classroom door opened and I heard her new teacher, Mr. West, speaking."

*"Thanks for stopping in, Mr. and Mrs. Engel."*
Just then, Veronica's face cinched at the memory. Richard recognized their faces as one of the mothers who always ignored Veronica in the school yard.
*"It was our pleasure, Mr. West. We're so happy to have you here. Our little Stephanie just can't stop bragging about you."*
*"Well, she is a great student. Take care, and I'll see you folks around."*
Just as Mrs. Engel made eye contact with Veronica, a mean sneer came over her face. She looked her up and down and rolled her eyes.
*"You absolutely will see us around, Mr. West. And if I'm not the one picking up my precious Stephanie after school, you know you will see my husband, Grant, here to get her. You know how that is, marriage and family life!"*
Neither Mr. West nor her husband didn't seem fazed by the comment, nor had they caught the sarcastic undertone that was meant just for Veronica.

Richard could see this Grant was more than just polite. He was absolutely taken aback by how stunning Veronica was. Even in her cosmetic uniform, she was a head turner. Richard began to see just why some of the mothers never gave her a chance.

Mrs. Engel grabbed her husband by the arm and pulled him out the doors. She did so quickly so her husband didn't have a chance to speak.
*"Ms. Chastain? Please come in and have a seat."*

Veronica entered into Gloria's classroom and was happy to see all the space and areas they had to learn. Between the classroom and the door was a small science area with a few seats, beakers, a sink and chalkboard. Once in the real classroom, she saw the desks in rows facing a large wall of chalkboard, the teacher's desk. There was also a small reading area to the left of the desk. In the back of the room, you could see easels and art supplies. Veronica smiled, envisioning Gloria having a painting frenzy and making the kind of mess only Gloria could.

Veronica sat in an adult-sized chair that was set up just in front of his desk, and waited for him to close the door and grab his seat.

*"Well, Mr. West, thanks for seeing me. I am really looking forward to—"*

*"Please! Ms. Chastain! The pleasure is mine really. Gloria is simply an important part of our class."*

*"Oh, that's so kind of you Mr.—"*

*"Oh no. Please. Only my students need call me Mr. West. My name is Alex."*

*"Oh, well nice to meet you, Alex."* Veronica was taken aback by how exceptionally warm he was. She was expecting him to be cold and standoffish.

*"I must say, you've done a wonderful job with Gloria. She is very intelligent for her age, and I feel lucky to have her in my classroom."*

*"That's wonderful to hear."*

Mr. West grabbed a sheet of paper off the top right hand corner of his desk. It was a page off a small pile of copies.

*"I have this handout for all my parents. I know they only schedule us fifteen minutes for these meetings, but I want you to know that my door is always open. This has our standard monthly curriculum here."* He pointed out each month laid out.

Veronica thought this was a great idea as no teacher had yet to be so thorough.

*"This is great, Mr. West. I appreciate this."*

*"Oh, it's nothing. I'll send home more detailed notes before the beginning of each month, in case there is anything special Gloria will need to have to participate in, be it in science or art. I am hoping to have some great field trips this year to a local nursery for our science class, and the main library downtown. I think the kids will have a blast."*

*"Oh, that's a great idea. We live downtown and Gloria just loves that library."*

Richard enjoyed the train of thought that Veronica had not shared with himself right now or Mr. West back then—that Gloria loved the library as it was next to the old court house and jail. What stories she must have learned and seen there!

*"Now, on the bottom is my home number if you need to reach out to me for anything after school hours. Don't hesitate to contact me if you have any concerns."*

*"This is fantastic! Thank you, Alex."*

Veronica stood up and shook Mr. West's hand and they said their goodbyes.

On the bus ride home, she couldn't help but think about how wrong Gloria was. She was certain it was just her not being able to read someone like Alex. So warm and open. So eager to help the children.

As soon as her bus arrived downtown, she went straight home to begin dinner for herself. She knew Mrs. Thompson would have fed Gloria, and Gloria would not be ready to leave Marcus the cat for the night. She pictured her cuddling the big orange tabby until it was time for Veronica to drag her home to bed. As she walked in the door, she heard the phone ring.

Veronica took off her shoes, went down the hall to the kitchen, and grabbed the phone off the receiver. *"Hello, how may I help you?"*

*"Oh, Veronica! Hi! It's Cathy!"*

*"Oh hey, hun, what's going on? How was your parent meetings? Any good gossip for me?"*

*"Oh, I'll get to that later!"*

Veronica could hear the excitement in Cathy's voice over the phone.

*"Don't waste another second—tell me what you think!"*

*"About what?!"* Veronica answered, no clue as to why Cathy was so worked up.

*"Hello!!! About Alex! Isn't he great?! I know it's only been a few months, but ... Veronica. This could be it! I think he really could be the one! We have so much in common. We both teach, never married, want children. We talk about everything!"*

Veronica laughed. *"Hey, slow down, it's only been a few months—more like two right? But I will say this—he is very charming and kinda cute."*

*"Oh my—kinda!? And his dimples!!"*

Veronica wasn't attracted to him at all but could recognize the charm he held by being so kind and polite. *"Well, he's your type, let's agree on that!"*

*"And, what about Gloria?! Did she like him? Oh, I bet she did. I told him all about her. I bet they get along just swimmingly."*

Veronica went silent on the phone, not sure what to say.

*"Hello? What's wrong? Did, did she say something?"*

Veronica still was stuck for words.

*"Come on, Veronica. You know I can't read anything over the phone. Oh God, she hates him. Right? Oh my. I should have known something was off when I couldn't read him."*

*"You couldn't read him either?"*

*"So Gloria said that? He couldn't be read?!"*

*"Listen. Calm down. Gloria is after all only eight years old. All she said to me was that it bothered her that she couldn't' read into him. You're the adult here. Trust your instinct. Get to know him. You have all the time in the world. There's no rush, right?"*

*"Ya, I guess. At least you like him. I'll find out more from Gloria tomorrow on how she sees him."*

*"There you go. So are you still taking her after school tomorrow? I have to work a little late tomorrow since I took Tuesday off for the first day of school."*

*"Absolutely. We'll be doing lessons at your place and starting supper. My fridge is empty from working so late with these parent-teacher nights."*

*"Sounds good. See you then. Good night."* Veronica hung up the phone and went to her room to get undressed.

As she took her makeup off at her small vanity desk, she stared into the mirror. She couldn't' help but think how odd it was that Gloria picked up on something so different than Cathy. Was this normal? Who was right, and who was wrong?

Richard had a hard time reading anything from Mr. West in the memory as well. He just assumed it was a little to do with how much he had to drink. He'd never encountered anyone else in all his years that had a block up like that.

"What did you make of him, in all honesty?" Richard asked.

"I personally thought he was a little over the top. No person is really truly THAT nice. I wanted to give him a chance as Gloria's teacher. The next night, however, things started to get strange."

# CHAPTER 20

# A Lesson in Darkness

The next day after work, Veronica got home just after supper time. The sun was just setting in the orange and pink fall sky. She entered their apartment building on Charles Street. After checking the mail, she went up to their apartment and could hear Gloria and Cathy talking. She slowly put her key in the slot, trying not to make a sound

"*I'm sorry, Miss Stevens. He's dark. Something isn't right.*"

"*When you see dark, what do you mean? I can't read him, even when I touch him.*"

"*What do you see?*" Begged Cathy.

"*I can't see anything. You know, I mostly hear when I read. But with him, it's like I hear soft fuzzy noise. The kind the TV makes on the wrong channel.*"

"*Miss Stevens, I don't know how I can make you understand. What I see or hear from him is dark.*" Gloria was being loud and firm. She meant it.

Veronica came in the room and let them know she was home. *"Hey, you two. How's things going?"*

"Hey, mom!" Gloria jumped out of her seat at the kitchen table and ran up to give her mom a hug.

Veronica hugged her back and kissed the top of her head.

*"I guess we are done here, Veronica. Gloria, can you go to your room for a second, please?"*

*"Miss Stevens, she's going to say yes. I asked her earlier, and I know you're a little scared, mom, but it's something I have to learn sooner or later."*

"Did I miss something?" Veronica looked at Cathy in confusion.

"Gloria, I hate it when you do that." Cathy looked annoyed at Gloria.

*"Sorry, I can't help it. Look mom, she wants to know if it's ok for her to try and teach me something."*

"Oh?" Veronica looked over at Cathy.

"Ok, Gloria, you might as well sit back down. Veronica, pull up a chair." Cathy reached beside her and pulled out one of the empty kitchen table chairs.

*"Ok, so I know I told you that I have a mentor. A friend who helped me learn how to use my gifts just like how I'm teaching Gloria. She lives in the States, and we only talk on the phone once a month now, the last Sunday of every month at 7."*

"I remember that."

*"But yesterday, she called me right after I hung up the phone with you. She sensed something and needed to talk to me about it. She's been helping me with Gloria's lessons."*

"She has? Will I ever get to meet this mystery lady?"

*"If you plan to go down to see her, yes. She is hopeful one day you and Gloria will come visit."*

"Well, one day, we'll see. What did she call you about?"

*"She picked up on what's going on here with Alex."*

"Who's Alex?" Gloria asked.

*"Sorry, Mr. West. She said Gloria is ready for a new stage of communication. One normally someone so young couldn't perform, but she felt Gloria is ready, and needs to know now for some reason."*

*"She wants me to get good at it, mom. Said in a few years I'm going to need it."*

*"Need what?"* Veronica asked the two of them.

*"Well, it's going to sound strange. My mentor believes I can help Gloria learn to project."*

*"Project what?"*

*"Well, when someone with the gift of insight can see images, they can project them to someone else."*

"What does that mean?" Veronica asked, sounding puzzled. A questioning look came over her face.

*"Mommy, it means I can show you what I see in my head."*

*"How on earth are you going to do that?"*

*"Mostly you have to be touching the person—just a handshake or a hug or something. It all depends on the person. Every person with abilities is different. My mentor thinks because I have insight as well, I can help Gloria work on this now. I just wanted to make sure you're ok with it."*

*"Well, I honestly don't fully understand, but of course. As long as it won't hurt Gloria."*

*"Goodness no. If anything, it's going to help her,"* Cathy said while shaking her head in a comforting way.

*"Ok. Well, I'm going to sit in the living room. I have some reading to do on a new face cream we have coming out, and I want to brush up on it for my clients."*

*"There is supper in the fridge for you, mommy. Miss Stevens made spaghetti. It's so yummy!"* Gloria blurted out.

*"Thanks, honey."*

*"Veronica, we won't be much longer. I'll head home as soon as we're finished."*

Veronica shook her head and got up from the table. She grabbed her bag from the front door area where she left it and headed to the couch. She sat down and only pretended to read her booklet. She kept staring at Gloria and Miss Stevens at the kitchen table, wondering what was going to happen.

*"Ok, Gloria, remember what we went over. Sylvia, my mentor, said to concentrate on channeling your conscious thoughts through your hand to mine. Visualize it. Put through a crystal clear image of something. See me see it in my mind. Focus. You ready?"*

*"Yes, Miss Stevens."* Gloria reached out her right hand and laid it palm up on the table.

*"Ok, you have the image in your mind? Start with something light and safe."*

*"Yes, Miss Stevens."*

*"Ok."* Cathy reached her hand out and clasped it with Gloria's. *"Now close your eyes and push. Make me see it. Remember your breathing."*

The two both closed their eyes and took slow deep breaths. At this point, Veronica wasn't even pretending to read. She closed the book and laid it on her lap. She was too interested in what she could witness.

A minute passed, maybe two.

*"Oh my, I think I see it! Are you sending an orange cat?"*

"Marcus?" Veronica said without even realizing it came from her mouth.

*"Mommy! Do you see it too?"* Gloria's eye flew open and looked at Veronica.

*"No, babe. Just a guess, you love that little guy,"* she said smiling.

*"Gloria, that was amazing. I could see it down to the detail. His little red collar, sitting on a floral print chair."*

*"That Mrs. Thompsons cat alright. That's her late husband's chair. He always sleeps in that spot."*

Gloria started clapping and squirming in her chair. She felt pride as she just accomplished what she was told most psychics can only do when they're much older.

*"Ok, Gloria, let's try it again. This time go bigger. Maybe a room. Think of all the details. What's on the wall? Where is the furniture? Are there any windows? Ok?"*

Gloria nodded her head. The two took position again and started to close their eyes. A few seconds later, Cathy sat up straight. Eyes still closed, she gasped.

*"Oh my God, Gloria, this is amazing!"*

Veronica got up from the chair and went into the kitchen. *"What is it? What do you see?"*

*"Gloria is showing my classroom. Her old kindergarten room. I can see everything. I can see the art section, the closets, the chalk—"* Cathy opened her eyes and leaned into Gloria. *"Gloria, I saw today's date."*

*"I know, you said show you a room. I thought you'd like to see one you knew so you'd know I was doing this right."*

*"No, Gloria, you are showing the room today. How are you doing this!?"*

"I am just going on what you said," Gloria said and slumped in her chair. She thought she was in trouble.

"No, sweetie, oh my God, no. This is not a bad thing, it's amazing. I don't even know what to say."

"What, what did she do?!" Veronica said loudly, a little concerned it was something wrong.

"Veronica, I don't even know if Sylvia can do that." Cathy Exclaimed.

"Who's Sylvia?!" Veronica asked looking at both of them.

"Sorry, she's my mentor. Her name is Sylvia. She was right. You are ready to work on this. Veronica, you need to understand. I just asked Gloria to project an image, a memory. That's all even some of the most clairvoyant people I've met can do. Well, she didn't just do that. She projected an image of what she can see in the room now. Like, right now. The sun is setting in the sky just like it is here now. This is, this is just incredible."

"Good job, babe." Veronica caressed Gloria's head to assure her she wasn't in trouble.

"Let's do more!" Gloria smiled and perked up immediately.

Veronica stood back and leaned against the counter, watching the two practice again and again. Gloria could only project a place she had been to, or something she'd seen in real life. Cathy told her that in a few years, she could see into any place she wanted or any person. One day, it won't matter if she's been there before, or even met the person before.

"Ok, Gloria, we will work on this more and more, until you've mastered it. I can't wait till we find out how far we go with this. What your limits will be."

Richard was taken back. Having not met Gloria while his abilities were in full tune like they were now, he only experienced her projection through Cathy in the memory. He was flabbergasted with her ability at only age eight. He hadn't been able to project until his late 20s.

"*Wow, Gloria, just wow. Say, want to try it on your mom?*" Cathy looked up at Veronica.

"*Uh, I'll sit this one out for now, but thanks—*" Veronica said back quickly.

"*Mom doesn't like this stuff. She'd prefer to watch rather than participate.*" Gloria finished her sentence for her.

Veronica looked at Cathy. "*She literally took the words from my mouth—literally.*"

"*Ok, Gloria, last one. It's what we talked about, ok?*" Cathy leaned in and looked at Gloria with a raised brow.

Gloria firmly shook her head. "*No, Ms. Stevens. You won't like it. You won't like what I see.*"

"*Come on, we talked about this. It's nothing to ever be scared of.*"

"*Miss Stevens, it's scary, I don't want to. Please don't make me.*" Gloria hung her head low and looked down at the floor.

Cathy grabbed Gloria's hand and looked up to Veronica. "*Gloria, we need to do this so I can understand. To see if I can help you.*" She made a facial gesture to Veronica to step in and help convince Gloria.

"*Gloria, honey, it's ok. Miss Stevens and I are both grown-ups. We're here to help you feel safe about it, ok?*"

"*Mommy, are you sure?*" Gloria looked up at her mother, then over to Cathy. "*It's scary. I don't want to scare you, Miss Stevens.*"

"*I'm a big girl, Gloria, I'm sure I can handle it.*" Cathy squeezed Gloria's hand.

"*Promise I won't get in trouble?*" Gloria looked at both of them.

"*Promise,*" they both responded in unison.

"*O-o-kkk-kay,*" Gloria said in a shaky voice. "*But, Miss Stevens, I'm worried. You won't like what you see and feel.*"

"*You let me decide that. Ok.*" Cathy closed her eyes, her hand still joined with Gloria's. "*Now show me what you see and feel when you are around Al—sorry. Mr. West.*"

Gloria took a big deep breath, Veronica noticing her shoulders go up and down. "*Well, remember I didn't want to do this. But, ok.*" She closed her eyes and furrowed her brow in concentration.

Veronica tensed as she watched the two concentrate. Her breath was the only thing that she could hear. She stared closely at Gloria who didn't move a muscle. Very subtly, she could hear Cathy take sharper, shorter breaths. She watched as all the hairs on her arm stood straight. All of a sudden, Cathy released Gloria's hand in a sharp, jerking motion and pushed her chair back as far as her hands could reach from the table. The screeching of the chair on the floor startled all of them. She was now panting in her seat.

"*I told you that you wouldn't like it,*" Gloria said in a shaky voice.

"*That was, what, what was that?! You, you see and feel that intensely?!*" Cathy asked, gasping for her breath.

Gloria immediately starting crying. Veronica acted quickly, trying to calm the two of them.

*"Gloria, honey, come with me. Let's get you ready for a bath."*

Veronica grasped Gloria's shoulders and pulled her from her seat. She was crying even harder then. *"Baby, it's ok."*

As she pulled Gloria from the kitchen to her bedroom, she nodded at Cathy who nodded back. *"We'll be back in a few. And hey, I have a bottle of wine in the fridge. Glasses are on the top of the far left cupboard."*

Cathy shook her head violently in agreeance.

Veronica gave Gloria a hot bath and calmed her down. She finally stopped crying when she stepped foot in the warm water.

*"Babe, mommy's just going to talk to Miss Stevens before she goes home, ok? You just have a soak here, and I'll be back in ten minutes to put you to bed, ok?"*

Gloria's face was red from tears. *"Am I in trouble, mom? I told you that wasn't a good idea."*

*"Not at all, sweetie. You just soak and relax, and I'll be back before you know it."*

Gloria didn't need to respond; she was too enthralled by the warm sensation from the water. She just nodded back at her mother. Veronica looked at her daughter calming in the bath until the last second before the door clicked shut. She turned around and went into the kitchen to find Cathy poised over the kitchen sink, a lit cigarette in one hand. To her right was the bottle of wine, half gone, and two empty glasses.

*"Cathy, what was that? What happened?"*

"There are no word to describe it, Veronica. What she sees, what she saw in Alex, was awful. Just awful. Pure evil if there is such a thing, Veronica. Pure evil."

"So why couldn't you sense it? Haven't you two… you know…"

"That's what makes it more awful. I've been with that, that, that thing!" Cathy turned around to look at Veronica. She had tears still streaking down her ghost white face.

As she turned around in the memory, Richard's senses were shaken. He could see what she was shone. It was as awful as anything he'd ever seen or felt since he realized he was clairvoyant. He leaned forwards and placed his coffee cup down on the table.

"Oh my God, Cathy! You look terrible!"

"Thanks."

"No, I'm sorry. I just—you look like you've just seen a ghost."

"I wish. A ghost is a welcome view over what I just saw."

She crossed over the kitchen after grabbing the wine and two glasses. She slowly sat down at the table as Veronica joined her. She poured them both a glass of wine and put out her cigarette.

"So what did you see?"

"Gloria was right. Just darkness. Pure darkness. Evil. Sinister vibrations. I never knew a human could come across like that. Just, disgusting."

"So what are you going to do?"

"There is nothing I can do. Tell people he's got a darkness inside him and stay away?"

"Well, it's a start! Don't you think other parents should know and protect their children?"

*"I don't foresee him doing them harm. Neither did Gloria. We talked about this before you got home. This is just something deep inside him. How he is."*

*"Well, I better call the school."*

*"And say what?!"*

*"Well, I at least have to get Gloria out of his class! She can't go to school and be around such a presence!"*

*"No, don't. She's fine. She even told me that. She said she has to stay in his class, and she wants to learn how to read vibrations like his better and control his from coming into her. She's right. It will just improve her insight in the long run. She's really wise for her age. I feel like I'm talking to an adult sometimes, not someone under ten."*

Veronica knew what Cathy meant. A lot of people always assumed Gloria was a lot older. But the mom in Veronica always saw her as a little girl nonetheless.

*"I'll talk to her about it when I put her to bed."*

Cathy held up her glass to Veronica. *"Here's to being single again."*

The two clicked glasses, and Veronica took a sip while Cathy downed the whole glass. She placed her now empty glass on the table and stood up.

*"I have to get going."*

*"Are you ok to drive?"*

*"Sober as a judge after that. There is a bottle of whiskey under my kitchen sink with my name on it. Don't think I'll be getting much sleep without it."*

*"Just be careful, ok? I'll come see you tomorrow when I drop off Gloria to school."*

*"Good night."*

Cathy collected her things and left.

Veronica went back to the bathroom to get Gloria ready for bed. Neither of them spoke. Veronica took her to her bedroom and got her dressed in her pajamas and tucked her in. She kissed her on her forehead.

*"Mom, I'll be ok. I'm going to learn a lot from Mr. West. I just don't fully see how yet, but it's important."*

*"Are you sure, baby? Just say the word and I'll call the school tomorrow and—"*

*"Mom, I'm sure. I love you. Good night, I need to sleep. I'm very sleepy."*

*"Good night, babe."* Veronica kissed her fingertip and touched Gloria's nose.

She left the room and went to bed herself.

The next day, Gloria didn't seem fazed at all like the night before. She seemed happy and chipper, like her usual self.

When they got off the bus and walked to the school, she saw Mr. West in the school yard talking to some parents. He noticed the two approach and looked up and smiled at Veronica and Gloria. Gloria didn't notice and ran off to talk to some friends. Veronica just glared at Mr. West who seemed put off by the harsh glance. She yelled goodbye to Gloria who waved goodbye and went around to the kindergarten door through the school yard. Veronica let herself in and went right to Miss Steven's class.

*"Hey, you. You look much better today. You ok?"*

*"I'm fine now. I think I was just in shock."*

*"I just saw Alex, it was awkward."*

*"Not as awkward as it'll be tonight when we have dinner."*

"You're having a dinner breakup? Hope it doesn't get ugly. What are you going to say to him?"

"Not sure yet. I'll think of something."

"Well, I'll be home tonight if you need to talk, ok?"

"Thanks. Wish me luck."

# CHAPTER 21

# Protective Mothering

*I think I need another drink*, Richard thought.

Veronica looked down and saw his empty coffee cup. "Did you want some more coffee, Rich?"

"Actually, I think I'll switch back to scotch if that's ok."

"Absolutely. SARAH!!"

In a flash, Sarah was in and out with another drink for Richard.

"So she broke up with him right away? What did she tell him?"

"She made up some excuse. It's too much too soon, I have to focus on my career. You know, the usual garbage someone says to someone when trying not to hurt their feelings."

"If you only knew how many of my patients come to see me when all they need is to accept that fact and they could move on."

"Really? Breakups are hard." Veronica started thinking about her breakup with Davian or the lack there of.

Richard heard her thoughts and quickly kept the conversation moving. "So how did he take it?"

"Oh, not well. As expected. But the brutal part of it was how he slowly started to take it out on Gloria."

"He did what?" Richard said in shock. Still not completely sober and having another drink, he didn't see that one coming.

"Yes, badly. I had to intervene a few months later into the school year."

"Why did he blame Gloria?"

"We weren't sure if he blamed Gloria, or he was just jealous of how close they were. After she broke up with him, she went back to her usual routine of two or three times a week after school with Gloria and some weekends. I think she used Gloria as an excuse to always be busy, and he started to resent her for it."

Richard looked in her memory at Cathy and that's exactly what happened. He was very jealous and it was consuming his every move.

"So what did you do?" Richard asked.

"Well, Gloria came home from school very upset a few times. She wouldn't talk to me about it. I had to ask Cathy what was going on and she told me. When I asked her why Gloria wouldn't tell me, she said she was afraid I'd pull her from his class."

"Was she right to think that?"

"I would have pulled her so fast her head would spin if she would have let me. But she made me swear not too. Although, she knew I had to step in as her mother. Psychic or not, she was still my little girl. It came in handy that he gave me his home phone number. I called him one night and set up a meeting for the next day after school. I knew from Cathy they had a staff meeting, so I asked to meet with him after so Gloria and all the other students would be gone."

A beautiful day in late March, Veronica got off work and came home. Mrs. Thompson had helped out by picking up Gloria from school and bringing her home. They were down the hall at Mrs. Thompson's place. Veronica knew it was so Gloria could play with Marcus. After she got out of her Lancôme uniform, she got dressed and grabbed the 1 Queen South bus and headed to the school. She was happy to see most of the teachers' cars were gone from the lot, and she headed to the Grade 4 wing and went inside. Mr. West was sitting at his desk, grading some papers.

She knocked softly on the door frame before walking in. *"Good evening, Alex."*

Mr. West looked up from his papers and frowned when he made eye contact with Veronica.

*"Please pull up a chair."* He pointed to the two chairs he had on the other side of his desk. *"And please, I prefer to be addressed as Mr. West."*

*"OOOK,"* Veronica said sarcastically. She took a seat.

*"So how can I help you, Miss Chastain?"*

*"I'm here to see why you have such a problem with my daughter. It's come to my attention you've been a little belligerent with her."*

"Belligerent? Me? That's funny as that's the exact word I would use to describe her behaviour in my class."

"I'm sorry, Mr. West, but what do you mean? You told me what a delight she is. I don't understand this."

"A delight? I'm not sure what teacher could find this to be true. Maybe months ago at the beginning of the school year before I got to know her. But those definitely aren't my words now. Since her first day, she has raised her hand every chance she could to either ask me a question or add a silly comment. It's so disruptive I find myself having to send her to the hallway to do her work."

"You gave my daughter a time out for being interactive with her class? What gives you the right?"

"I am the one trying to teach these children. You daughter lacks discipline. She needs direction. She is off in her own little dream world all day, and she needs to focus on the work I am giving her."

"Mr. West, you'll have to excuse me, but don't you think you're being a bit extreme? This all seems completely unnecessary."

"Ms. Chastain, your daughter is a bad seed. I bet the apple doesn't fall far from the tree is my guess." Mr. West laughed and shook his head.

In this memory, Richard could see how he interacted with her. His personality was void of any sense of humour or humility. He was enjoying being mean and condescending to Veronica. Richard thought to himself about how much he could have used therapy back then. Maybe had he gotten help, the future would not have unfolded the way it did for this awful man.

"Mr. West, I—"

"Please, Ms. Chastain. Goodness, you're as bad as your daughter. I see where she gets it from! She needs to focus on the *studies I give her and not be so obnoxious. She raises her hand before I finish asking questions, and she challenges me on answers. Answers on things she possibly couldn't know about. In our history lesson the other day, she even said I had the wrong date about something in the war! I know my facts and don't appreciate being second guessed!"*

Veronica understood all too well when he said she was trying to answer questions before he could finish asking them. It's because she knew the answer before he even spoke the words. It wasn't her fault.

*"Look, Mr. West, I appreciate your concern. But, Gloria is my child. It's not your place to discipline her just because she gets on your nerves. She is bright, smart, and has the compassion of a saint. I've noticed her behaviour at home is very suppressed, and now I know why!"*

*"Well, it's good to know she is learning SOMETHING from her time in my class."*

*"Listen, Mr. West, you're new here, and I am going to give you benefit of the doubt. You just need time to get to know Gloria and how she interacts as a student here at Southridge. She is going to come to class, and I will speak with her about her hyper behaviour during lessons. I promise she won't raise her hand too often and she won't speak out of context. But this is what's going to happen. You will not pick on her, punish her or make her feel bad any more about how bright she is. Do you understand me?"*

*"Well, well, you do have a back bone after all. The other parents here don't speak highly of you, you know. The parents I've met have all had concerns over you and your daughter being a part of this community."*

Veronica started to get mad, really angry. She felt like something had snapped in her head, and now she had truly had enough with keeping her head down with this school, the parents, and now this teacher. She stood up and placed her hands firmly on his desk and leaned in and got in his face.

*"Good to know I'm not winning any popularity contest here, because I never entered to win! But mark my words, Mr. West. If I ever see Gloria leave school looking upset after being in your class, I promise you that you'll regret it."*

*"Making threats are we, Ms. Chastain? Not sure if the principal will like this. I can't wait to discuss this with him after you leave."*

*"Well, Mr. West, should you feel it necessary to do that, I'd have no choice."*

*"No choice but what? Move and take your weird little kid to another school? Please, that would be a blessing as far as I'm concerned. And I'm sure the other parents would see it that way as well."*

*"No, no, Mr. West. Nothing that easy. You see, I work downtown at Eaton's. I work in the cosmetics department for Lancôme. It's a huge beauty brand from France, and they love to empower women who work for them. In fact, my department manager, Mrs. Charlton, is married to Mr. James Charlton. Have you heard of him?"*

*"You can make up names to scare me, Ms. Chastain, but let me assure you—"*

*"Oh no, let me assure you. When I leave here, I encourage you to pick up that phone on the wall and ask secretary Janson to get you an outside line. She will ask you whom she should call. Ask her to grab the phone book in the office. It's right on the shelf beside the window. I know the office well as I have been coming to this school for years. You will ask her to look up the Waterloo Regional*

*School Board head office in the yellow pages. She will dial the local number and when the receptionist picks up, you will ask to speak to the Regional President Mr. James Charlton."*

As she went on, Mr. West lost his smug facial expression. He started to look a bit pale.

*"So you see, it's up to you if you ever want to get hired at any other school in the district, or any district for that matter. My boss, Mrs. Charlton, and her husband, Mr. Charlton, have me over every few months for dinner and always ask me to bring my Gloria. With no kids of their own, they absolutely adore her. I wonder how the head of the Waterloo Regional School Board will feel when I tell him how much you've hurt Gloria's feelings and how you've been treating her. I'm not sure that will help your chances of getting a job, ANY job again. Do you?"*

A bead of sweat started down this little rat of a man's forehead, and she knew he understood how serious she was.

"Was this true? You knew someone on the school board back then?"

"Well, no, not exactly. Mrs. Charlton was my boss, that was true. But her husband, Mr. Charlton, worked somewhere I presumed, that is before he passed away two years prior."

Richard burst out laughing.

"You mean to say you made all that up to scare him?"

"You bet I did. I was protecting Gloria, and I would do it again in a heartbeat."

"Ok, well I don't think that will be necessary. I will adjust my lesson plan to make Gloria feel more comfortable and if I have any more issues with her—"

"There won't be any more issues. And if you feel she needs more 'discipline' and I quote, you'll address me going forward. Is that understood?"

"Yes, Ms. Chastain. Have a good evening."

Veronica walked out of the room and slammed the door.

Richard watched in his mind how Mr. West got the message. Despite not being able to read him either, the expression on Mr. West's face said it all.

"Good for you, Veronica. That took guts."

"I still don't know what came over me. But from that day forward, I didn't hang my head down and let people bother us. We were our own family unit, making the best of the things we were given, and I wasn't going to feel ashamed anymore."

"So what happened the next day?"

"The next day, I was stressed all day when she was in school. I didn't have to work that day at the Lancôme beauty counter in Eaton's, so I was left alone to pace my kitchen. It felt like such a long day. I took the 2:30 p.m. bus to make sure I was right outside the school doors when the bell rang. I got there early, but I didn't care. The bell rang and my heart lifted. One of the first kids out the door was Gloria who came running up to me. She was back to her old self."

"Mommy!!"

*"Hi, baby. How was your day? Did you have fun?"*

*"Ya! Today was art lessons in the afternoon and I got to paint a picture. Mr. West said it was really good and he hung it on our board in the hallway!"*

*"That's incredible, sweetie! Why don't you show me!"*

With that, Gloria grabbed Veronica's hand with all her might and dragged her into the school hallway. Her door was second on the left and was clearly visible when anyone entered. There on Grade 4 class board was a big painting of Marcus, the big orange tabby that belonged to their neighbour Mrs. Thompson.

Veronica looked inside the classroom and saw Mr. West. He didn't look up at her or move a muscle, no doubt busy at his work.

Richard knew better. In the memory, he could see how uncomfortable the man was with her around. He was trying to look busy but really was staring at blank papers.

"Gloria and I left and took our bus home. We made supper, and all night, she talked about school and how much fun art and science was. I was happy I made things better for her. Even though she probably knew what I did."

"She went to bed at her usual time of 8 p.m., but she begged me to stay up a little later because it was Friday after all. I negotiated some extra chores that weekend for one more hour with me. She fell asleep on the couch watching TV with me and I took her to bed."

# CHAPTER 22

# Night Terrors

"Things were starting to get to our normal, but just as we settled into our new routine of for Grade 4, Gloria started to develop insight in her sleep. Cathy had warned me this would happen one day, but knowing it would come didn't make it any less terrifying for me.

"One night at 1 a.m., I woke up to her screaming. Screaming so loud and sharp it made my heart stop. Only when she stopped to take a breath could my brain compute it wasn't a dream, and I got out of bed and ran into her bedroom. I ran over to Gloria who was in her bed but screaming in her sleep. I reached over to her in the dark room and woke her up. Once I touched her, I noticed she was sweating and had wet the bed. She hadn't done that in years. She woke up out of her daze and started crying. She kept saying over and over—"

*"The door, mommy, the door!"*
*"What door, baby? What door are you talking about?!?!"*
*"The door, mommy, when he's angry, he's behind the door!"*

As she started to fully wake up, she calmed down. Veronica reached beside her bed and turned on a light. She looked so confused and tired.

"You ok, honey? What man is angry?"

"Yes, mom, sorry, I just see this door. It's in a dark place. In the ground somewhere. It's old and wooden. It's locked. I'm scared of it. I've never seen it before, but it's bad. Really bad."

"How can you tell, honey?"

"Mom, Miss Stevens told me this would start soon. She told me it would be the scariest thing ever. Mom. I've never been so terrified. Ever. But more will come to me until it makes sense."

"Baby, are you sure you're ok? You want to come sleep with me tonight?"

"No, mom, I'm ok. Ms. Stevens told me not to be scared but to try to understand why I'm seeing what I'm being shown. I didn't mean to scare you."

"She gave me a quick hug and we got her all cleaned up and changed the bed. She was so exhausted and laid back down to instantly fall sleep. I left her room in a state of shock."

"Were you shocked because she was finally having nightmares?"

But Richard already knew her answer. She was shocked in how well Gloria took her nightmare. She sounded like a young adult, not a child of only eight years old.

"No. I was shocked at how well she handled her nightmare. I know when I was that young, it took my mom all night to calm me down. I felt, I don't know, almost a little useless when it came to her developing abilities."

"So you were starting to accept them and welcome them a little more at that age?"

"Yes, it was so hard not to. She was growing stronger and much more aware of her special talents—I called them talents then, and her and I called it that to not sound crazy if anyone ever heard us speaking about them."

"Did you speak of them often?"

"Not too often. I talked more about it with Cathy who assured me how normal it was. I was just starting to find a rhythm in our lives that was working out well for both of us. We had friends, I had a job, and Gloria was doing well in school. Once her first night terror episode had happened, we had a talk about things the next morning. She wasn't old enough yet to fully understand her power, but she was old enough to understand it had to be kept secret. Luckily, Cathy made it a priority early on in her lessons that she was not to talk about her "talents" to friends. Only Cathy, myself and Gloria knew what she really was."

Richard took a moment in Veronica's memories and explored that breakfast talk on his own, as she seemed to not want to discuss it with him. He could feel her resistance to speaking about it, and he wondered why.

He could see Veronica in their small kitchen making breakfast. He noticed the time was 8:30 a.m. and remembered her saying it was the weekend. She had let Gloria sleep in.

*"Hi, sweetie. Did you get more sleep last night?"*

*"Yes, mom. I feel good. Wow 8:30? I must have been tired!"*

*"I didn't want to wake you. We have no plans today. But, I did want to talk to you about last night, honey."*

*"What's there to talk about mom? I will be fine."*

*"Well, you know nightmares are normal, right? Even mom here gets them from time to time. It's very normal when you're stressed. Is everything ok? Nothing is bothering you? Is Mr. West being nice?"*

*"Mom, everything is just great. Mr. West is fine, but I sense he can't wait for school to be over for the year. He keeps saying 'Only a few more weeks and you're out of my class and on to another teacher.' Do you think he likes being a teacher?"*

Veronica grunted under her breath and turned her back to Gloria so she wouldn't see the face she couldn't hold back from making. *Who knows with that one,* she thought to herself.

*"I'm sure he likes being a teacher just as much as anyone else at Southridge. Are you looking forward to summer? Or are you stressed about spending more day time with Mrs. Thompson down the hall while I'm at work?"*

*"Mrs. Thompson is great, mom. I have fun there. Plus, she said she is going to take me swimming at Woodside pool on the really hot days!"*

*"Well good, I'm glad to hear you say that. But, honey, last night you gave mom a little scare. Do you remember anything about your dream? Anything about the door?"*

*"I don't know. When I first wake up, I remember more, but now it's all a little fuzzy. All I can remember is this door is brown in colour. I can see it's wood, but I don't know if it's been painted or not. It looks rough to the touch, not like the doors here at home*

*that are smooth because of the white paint. And the doors at school are all metal. This one looks old. And it's locked. The lock is really neat, it looks like one in a cartoon with an old key hole. Like the one in* Cinderella *you took me to see."*

Veronica was nodding her head, trying to picture the door. She took Gloria to see Disney's *Cinderella* that spring when it was showing just a few blocks away at the Capitol Theatre downtown. She loved that theater since she was child because it had a really old fashioned feel to it as it was built in 1921.

*"Ok, honey, do you think you've seen this door before?"*

*"No, mom, I've never seen it."*

*"What about the man?"*

*"What man?"*

*"You said there is an angry man behind the door."*

Richard could see Gloria at the age of eight concentrating and looking confused, sitting at their kitchen table.

*"I don't remember that. All I know is the door is bad. Really, really bad."*

*"Well, I'm glad we can talk about these things, aren't you?"*

*"I am, mom. But I really wish I knew someone else who was like me. Ms. Stevens has been a great help, but she said she can't help me anymore. Mom, is there anyone in our family like me? Was grandma or grandpa like me?"*

*"Gloria, we've talked about this before. No one in my family is special like you. No one has* talents*."*

*"What about my dad?"*

Oh, right there. That's why she didn't want to open up about this memory. It involved Davian. Richard didn't move a muscle in front of Veronica, as he didn't want her to pick up on his abilities. She might not be willing to open up if she knew he was psychic as well.

Deeper in her memory, he could feel her heartache. She never spoke to anyone about Gloria's father. Rather, she buried his memories so deep in her head so she wouldn't think about him. It was really hard when she would look at Gloria while she was growing up and she'd see small resemblances. But she always kept that to herself. Gloria didn't ask about him often. Richard's guess was she could sense how much it hurt her mother when she did.

*"Baby, your father is gone. We promised never to ask about him, remember?"*

*"I know but—"*

*"No buts!"*

Gloria slump down in her chair, and you could tell she wasn't going to ask again.

*"So, honey, you need to make mommy another promise, ok?"*

Gloria sat in her chair and very calmly shook her head. A very serious look came over both their faces.

*"I know Cathy tells you often you can't talk about what you two do in your study time. But I need to know you understand why."*

*"Why, mom?"*

*"Honey, not everyone out there is going to understand. It's very—unique and special how you sense things other people can't. And I know you've always seen things. But now, seeing them while in dreams? You can't tell other people."*

*"Mom, I—"*

*"Honey, this is the first and hopefully only time I ever ask you to use your . . . intuition or talent for something, but look inside*

*yourself, you know I'm telling you the truth, right? That only bad things will come if you tell friends or teachers at school?"*

Gloria sat and looked down at their kitchen table. She made both of her hands into fists and closed her eyes. She took a deep breath. Veronica could see her eyes moving under her closed eyelids as she concentrated.

*"Mom, I get it. Don't worry. I see what happens when I tell certain people and you're right. It will be a few years until I am able to be more open about what I can, or what I will be able to do."*

*"God, you sound like Cathy."*

*"Well, she has taught me everything I know."*

Veronica laughed and walked over to Gloria at the kitchen table. She bent over and kissed her on her forehead and embraced her cheek in her right hand. *"I'm so proud of you."*

*"I know."* Gloria smiled and looked up into her mother's eyes. *"I'm going to go get dressed, ok? We're going to the farmers market. Make sure you bring the big umbrella. It's going to rain when we walk home."*

Richard marveled in Gloria's abilities again in her youth. As it stood to date, no documented psychic could properly predict weather with accuracy until past their teen years. Due to the way the body and mind develop at younger ages, there is too many shifts in hormones and cognitive functions to be able to pick up on meteorology, the jet stream or plate tectonics. He wondered what other major weather anomalies she could sense at such a young age.

## CHAPTER 23

# A New Best Friend

"By the time Gloria was heading for grade 6, things for myself had gotten much better for us. I had finally managed to move us from downtown, and we were living in a small bungalow in an area behind the school call Forest Heights. It wasn't much, but the year before I had met a sales rep at my job at Eaton's. He was constantly on the road. He was never married and lived alone in the house he inherited when his parents passed way a few years ago. He had a small separate living space that he lived in while his parents were still alive, as he would help take care of them in their final years. After they both passed, he moved to main part of the house, and the apartment in the basement sat empty for a few years. He gave me an excellent price that I could afford, and in truth, I think he appreciated the company when he would be home. I would make him meals and we would have brief but pleasant little chats. I had been working hard at Eaton's and picked up extra shifts any time I could in the department store. I mostly worked at the Lancôme makeup counter, but sometimes they would need help in shoes or hosiery, and I would work to save money. It really paid off when I was finally able to afford a small used car.

"Another great perk was one of our neighbours. She was an elderly lady in her 50s named Trudy. She was a lot like Mrs. Thompson who lived in our building downtown, but sadly passed a few months prior. Trudy's husband was still alive, but he was a quiet, timid man. They never had children, and any family they still had didn't live near Kitchener. I think she just loved having us around. We kept her company once we got to know her, and she would watch Gloria anytime I needed her too. She too felt like family after a while, not a neighbour."

"Was this one of the houses Gloria bought and donated to the local families on her Christmas Special in 2017?"

"Yes, those are them. I found it funny she bought a row of houses in the first place. But when I think more about it, she had a very happy time in those houses, even if it was only for a few years."

"If you were both happy, why didn't you stay longer?"

"I'm getting to that part." Veronica looked a little annoyed at Richard.

He could sense she was a little irritable. The many martinis she'd had didn't help.

"Anyways, it was the late 70's. So many things in the city were changing and developing. The mall where I worked was originally built mostly as an outside shopping centre. Some developer bought it and was enclosing it with a fortress of green glass. They called it the emerald city. It was really neat to go watch as they built the structure. I would take Gloria down on my days off to get my paycheque, and we both loved sitting outside watching the crews work. It was really neat that they were attaching the Valhalla Hotel next door and anther office building across the street. It really felt new age.

"Any ways, Gloria was in Grade 6 now. A week or two after the first day of school was the usual parent-teacher night. I always enjoyed these nights, except for Grade 4 when I had the displeasure of meeting Mr. West."

"Was he still at Southridge?"

"Oh yes. He never bothered me or Gloria. He always avoided me at school events and pageants, and if he was forced to see me, he would be polite with a tone of hatred in his eyes. That man gave me the creeps."

Richard could sense the unease in her brief memories of running into him when she would come to the school to watch Gloria in a school event, or at the book fair. He really was a strange man.

"So I arrived to parent-teacher night, and I knew what to expect this time around. I decided to go later in the day in hope to be one of the last parents to be seen. Gloria was at our neighbour's house, Trudy, who agreed to keep her for the night. It was much easier that way. She knew going there meant some new toys, staying up extra late, and it was almost a guarantee at some point they would gorge on ice cream."

"Kids, so easy to please," Richard said.

Veronica laughed.

"So I was in the hallway and saw the usual chairs outside the classroom doors, and I took a moment to look at the project board outside the 6 Grade class door. Lots of picture and cut and paste projects. I noticed one very bright and beautiful cut and paste project hanging from the wall about halfway down, right in the centre. It really stood out and was quite impressive, and I could immediately tell it was Gloria's work. She loved to use glitter and her favourite colours. What made it obvious it was her though, was there was a lot of orange in all shades and textures of paper. She was the only little girl I knew who was obsessed over the colour like that. Most girls were groomed into loving pink at an early age. Toys, clothing and anything you could think of for a girl was pink. But Gloria loved orange. I bent in closer and sure enough, there was Gloria's little scribble of her developing signature. But strangely, I made out a second name, Stephanie, and didn't know why.

"I stood in the hallway trying to process this new tidbit of information, and I could hear voices coming to the door. I took a step back."

*"Thanks again, Mrs. Kropf. Grant and I are so happy to have you as Stephanie's teacher this year. We think she is going to do wonderfully with her studies, and we can't wait to see how you help her develop."*

Veronica could hear the dry, shallow laugh that only Nicole Engel was capable of.

*"It was nice to meet you, and this year will be great for the entire class. We'll see you next at the school fall fair."*

*"I look forward to it."*

Just then, Mr. and Mrs. Engel walked out the door, and Nicole Engel stopped dead in her tracks. Her husband, Grant, ran into her, almost knocking her over. She just looked at Veronica, with her usual sneer, gave her a mocking grunt, and carried on down the hall.

Mr. Engel looked at her and said, *"Good evening, Veronica, nice to see—"*

*"Don't keep me waiting, Grant! You know the kids like ME to tuck them into bed, not the sitter!"*

*"Yes, dear."*

Mr. Engel looked at Veronica with an apologetic face and hurried after his wife, who was clearly annoyed.

*"Miss Chastain, please come in!"*

*"Oh, hi. Please, call me Veronica."*

*"Well in that case, why don't you call me Samantha?"*

*"Thanks, Samantha."*

*"Come in and take a seat. I just have to lock the doors behind the Engels. We're the last ones here other than the janitor, but he starts cleaning at the kindergarten wing. He'll be at least an hour."*

Veronica walked over to the adult-sized chair set up right in front of her desk that was at the front of the classroom. She didn't see her come back into the room, but she looked up when she heard her shut the door.

*"No, no! Not there!"*

Veronica was a little confused and watched her walk the length of the room past the desks to the book shelves near the back, and she went to the other side. Curious, she got up to follow her. Behind the book shelves was a long couch. She was sitting at one end and made a hand gesture for Veronica to sit with her. She grabbed a seat.

"I've never seen a couch in a classroom before. This is a first!"

"Let me tell you, I've been teaching a few years, but I baby sat all through high school and college. If there is one thing I've learned, it's that a tired child is a cranky child. And a cranky kid is, well… There are a few choice words I'd use, but I just met you and don't want to make a bad impression as your kid's new teacher."

"An asshole?"

Samantha looked at Veronica like she had two heads.

"What?"

"A tired kid is a cranky kid, and cranky kids are assholes." Veronica suddenly felt regret saying that, not sure how she'd take it.

Mrs. Kropf burst out laughing. "Oh my, as long as you said it first!" She laughed until a tear ran down her cheek. "Honestly, a lot of the other teachers make fun of me. They think I'm nuts. But I tell you. More often than not, if I have a student acting out, I tell them they are being punished for their actions and make them stay behind while I send the class to the gym or the library. I tell my student—or the asshole as you put it—to read a short story and that I expect a verbal report when I get back. I dim the lights in the room and turn on the fan in the corner over there. I sneak back before the rest of class, and almost every time when I get back, they are out cold. They usually wake up and forget I asked them about the book. I ask if they're sorry, and they are sincerely apologetic and go back to their desk and—ta-da! It's like starting the day over."

*"I have to say, that's genius. While my Gloria thinks she's too grown-up for naps, sometimes I force her to bed and it's like night and day when she gets up."*

*"Right? And don't get me started on those plastic chairs. They were uncomfortable when I was a kid. Let alone now and with the size of my behind."*

Both women paused for a second, then broke out in hard laughter again in unison.

*"Samantha, I think I'm going to enjoy having you as Gloria's teacher."*

*"Veronica, you're like a breath of fresh air for me. I mean, the parent I had before you ... oh my."*

*"Mrs. Engel?"*

*"Oh, I'm sorry, I shouldn't have said that. Are you a friend of hers? Oh no, I'm sorry if I said something to offend you."* Samantha started to rub one of her temples in stress.

Richard could see she really felt comfortable around Veronica, and could tell Veronica immediately felt the same.

*"Me and Nicole Engel, friends? Hardly! She's barely said a few sentences to me and our daughters have been in the same class since kindergarten. I'm one of, if the only, single mother she knows and she doesn't seem to approve of my situation."*

*"Can I be blunt, Veronica? She made it clear to me she feels that way as well."*

*"This is not the first time a teacher told me this, I'm used to it. But out of curiosity, what did she say this time?"*

*"I have to blame myself, really. Did you happen to see the artwork outside the class?"*

*"The paper and paste thing? Yes, I could tell it was Gloria's work right away. Now that it's the subject at hand, why is*

*Stephanie's name on it? I know Gloria's style, and that little masterpiece is Gloria's work all the way, and only Gloria."*

"Well, I try and mix it up with the students. The social food chain is obvious at an early age and these kids are about one year away from junior high. Junior high is going to be like a shark tank. It always is, don't you remember? There is a pecking rank to say the least."

"Oh, I remember that."

"There's always one student who is nice, but that fake kind of nice you're afraid to stand up to as a kid. I'm sure you had girls like that when you went to school."

Veronica nodded, she understood and could relate. "Yes, not so much in grade school or junior high, but by high school I definitely got a taste of that and worse."

"I thought it would be good for little Stephanie Engel to just work on some different projects with lots of different students in the class. Give them all a chance to get to know each other and maybe form a few new friendships."

"Fair enough."

"Well, I thought it was going well until I observed Gloria being too nice. It was like she didn't notice that Stephanie made her do all the work while she sat and talked to her other friends. She was pretty manipulative, in Gloria's defence. She'd say, 'Good job, Gloria, oh that's awesome. I can't wait till we show it.' Gloria was just happy to be appreciated by Stephanie. She didn't see how she'd done 90% of the work. But, don't you worry, I've got my eye on Stephanie and that won't happen again. And I probably shouldn't tell you this, but after meeting Mrs. Engel, it all makes sense."

Both woman laughed and sighed. Veronica more so to herself, knowing Gloria could read Stephanie's mind and probably knew the whole time that Stephanie was using her.

"But, let's talk about Gloria, shall we? Say, would you like a drink? There is some cold drinks in the teachers' lounge down the hall, I could use a little sugar. I grabbed some cold pop after I locked the door behind Mr. and Mrs. Engel. Would you like one?"

"Actually, that sounds amazing. I could use the caffeine."

Samantha got up and grabbed the two cans of pop she had put on her desk and walked one back and handed it to Veronica.

The crisp click of the cans opened in unison and they both had a sip.

"So, Gloria, she is very bright. You should be proud of her."

"I am. She is my everything."

"Her skills are right where they should be. Her math and writing is on point. "

"That's so great to hear. She just loves going to school here."

"She is just going to love some of the field trips I have planned this year. One is to go to Centre in the Square, have you heard of it? It's a new state-of-the-art entertainment facility they are building down on Fredrick Street. I looked at the first few months of shows they have planned, and I think the students would get a kick out of seeing one."

"What kid wouldn't!? I'm anxious to go there too."

"Well, I guess I can confirm you as one of my parent chaperones then? It's not for a few months, lots of time to make arrangements at work. That is, if you work? Do you work, Veronica?"

Veronica sat up a little when she was asked this. "Yes I do. I work for Lancôme cosmetics down at Eaton's."

"REALLY!?" Samantha gasped. "Oh my God, I just love their stuff. I treat myself once and a while to lipstick or perfume *from there. But only when I can hide it from my husband."* She laughed.

Veronica raised both her brows. *"Well, you now know someone who can get you some freebies, so come see me."* She winked at Samantha.

*"Done! But in all seriousness, Gloria is wonderful. I have no complaints and am truly happy she'll be in my class this year. It's getting late, and I think I hear the janitor making his way up this wing. Did you have any questions for me?"*

*"No, not really. Just please, if you ever have any problems or concerns, will you come to me first?"*

*"Of course I will. I'd rather talk to you any day of the week than the other parents."*

Richard could see in the memory that the two had instant chemistry. The type of connection you could tell when you've met a true friend.

Veronica got up off the couch and headed to the door. She turned and faced Samantha one more time.

*"Have a great night, Samantha. Do you need a ride home?"*

*"Actually that would save my husband a trip to pick me up. I usually walk home just not this late. I don't live far, do you?"*

*"I'm just over in Forest Heights, behind the high school off McGarry Drive."*

*"Get out! I live off McGarry too!"*

Richard saw in Veronica's memory that was only a street or two over from where she lived with Gloria at the time.

*"What a small world!"*

*"Ok, I'll just head to the teachers' lounge and call my husband and let him know. Be right back. Should I meet you at your car?"*

*"Sure. My car is probably the only one left out in the lot on Queen Street. I'll flash my lights if you don't see me."*

*"Great, see you in a sec!"*

Veronica left the school and got into her car. Sitting there, she really felt for the first time since high school that she had made a true friend.

A moment later, Mrs. Kropf was at her passenger door. Veronica reached over and unlocked it and Samantha got in. She directed Veronica to her house and pulled the car into her driveway.

*"Thank for the ride. My husband really appreciated it too. He got our kids to bed and didn't want to wake them for the car ride just to come get me."*

*"Anytime."*

Richard felt the surge of anxiety wash over Veronica then in her memory as she explained what happened next. Why was she so nervous?

*"So Samantha, my neighbor Trudy likes to have Gloria over for a sleepover once a week. See, she never had kids, and she's not married, so she just loves spoiling her now and then. Gloria just loves her too. I like her and she is a friend of mine, but she's a lot older than I am. Next Saturday, she has Gloria overnight, and I was wondering if you maybe would like to do something?"*

*"Oh. My. God."* Samantha just gasped.

*"Too soon? I'm sorry, I didn't mean to be too forward. I just thought—"*

*"No, no! I mean oh my God, YES!!! All my friends are too— mommy this, baby that. Don't get me wrong, please. I LOVE being a mom and wife. But, I'm still a woman! I NEED time away from that part of my life, and my sanity has been tested lately. I work*

*with kids all day, then come home to kids all night. This is exactly what I need, you have no idea."*

*"Really? You think you could get your husband to watch the kids?"*

*"Uh, I'm not asking him. He has poker night, football Sunday, and hockey twice a week. I haven't had a night to myself in forever. Hey! Let's go dancing!!!! Have you been to Valhalla before?"*

*"Valhalla? Of course I've been there. But never stayed overnight. Why would we go there?"*

*"Oh my, Veronica. What do you do with yourself on weekends!? We're not going to the hotel silly, but the bar there. It's called Schatzi's. Live music almost every night, dancing, you're going to love it!"*

Just there in her thoughts, she felt how sheltered she'd kept herself. It was time to change that. Her and Cathy were friends, but more through her connection with Gloria. They never went out together, not without Gloria.

*"Sounds like fun! Well, what time should I come and get you?"*

*"Veronica, no way. We will get my husband to drop us off. He owes me a LOT of rides. We'll just share a taxi home, ok? It might be like $6 with the tip, but trust me, we aren't driving home."*

*"Well, ok. Are you sure I can't drive?"*

*"Veronica, we're going dancing at a bar. What do you think we'll be doing?"*

*"Um, drinking?"*

*"Hello! We're two adult woman on the town, of course we'll be drinking!"*

Veronica was wide-eyed and nervous. *"I've never drank before."*

*"You never had a drink before?"* Samantha's jaw dropped in shock.

*"Well, not never. A glass of wine here and there. My old neighbour Mrs Thompson and I would have wine on the weekends together. But since we moved, I've barely touched it. I've just never been out dancing or to a night club. Nothing like that."*

*"Ah! I am even more excited now! You're going to have so much fun! I can't wait to show you around and introduce you. I don't know a lot of people like I used to, it's been years since I was out regularly. But Kitchener isn't that big, so were bound to run into some people we know!"*

*"Ok, I'm excited!"*

Richard could sense her excitement but also insecurity. She'd never been out dancing before. She didn't know what to expect. She was also unsure about running into people from her past. Old friends from high school, for example. Veronica thought this was the best for her to brave it. The psychologist in Richard was in compliance with that idea. That's exactly what she needed to grow and move on from Davian.

*"Good night, Samantha, and I guess I'll see you next Saturday!"*

*"I'm sure you'll see me at the school before that, but next Saturday is going to be one to remember!!!"*

## CHAPTER 24

# The New Veronica

"So the next week or two seemed to drag on for me. I was equally excited as I was nervous.

I was working the day of our big night out. Janet could sense I was in a particularly good mood."

*"Hey, Roni, what's going on with you today? You seem like a kid on Christmas morning. Your cheery mood is out selling me two to one. What's your secret?"*

*"You know how you and all the girls here are always on me to go, get out and start having a life?"* Veronica laughed and let out a huge smile.

*"Oh my gosh! Do you have a date? I can't wait to tell everyone! You know, I've bothered you about this for the past seven years I've worked with you. It's about time. You're too young and too pretty to not be dating and out having fun. When I was your age, I went out to the disco with my girlfriends as much as I could before I got married. If I was young, single and pretty like you, I'd be out all the time. It's time you let loose and live a little."*

*"No not a date!"*

*"Oh, well whatever. What is it then?"*

*"It's not a date. Well, not like that. I made friends with this girl Samantha who is Gloria's teacher. We're going out for a girl's night."*

*"Oh that's exciting! What are you two up to? Where are you going?"*

*"Have you ever heard of Schatzi's? She said it's the bar inside the Valhalla hotel across the street."*

*"I live in Kitchener, Veronica. Of course I've heard of it! Are you going to see a band there? What night are you going?"*

*"Tonight. She didn't say anything about a band. I'm nervous. I've never been out dancing. Unless you count dancing to the radio in my pajamas with Gloria in our living room."*

*"Oh Roni,"* Janet laughed and shook her head. *"You're like an old woman trapped in a young girl's body. You're not even thirty, go have fun! What are you going to wear?"*

*"To be honest, I hadn't thought about it."*

Janet looked Veronica up and down. *"Seriously? Oh, that's it. We're getting you done up for tonight!"*

Veronica looked up at the mirror behind the counter. She couldn't see much as the mirror was the display for all the wonderful perfumes they sold at the Lancôme counter. She looked at herself and thought she looked nice. Her hair was up in a bun as she always had it. She hadn't cut her hair since before she got pregnant. She simply took scissors to it in her kitchen once or twice a year to keep it a few inches past her shoulders.

*"I have the best idea, Roni. Hang on!"*

Just then, Janet went to the PA mic for the entire store and picked it up.

*"Attention, Eaton's staff. Could I have Stacey and Kelly to cosmetics, please? That's Stacey and Kelly to the cosmetics floor. Thank you."*

*"What are you doing, Janet!!?? We're going to get in trouble!"*

*"Relax, would you? First, Mrs. Charlton is off this entire weekend. Second, we have hit our sales target of the day, and third, you never do anything nice for yourself. You never let yourself come to a launch party. You never come with us for drinks after work. You have picked up shifts for me and all the other girls here, and so it's about time we did something nice for you. Roni, I swear. It's like you punish yourself or something."*

*"What are you talking about?"*

*"Just let me take care of this."*

About three minutes later, two other coworkers came to the cosmetics department.

*"Oh, and Miss Veronica?"* Janet said while raising one eyebrow. *"Don't think of even trying to say no to coming out with US girls next time. Now that I know you are no longer afraid of a social life, we're going to ask you ALL the time."*

Veronica laughed. *"Ok, ok, Janet. I know I've been a bit of a stick in the mud, but I'm working on that."*

Veronica looked like a deer in headlights as both Kelly and Stacey walked up and had a sudden look of worry on their faces.

*"Hey, Janet, hey, Roni. What's up? Why'd you page me and Kelly? Is Charlton back?"*

*"Stacey, Kelly. You'll never guess who's leaving her cave for once and going dancing tonight at Schatzi's next door!?!"*

Both women started to giggle and jumped up and down.

*"Oh my God! Finally!"* gasped Stacey.

*"I knew you'd one day break out of your shell!"* chirped Kelly.

*"I mean, I knew I was anti-social, but not that bad,"* Veronica said defensively.

*"Relax, Roni. We're just teasing you. Okay ladies. Let's divide and conquer. Kelly, you go pick out a dress. Stacey, find her some hot heels. What size are you, Roni?"*

*"Um, 8? I think?"*

*"She's an 8,"* explained Stacey. *"I always help her with her shoes."*

*"I know exactly the dress that will make you look like a million dollars. We just got them in, and they don't go on the sales floor till month end. No one will be in this dress. It's to die for,"* said Kelly.

*"Hey, I can't afford any of this, you guys! Seriously, I appreciate it, but I can't."*

*"Roni,"* Kelly said, looking half-annoyed and half-baffled. *"Seriously. You're just going to borrow them and bring them back. Just don't wreck anything or you will have to buy it. Everyone does it."*

Veronica looked up at the three women determined to give her a makeover. All three of them stared at her impatiently.

*"As long as I won't get in trouble."*

*"Roni, it's not like we do this all the time. Relax. Trust us."*

*"Well, ok, let's do this."*

Veronica didn't want to admit it, but she was excited.

*"Ok girls, you get busy. I'm going to do her makeup, and I'll have to do something with this hair. Say, is Dave working up in the salon? He owes me a favour."*

*"Yes, he's here till four,"* said Stacey.

*"Perfect. Ok, Roni, you take your lunch break, and I'll cover for you. Head up to see Dave right after you punch out. I'll call the salon right now. When you're done, go punch back in and come back down here. I'm going to do the most awesome makeup on you."*

*"Ok! Wow, this is so great, ladies, thank you so much!!"*

They all looked at Veronica with the warmest smiles.

*"Roni, you go above and beyond for everyone here. Eaton's wouldn't be the same without you."* Janet gave her a huge hug after that.

*"Thanks, girls. Ok, let's do this!"*

"I was so excited that I think I ran to the punch clock. Eaton's was four floors of shopping, and our staff area for cosmetics was on the third floor. In the basement was furniture, the second floor clothes, shoes and jewelry, third floor was cosmetics, the salon, and household items, and the top floor was undergarments, travel and menswear and a restaurant named Timothy's. Over the years, it all moved around, but that was the layout when I got there. You could leave the mall to go outdoor shopping on level two and three, and they were currently converting the shopping centre indoors. Like I said, over the years it all moved around, but that was the layout when I got there."

"I'm happy to hear at some point you made yourself a priority. You were a young mom. You deserved to get out and have some fun," Richard said.

"Well, I went all out that day. I went to the salon and got my hair done for the first time. My mother cut my hair when I was young, so it was such a nice experience," Veronica said while smiling.

On her scheduled lunch break, Veronica punched out as Janet told her to. She went immediately to the salon.

"*Hello there, Veronica,*" a man in his late 30s said, standing beside a stylist chair.

Veronica and Dave had chatted here and there over the years, but they didn't know one other too well.

"*Thanks for doing this, I really appreciate it.*"

"*Hey, any friend of Janet is a friend of mine. I owe her one anyways, well, more than one. You're helping me really, by evening the score. Come sit, will you?*"

The salon in Eaton's was nothing like the majestic spas or salons of today. The salon was very simple. Only two stations with chairs for cutting and styling hair. There was only one wash sink along the back. Large framed posters hung around the salon featuring the lasted hairstyles and products. Veronica always seemed to notice these in any beauty salon, then as well as now. It was because she worked in the industry. She appreciated it.

Dave extended his arm to his station. It was a large green chair made up of plastic-covered cushions and chrome metal. She sat in his styling chair facing him, and he turned her around to face the mirror. He placed a cape over her, only exposing her from the neck up. He took her hair out of the neat bun she usually styled it in, which was at the base of her neck. He tousled her hair around and looked at her like she was a project of his.

*"My, you simply have gorgeous hair. It's so healthy and thick. Is this your natural colour?"*

*"Yes. I haven't had my hair coloured in my entire life. I cut it myself."*

*"Well, for a self-made beauty, you're not doing too bad of a job. But, I really think we could do something to bring you into the now. The 80s are just around the corner, and you women have endless opportunities to be trendy and modern with your hair. Will you trust me?"*

Veronica was nervous, but gave herself a good long stare in the mirror that day. She knew she wasn't completely shorted in the jean pool when it came to good looks, but she was never overly confident.

*"Dave, I'm at your mercy. Just nothing short, ok?"*

Dave smiled. He turned her chair around and didn't let her see anything while he was working.

Over the next hour, her hair was washed, cut, styled and sprayed. It was mostly down but a few pieces he'd pinned out of her face on her left side. Veronica could see big piles of poufy dry hair on the floor and was nervous to see how much length he had taken.

*"Ok, my dear, you're all done. It's one of my best cuts. We didn't colour you, as your natural colour is what most of my clients pay me for. You're such a natural beauty."*

*"Ok, let me see!!"*

*"Oh no, sorry. I can't. I've been sworn to keep you in the chair until Janet gets here. She should be here any second."*

*"What? Why?"*

As soon as Veronica spoke those words, Janet came into the salon in her Lancôme jacket. In one hand, she had a cup of makeup brushes, and a travel kit of makeup was in the other. She looked like she meant business. She looked at Veronica sitting there in Dave's chair.

"*Oh my God, Roni! I love it! Dave, you outdid yourself!*"

"*Don't thank me, she just makes my work look so good!*"

"*Well, I don't know about that Dave, but it's outrageous. You look like you could be a model.*"

Veronica felt her cheeks burning. She heard more footsteps coming into the salon and looked over to see Stacey and Kelly, both of them with large Eaton's bags in hand.

"*Janet, shouldn't I punch in and we'll do this down at the counter?*"

"*Relax, Roni, Klaus from fragrance is covering me. It's dead today, anyways.*"

"*Girls, what's all that? You didn't have to buy me things!*"

"*Honey,*" spoke Kelly in a soft tone, "*if we told you we were buying this stuff for you, we knew you'd never let us. I speak for all of us when I say we were teasing you by saying we'd borrow this. We're not like that. Sweetie, this makes us feel better. You do so much for all of us around here.*"

"*Come on, you guys…*"

"*Sorry, Roni, tags and stickers are all cut off. You're stuck with all this. I can't wait to see you all done up!*"

Veronica couldn't say no, and she knew they wouldn't take no for an answer anyways.

Janet came over to the chair and pumped it high for her to do makeup. Dave moved aside and went to greet his next client at the entrance.

"*Oh, this is so exciting. I can't wait for you to see yourself. I won't take long. After makeup, we have your dress and shoes with a light jacket. You're going to look so sexy. You will meet someone tonight, I just know it!!"* Janet was almost jumping up and down again.

What seemed like seconds was probably a half hour. After the makeup, the trio of girls took Veronica to a changeroom upstairs, all the while avoiding any possible reflections. The outfit Kelly picked was something Veronica wouldn't have dared to even look twice at. It was a champagne colour dress. It reminded Veronica of a robe the way you tied it up at the side after wrapping it around your body. Kelly had to come into the changeroom to help show her how to do it up. She pulled one long tie through a small slit on the other side of her waist and tightened it. She helped align the thick shoulder pads; Veronica looked at them strangely as Kelly adjusted them.

*"Hey, trust me, these are the biggest things in fashion since bell bottoms. Farah Fawcett is always wearing them to parties."*

The dress felt tight. Veronica started to move for the door when Kelly grabbed her arm.

*"Wait! Not so fast. I have this blazer for you to wear, and Stacey has the cutest platforms."*

Kelly pulled out a cute short-cut jacket for her. It was tan in colour and a perfect complement to the dress. The dress was tight and a bit low-cut, so the jacket made her feel a lot more comfortable. The jacket had big metal buckles and a belt that hung low. She thought it looked really cool.

*"Stacey! She's ready!"* exclaimed Kelly from the changeroom.

Stacey emerged with a pair of platform shoes. Tan with laces and not too high. Veronica had seen women, and even some men, wearing them in the store and around town. She really liked them right away.

"Wow! I hope I can walk in those!"

"Oh, platforms are easy, and these are mini platforms. I didn't get the big guns just yet for you. I know you've never worn them, or heels for that matter. And here, I noticed you had your ears pierced. Here some hoop earrings and these are called bangles. It's basically a bunch of bracelets you wear at once. It's so fashionable."

"Ok, Janet, she's finished!" Kelly looked at Veronica with a reassuring smile. "Are you ready!?"

Veronica nodded her head but was so nervous. This was more attention than she was used to. She stepped out from the back room and looked at Janet who gave her the biggest smile.

"Wow. You look fabulous! God, I wish I had your figure! No more hiding, Roni!! You got it?"

Before she could respond, she grabbed Veronica by the arms and pulled her in front of a mirror.

"Well, what did you think?" Richard asked Veronica. He watched her tell this part of the story with a smile on her face and a warm flush in her cheeks. He already knew how she felt. She was shocked. She didn't think she could look this pretty. Richard thought she was stunning. Like a model he would have seen in old magazines when he was younger. In 1979, he was barely a preteen, but he knew he would have noticed her then.

"The hairdresser, Dave, told me how stunning I was, and my little group of friends all made a big deal. For the first time ever, I felt as pretty as people told me I looked."

Richard was glad as he experienced her new surge of self-confidence. He couldn't help but think that this was such a good thing for Gloria. The hardships she would face in her life were trivial in her development as the psychic the world knew her to be. She needed a strong female figure to look up to.

He shook his head as the hair on his arms stood up.

"Are you ok?" Veronica was staring at Richard, looked very concerned.

"Me? Oh yes, sorry. Sorry. I was just daydreaming, I don't know what that was about." Richard was generally confused on where his mind just went. "Anyways, I was excited about this moment for you."

Richard scanned her thoughts. She bought it, but not fully.

"So what did you do then? Head home or??"

"Oh, well, I had to go home and take Gloria to Trudy's. Trudy babysat all day for me so Gloria could do her homework at our home, but she always preferred to be at her place for bedtime. I didn't mind, and Gloria thought a sleepover was always the coolest thing.

"I left Eaton's and drove straight home. My plan was to call Samantha right away to let her know what time I'd be ready to leave. I got home and walked in the door with all the Eaton's bags from the clothes and shoes all the girls had just given me. I entered the side door of the home and went down the stairs to our little apartment area. When you walked in, there was a small closet on the left, and then you were in the living room/kitchen. Trudy sat on our little sofa and looked up at me when she heard the door open and the sound of me rustling bags."

*"Hey, Veronica, how was—wow!!! Did you buy the entire store?"* Trudy hopped up and ran over to her to grab some things out of her hands.

*"No, the girls at work treated me to a makeover. What do you think?"*

Once Trudy had the bags out of Veronica's hands, she could see the new Veronica.

*"Wow, you look amazing! You sure do clean up nice. It's nice to see, Veronica. You stay home way too much. Where are you ladies off to?"*

*"Some place called Schatzi's in the Valhalla Hotel. Have you ever been there?"*

Trudy laughed out loud.

*"My goodness, maybe in my younger years. I went to wedding at the hotel a few years ago, and I went there for a drink with my brother and his wife. They drove in from up north and were staying there too. It seemed like quite the hip spot. Do people still call things hip? I don't know, I'm so out of touch."*

Veronica giggled and made her feel good. *"Hip? Oh yes, hip is still in."*

Trudy took the bags down the small hallway to Veronica's room and yelled for Gloria. *"Gloria! Come see your mom! She looks like a movie star!"*

Gloria came full steam from her room and stopped like a statue in front of her mother.

*"Mommy!!! You look so pretty! Like a doll, mommy!! I love it! Can I come out with you tonight too? I'll put my orange dress on!"*

"Richard, I tell you. If there is one item from those years I would buy at auction for sentimental reasons, it's that dress."

"Why is that?" Richard could see in her memories that Gloria wore that dress to so many events at her age. It was knee-length with gig puffy sleeves and lace trim. She beamed with happiness when she wore it.

"I just remember her in her youth wearing this specific orange dress. She was so happy when she wore it. It always made me smile. She was so sad when she grew out of it. But it was her age."

Richard made another mental note about the details of her orange dress. *This would also be helpful when I get the chance to see her,* he thought.

*"Gloria, tonight is for us big girls. You're going to have a great time with Trudy. I think she even has plans for popcorn tonight. Isn't that right, Trudy?"*

*"Oh yes, Gloria, and I have a surprise for you too."*

It seemed to work. Gloria was excited to spend the night with Trudy.

*"Ok young one, grab your bag and let's get going. These old bones need to get home."* Trudy gave Gloria a warm smile and patted her shoulders.

*"Ok, Mrs. Trudy. One minute!"* Gloria ran down the hall to her bedroom to collect her things.

Veronica looked at Trudy and grabbed her hand.

*"Thanks again, Trudy, I wish you'd let me pay you to watch Gloria. You help me all the time."*

*"Dear, I have no one else who visits me. My brother and his family are a three-hour drive away, and I don't want to go up north where there is even more snow in the winter than we have here. And*

*besides, I think I have more fun with Gloria than you realize. The pleasure is seriously all mine."*

Veronica knew she meant it. Trudy collected Gloria and her overnight bag, and the two of them set off for the house four doors down.

*"Bye, baby, you have fun tonight, and be on your best behaviour for Trudy, ok?"*

*"Yes, mom. Have lots of fun tonight! I love you!"* Gloria ran up to Veronica and they gave one another a tight hug.

Veronica noticed Gloria squeeze a little tighter than usual. She seemed to not want to let go.

*"I love you too, baby. Gosh, now get going, or Trudy will be at her house before you even leave our front door!"*

Gloria let go of her mother and looked up at her with a blank expression on her face.

*"Gloria, honey, don't keep Trudy waiting. It's rude."*

Gloria shook her head as though she was deep in thought and ran up the stairs out the door behind Trudy. Veronica followed behind and was about to lock the door when all of a sudden, Gloria came bursting back in.

*"Gloria, what in the world is going on? Where's Trudy?"*

*"Mom, I told her I forgot my sweater and to wait on the sidewalk for me. You told me never to talk about certain things unless we were alone."*

Veronica tensed up right away.

*"What is it, baby? What did you see?"* Veronica moved back down the stairs toward the sofa and took a seat. She grabbed Gloria's hand and pulling her alongside her.

*"It wasn't a dream, mom. I'm seeing more things when I'm awake. I can't explain. You know I don't pry unless I have*

*permission, but when you hugged me, mom . . . something came through. Touch is always strong for me. I usually am aware of that at school or with grown-ups, and especially with you, like you've always asked me to be."*

"I know, honey, and I'm so proud of you for that. What's personal to people is just that—personal. You'll understand that more as you grow up."

"Mom, believe me, I see and hear enough from the outside world right now than to let people's petty thoughts come to my mind."

Veronica gazed at Gloria as she often did when she spoke about control over her power. She was proud at how much self-control her daughter had at such a young age. She knew Gloria never used her abilities to cheat at school, or foresee presents under the tree at Christmas. Cathy had just taught her so well.

"Mom, I don't understand. Are you going to a zoo tonight?"

"A zoo? What on earth makes you see a zoo??"

"I just keep seeing an alligator, mom. I can't explain it. It's not clear, just that it's not safe."

"An alligator. Honey, I'm going dancing. I will be nowhere close to an alligator."

"I just see an alligator, maybe even in a cartoon or something. I feel it, and I feel you. Hurting. A LOT."

"Ok, honey, well, I'm glad you told me. And you were right to do it in private. I'm only going to the hotel beside mommy's work tonight for a little bit with a friend. Nothing to worry about. There will not be any alligators there, I promise. And if mommy decides to run away to the zoo, she'll be extra careful, ok?" Veronica tried laughing it off.

Gloria's face and body language made it clear she didn't find anything funny. "*Ok, mom. I'm sure it's nothing. I guess, maybe I'm just being silly. Have fun, mom. See you in the morning.*" Gloria turned to leave again, very reluctantly. She turned back around one more time. "*You sure you have to go, mom?*"

"*Honey, you know how excited I am for tonight. The girls got a lot done for me today to help. But if you really think I need to stay home, I will.*"

Gloria looked hard and intensely at her mother. "*No, no, mom. It should be ok. Just go, have fun.*"

"*Are you sure, baby?*"

"*That's the problem, I can't see it clearly. But if you're not going to a zoo tonight, maybe this is something about another day.*"

"*Ok, honey, and again. I'm glad you told me. You can go into this more on Monday after school with Cathy, ok?*"

"*You're probably right, mom. Love you. See you in the morning.*" Then Gloria ran out to meet Trudy who was waiting outside.

"What did it mean? An alligator?"

"To this day, I still don't know. Must have been a vibration she picked up for something else. It never made sense."

"And you said to her you were going out with a friend. Did she know you were going out with her teacher, Mrs. Kropf?"

"No. I didn't tell her. I didn't want any of the kids or teachers thinking she was getting special treatment because we were friends. I just thought it was better that way."

"Don't you think Gloria knew? Like, she could sense it?"

"Well, Cathy always instilled in her that she should not read people's minds. When she was young, she never did it for any reason. That I was sure of before she hit twelve."

Richard picked up on the 'when she was young' part. "Only when she was young?"

"Please, Richard. Once she hit puberty, she rebelled and did whatever she wanted. But you know this already, that's all published material."

"Of course." Richard responded.

Anyone who read up on a Gloria knew about her teen years helping the Waterloo Regional Police as it was highly documented. It was the first time any local law agency around Southern Ontario used a psychic to solve a case.

"So, I let her leave the second time and I locked the door. I went into the kitchen and called Samantha. Samantha said her and her husband would be leaving around 7:30 to pick me up, and that her in-laws had come to spend the night to help with the kids. This gave me an hour to eat and have some time to myself before going out. The time seemed to drag on from nerves, and I thought about cancelling."

"How come?" asked Richard.

"I was just so nervous and didn't know what to expect. And what Gloria told me had me a tiny bit rattled. I couldn't deny that."

# CHAPTER 25

# Girls' Night Out

"Anyways, at 7:30 sharp, I heard a car horn and ran up to see Samantha in the passenger's side, and her husband driving. As I walked to the car, Samantha rolled down her window."

*"Wow, Veronica, holy. I look like a bum next to you! You look awesome! Honey, tell her she looks amazing!"* Samantha smacked her husband's arm who barely flinched.

He didn't even look at Veronica as he was too enthralled by the radio and the hockey game that was on.

*"Yes, dear, she looks great. Come on, you idiots, shoot the puck!!!!"* Samantha's husband, Greg, yelled at the car radio.

Veronica climbed in the back seat and Samantha turned around. Her husband put the car in reverse and they were on their way.

*"You morons, block the net!!"* Greg yelled while flailing his hand in the air.

*"To the Valhalla, hun,"* Samantha told her husband.

*"Ya ya, I know. You told me a million times. I still can't believe you're leaving me with my parents and the kids."*

*"Uh, Greg, you know I never get out. This is only fair. "*

*"Ya well, my mother better let me watch the game when I get home, or I'm coming to join you ladies."*

*"Don't you dare! This is our night. That's that. So are you excited, Veronica?"*

*"Yes and no. Hey, make sure I don't fall on my face in these shoes. I'm wearing platforms. This is all new to me."*

*"Those aren't platforms. Wait till you see my shoes. I'm practically 5'10"!!! I can't wait to dance!!"*

It only took a few minutes in the car to get to the Valhalla. Samantha's husband pulled under the overhang of the hotel doors.

*"Good night, honey. I'll try not to wake you and the kids when I get home."* She leaned in and gave him a quick kiss on the cheek.

*"No problem. You girls behave."*

Veronica heard the radio murmur something about the hockey game.

*"You idiots! Do you know where the net is!?!?!? Fuck, at this rate, they might be into overtime, and I could still be up when you get home. Don't be too late, ok?"*

*"Night."*

They both hopped out of the car and watched him speed away.

*"Finally."* Samantha grabbed her purse and pulled out a pack of cigarettes.

*"You smoke?"* Veronica asked her in disbelief.

"God, no. I used to in college a little. Now I just have one once and while, on special occasions. I loved smoking, but it makes your teeth yellow and you smell bad."

"So why the cigarettes now then?" Veronica asked, puzzled.

"Wait and watch, my dear Veronica."

She led Veronica away from the main entrance of the hotel.

"Hey, where are we going? Isn't this place inside the hotel?"

"Yes, it is, hun, but the main doors are off of King Street around the corner. Follow me!"

They walked twenty feet from where her husband dropped them off and came around the corner of the Valhalla hotel. As soon as they rounded the corner, she could hear music and see a lineup of people.

"Not bad considering how early it is!" proclaimed Samantha.

"Is it always like this?"

"There is only a handful of really popular places in town, Veronica. The Evergreen Hotel, the Coronet, or we could have gone roller-skating at Bingemans. This is my favourite though. Live music, dancing, and it's so classy inside. I wonder if we'll run into anyone we know."

They walked up to the lineup, and it moved quickly, getting them in. There was a small set of stairs right inside the doors. Veronica couldn't see anything except shoes and some flashing lights. The door man let them inside and didn't ask anything. Once they got up the stairs, Veronica was overwhelmed.

In the memory, Richard could see for himself. The place was packed and lively. To the right was a huge bar made of rich wood with beautiful brass trim. Most bars had this look around that time. Straight ahead was a dance floor packed with people getting along to the music. Over to the right past the bar was a huge piano, and beside that was where the band played. It was loud and boisterous, a typical nighttime hot spot.

*"Let's get a drink!"* Samantha went straight for the bar. She moved her way right up front and the bartenders looked slammed. *"What do you want?"*

*"I'll have whatever you have."*

Samantha grabbed a cigarette from her pack. She put one in her mouth and pretended to look for a lighter. Just then, a handsome stranger extended his hand out with a light for her.

*"May I?"* asked the man.

*"Thanks. I'm Samantha, this is Veronica."*

He lit her cigarette and pointed at Veronica. *"Nice to meet you, ladies. Care for a drink?"*

*"Two rum and Cokes, please,"* Samantha blurted it out without missing a beat.

The man signaled the bartender and got them each a drink. While speaking to the bartender, he didn't notice Samantha drop the lit cigarette to the floor and put it out. After paying, he handed them out to each of them.

*"Here you are, ladies, care to join my friends and I?"*

Veronica started to feel flush with anxiety. She wasn't ready to just join a table of guys. She was worried, thinking she stepped way too far out of her comfort zone.

*"Oh sure, we'd love to. But my friend and I need to find someone first. Where are you guys sitting? We'll come find you in a bit, ok?"*

"Yes please, ladies, do come find us." He grabbed Samantha's hand and kissed her knuckle, barely noticing her wedding ring. He stared deeply at Veronica. *"And please, make sure you stop by our table."* He grabbed Veronica's hand, and it was an awkward pause before he tried to kiss it. She pulled away before he could make lip to knuckle contact.

*"Sure thing, we'll look for you. Bye!"* She sounded a little short and turned and walked away, dragging Veronica with her.

Veronica was relieved to hear her say this. She politely smiled at the man as they went their separate ways.

*"Now I understand why you brought your cigs. That was genius."*

*"Right? Don't worry, Veronica. We're going to have a blast. Nothing but innocent, harmless fun. I'm married after all. But you can do whatever you want!"*

Once Veronica realized Samantha really was out to just have fun, she relaxed and let her guard down a bit. There was nothing to be afraid of. She was a grown young woman with her life on track. Maybe she was a single mother. But, they had a nice place to live, she was working, and now she even had a car. Not to mention how great Gloria was turning out to be as a young adult. She realized in that moment that she should give herself more credit.

In the memory that played out in Richard's mind, he saw her look at herself in the mirror behind the bar. She was starting to understand how great she really was doing. He picked up on her inner turmoil as she started to let go. Such a healthy thing to do. He still found it odd how she didn't notice the attention men gave her. On a daily basis, she turned heads whenever she walked into places. Tonight, she looked exceptional, and there wasn't a man, or woman for that matter, that didn't look twice at her.

*"Come on, let's dance!"* Samantha led Veronica to the packed dance floor.

They went out and made their way to the centre of the dance floor. The music was so loud and upbeat. The band was amazing. Veronica looked over and saw a poster saying, "Live Music Monday To Saturday. Featuring Kitchener's Very Own *Gemini*!" They played everything she knew from the radio. Queen, Abba, lots of rock and roll. It was such a magical night.

*"I'm thirsty!"* Samantha shouted, holding up her empty glass.

Veronica had barely touched hers. *"Oh ok, let's go to the bar."*

This time, they bought their own drinks. Veronica pushed their way up to the bar and Samantha followed.

*"Two rum and Cokes, please."*

*"Look at you! Say, you should order us shooters!"*

*"What's a shooter?"* Veronica asked, having never heard of the term.

*"Oh my, Veronica, if there was any part of me that doubted you were just kidding by saying you'd never been out drinking—well,*

*that part of me has zero doubt now. Trust me! They're tasty! Two B-52s as well!"* she shouted over to the bartender who was making the fresh rum and Cokes.

Once he finished making the rum and Cokes, he placed them on the bar. Samantha drank hers in one or two gulps.

*"It's so hot in here, these are going down like water!"*

Veronica wanted to try to keep up with her and tried to drink hers just as quick. She got one big gulp down and that was all she could do. She just wasn't used to drinking alcohol like that.

Veronica looked up at Richard, and raised her martini.

"I think I've mastered that skill now, what do you think there, Richie?" she laughed.

"I'm choosing not to say anything out of fear you'll cut me off, Miss Chastain." Richard raised his glass back at her.

They both had a laugh.

"So the bartender still had his back to us. He was facing this wall of liqueurs and glassware. I could see his arms moving around, working fast in a frenzy. He turned around with two small glasses that had an orange liquid on top, a cream-coloured middle and a dark bottom. I had to order one more rum and Coke for Samantha. She paid the bill, and I looked at her for direction."

*"Ok, so for a shooter, it's called this for a reason, Veronica. You just shoot it back in one sip."*

*"One sip? This whole thing? But it looks so pretty!"*

*"Yes, or one gulp. Just shoot it back, you can do it. Ready?"* She held her glass up, waiting for Roni to cheers. *"To our first, but definitely not last, girls' night out!"*

They both picked up their small glass and clicked them together in a toast.

*"Cheers!"* Samantha shouted over the loud music.

"So what did you think?" Richard asked her, trying to hide his grin under his hand.

"I loved it. It tasted like chocolate milk to me. Cold and creamy. I just didn't expect how fast the booze would hit me. Keep in mind, I had never really had a night out drinking before. Within a few minutes, I took a break from drinking. I just drank three drinks in the first thirty minutes there. Samantha didn't seem to slow down for anything."

*"Ok, let's get a table, and we can take off our jackets and relax a bit. Then we'll dance some more!"*

Veronica really wanted to sit down, as her feet were starting to hurt. She expected as much as she'd never worn anything with even a slight heel before, let alone a platform. She also suspected that if they lingered by the bar much longer, Samantha would get them more drinks.

*"Sounds amazing!"* Veronica said, just wanting to be agreeable. She liked Samantha, but still was just getting to know her.

They found a table down some steps to the left of the dance floor. The bar was really beautiful and had a lot of levels. They took a seat and a waitress came over before they took off their jackets.

In the memory, Richard was delighted when he saw the name tag on a much younger Carol. *She really did work there all these years!* Seeing someone in that concept of a memory was rare for him.

"Two rum and Cokes, please," Samantha ordered, and she didn't even notice that Veronica had not touched her drink they had gotten at the bar.

The waitress was out of sight in seconds.

"*So what do you think? Fun, huh?*"

"*Yes. It's surreal that I'm here. Out on a weekend with someone my age. Not at home watching TV with my ten year old.*"

"*Veronica, you and I both need this. I can't do this every weekend, but once and while, we have to make the time. Heck, we should make this a once a month thing.*" All of a sudden, her face went sallow and she spoke under her breath. "*Oh Jesus, whatever you do, don't look up.*"

Naturally, Veronica looked up.

"*Well, isn't this pleasant. My child's teacher and current mentor, out socializing with the likes of you.*"

Veronica looked up and saw Mrs. Engel.

Richard saw it. Veronica looked up to see the horrible woman staring down at her with disgust. Using his talents, he could see into her mind. She was jealous. Beyond jealous. And seeing Veronica all dressed up pushed her over the edge. She'd also had some drinks which made her extra vicious.

Veronica stood up to try and be the bigger person.

"*Nicole, hi. Would you like to join us? It's so nice to see you outside of school.*"

As Veronica stood up, Nicole Engel looked at her once over. Head to toe. As she did this, she noticed all the people nearby looking at Veronica. She was furious.

Richard could see back in her day. She was prom queen and the most popular girl in school. Like so many people, she peaked in high school. But time was not kind to her, and her personality eventually shown through. Her beauty was a dim beaker of light compared to the burning sun that was Veronica.

*"Please, I have better things to do. My husband works here as the manager. Anyways, I have to go. Mrs. Kropf, it was good to see you. Can I give you a ride home to get you out of here?"*

*"No thanks, Mrs. Engel. I'm perfectly fine here with Veronica."*

*"Suit yourself. Good night, Mrs. Kropf."* She turned to Veronica to give her one last dirty look and disappeared into the crowd.

*"Oh my, she hates you."*

*"Really? I hadn't noticed,"* Veronica replied sarcastically, raising her brow in frustration.

The two woman laughed, and the waitress, Carol, just made it back with their drinks. While Veronica was paying for the drinks, she was distracted enough that she didn't notice that Samantha had already drank her old drink.

*"Let's dance, Veronica!"*

They made their way to the dance floor. As they got into the thick of the crowd, someone bumped Veronica's arm, and she watched her drink spill all down their leg.

*"Oh my, I'm so sor—"* Before she could finish apologizing, she found herself looking into the face of

the most handsome man in the bar. Her eyes widened and she stood up taller.

"*Please, don't be sorry, miss…*" he trailed off, waiting for her to say her name.

"*Oh, hi. I'm Veronica.*" She looked over and saw the back of Samantha's head disappearing quickly into the crowd.

"*Pleasure, Veronica. My name is Connelly.*" He stared at her with such intensity, making her blush.

"*Well, nice to meet you, Connelly, and I'm sorry about that. I really should go though, I don't want to lose my friend.*"

"*Maybe I'll see you around then, Veronica.*"

"*Ya, maybe. Bye!*" She briskly walked to catch up to Samantha, and turned around and saw Connelly staring at her.

Richard tried to scan into Connelly's consciousness, but the memory had too much going on, and the interaction happened too quickly. There was also loud music, and Veronica was a little intoxicated and still running high on anxiety. He could only pick up on how beautiful he thought she was.

Samantha and Veronica danced all night. She had most fun she'd had in years. The two women laughed, danced, and really got to know one other.

"Did you tell her about Gloria and her talents?"

"No, that came later. I didn't want to scare away my only friend. As the night went on, I kept catching my handsome admirer staring at me from across the bar. It was such a strange feeling. I'd make eye contact and I would blush and look away."

*Seeing Through Doors*

"You were flirting," Richard said insistently.

"I know. And I liked it. For the first time in my adult life, I was flirting."

"Did he come back to talk to you again?"

"Well, he came back to talk to me again, but not to flirt."

"So what did he say?" As soon as Richard asked, the memory showed him.

"Well, I knew I was a little bit tipsy, but Samantha—oh my, that was a different story. At our table, she could barely keep her eyes open. She was slurring her words and making little to no sense. Just then, I heard a voice over my shoulder."

*"Hey, is this Samantha, Greg's wife?"*

Veronica looked up and was staring at her handsome admirer again.

*"You know her?"*

*"Yes, I am a friend of her husband's. I've worked with him for a few years. Need some help getting her home? I drove my car here. It's parked in the hotel lot."*

Veronica was so nervous and didn't know what to do. She couldn't handle Samantha this drunk on her own, but she didn't know this guy.

*"Hey, I get it. You don't know me. Tell you what, here is a quarter, and here—"* He was writing something down on a piece of paper. *"Why don't you go to that pay phone and call their house. Greg will answer. The game is still on."* He pointed to a TV behind the bar, still showing the hockey game in over time. *"I'll watch her, and you can ask Greg if I'm a murderer, ok? I know where they live off of McGarry Drive."*

Veronica reluctantly took the piece of paper from her handsome stranger's hand, but relaxed when she recognized the phone number. It was indeed Samantha's home number. She still walked to a pay phone not far from their table, where she could still keep an eye on Samantha. She watched as Connelly sat beside her, trying to hold her up.

He was right, Greg picked up in two rings.

"*Hello?*" Greg answered.

"*Hi, Greg!? This is Veronica, how are you!?*" Veronica screamed into the phone. The music from the band was still blasting.

"*What's going on, is Sam ok??!!*"

"*No, she's fine. Well, actually, she's really drunk.*"

"*Oh geese, did she get into the shooters again?*"

"*Ya, a little maybe?*" She tried not to laugh. She didn't want to make light of the situation. "*So there is a guy here named Connelly who said he works with you, and he'd be safe to drive us home.*"

"*Connelly? Oh ya, I know him. He works with me.*" He sighed in relief. "*He's ok, Veronica, but I'm glad you called me. You can never be too safe. I don't know him well, but he's a solid guy. Please get her home before she starts to get sick. I'm warning you, that's the next phase of my wife having a good time. I hope she doesn't throw up in his car! Why, Samantha, why!!!! Sorry about this. I'll watch for you guys at the door, ok? Just be quiet. If she wakes my mother upstairs, I'll never hear the end of this.*"

"*Ok, Greg, see you soon.*"

Veronica hung up the phone and went back to the table where Connelly was now trying to feed Samantha a glass of water.

*"Well, you checked out. Greg says thank you. Now, let's get her out of here."*

Heads turned from all directions as Samantha was barely standing. One of the door men approached them.

*"Hey, she's gotta go."*

*"I know, we're leaving,"* Connelly said sternly.

Veronica was suddenly so glad that Connelly was there. She wasn't sure how she would have handled her friend without his help.

They walked her out of the bar, both of them being a human crutch on either side of her. They found a bench outside on King Street and both sat her down.

*"Ok, you stay here and I'll go grab my car. Are you ok?"*

*"Me? I'm fine. I didn't do half the shooters she must have."*

Connelly laughed and shot her a huge smile. *"Hey, last year at our work Christmas party, she got a lot worst. She's a bit of a legend at staff events. Greg is not the happiest of how she gets. I'm sure she's in a bit of hot water when she gets home."*

Veronica couldn't help but laugh and look at her friend who was passing out on the bench. *"Just go get your car."*

*"Ok, I'll be right back."*

A few minutes later, Connelly pulled up in his car. He got out and helped Veronica get Samantha into the back seat. She was incoherent but able to move a little on her feet.

"So, did you two have fun at least?" Connelly asked Veronica as they drove to Samantha's house.

*"I did, it was my first time out!"*

*"Really?"*

*"No, I mean at Schatzi's,"* she lied. She didn't want him to know she never got out.

*"That would explain why I've never seen you before. But, I've never seen you out before at all. Where do you like to go out?"*

*"Oh, you know, wherever."*

*"So, are you married?"*

*"Me?"* Veronica gasped. No one had ever asked that before. *"No. I'm not married."*

*"Single?"*

*"Yes, I'm single."* The words were hard to spit out. She *was* single. Saying it aloud only made her think of Davian.

*"Good to know,"* he said, and Veronica could see a smile come over his face.

They pulled up to Samantha's house, and Veronica saw Greg waiting at the front door with the lights on. He came out as soon as he saw car lights in their driveway. Connelly and Veronica both got out of the car.

*"Hey, Connelly, thanks, buddy. So sorry about this. I am so glad you were there tonight. You know how she gets."*

*"Hey, buddy, it's cool. She was better behaved than the Christmas party of '76."*

Both of them had a laugh. They went to the car and grabbed a snoring Samantha out of the back and took her inside. A minute later, both of the men immerged and said their goodbyes.

*"Have a good night, Veronica. Connelly, see you Monday. Make sure you get Veronica home safely."*

Connelly and Greg exchanged a firm handshake. He then came over to the passenger side door, opened it for

Veronica, and she got in. He shut the door and went and got into the driver's side.

*"Where to?"*

*"The end of the street here and go left."*

He followed her directions, and they were in her driveway in minutes. Her heart was pounding the whole way home; she wasn't sure of what could—or should—happen. She'd never been on a date before and had no idea what etiquette she needed to follow at a moment like this. He pulled up close to the house, and her heart skipped a beat in terror as he shut the engine off. What was she supposed to do or say? Her cheeks flushed as she stared at the beautiful stranger beside her.

*"Veronica?"*

*"Y-yes, Corry? I mean Connelly, Connelly? Sorry, that was stupid."*

He let out a gentle smile.

*"Calm down, Veronica, I was just going to ask if I could use your washroom. I was going to ask Greg if I could use theirs, but Samantha woke up as soon as we got in the house and ran straight for the bathroom to get sick. It was a little awkward."*

*"Oh."* Veronica felt stupid, thinking she misread the situation.

Veronica decided to let him in. It was only 12 a.m., and seeing how Greg trusted him, Veronica thought it was ok to let him use the washroom. Greg had shown no concern about her leaving with him alone.

Richard squinted his eyes deep in thought. He was interested in her, but his inner vision was muffled. There was something he couldn't pick up on yet. Something was off. He could feel it. Richard's reading of Greg were very clear. He was a good man, he loved Samantha very much and seemed to have a good sense of character. He was a solid guy. Greg did trust Connelly. Then what was it that Richard was picking up on?

They went to the side door and down the stairs to the apartment. Veronica unlocked the door, held it open and told Connelly to come inside.

"*It's down the hall, first door on the right.*"

"*Cute place. Is it just you here?*"

"*Me and my daughter.*"

"*Daughter?!*"

"*Yes. She's ten. She's in Samantha's class. That's actually how we met.*"

"*Very nice. Samantha is great.*" He smiled at Veronica.

He went down the hall and shut the door behind him. Veronica went into the kitchen and started going through the fridge like a deranged woman. She thought it was appropriate to at least offer him a drink or snack. Her mind was running wild. *When do I ask him to leave? What if he doesn't ask to stay? What if he does? Do I offer alcohol?*

She was practically pacing the kitchen when she heard a knock at the apartment door. She jumped up in shock. It was so late—who could it be? As she walked up the stairs to the door, a little sense of relief came to her from knowing she wasn't alone. She warily opened the door with extra caution.

As it swung open, she was worried when she saw who it was. There, after 12 a.m., was Trudy and Gloria both in their pajamas. Gloria's face was streaming with tears.

*"I'm so sorry, Veronica. I didn't know what else to do. I tried calling you, and when I saw the lights in your driveway, I just came right over."*

"What is it? What happened? Is everything ok?" She stepped out the door and embraced Gloria who was sobbing.

*"Baby, babe, what is it?"*

*"Nothing, mommy, I just had to come home. I need my own bed tonight. I need you."*

*"Ok, honey, just go to bed. Mommy has a friend in the washroom, so don't be alarmed. Go tuck yourself in, and I'll be there in a minute."*

She ran inside and Veronica stepped out to talk to Trudy.

*"What the hell happened?"*

*"I don't know. She's never been like this before. She went down to bed just fine like always. Then, I was going to bed myself when I heard her screaming."*

"Screaming?" Veronica stopped moving every muscle in her body. She hated when Gloria had her night terrors, especially about the door she'd been going on about for over a year.

*"Ya, screaming! She terrified me."* Trudy's face was grim and serious.

*"Was it about a door?"*

*"A door? No, she was out of control. She was hysterical. It terrified me and my husband. I don't know what to say, Veronica."*

*"Trudy, I'm so sorry. She's ten with an active imagination."*

*"You didn't hear her screaming, ok? And she wouldn't let me calm her down. She refused to go back to sleep. She went down to put her coat on, and I was trying to stop her. She was not letting me. I was trying to phone you when we both saw the lights in your*

*driveway. She nearly walked here by herself. I barely had enough time to put on my shoes."*

*"I'm sorry, Trudy. I don't know what's gotten into her today. I'll talk to her about it in the morning. Come over for breakfast, won't you?"*

*"Have a good night, Veronica. I'll, I'll call you tomorrow or—something. We'll see."*

But Richard could see in Trudy's eyes that she was scared of Gloria. She'd never witnessed such a scary tantrum. She didn't need to have children to know this wasn't normal. Richard played the screaming over in his head and it gave him the chills. The hairs on his entire body stood on end. Her screaming.

Veronica walked back down the stairs to their basement apartment. She was so worried about what was happening that she stood at the bottom and tried to figure out what to do. Just then, she heard some glasses smash on the ground in the kitchen. She ran in and stopped before getting too close. That's when she saw Connelly, shaking there in the dark. He was staring straight ahead into the empty hallway of her apartment. He didn't break his gaze when she entered the kitchen. There was broken glass and an orange liquid all over the floor.

*"Connelly, what happened?!"* As she shouted, she saw the glass juice container on the counter beside him.

*"I, I just wanted to make you, thought, thirsty…"* His words were cut off as he was gulping to catch his breath. *"I have to go. I have to leave and go."*

*"Leave? You just got here. Look, it's just some glass. I can clean it up."*

*"No, I have to leave. Leave here. Kitchener."*
*"What's wrong with you?"*
*"Nothing."* He shook his head and sniffled.

He ran past Veronica and headed to her stairs. She turned and followed him and grabbed his arm. He paused and turned around, and she could now see tears running down his cheeks. She scanned him up and down, trying to think of what to say. After a pause, he jerked his arm free in a gentle manor and ran up the stairs and out the door.

"What do you think happened?" Richard asked as she finished explaining the incident.

"As best as I just tried, no words can accurately describe what I saw. It was too strange. I'm still not even sure what I saw. I come into my kitchen and this man I just met is frozen in trauma. I still wonder to this day if maybe he had a seizure."

Richard saw the scene. He knew what was happening. He didn't say a word to Veronica.

"Wow, that's so strange. Guess we'll never know. Say, Veronica. I need to use the washroom, would you please excuse me?"

"Of course. I could use a little refresh too. Guest washroom is down the main hall, second right. Then third door on the left."

"Thank you."

Richard followed her directions and found the washroom no problem. *How big IS this place?* he wondered. He could smell the nearby pool. She wasn't kidding. She made them put a pool on her second floor. Incredible. He put his thoughts back to finding the washroom before he got sick. Dizziness was starting to sink in. *Focus, Richard.* He found a bathroom, unsure if it was the one he was directed to. His state of mind was going in and out. He shut the door behind him firmly and ensured he locked it. He turned on the tap and gripped the porcelain sink. The coolness of the porcelain centred him a little, helping him to calm himself. He splashed some water on his face and took a deep breath.

*That power. Oh my God. Ten years old. What did I just see?* Richard was overwhelmed. In the memory, when Connelly looked in Vernonica's eyes, Richard saw what had happened. He felt it. Everything.

As his nerves calmed, he felt his sense of balance slowly return. He turned off the sink and went over to the toilet and put down the seat. He sat and cleared his head in order to replay the memory at full clarity, with no distractions from speaking to Veronica.

Connelly walked into the apartment, looked around at the tiny little place and thought, *how sad. She must be poor as hell. How easy it will be to please her. Doesn't even look like she can afford to put food on the table.* He quietly grunted a laugh to himself.

"It's down the hall, first door on the right."

"Cute place. Is it just you here?"

"Me and my daughter."

"Daughter?!"

"Yes. She's ten. She's in Samantha's class. That's actually how we met."

"Very nice. Samantha is great."

He headed to use the washroom and a thought came to mind. *Daughter? Fuck. That could complicate things.* He had never dealt with children. But he was still confident in his position. He'd dated many difficult woman. How hard could a ten year old be? Anyways, she wasn't here tonight. One night was all he needed.

He finished up using the washroom and headed into the kitchen. He looked in the cupboard and grabbed a couple glasses. He went to the sink and turned on the water. *Shit, it never mixes right in water. I wonder what she has in the fridge.* He walked over to the small fridge and opened it to find a glass jug of mixed orange juice. *Perfect*, he thought. He poured some juice, then he set the bottle down and reached into his inner jacket pocket. He pulled out a small glass vile of powder and put in his usual amount. He stopped and added more. More than usual. *This will make her sick for a day or two. Just the time I need.*

Richard spoke aloud, "Need for what?" He was processing the memory as fast as he could. "What did he plan to do?"

Connelly heard the side door knock and started to work quickly. He put the vile away as fast as he could and stirred the drink with his finger. In the background, he heard a woman's voice coming from the door.

*"I'm so sorry, Veronica. I didn't know what else to do. I tried calling you, and when I saw the lights in your driveway, I just came right over."*

*"What the fuck,"* he spoke the words aloud.

As he spoke, he looked up. Standing in the hallway, he saw young Gloria with her golden brown hair, in her pajamas, staring at him. He jumped back a little bit. He quickly hid the glass vile in his palm and slid it into his pant pocket.

"Well, hi there, sweetheart. Who are you?" *This must be the brat*, he thought.

Gloria just stared back at him.

"I'm your mom's friend, Connelly. What's your name?"

"I'm Gloria. Veronica's my mom. You're no friend. I think you should leave now."

"Leave? I just got here. Would you like something to drink?"

Connelly thought he would just pour her a glass with a touch of his powder, and she'd be out like a light. Maybe she would think him being there was just a dream. *Stupid little bitch.*

"I think you want to leave, Connelly, trust me."

"Now, young lady, who are you to tell me to leave? That's not very nice. Your mom wants me here. Tell you what, I'll make you a special drink, and you'll go right to sleep. How does this sound?"

"Is it like the one you made for my mom?"

"How the fuck? Listen, you little brat." He took one step toward Gloria, and that's when it happened.

She reached out and grabbed his arm. She squeezed with all her might. He stood there, paralyzed in fear. They stood there a minute, and then his body started to shake.

"You're going to leave and never talk to my mom again. Do you understand?"

"Y-y-yes," he said. His eyes were wide and fully dilated.

"You're not going to touch my mom, or any other woman again, do you understand me?"

"Yes."

He shook and his body convulsed. She moved his arm with her hand, knocking over the glasses of juice on purpose. Spilling it all over the kitchen floor where they were standing. As the glasses emptied, they slowly rolled to the edge as she let go of him and left the kitchen. The glasses shattered as they hit the floor. Gloria was out the kitchen and in her bedroom before the sound of broken glass filled the apartment.

Richard jolted. *Oh my*. Taking in the memory with more detail, he was overwhelmed by the amount of power. Her strength of that nature. She was trying to scare Connelly. He marveled at the fact of how strong she was at ten, and he was only experiencing this in a memory. The real ordeal must have been way more traumatic.

Richard took a deep breath. This was going to be intense. He relaxed his body and his mind to take in what Gloria was showing Connelly.

Rape, violence. Brutality. Connelly was a monster. He had been drugging women for years. Having sex with them when they passed out. But, it didn't stop there. A few of them he dated. He would drug their drink so much, they would be sick for days. They would wake up, not knowing what had happened to them. He'd stay the night and play the hero. "You were so sick, how could I leave you? I stayed to make sure you were ok." These women, they had no idea. They'd invite their attacker to stay, and get close to their abuser. Let him into their lives. Once trust was earned, his true nature never came out. He'd drug them first. Always keeping his mask on. He'd beat them. Degrade them. Then when he got bored, he'd move on to keep feeding his predatory appetite. None of them ever knowing the brutality they endured. But his appetite was getting worse, more intense. Gloria knew that. Veronica was to be his first. Not his first victim, his first kill. He had it all planned out. The thought excited him. Even when he found out she had a daughter, he thought it made the game more exciting. More of a challenge.

Richard felt a tear run down his cheek. The sick things he saw Connelly do.

The memory played on, and when Richard saw Connelly's tears as he left the apartment that night, he understood why. Gloria didn't just show his past victims. No. The narcissistic bastard trembled over what would be his fate. She showed him what happens to him when he gets caught. See, Connelly was clever. He never left evidence, and none of his past victims even knew what happened. None of them knew he raped them the night they met him. They had no idea they were victims. But, Veronica wasn't going to be his only kill. He would go on to kill seven more women. After that, his growing appetite wanted more. His first attempt for trying to lure two women in one night proved to be too much. In 1987, he would drug two girls back at their apartment after meeting them in a bar. What he didn't know was one girl wouldn't digest the drug and would get sick in her unconscious state. She would wake up and see her roommate being raped and take quick action. She'd bash him over his head with a lamp, and the two girls would safely make it out to call the police. He would get arrested and charged for multiple murders and sexual assaults. As he confessed to how he abused his victims after drugging them, a few whom he dated would come forward to be investigated. Ones that were left unsettled by how things ended. They felt abandoned, and now knew why. By 1989, he would be sentenced to life in jail. The guards all hated him. Despised him for the monster he was. The other prisoners all hated him too. In 1990 when his brutally beaten, sodomized and castrated body is discovered in a shower room, there is little to no investigation. It was deemed a "Clerical Error" in his rotation schedule at Kingston Penitentiary that he went unaccounted for when he was killed.

When Gloria touched him, she showed him his horrible fate. He was so confused and scared. He left Veronica's that night and took an oath. He vowed never to hurt another woman again. He lived and felt the abuse that would come no matter when he was caught. He couldn't live all the flashes out in his head, but Richard knew Gloria showed him. No matter what or when, this is what will happen to you.

After Richard lived out the memory in detail, he collected himself and went back to sit with Veronica. He sat back down across from her and anxiously grasped his drink. He drank the rest of what was left. He happily noticed a fresh drink waiting as well.

"Find it ok, Rich?"

"Yes, Veronica. Stunning place here you have, really."

He looked into Veronica's eyes, and she was still focused on the memory. She held something back. *What was it?* He focused hard and concentrated until he saw it. In her eyes. It was the last thing she saw of Connelly before he ran out of her apartment.

*"Connelly, what's wrong? Are you crying??"*

He stood there frozen, staring into Veronica's eyes.

His bottom lip was trembling, and he was drooling, barely making sense. The only words he could get out between gasps of hysteria were *"She."* Gasp. *"I."* Choke, gasp. *"No one knew. No one."* Liquid was oozing out of his eyes ears and mouth. *"How!??! HOW??!!"*

Veronica stepped back. She looked at her would-be guest and took in every detail. He was wearing very nice clothes. Leather coat, designer shirt. Pressed slacks. And his whole outfit came together. She noted every last detail, including the small embroidered alligator on his shirt.

## CHAPTER 26

# The Field Trip

"Hope you don't mind. I asked Sarah to make us a fresh drink."

"Oh, that is just great. Like music to my ears." Richard was completely scared sober now. "By the way, I could smell the pool from the washroom."

"I never use it. I just wanted it."

"She can afford it, right?"

"Now you're catching on. So where were we?"

"It was just the night you met Connelly. But I am curious, did you ever find out what happened to him? Or what Gloria was so worked up about? About seeing an alligator?"

"As far as the alligator was concerned, it never came up again. She was still just a little girl. Not everything had to do with her psychic power. I'm pretty sure she was just insecure about me starting to go out and potentially start dating."

Richard knew why she didn't tell him. She was embarrassed that she hadn't trusted Gloria.

"What about the Connelly character you met? Ever hear from him again?"

"Well, I called Samantha the next day to make sure she was ok. She said she was nursing a bad hangover. Her husband didn't hear from Connelly all weekend. I just assumed it was because he wasn't interested in me. I was relieved when Sam told me the following Monday that he had quit his job. Said he had to leave town right away, I guess his mother was sick. Probably for the best. I don't feel like I was ready to date anyways."

Richard was glad Veronica didn't know the real horror. She had no idea how close she came to just being another statistic.

"Well, not much is left from her years in Southridge. It was her last year there, before heading off to junior high just down Queen Street at Queensmount Public School."

"Oh, the stories you can find from her time there and her time in high school at Forest Heights Collegiate are fascinating."

"Yes, I've read a few, but living them is very different than simply reading them on paper. But, none of those times would be relevant without what took place on her spring field trip, and the summer's end BBQ for her Grade 6 class."

Richard perked up in interest, knowing he'd never heard about the field trip. The BBQ was urban legend, as there was no tangible proof of anything. All just hearsay.

"One of the field trips the Grade 6 class always looked forward too was the winter's end day trip to ice skate at Queensmount Junior High. Most of the students at Southridge would go on to Grade 7 there. This field trip was an annual one organized by the faculty that allowed the students to get familiar with their next school, and get excited about seeing how much bigger it was than their grade school. Both Cathy and Samantha explained the politics behind the school's choice for doing this, and you could tell the Grade 6 glass was excited to go as well."

"I think a lot of grade schools did that back then."

"Well, this was around the end of January, when the school year was about halfway done. Gloria was doing well in class, and while her night terrors about the brown door weren't as frequent, they were getting more intense and more detailed. Each time she woke up, her scream was even more bloody than the time before."

Listening to the screams in Veronica's memory made Richard very apprehensive about what they were about. They scared him too.

"It was odd to have a new student join the class mid-year, but that year, a young boy and his family moved to the area. Reggie Holtom. His mother and father moved from some place just outside of Windsor, so they didn't know anyone. For whatever reason, Gloria was drawn to him like a moth drawn to light. As soon as they met, they became thick as thieves. She had many friends over those years, but none of them ever got as close to her as Reggie."

The memory of Reggie in Veronica's mind was clouded. Muzzled. The block Gloria put on him regarding anyone who knew of him was still intact after all these years. Richard's memories of him were the same, so this came as no surprise.

"Gloria made friends growing up, but not like Reggie. No others are worth mentioning. The two were inseparable. If she had free time after homework and work with Cathy, she wanted to be around him. Him and their family cat. A big fat boy named Sydney. She finally had a new animal to obsess over since she didn't see Marcus anymore. With the kids, nothing romantic as far as I could tell, both of them too young really. But a bond I could never make sense of. Sometimes, he even hung around outside the door while she worked with Cathy. They both swore he never knew what they were doing, but it never sat right with me."

"Do you think they told him in secret?"

"I don't think so. But who knows. I never really took interest. It was just an observation."

Richard saw in memories Veronica coming home and Reggie waiting outside, playing in the driveway. He always seem content, so she never thought anything out of the ordinary.

"By the time March rolled around, it was time for the annual day trip to Queensmount for a few hours of skating in the adjacent arena, followed by a school tour." Veronica laughed. "You know, she was so excited that day. Beyond energetic. I will always wonder if that's why she didn't see it coming."

Richard sat back and took a quiet deep breath, not wanting to arouse suspicion. He didn't want Veronica to know that he was actually in Gloria's Grade 6 class. It's how he knew her. How the council thought it be best he do the investigation. His family moved to Kitchener for one year, his Grade 6 year. In the summer before Grade 7, his mom and dad divorced, and he moved with his mom to Cambridge. His father became estranged from his family. He didn't start to develop his abilities until high school, so none of his gifts we're helpful with his own recollection of that time, nor did peering into his memories. He'd worked with my different psychics over his career to no avail. He wasn't able to have clear memories of years before that either. Flashes here and there, but he was never able to figure out why. With Veronica now talking about school memories, he started to relive some with her. He didn't remember what happened on the school trip, but he did remember Reggie, and the horrible fate awaiting him and his family.

As he asked questions now, it was for his memories' sake too. He had to as he couldn't get a clear reading. It was like there was a muffle on his visions. He'd never experienced this before when treating a patient or speaking to someone in general.

"So what was Reggie like?"

"He was a sweet, well-mannered young boy. He was never anything but polite and pleasant. Samantha said the same of him while he was in her class that year. He never caused problems. She also made jokes about how close Gloria and he had become. He came from what I thought, at least at first, was a normal family. Until, well, until we all learned the truth. His parents were one of the few who said hello to me outside the school in the morning when I'd drop off Gloria, and they had a younger son in kindergarten that year in Cathy's class."

Richard had to slow down his breathing as his memories of Reggie and his family sharpened with Veronica's descriptions. He'd hadn't been able to have clarity around them since they happened over fifty years ago.

"So it's now the day of the field trip. Samantha had asked to chaperone, but couldn't get off work that day at Eaton's. I didn't mind once I found out Cathy was one of the accompanying teachers, as she only had class in the mornings that year, and they were going in the afternoon."

"Queensmount Public School was further north up Queen's Boulevard. That was the bus route we used to take to grade school when we were living in downtown Kitchener. We passed by the junior high but never went inside the school. It was built a few years before Southridge, in '65 I believe. I'd only every taken Gloria there once to skate. We just went to try it, but she still preferred to skate outside on the pond at Victoria Park. We used to love to skate when she was little."

Veronica's mind slipped away from her train of thought, and she was silent again.

"Veronica, what's wrong?"

"Oh, I'm just wondering if it would have been different had I gone that day."

Richard didn't know what to say.

"Anyways," she shook her head and was out of her daze once again, "I was even happier knowing I wasn't going when I heard that Mr. West was one of the other teachers going."

"I bet. You dodged an uncomfortable afternoon for sure."

"I know. I worked that day and didn't rush home as I knew Cathy was taking her home from the school trip. I had to sign a permission form for the school, even though Samantha knew it was fine. It was just a formality. I figured she'd be tired and want to lay down after the trip that was slated to be finished around 4:30 p.m. The rink was rather big, so imagine how much energy she'd burn in a few hours, topped off with her excitement. I finished my shift after 5, punched out and left the mall. It only took me about fifteen minutes to get home. As I pulled my car into the driveway, it was nothing out of the ordinary to see Cathy's car out front on the street. But, this was far from an ordinary day. So far, so, so far."

Veronica went into detail while Richard closely paid attention. He was living the experience firsthand through Veronicas memory.

It was after 5 p.m., and the sky was turning a little dark. While the sun was barely still in the sky, Veronica was happy the days were slowly getting longer and longer. She parked her car and locked the door behind her. She walked through the door and headed down the stairs. She saw Cathy sitting alone in the dark, grasping her head with her arms, slumped over between her knees. Veronica saw no other lights on, and Gloria was nowhere to be seen. The smell of cigarettes lingered in the air.

"Cathy? Hey, are you ok? Where's Gloria?"

Cathy sat up and turned around to face Veronica, the reflection of the doorway light shining onto her face. It was beat red with streaks of tears flowing down it. She'd been crying a while. Veronica took one look at her and ran to the closest lamp. She clicked in on and ran up to sit beside Cathy.

"Cathy, what is it?" She hugged her.

Then panic set it as Gloria wasn't there. She pushed back from her and was about to get up.

"Stop. Sit. Gloria is fine. She's asleep in her bed. She's fine. Don't worry."

"Then what the hell is going on here, Cathy?!" she raised her voice a little.

"Ok, first, calm down. Gloria is 100 percent ok, but something happened today to Gloria. Something big, and a lot of people noticed."

"What does that mean?!" Veronica snapped back.

"Let's just calm down, and I'll do my best to explain. Say, have anything to drink?" Cathy asked. "My cigarettes just aren't cutting it."

Veronica's sense of worry immediately heightened. The last time Cathy had ever asked for alcohol was when Gloria pushed something onto her senses.

"Um, ya. Ok. Just a minute."

Veronica got up off the couch and went into the adjacent kitchen. Under the sink, she had a few bottles of spirits. Most of them were gifts given to her that she just rarely drank. She grabbed a bottle of Seagram's whiskey and two short glasses from the above cupboard. She walked back over and this time sat across from Cathy so she could see her face. She poured them each a full glass, and they both took a big sip. No toast, just eye contact.

Cathy let out a huge sigh. *"Thanks, I really needed that. I wish I knew that was there a few hours ago when we got back."*

Veronica looked at her clock in the kitchen. She did the math in her head and it didn't add up. The two girls were supposed to be at the school tour until 4:30, so they shouldn't have been home for even an hour yet.

*"Hours? But you only should have gotten home close to 5 after the school tour."*

*"The tour was cancelled. We all got sent back to the school. Thank GOD you signed that permission form to let me take Gloria home, or she would have had to sit in the principal's office and try to explain. At least this way, we can think of something to say."*

*"Cathy, you'd better explain and you'd better explain fast. You're scaring the fucking shit out of me."*

*"Whoa, ok. Well, after the ambulance left—"*

*"The ambulance—what ambulance!!??"*

*"Stop yelling at me for fuck sakes!! This isn't easy for me to explain!"*

Both Veronica and Cathy only swore when they meant it. Each of them calmed down a degree to try and give one another a chance to speak.

*"Anyways, after the ambulance left the arena, Samantha assured all the faculty left and the other parent chaperones that I had written permission to take Gloria right home. Honestly, it was like a wild mob. I got her out of there as fast as I could, away*

*from all the screaming. I swear, Veronica, things were about to get violent."*

In Cathy's eyes within Veronica's memory, Richard could see the angry mob. Details that Cathy never fully went into to protect Veronica's feelings. The front foyer of the skate arena with the 12–15 parents and teachers screaming at Cathy. Samantha acting like a human shield. 'Freak!' 'Retard!' 'what the fuck is wrong with her!' 'She better not be at school with MY children anymore!' and more vile profanities Richard selectively chose not to listen to.

*"Ok so an angry mob came after my daughter?! What did she do!!??"* Veronica yelled.

*"I got her out of there as fast I could. It all happened so fast. We drove right home and didn't say a word. We communicated in our minds as we were both in too much shock to speak. I asked her what happened, and she said she couldn't talk to me. She had to show me."*

*"Show you, like the special showing she does?"*

*"Yes."*

*"Like that time in the kitchen at our old place?"*

*"Yes."*

*"Ok, I get why you needed a drink. So what did she show you?"*

*"This I can't tell you. She has to."*

*"Well someone tell me something!!! You're scaring the shit out of me, and I don't know if I need to call the school or the police!!"*

Cathy got up off the couch and grabbed Veronica's head between both her hands, cupping her ears. She firmly forced Veronica to look at her and Veronica immediately calmed down. Cathy was using her abilities to calm her.

*"Now look, Veronica, what I'm doing now is a calming push on you. What Gloria is about to show you, you're going to need it so you can listen, do you understand?"*

Cathy's touch was like morphine. It dulled Veronica's sense of panic and subdued her to a submissive state.

*"Now I can't show you things, or I would and edit what you see. Only Gloria can show you things. I am going to keep you calm so you can take this all in. You sit here, and I will go get Gloria. She needed rest in order to show you. Showing me took a lot out of her."*

Cathy left Veronica in the chair, and she completely relaxed into it. She had no idea how Cathy's powers worked at all, but she felt that Cathy was still lying a little about what she could really do.

*"Ok,"* Veronica said, sounding a little drunk from the cohesion to a calmer state.

Cathy went down the hall, and Veronica heard her speak to her daughter.

*"Yes, hun, she's home now."*

Veronica was subdued by hearing Gloria's response.

*"Yes, you have to show her, it's the only way. Come now, I pushed her to a calm state so she will be ok while you show her."*

Veronica heard the rustling of Gloria's mattress springs and bed sheets, then saw her and Cathy coming down the hall hand in hand. Veronica felt a tinge of jealousy seeing them hold hands.

Gloria stood beside her mother, noticing the mental push Miss Stevens had given her mother.

*"Mom, I'm sorry I told Cathy to do that. It's the only way you won't freak out. You're not used to this stuff, and today was intense. It's been building for a while now."*

"*Baby, it's ok,*" Veronica said. She was lying but could not get upset no matter how hard she tried. She didn't understand what she meant by building up.

"*Mom, your state of mind has me reading you like an open book. I won't pry, but I can hear your thoughts loud and clear. But, I'm not going to read you. Instead I'm going to let you in on what I've seen. Mr. West. His anger with me and Miss stevens has been getting worse.*"

Veronica calmly and matter-of-factly looked up at Cathy. "*You knew about this?*"

"*I knew a little, but I didn't know how bad it had gotten. Gloria's gifts are so far past my own now that I can't read anything from her. But, she has been strong. And, Reggie is always around her. It's like he's been protecting her.*"

"*Oh, well isn't that nice,*" Veronica calmly spoke, thinking full well when she was out of this trance that she would become furious.

"*Mom, Cathy is going to keep you centred while I show you what happened. It was my idea as you have no third sense. This could overwhelm you and change you forever. I'll show you a few run-ins with Mr. West and what led up to today. It wasn't my fault, and no one saw it, not even Reggie. He was off getting us some snacks in the lobby. So no one will believe me when I tell my side of the story,*" Gloria said, looking at her mom straight in the eye. She sat down on the coffee table and turned toward Veronica and grabbed both her hands. "*Be still, mom, and know none of this is real.*"

"*Ok,*" Veronica said with no expression.

Gloria nodded at her mother, then looked over at Cathy and nodded. Cathy nodded back and placed her hand on Veronica's shoulder. She closed her eyes and shook her head while communicating with Gloria telepathically to go ahead.

*"Ok, mom. Stay still and concentrate. Close your eyes."*

Once Veronica closed her eyes, she started to see and feel Gloria and her memories. She started to flush with panic, only to feel the soothing calm sensation Cathy continued to push on her.

At first, a few visions of memory flashed of Mr. West in the halls at Southridge. He was yelling at her to slow down, pulling her aside and belittling her in the hallways full of her fellow students. Cathy was never around to see it, nor were any of Gloria's friends. Veronica could hear what Gloria heard on a daily basis. Try as she might, some would come through. 'She's a loser. So glad Mr. West hates her too.' 'Maybe Mr. West can have her thrown out of school and we can have a party.' 'Serves her right, she's a freak' and all sorts of hateful things. This happened on more occasions than not. Mr. West took every chance he could to humiliate her. Not just in the hallways, but also at assemblies and school functions. Even in the relaxed trance she was in, a tear still flowed down Veronica's cheek as her heart broke hearing what vile things were thought about her daughter.

As Veronica conscientiously went through Gloria's memories, Gloria showed her how she could see auras around people. Some were bright and colourful. Others, dark and dimmed.

*"Are there that many bad people in this world? That makes me sad."*

"No, mom. People's auras dim mostly when they do something bad or their emotions turn them dark. It doesn't last. Most people are good until they take a dark path. Sadly, if they do, they either choose to in their life plan or were influenced by those who are really dark."

After being told that, she could see that in the memories of Mr. West berating her, the people around him were dark and dim.

"See, mom, he always knew what people to pick on me in front of. He always did in front of those who never told or defended me. I suspect he can see auras too, or at least pick up on people's vibrations. Whether they're not good people, or just people with hate in their heart."

Veronica immediately thought of Cathy and why she didn't rescue her.

"Now, mom, Cathy interjected whenever she witnessed it, but he's clever. It was never around teachers or students who liked me. He always knew when he could get away with it, and I never saw it coming. It started to make me angry. Really angry. But Miss Stevens has always shown me how using my power for something dark will always come back to me. It's called karma, mom. And it's real and it exists, though most people don't believe it."

Veronica felt the sense of clarity knowing how someone like Gloria senses energies.

"Mom, listen, what you put out there comes back to you. Every. Single. Time. No exceptions. But strangely, Mr. West got better when Reggie came to school. I don't know why, and I can't read into it, neither can Miss Stevens. As you know, what Sylvia has taught her, which she has taught me, is that some things happen for a reason. Some bad things are meant to happen, and they have to. It's human nature, and no matter what I see, I won't always see *everything and anything. That will never change no matter how strong I grow to be either."*

Veronica nodded, feeling the emotions and practical sense that Gloria was letting her in on. She understood why they had to show her this way. It was the only way Veronica could comprehend what they had to say.

*"So today at the arena, me and Reggie were having the best time. We were skating to the loud music that was playing, and we felt so excited knowing that next year we'll be in junior high together. We were talking about all the cool stuff we'd do this summer when the bell rang. It was time for the Zamboni to come brush the ice."*

Veronica could smell the arena. The smell of the ice, the loud music pumping in the echo of the cathedral height ceiling. The happiness and joy Gloria felt when around her friend Reggie. They really did have a bond. The loud buzzer going off in Veronica's head made her body jump a little. She felt the squeeze on her shoulder and settled right back in the chair in the apartment.

*"Gloria, you go over there and wait for me,"* Reggie said and pointed to a gate opening off the ice that was away from where all the other kids were getting off the ice. *"I'm gonna go get us some snacks, and I'll walk around and meet you. I saw a bench there on one of our laps."*

*"Sounds good, Reg. Get me a chocolate bar, I'm hungry."*

Veronica saw the vision of the bench Gloria got from Reggie's mind and felt the gurgle in her stomach that Gloria did at that time.

Gloria got off the ice and went to the bench. She sat there only a moment when the smooth sound of the Zamboni fired up and started to drive over the ice. It passed where Gloria was sitting, and she waved at the driver who waved back with a lit cigarette in his hand. *Pour guy. Wonder if he knows those things will kill him by next year if he keeps smoking.*

While Veronica was experiencing how Gloria received some messages in her mind, she was distracted, just as Gloria was, and didn't hear someone approach her. The firm grasp on her arm shook her out of her concentration on the man driving the Zamboni.

*"Funny I run into you, you little liar."*

The wave of darkness that Gloria and Cathy tried to explain to Veronica was now apparent. Luckily, he didn't make physical contact long enough for Veronica to truly experience what Gloria could sense.

Gloria's sense of confusion and the innocence of her youth showed through first. *"Mr. West, I just don't get it, why don't you like me?"*

She was trying so hard to read him, only to be blocked by his dark vibrations. It was like she was trying to see through a wall of black steel that was cold to her psychic touch and told her it was unsafe.

*"You little shit. You know what you did. We were perfectly happy until you messed with it,"* Mr. West said.

Veronica looked in his eyes through Gloria, and they were black with rage. His aura was nonexistent.

*"You mean you and Miss Stevens?"*

*"Well, I see you're not completely devoid of reality. Of course Miss Stevens. She and I could have been happy for the rest of our lives, you know. I was going to ask her to marry me, and now she won't even talk to me! And it's all because of you!"*

*"Mr. West, stop yelling at me. You're scaring me."*

Gloria looked around to see who would come to her rescue. With the rest of the class and chaperones on the other side of the rink, she realized no one could hear him yelling over the sound of the Zamboni.

"*Good. You should be scared. I'm going to ruin you.*" He bent over and got face to face with Gloria.

She could smell his foul breath.

"*You and that slut of a teacher, Miss Stevens.*"

He reached out and violently grabbed her elbow. The darkness rushed into her mind, but luckily, her fear was blocking it out in a protective mode. He yanked her closer to him, so close as he bent over, now fully in her personal space.

Inside Gloria, the fear was turning to defense. She was getting angry, really angry. He was not only insulting her, but her mentor, Miss Stevens.

"*I'm on to her and you. Don't think I don't see what you're trying to do.*"

"*Mr. West, I'm not doing anything, and you're hurting me. You better stop. I'm warning you.*"

"*Warning me? What are you gonna do, stick your boyfriend after me? The only reason I don't say anything in front of him is that I know he'll take your side. He'll rat me out like the little rat bastard he is.*"

Gloria's rage was more intense. Now he had put down her best friend, the only close friend she'd had in her life.

"*Mr. West, this is your second warning. Don't push me.*"

"*Push you? You have no idea how I plan to push you. I'm going to ruin you. You don't know it, but you're about to be expelled for stealing. I have it all worked out.*"

*"What are you talking about? I didn't steal anything."* Gloria felt so frustrated not being able to read what he meant. He was the only person she'd encounter who could block her.

*"Like I'd tell you what was going to happen. You'll know when it happens. You and you mother will be ridiculed and chased out of this city so fast it will make your head spin."*

Gloria's burning hot emotions were on fire. She'd never been this angry in her entire life. All her energies, physically, mentally and psychically were fusing together in red hot frustration. Her aura was burning so bright that even she could see her own colours in her peripheral vision.

Her jaw was fully clenched; she could barely push out the words. *"Not another word, Mr. West. This is your last chance. Let go of me, walk away, and leave me alone."*

*"You fucking little bitch. I'm not afraid of you. You or your filthy liar of a mother. Fuck her. Made me think she could affect my career. Well, this is me getting the last word in. On both you pieces of shit."*

*"That's it, Mr. West. I'm done playing nice."*

Gloria spun around on the bench, freeing her arm from Mr. West's tight hold. She started to concentrate. Her anger and rage blew past any mental blocks he had. She didn't need to touch either. Her negative emotions amplified her visions, and she was communicating deeply with Mr. West's conscious and subconscious mind. He stood up and took a step back in pure animal instinct. Like an animal of prey from its predator about to strike.

She searched his memories for fear. His whole being was consumed by it. He was petrified. She was in control. She had power. And he better fear her. He better be afraid. She could destroy him in the blink of her eye. He would never be able to speak again. Be locked in a permanent state of mental paralysis if she felt like it. She gave him a taste of what a lifetime of that felt like and didn't hold back.

He fell to his knees and couldn't speak, drool starting to stream down his chin while he gasped for breath.

Gloria took no pity on him, too enthralled with her anger. She looked at him mercilessly on his knees in front of him, no one around to see the final act.

*"I don't like you, Mr. West. I don't know what's wrong with you, but something is wrong. You're a danger to me and anyone I love. You're also a danger to yourself. I'm going to save you from that fate, Mr. West. The way I see it, I'm doing the world a favour."*

She walked up to Mr. West and placed her right palm on his forehead, pushing more intense psychic power through her touch.

*"Ah, there it is. What you fear most. It's what caused that scar on your face isn't it?"*

Veronica watched what Gloria saw. Something happened to him as a child. The memory flashed to quickly for Veronica to make sense of it. She felt Glorias anger centre and intensify. It was enough to push through a flash of light so bright and intense that Mr. West lost all his memories. His eyes rolled into the back of his head, and he urinated in his pants while all his memories were cleaned from his mind. As Gloria held him in place for longer, his hair turned from black to completely white. And not just the hairs on his head, but every hair on his entire body.

*"Enjoy those thoughts everyday for the rest of your life. I hope you do Mr. West. Ophidiophobia is unlike other phobias. But you'll have time to reflect on that for the rest of your life. You won't have any other thoughts other than those, forever."* Gloria didn't break from the lock and gaze she was holding, looking down at him until Reggie came around the corner.

"*Gloria!!!*" He dropped everything in his hands and ran toward Gloria.

Gloria let go of her hold on Mr. West and he fell to the ground completely unconscious.

*"What are you doing!!?? What happened to Mr. West!?"*

Gloria was shaking, having temporarily lost her memory of the last few minutes. Only later when she got home and Miss stevens calmed her, would everything come back to her.

"*Reggie, what?!*" She looked around in shock, not knowing what happened either.

The two children sat there speechless as they heard high heels come around the bend.

"*Reginald Holtom. I told you to stay in the foyer as we're about to leave to tour the school!*"

It was Mrs. Engel, their class peer Stephanie's mom. She was one of the parent chaperones. As she rounded the corner in better view, she saw Gloria and Reggie. Or as she referred to Gloria—that vile daughter of Veronica Chastain. She glanced harshly at Gloria then saw the Mr. West convulsing at their feet.

*"Gloria, what are you doing—"* she inhaled and gasped. *"Mr. West!"* She ran over and threw herself over his body. *"What did you do?? You did this, I know you did!! You're evil, I can sense it!!"*

Veronica noticed how dim and dark her aura was, knowing it was how Gloria had always seen it.

*"I don't know what happened, Mrs. Engel! I-I don't remember!"* Gloria said, tears starting to build in her eyes. *"He just collapsed!"* she said and looked at Reggie.

He knew that look, it was a look for help. *"Ya, Mrs. Engel. I was coming to get Gloria for the tour next door and found him laying here just like this. Gloria didn't do anything. I would have seen it."*

Mrs. Engel's face was red with anger *"I know you did this!"* She glared at Gloria a little longer, then placed her ear by Mr. West's mouth and nose. *"Oh thank God, he's still breathing!"*

She grabbed the whistle hanging from her neck. Every parent and teacher had to wear one for emergencies just like this. The scream from her whistle quickly drew all the other parents and teachers over to the scene on the other side of the ice rink. As they came around the corner and saw the scene, they all stood frozen in their tracks.

Mrs. Engel yelled at one of the other teachers, *"Well, don't just stand there! Run and call an ambulance!!"*

The teacher was in shock having seen that Mr. West had peed himself. But even more shocking to the entire crowd was that his hair was fully white. Bright, crisp white.

"*Go now, you idiot!! He could be dying!!!*" shrieked Mrs. Engel.

The teacher snapped out of their daze and ran to the foyer to the pay phone.

Confusion and panic started getting the entire class and faculty going. Veronica could hear what Gloria heard. '*Is she a witch?*' '*Omg, she's a nightmare*' and much worse.

Reggie moved into Gloria's sight and looked her deep in her eyes. "*Gloria, I think you should run the other way and find Miss Stevens. Get out of here.*"

Gloria didn't say anything; she just listened to the sound advice of her friend. She ran like the wind the other way around the rink in search of Miss Stevens. She ran right into her open arms and was crying uncontrollably.

"*Sssh ssh, calm down. I heard their angry thoughts. I knew you'd come this way. I can hear you a little right now because you're so afraid.*"

She comforted Gloria and took her aside, hiding behind the snack counter in the foyer of the skating rink. After a few minutes passed, she was able to calm Gloria down enough to stop crying.

"*Quiet, the ambulance is already here.*"

Gloria started to cry loudly again.

Miss Stevens grabbed her by the chin to make eye contact. "*Gloria, be quiet. The ambulance is taking Mr. West and I can hear the thoughts of the angry crowd just like you can. We have to get out of here and fast, ok? Here are your boots, take off your skates.*"

"Yes, Miss Stevens," she said while sniffling.

She quickly took her skates off and put on her boots like she was told. A few minutes later, they heard the gurney roll by with a few pairs of footsteps running beside it.

"*Go. Move!*"

They almost made it to the door before Mrs. Kropf, Samantha, came back inside the doors.

"*Gloria, what happened back there? Mr. West is, he's, he's a mess! I'm hearing a lot of things said right now I hope aren't true.*"

"*Samantha, please. I have to get Gloria out of here. Those parents and teachers are angry. They're scared. They think Gloria did something.*"

"*I know what they're saying, and it doesn't make sense. Gloria is just a kid, Cathy.*"

"*I know that, Samantha. Please, let us go!*"

"*Cathy, look. I know you are close with Gloria, but she needs to come to the school and fill out an incident report. You know as well as I do that that is school policy! Just because we're close to her family doesn't give us the right to bend the rules. And given the severity of what I just saw, I think it's important we hear from her what she saw?!*"

The rustle of more footsteps and angry voices grew louder. It wasn't just the teachers and parents in hot pursuit, but the entire Grade 6 class behind them, eager to catch a glimpse of what could transpire.

"*There she is! Don't let her go!*" yelled Mrs. Engel. "*She did something to him—I saw it!!*"

Veronica felt rage overpower Cathy's calming trance as she was hearing someone lie like that.

Samantha looked past Miss Stevens who was hold a trembling Gloria.

*"Samantha, please. Those are angry, irrational adults. You know I have permission to take her home. Please. I will bring her to the office first thing in the morning myself."*

Samantha looked confused, but was startled by how hysterical everyone was in the crowd that approached them.

*"Please, Samantha."* Cathy reached out and touched Samanthas arm, using a bit of calming push.

Samantha didn't know why, but she let them go. *"Ok, get out of here. Tell Veronica I'll call her later. Let me see if I can handle this."*

Miss Stevens mouthed the words *thank you* and ran past Samantha out the door.

Over her shoulder, she heard Samantha yelling as she blocked the only exit doors that could lead to the parking lot. *"Everyone just calm down! No need to overreact!"*

Miss Stevens and Gloria heard the rest as they sped away in her car. Her tires spun and left marks as she pulled out of the school parking lot and drove down Queen Street.

*"That little witch did something to him. I saw it!"* screamed Mrs. Engel as she tried hard to push past Samantha who firmly stood her ground.

*"Mrs. Engel, you need to relax."*

*"I won't relax until that thing doesn't go to our school!"*

Other parents were shouting their support. *"Ya, something's wrong with her!"*

*"She's always been off. I'm not the only one who's noticed!!"* more parents were cheering her on.

*"Ya, it's not safe with her at Southridge! What if she could do that to my kid?!"*

There was more shouting and pushing, but Samantha wasn't having it. *"Shame on you! Shame on all of you! Gloria is a wonderful, bright young girl and she would never hurt a soul."*

More murmurs came from the crowd, this time less intense.

*"Mrs. Engel, I know you're jealous of Veronica and that's all this is."*

The crowd went silent after such a harsh remark. The parents and teachers had all seen over the years how Mrs. Engel treated Veronica.

*"I have no idea what you're talking about, Samantha. And I will surely follow up with the principle about you making such wild accusations,"* Mrs. Engel said while crossing her arms.

*"I'm making wild accusations? Have you listened to yourself? You're the one going after a eleven year old girl, claiming she somehow caused a grown man to have a medical emergency,"* Samantha said, looking at all the parents and teachers as they started to back up and look at the ground.

The Grade 6 class was silent in the back of the foyer, still in their ice skates. Her friend Reggie was front and centre in the crowd.

*"Please, everyone here knows Veronica is trouble and Gloria is weird. No kids in the class like her,"* she said smugly, looking at some of the parents who agreed with her. She looked over her shoulder and at the Grade 6 class. *"Right, Stephanie?"* She looked at her daughter.

*"Ya, she's so weird. We don't ever like to play with her. I hate when I get stuck on a project with her."* Just like her mother, Stephanie looked around at her friends who chirped along with her.

"*Ya!*" three or four of them shouted.

"*See, Samantha?*"

"*I like her! I like her a lot! She's my friend!*" Reggie shouted from behind Mrs. Engel.

A few other students agreed with his side.

"*Ya!*" Half the class seemed to yell.

"*Mrs. Engel. Me and half of the faculty don't like you. You come to school and push your daughter into every club, every school event. You think she's mighty talented and knows all. Fact of the matter, most of us can't stand her, just like we don't enjoy dealing with you.*"

As she said this, Mrs. Engel looked at the present teachers on either side of her. None of them would make eye contact with her. Her daughter, Stephanie, ran out of the room, clearly about to cry.

"*Ya, well what do I care what a bunch of washed up scholars who teach at a grade school think of me and my daughter? She'll be something. You'll see.*" Mrs. Engel stormed away to go console her precious Stephanie.

Once she left, the tension in the crowd faded.

Samantha shouted over the parents and teachers still huddled in front of her. "*Class, go get your boots, ok? The school tour will be postponed in light of Mr. West being sick.*"

The class all groaned in disappointment.

"*NOW, CLASS!!!*" she yelled with authority.

The children all dispersed into the changeroom to remove their skates.

Now with only adults present, she looked at them all in dismay. "*Now, come on people, Mr. West clearly had a stroke.*"

No one said a thing.

"*Seriously?! Do you really believe a little girl could have caused that? Think what you want of her, strange or not. There is no way she could have caused this.*"

A few parents and teachers nodded their heads once they heard how silly they acted.

"*She is a bright student in my class, and there is no way—zero possibility—that this was her fault. And you all acted worse than the group of preteens did that were behind you.*"

The group of parents and teachers came to realize how harshly they reacted. They all retreated to the changerooms to collect the students.

# CHAPTER 27

# Year-End BBQ

Veronica slowly looked at Richard. She hadn't noticed that he had closed his eyes while listening to her. "Richard?" He didn't respond. "Richard?" Still no response. Veronica set down her glass and walked over to Richard, sitting in the chair across from her. She gently shook his shoulder. "Richard?"

Richard immediately jumped in his seat. He didn't notice how the memory had pulled him into a state of trance too, just as Veronica relived it in her head. "Oh, oh my! Sorry. I was just so fascinated to learn this history. Nothing on the dark web comes close, not even close. I was just trying to take it all in."

Veronica looked strangely at Richard. "Are you sure we haven't' met? When you were out like that, it gave you a different look. Your expressionless face made it so I could see you in a different light."

Richard quickly pushed on her with a bit of compulsion. "No, definitely not. I am certain we haven't met before today." He pushed his tone more firmly.

"Please, take a seat and tell me what happened after you woke up."

Veronica went back to her seat and seemed out of it. "Yes. Yes." Slowly, she came back to awareness. "Yes, so I came out of the trance and felt off. Really off. I looked around the room and felt dizzy.

Gloria let go of her mother's hands and Cathy let go of her shoulder.

*"Veronica? Veronica? You ok? Say something."*

Still too dizzy, she didn't speak. Her eyes were spinning in their socket.

*"Mom, mom! It's ok. Come back. It's just compulsion sickness. It will be over in a bit. Maybe longer as we pulled you in deep."*

Veronica's eyes slowly came back into focus. She looked at Gloria. *"Compulsion sickness?"*

*"Mom, it's kind of another weird way of nature having its own natural karma. If people like us use people like you—like mind control—you get sick, and we get tired, really tired. It doesn't last long and when you come to, the sickness and our apparent exhaustion is sort of a warning sign. So we can't use it much or at all."*

*"Whatever you say, Gloria."* Veronica was still a little disoriented.

*"Speaking of tired, Gloria, it's late. I know that took a lot of energy,"* said Cathy.

*"It didn't, really. Well, not physically at least. It dulls my other senses. Like they're tired and they need rest."*

*"Well, whatever it is, just get to your bedroom so I can talk with your mom, ok?"*

Gloria looked up at Miss Stevens. "Ok. I love you, mom." She stood up off the coffee table and hugged her mom and went to her room.

Miss Stevens stood waiting until she saw Gloria's door close behind her. She walked around Veronica to sit across from her on the couch. She reached over and grabbed their glasses of Seagram's, both still half-full.

Veronica drank it back in one gulp.

"*I know how you feel,*" Miss Stevens said wide eyed at Veronica, and shot hers back too.

"*Cathy, I had no idea. I didn't know what it's like. To be like you or her. I'm so sorry if I ever questioned it.*"

"*Never apologize, Veronica. Ever. You have been more understanding about this stuff then anyone ordinary I've ever met.*"

Veronica felt that the word ordinary was condescending.

"*Oh it's nothing. Just a term used by those of us who are different. It's what we call people with no abilities.*"

"*It's derogatory. I don't like it.*"

"*Fair enough. It's just a word we've used as most people like you aren't as open to what we can do. People like us get persecuted a lot. Like you just witnessed...*"

"*Fair enough.*" Said Veronica, still a little offended.

"*Look, I won't use it again with you. I promise.*"

"*Thank you.*"

The phone then rang and Veronica got up. She crossed the living room and took the phone off the receiver in the kitchen. It was Samantha on the other end of the line.

"*Hey, everything ok? How's Gloria doing? Did Cathy tell you what happened?*"

"Oh hey, Samantha. Yes, Cathy is still here. Gloria is in her room."

"Did she explain what happened? With Mr. West?"

"Yes, she told me he had a stroke. And that Mrs. Engel basically pursued a medieval witch hunt after my daughter." Veronica sounded cold and angry. She pulled the long phone cord and sat down beside Cathy, tilting the phone receiver so that they could both listen. "Listen, Cathy is here, I'm putting her on the phone with me."

"Look, yes that did happen, but honestly, it was a good thing for Gloria that it did."

"Excuse me? For a second there I thought you just said it was a good thing this happened to Gloria." Veronica looked at Cathy as she shook her head.

Cathy's face immediately looked just as confused. But her eyes were shifting. Then she looked at Veronica and shook her head.

"I know that sounds mean, but hear me out. The hospital called the school where we were having an emergency meeting. Mr. West did suffer a massive stroke. It nearly killed him."

"Oh dear," Miss Stevens said aloud.

"Yes, Cathy. We are all scrambling trying to find subs for his school activities and are writing tomorrows PA announcement as we know how the rumours are already flying."

"Did they say if he'll make a full recovery?" Veronica asked.

"Sadly, they don't think he will. The damage was so bad that it showed on an X-ray, and they think he may never walk or speak again."

"Oh my God," Cathy gasped.

"It was a ticking time bomb. His family came to the hospital and said it's genetic. Many, many people in his family on both sides *lost their lives this way. Both his parents died from a stroke in the last ten years. It's a miracle he is still alive. If that's what you want to call it."*

"So what are they going to do?" Cathy asked.

"Well, his insurance with the board is extensive. They are going to keep him on life support. His brother is now his power of attorney and said he would keep us informed."

"Thank you for calling me, Samantha. I think I'll keep Gloria home from school tomorrow in light of what's happened."

"No, Veronica. Please don't, that's the other reason I'm calling."

"What?"

"All the parent chaperones, and I mean all of them, phoned me at home tonight. In this emergency situation, they looked me up in the phone book. Even some parents who were not on the trip got wind of the situation and called me too. This is why I said maybe it was good that it happened."

"What did they want?" Veronica asked.

*"They all wanted me to know how terrible they felt about their actions. They felt awful for how they've all treated you all these years. You specifically, and not just Gloria. They all know we're friends, and they all asked me to tell you to be sure to come to school tomorrow. They all want to see you there. I think they want to apologize in person."*

"All of them?" Veronica asked.

"Well, almost all of them called."

"Let me guess, Mrs. Engel didn't give you call?"

"It is what it is, Veronica. She's just a miserable soul. She's had it out for you since God knows when."

"Kindergarten at least," Cathy piped up.

*"Well, good night, ladies. I'll see you in the morning. You'll see. In a few days, this will be old news. Good night."*

Veronica hung up the phone.

*"Well, we owe her one. She handled that perfectly,"* Cathy said, pouring more Seagram's. She looked up at Veronica watching her pour the whiskey. *"Hey, relax, you know I don't drive if I've had too much. I swear."*

*"No, you better pour me one too."* Veronica sat down beside Miss Stevens, and they both drank in silence into the night.

"I don't think any of the field trips I went on with my sons were as wild as that." Richard looked at Veronica with concern. "I'm not sure what I would have done if an angry mob of adults came at my children."

"I wasn't there to witness that part firsthand, so I don't really know what I would have done either."

"Did you feel closer with Gloria after that? After experiencing her abilities firsthand, so to speak?"

"Not closer necessarily, but I definitely understood her better. It made her night terrors easier for me to handle after that as I had more compassion. She had the worst one that very night while Cathy was still over."

"Did she? What did Cathy do?"

"We were both helpless, but we calmed her down. But that scream though. Her scream. I was not sure if I was still off from being under compulsion, but after we got her back to down to sleep, Cathy told me she'd never heard a scream like that either."

Richard got the chills as Veronica replayed the sound of Gloria's scream in her mind.

"So, did things change for you at school after that?"

"Drastically. The following morning, I dropped Gloria off at school. The Grade 6 wing was the closest to the main parking lot. I pulled into a spot like I always did. But, she never got out before I got to say goodbye for the day."

*"How you doing, hun? You sure you're ready for this? If you want to go home, you just say the word."*

*"Go home? Why would I want to do that? Everyone is going to be nice to me today, I can see it. Besides, I didn't get to talk to Reggie either, and he's worried about me. I can feel it."* Gloria leaned in and gave her mom a hug, then she hopped out and closed the door. *"Bye, mom!"* she yelled through the open window and rushed off into the school yard.

As Veronica put the car in reverse, she slammed on the brakes as someone patted the hood of her car.

Through the open driver's window, she heard a familiar voice.

*"Hey, Veronica! I'm sorry if I scared you. I just wanted to catch you before you left."*

Veronica looked up at the woman beside her car. Her name was Mrs. Miliz. She was the mother of a boy named Tyler who was in Veronica's class. The two had never really spoken.

*"Oh hi, Mrs. Miliz. Can I help you? I have to get going."*

*"Oh, please. Give me a minute? Well, not just me, us?"* She stepped away from the car, pointing to a group of gathering women in the parking lot.

The school bell rang and the herd of young kids flooded into the school in under a minute.

Veronica nodded and put her car back in park. She felt apprehensive about what to expect. Most of these women never gave her the time of day, let alone had a full conversation with her. She got out of the car and walked a few spots over where the group of women stood on the grass.

*"Look, I speak for everyone here. Some of us were there yesterday, some of us were not. But we all know what happened and we feel terrible. We don't know why it took Mrs. Kropf talking some sense into us, but now we truly and honestly see the fault in our ways."*

Veronica stood there looking at all of them. She wasn't sure what to say, but an *"ok"* just slipped out.

*"It's not ok, Veronica. And we all want to make it up to you. Please?"*

"Ok," she said, nodding her head and trying to look serious.

*"Please, say something other than ok. We really feel bad!"*

Veronica wasn't good at speeches and tried to think of something forthcoming to say. *"Well look, I have no hard feelings. We all just didn't get the chance to get to know one another. I'm to blame for that as well. But more importantly, I just want the class to be a little more accepting of my Gloria. She is the one in school here, not me."*

"Oh, that is so classy of you," one of the other mothers added.

"Yes, only a true lady would say that." another added.

They all started talking amongst themselves. Veronica felt awkward and didn't care what these women thought of her. But, she felt happy that they all were coming around and things would get better at school for Gloria.

*"Well, ladies, it was a pleasure. I should be going now."*

A whimsical roar of goodbyes came at her from the group as she headed back to her car. It made Veronica smile too. She got in her car and pulled back and waved, a slew of hands eagerly waving back at her. She was in a great mood the whole way home.

"So did it last?"

"They were true to their word. It was refreshing." Veronica smiled while seeing the moment in her mind. "For the rest of the school year, it was night and day for me and Gloria. She got invited to every birthday party after that. I got invited along to most too."

When she spoke those words, memories of seeing Veronica with Gloria at a few birthday parties came back to him. He wondered if his mother was one of the ones in the parking lot that day.

"I didn't go to many as I still had a slightly jaded perception of my new so-called friends. It was hard to forget how cold they were to me for years prior. But I made it my business to go to any birthday parties that were a sleepover to ensure I took the blame for Gloria not being allowed to stay."

"Night terrors?"

"The closer we got to the end of Grade 6, they started happening two to three times a week. I would have taken her to the hospital if Cathy hadn't talked me out of it."

"How did she do that?"

"She knew the kinds of medication they would have given her. They would change her personality. She knew from experience. It also muted her ability to receive and clarify any type of messages or vibrations that came to her."

"So you didn't want her to have them subside?" Richard asked.

"Never. Being psychic was what made Gloria herself. It was who she was, and I understood that then better than ever. Also, Cathy warned me that the vision in her sleep was not just a nightmare. It was a warning."

"What did she think it was a warning of?"

"She couldn't say. Obviously, Gloria had no idea either. But Cathy made it clear. Gloria should be at full alert when she picked up on anything that might explain the terrifying warnings."

"She was right, you know. I learned about those medications prescribed then back in historical medicine classes in med school. The medical profession is far from perfect. But it is one profession that learns from its mistakes." Richard added.

Veronica looked away at Richard when he said that. He couldn't blame her. The masses still held judgments on unjustified medical practices of the past—those practices that psychics and the truly mentally ill were subjected to.

"With the last day of school just around the corner, I heard about a big backyard party for students and their parents on the last day of school. I was happy to learn it was going to be held at Reggie's parents' house. At least it was going to be at my daughter's best friend's house where I could let go of all pretentious thoughts."

"I can see where you would get the comfort from," Richard said, putting his therapist's way of thinking into perspective.

"The final week of school was here, and the summer weather was in full swing. The school was getting warmer, and the students couldn't wait be done for two months off school. All the buzz was about starting junior high—the precursor to high school."

"Hard to think we were that age once too."

"Wait till you're my age and say that! Anyways, a letter was sent home with Gloria before the last day with the address and time. School was officially done at noon on the last day, with the invite to the party saying to show up around 2. The last day of school came, and the morning was such a happy time. If only the rest of the day would have kept the same momentum." Veronica paused. "Sarah!!" She turned to Richard. "You're going to want another one. A strong one. Trust me."

"Oh," Richard said and looked at Sarah walking into the room. "Make mine a double."

"Me too." Said Veronica.

Sarah collected their empty glasses and scurried out of the room. She was back quickly. She set the glasses on the coffee table and promptly excused herself from the room once more.

"So on the last day of school, I always took Gloria out for lunch. We did it every year. Her favourite place to go was this cool place called the Ali Baba. Did you ever go there, Rich?"

"Of course. Everyone from Waterloo to Cambridge went there. It was so unique. The best steaks outside of Charcoal Steak House, and the only place a server tossed fresh Caesar salad right beside your table."

Richard had fond some memories of that place. His mother took him there on special occasions.

"That was one of Gloria's favourite spots for that reason as well. So we had a delicious lunch and headed home to get our things for the pool party."

"It was a pool party?" Richard was genuinely shocked. He had no recollection of that.

"Yes. Reggie's family lived off a street called Birchcliff Avenue. It was right behind Southridge and so close to our place. We packed our bags the night before so we just had to run and get them. She of course wore an orange dress that day. She outgrew her first one she loved so I had to replace it. I bought it at Eaton's for an end of school gift. I don't think I could have slowed Gloria down if I tried. She was jumping at the chance to go swimming. We arrived at the party just after 2:30, so most of her class and the parents were already there. We had to park a little down the hill, but it was just a few houses up the street. I put the car in park and pulled the parking break lever, and Gloria opened the car door immediately."

*"Hey, Gloria! Slow down! The party will still be going on in five minutes, ok? Get back here and help me grab some stuff."*

*"But, mom!"*

*"No buts! Just get your butt back here and at least grab your towel."* Veronica laughed, seeing her daughter smile.

"*Fine!*" She defiantly stomped back to the car and helped grab some bags.

"*Thank you.*"

Gloria grabbed what bags she could. Veronica grabbed the rest and a small Styrofoam cooler she had brought with cold drinks.

As the pair walked up to the correct house number—302—Veronica was taken aback by how huge the house was. It was dark brown in colour and two stories high. A two-car garage was attached to the home with a huge front porch.

"*Gloria, is this really where your friend Reggie lives?*"

"*Ya, mom. I've been here after school to do homework before, remember?*"

Veronica thought back and remembered. She regretted always letting Reggie's mother drive Gloria home and never offering to pick her up.

"*I know, babe. It's just a nice place. I'm impressed. What does Reggie's parents do for work?*"

"*I don't know. His mom is a nurse at St. Mary's hospital, but his dad is never home when I'm there to ask.*"

"*Can't you tell by being around Reggie?*"

"*Normally I could, I can tell what all the other dads do when I'm around the kids in my class. But he's not very close to Reggie. He's always travelling for work. Come to think of it, Reggie doesn't even know what his dad does.*"

Veronica found that strange.

"*Now, come on, mom! Wait till you see the inside! And I can't wait to swim. The pool wasn't open the last time I was here, and I can't wait to see it!*"

Gloria let go of her mother's hand and ran off into the house. Veronica stood there in awe of the beauty of not only the home, but the property too. It was a big lot with mature trees. She could hear the sound of kids jumping in the pool in the backyard.

"*Veronica, is that you?*" At the front door stood Reggie's mother. "*It's me, Angel!*"

Richard focused on the memory of Reggie's mother, and it was blurred too. The voice muffled. He couldn't make out anything, just like Reggie. The work of Gloria's block on Veronica's memory showing again.

"*Oh hi, Angel. Say, your home is beautiful. Thank you so much for inviting us. Gloria ran off already, the sound of the pool calling her.*"

Angel laughed. "*Oh, I saw her run by, not to worry. And of course we want you here! Gloria is Reggie's bestest friend, you both had to come! Wouldn't be the same.*" Angel held the door open, and as she did, their large Siamese cat ran out the door like a bolt of lightning. "*Sydney!!! Oh sorry, hun, that stupid furball just got back from three days on the prowl. He probably wants out of here with all the ruckus from the party.*" She grabbed some bags from Veronica's hand. "*Here, let me help you. What's all this for?*"

"*I know the invitation said not to bring anything, but I wanted to contribute something. It's just some bottles of pop from the Pop Shoppe. Gloria helped me pick out the flavours. I wanted to meet Sydney! Gloria said he's such a sweet cat.*"

"*Ooo, the Pop shoppe! I keep hearing about that place. The moms all tell me it's where you can get fresh fancy sodas made!*"

*"Oh, it's so delicious. Tell you what, each glass bottle is a 10 cent deposit. Use them as initiative to get yourself there to finally try it! It's just over off Mill Street."*

*"You're so thoughtful. Thank you, I will! As for that mangy bag of fleas, God knows I love him, but he takes off on hunting sprees whenever he gets the chance."*

Angel led Veronica down the hall to the kitchen which had a huge bay window looking out onto the backyard. Veronica saw the entire class and their parents by the pool and on the patio. All eighteen of them—and their parents, including Mrs. Engel. She was gazing off into the yard while Angel put all the pop in the fridge and emptied the ice from the cooler into her kitchen sink.

*"Here you go, Veronica."*

Veronica didn't grab the cooler right away. She was looking at Mrs. Engel in the back yard. She was lucky not to run into her at the school after the last field trip. Cathy told her she was avoiding her and dropped her kids off back at the kindergarten wing to do so. Veronica was intensely looking at the woman who tried to attack her daughter.

*"Veronica?"* Angel looked in both directions, seeing what was distracting Veronica. *"Oh, don't worry about her. She's on her BEST behaviour. We only invited as a formality. That and we didn't want Stephanie to suffer for her mother's delusional way of thinking."*

*"Stephanie is no saint either."*

*"Look, I know that, Veronica. But please, how about we let that go for the sake of the kids today, ok? Just look at Gloria and Reggie having fun out there."*

Veronica was too caught up to notice her daughter and Reggie laughing and carrying on. Jumping in the water again and again. She knew Angel was right and to just ignore Mrs. Engel if she said or did anything. She then looked around the yard and saw how large it was. A nice fence all around, more trees, and a large shed in the back corner. They had streamers and balloons hung wherever they could, and they had a long table set to the side of the patio with plates and dishes all decorated for the party.

*"Angel, I love the decorations, and your backyard is huge! And I think your shed is bigger than the house we live in!"* Veronica said laughing, trying to change the subject from her nemesis.

*"What? Oh, you mean the pool house. We don't need a shed with the size of our garage."*

Veronica's jaw dropped a little in her mouth. *"A pool house?"* She couldn't believe they were so well off to have a second "house" on their property.

*"It not much. It houses the pool pump and all our equipment. The previous owners built it for a spot for guests to get changed and keep their belonging safe and dry. Good idea if you ask me."*

Veronica took a moment to realize Angel wasn't being smug about their home; she was just speaking in context about it.

*"Let's go outside and check on the kids, shall we? I'm sure the rest of the parents want to say hi to you too."*

*"Sure, sounds good."*

Veronica knew Gloria never got to have fun like this. Not with all the work she did with Cathy and at school. It was nice to see her be a kid once and while.

Angel led the way down the hall and out the back door. Veronica took notice of the beautiful furniture throughout and all the latest stereo equipment.

"Wow, Angel, you neighbours must hate you!!"

Angel laughed and held open the back door. "*They would if I knew how to use it! I never touch that stuff. It belongs to Jim. I don't even know where to turn it on. I'm too afraid I'd break it.*"

"*Speaking of Reggie's father, his name is Jim?*"

"Yes."

They entered the patio where most of the parents were standing around.

"*Speak of the devil.*" Angel said.

They cut over to the BBQ where Jim was grilling away. He had on a BBQ apron that read **WORLD'S GREATEST CHEF**.

"*Hey, honey. This is Gloria's mother, Veronica. Veronica, meet Jim. Jim, Veronica.*"

Jim put down his tongs and held out his hand to Veronica.

"*Veronica, lovely to meet you.*"

"*You have a lovely home.*" Veronica shook his hand.

"*Thank you, we like it here too. And I must say, Gloria is just as lovely.*"

"*Thank you.*"

"*We like it here for now, right, honey?*" Angel tenderly jiggled her husband's forearm.

"*For now?*" Veronica asked.

Jim went to speak and nothing came out. He licked his lips, then responded. "*You'll have to forgive my wife. She's a kidder. But, my job does force us to move around a lot,"* Jim said, not even looking up from the grill and clearly annoyed.

*"I was meaning to ask by the way, what do you do for work?"* Veronica asked to try and ease the tension.

Angel stood there and crossed her arms and looked away. Veronica figured this was a common argument they had.

*"I am in medical sales. I go from different hospitals and private practices and sell equipment and supplies. I'm on the road five to six days a week, depending on what area I cover."*

*"Yes, the man always seems to go longer than needed. But, I guess band aids are a hot commodity nowadays,"* Angel viciously responded.

Veronica took a step back, trying to think of an excuse to get away. She felt so uncomfortable. She was grateful for the all noise the kids were making splashing in the pool.

*"You'll have to excuse us, Veronica, it's just that Jim here hasn't been home for over three weeks, and it seems he has to leave town again tomorrow!"*

Jim put the BBQ lid down and set the tongs and brush on the side of it. He looked at Veronica and shot a quick smile. *"Veronica, would you excuse me and my wife? I think we have to go inside and check on the rest of the food."*

So relieved they excused themselves, Veronica didn't try and stop them. *"Hey, no, it's fine. I should go check on Gloria anyways. See if she needs a drink or something."*

*"Great,"* Jim said, wrinkling his nose at Veronica. *"Dear—"* Jim placed his hand on his wife's hip, ushering her inside.

Veronica stepped aside to let them pass and went and said hello to a few more parents. She kept close watch on Gloria, not wanting to interrupt.

A few minutes later, some yelling came from inside the house in the kitchen. The kids didn't notice, not over the sound of the water. But, all the parents did. They all kept trying to carry on and pretend they didn't notice. Veronica was speaking to some of the moms when she looked over at Gloria, just standing on the pool deck and staring blankly at the kitchen window.

"*Ladies, would you excuse me?*" Veroncia politely shrugged her shoulder and squeezed through the group. "*Thanks.*"

She grabbed a towel from their bag at one of the green and pink folding plastic lawn chairs and headed over to her daughter.

"*Hey there, my little mermaid, having a good time?*" She whipped open the towel, giving it a fluff before wrapping it around Gloria's shoulders. "*You know, it's not polite to stare.*"

"*They fight over moving all the time.*"

Surprised Gloria could hear them over all the commotion, she looked over her shoulder to see if she could make out what they were saying. She looked in the bay window and saw Jim pacing the floor while Angel was yelling. Her hands were flailing in the air. He was talking back at her, his finger in her face. He looked up at his wife and passed her, noticing Gloria and Veronica looking at them. He turned and walked over to the window to shut it, and they went right back to fighting. Veronica looked back at Gloria.

*"You're not hearing them with your ears, are you?"*

*"Mom, it's so weird. I couldn't read anything off Reggie about his dad until I met him. He's really weird, mom. He's never home, and when his is at home, he likes to blare music in their living room and go into the basement."*

*"Did Reggie tell you that?"*

*"No. It's like it's his only real memory of him. They move for his dad's job, but that doesn't make sense."*

*"How would you know?"*

*"Well, I see conversations in Reggie's memories, and I read Angel just now."*

*"Gloria! You know you shouldn't do that! What's on her mind is private!"*

*"I know, mom. I've been able to be selective on what I pull from someone. I have for quite some time."*

"Oh," Veronica said, feeling unaware of where her daughter was at with her lessons with Cathy again. *"What did you see?"*

*"I listened to their fights. She always makes comment like how come they move every year or two when he travels for work? Why do they have to move when he's on the road anyways? Mom, that sounds weird and it's strange. Don't you think?"*

Veronica just thought it was a private fight and didn't want Gloria to think more about their grown-up problems than she already had. *"Honey, that's really none of our business. Seems like a private matter to me."*

*"Ok, mom. But mom, not since Mr. West........"* Gloria eyes were still glued to the kitchen window.

*"What honey, what about Mr. West?!"* Veronica stared at Gloria nervously.

*"Nothing Mom. I have to figure this out."*

Gloria and her mom walked away from the pool and headed to a table where their bags were and sat down.

The angry fighting couple must have worked things out.

Suddenly, Angel slid back open the glass and yelled to everyone, *"Hey, guys, food is ready! Get out of the pool and grab a seat! We'll be right out!"*

There was a lot of commotion for the next while. Kids got out of the pool and changed. Some of the parents helped bring all the food out. The kids ate quickly, and the parents helped oversee their own children eat before grabbing a plate themselves. Jim and Angel looked out for Reggie and Oliver too. As their boys sat down to eat, Jim stood up to the group to make a speech, still in his BBQ apron.

*"Everyone, thanks for making Grade 6 and kindergarten a great year for our boys. We are happy to have met you all! Now folks, when the kiddos are done eating, we have some games set up in our rec room for them to play. So kids, follow Reggie downstairs. And parents, we're going to play bartender for a little while."* He smiled a crooked smile and winked to the group.

The adults all clapped at the sound of drinks, and the kids roared over games.

One boy in the class asked, *"Can't we swim, Mr. Holtom?"*

*"You kids can swim a little later, but not right after you eat,"* Angel said.

*"What she said,"* Jim pointed to her and laughed.

Veronica could tell it wasn't sincere.

After everyone ate, the kids went into the basement, and the parents all grabbed some food. Veronica had just sat down to eat when Mrs. Miliz came up to her.

*"Hey, Veronica, sorry to bug you. But I just went inside to use the washroom and saw Gloria standing at the top of the stairs to the basement. I asked her if she was ok, but she said she needed to see you. She asked me to come get you."*

*"Oh, thank you."*

*"Is she ok? Is she sick?"*

*"I'm sure she's fine."* She looked down and saw Gloria's summer sandals. *"Look, her shoes. I bet that's what she wants."*

*"Ah, kids! I swear mine go through five pairs a year!"* both woman have a little laugh.

Veronica got up and headed inside the house. She had to have a little look around until she found Gloria, just standing at the top of the stairs in her little orange dress. She looked ok, but was looking at the basement in a cautious way.

*"Hey, babe, what's going on? Did you forget your shoes?"* Veronica said and knelt down and put them on the floor.

Gloria looked at them and stepped her feet in one at a time. Veronica helped her put them on.

*"Mom, I'm scared something is down there."*

*"Baby, what could be down there? All your friends are waiting to play games with you."*

*"No, mom, it's something else. I can feel it."*

*"Babe, are you sure?"* Veronica pleaded with Gloria.

One of the other parents stuck their head inside from the backyard. *"Veronica? What would you like? Jim is taking orders!"*

*"I'll be right there!"* she yelled over her shoulder. She turned her head back to face Gloria. *"Honey, think you could just try and have a little fun? Reggie's feelings will be hurt if you leave now. Right?"*

Gloria stood there and thought, seeing that Reggie would be upset. *"Yes, he would, but I don't have a good feeling about this."*

*"Gloria, just go play games. One hour is all I ask, ok? Just one hour and I'll take you home. Mommy just wants to hang with the grown-ups for a little bit, ok?"*

Gloria hummed and hawed. *"Ok, mom, but please one hour, ok?"*

*"Babe, why now? You've been here a few times and never seem to be bothered."*

*"We never came to the basement. We always did our work at the kitchen table. And I read things differently when Reggie's dad was not here. Now that he's here, things are different. They're off."*

Gloria could see the disappointment on her mother's face and could read it off her. She really wanted to stay at the party. *"But, I'm sure I'll be fine one more hour. Go, mom, it's ok."*

Veronica smiled, knowing that Gloria was willing to stay for her sake. *"Thanks, babe. I owe you one."* She held up her hand with just her index finger in Gloria's face. *"One hour."* And she bopped it off Gloria's nose.

She watched Gloria run down the stairs and around the corner.

Veronica got up and went back to the backyard where all the adults were mingling. Angel ran up to her as soon as she stepped outside with a blue drink. It was in a fancy tall glass with a wedge of fruit and cherry on the rim.

*"Here, Veronica. This is Jim's famous Blue Hawaiian. It's so good that you wouldn't even know there's alcohol in it unless I*

*told you! But be careful, they sneak up on you fast. I know from experience."* She laughed and walked away.

*"Thanks, Angel."* Veronica immediately thought of Samantha, and how she'd love these cocktails.

She wished she could have come to the party, but her husband took their family to their cottage as soon as school got out at lunch. She quietly laughed to herself as Angel went around helping hand out the fancy cocktails. Veronica admired how she put on a good front while clearly in a fight with her husband.

If she knew her better, she would have asked her if she was ok. But she thought it was best she leave it alone for today, especially after seeing Angel gulping down a glass of brown clear liquor.

She took a sip of her blue drink and marveled at it. She walked over to a few other mothers drinking the same drink and made small talk.

*"Oh my, I see what Angel meant about not knowing there is alcohol in it!"*

They all laughed and started chatting. Veronica was so glad she got to stay and relax by a pool for an afternoon.

About twenty minutes went by and Veronica was on cocktail number three. Angel kept walking around with pitchers and filling everyone's glass. All the parents were laughing and having a great time. Jim went in and turned on his fancy stereo, blasting some music. He just stepped back outside when his wife, Angel, got upset.

*"Not too loud, Jim, you'll bug the neighbours!!"* she scolded him.

Jim rolled his eyes and turned around. "*Yes, dear.*" And he muttered some profanities under his breath.

All the adults either pretended not to notice or didn't care.

Everyone, including Veronica, were enjoying the music and drinks when the loudest scream came from inside the house. It let out for almost ten seconds as everyone was still in shock, not sure what was going on. Veronica dropped her drink, the glass smashing on the patio concrete. Glass and blue liquid splashed everywhere. It broke everyone's daze momentarily.

"*Hey! The glass! My pool!*" Jim screamed from the other side of the yard.

Jim yelling snapped Veronica into motion as she ran into the house toward the basement.

"*Gloria!!!*" she screamed inside the door over the loud music.

As she took one step inside the door, another scream came from downstairs.

"*MOM!!*"

Her head was now spinning from hearing Gloria's scream as well as hearing the scream that Gloria telepathically sent her. She started running toward the basement.

"*Mom!! Help, I'm trapped!*" She was now hysterically crying.

"*Where are you??!!*" she yelled while rushing down the stairs.

The sounds of her sobbing were getting closer. When Veronica got to the bottom of the stairs, she looked to the right and saw all the kids huddled around.

All the kids, but not Gloria. They were scared and didn't know what to do. She could hear Gloria but didn't know where the sound of her crying was coming from. She looked in every direction of the room.

*"Gloria??!!"*

Gloria was crying too loud to hear her mother call to her. The music was still blaring upstairs and it was disorienting her, and so was the third cocktail she wished she hadn't drank. She scanned the room and tried to calm herself. Reggie!

*"Reggie, Reggie!! Where are you!!??"*

He stepped out from the back of the huddle of children.

As she lunged toward him aggressively, her actions scared all the kids. They all started running for the stairs, and ran up and outside. A few parents were coming down the stairs to see the commotion.

He was shaking. *"I'm sorry, Ms. Chastain. We were just playing hide and seek."*

*"Gloria, where is she!? Where is she hiding??!!"* she screamed at him while shaking him hard.

So hard that his head whipped back and forth.

*"Let go of my son!!"* Jim yelled from the staircase and came running at them after witnessing her shake his boy.

His wife Angel right behind him.

Veronica didn't let go. *"Not until you tell me where she is!"*

Reggie was so scared that he couldn't speak. He pointed to a white door at the end of the long basement rec room. As he pointed, Jim was beside him and picked him up out of Veronica's grasp. She could smell the bourbon on his breath.

"*How dare you!*" he snapped as he pulled his son into him.

Veronica didn't pay any attention and ran to the door, pulling and twisting at the knob profusely. It was locked.

"*She won't be in there! I always keep that door locked, and I have the only key!*" Jim yelled at her while comforting his son who nuzzled his head into his father's stomach.

Someone upstairs finally thought to turn off the music, and Gloria called out to her mother from behind the locked door.

"*Mom, please! Help me! I'm in here!*"

"*How in the?!*" Jim snarled, pushing his son off him.

"*I'm sorry, dad!*" Reggie yelled out to his father, tears now streaking his bright red face. "*I think she went in there to hide!*"

"*How did she get in there?*"

Reggie shrugged his shoulders. "*Maybe the pet hole?!*"

Jim looked all around the wall. When he stepped forwards and looked again, he looked down and to his right and saw the open hole in the wall the previous owners had for their cat to get in and out. "*Fuck, I thought I filled that thing up!*" Rage and anger took over as he remembered how many times he put it off.

"*Jim-language!*" Angel yelled at him.

"*One second.*" He wrestled in his pant pocket, the sound of coins and keys tossing around, pulling all the contents of his pocket out into his hand.

Gloria was crying so hard, and she was still screaming, *"Let me out!! Let me out!!!"* Her voice was cracking with every word.

*"That room is off limits, you hear me!! Off limits! You have no right!!"* he yelled while fiddling in the palm of his hand. Finally, he found the key.

*"Don't you fucking yell at her! What if she's hurt! What the fuck do you have in there?"*

*"Don't swear, Veronica! There's children!"* Mrs. Holtom hissed at Veronica, her teeth clenching.

Veronica couldn't believe she nitpicked her over a swear word. *"You fight with your husband in the middle of a party, and you have something to say when I say fuck!!"*

The tension in the room was high enough that you could cut it with a knife.

Angel didn't say anything in response.

A loud click came from the door and Veronica stepped back. Gloria must have been pressing all her weight and strength against it, and now she fell out onto the floor. She passed out immediately.

*"Gloria!!"* Veronica sifted down to check on her daughter. *"Oh no, what have you done to her?!!"* She sobbed while looking at Jim.

*"Oh my God!"* one of the mothers screamed.

The murmur of the adults took over the sound of the room as they all speculated.

*"What I've done to her?! I was outside!"* Jim exclaimed. Furious with anger, a vein was bulging in his forehead.

Veronica picked up Gloria's lifeless body and just cried.

Another mother ran over to Gloria, who laid in her mother's arms. She instinctively checked her pulse.

*"Look, for all we know, she's just a little afraid of being locked in a place. My mother has it, it's called claustrophobia. She has a strong pulse. Let's get her outside and let her get some air. Honey?"* She turned around and her husband came running over and grabbed Gloria from Veronica's lap.

*"Here, Veronica, let me take her. We can sit her up outside and some cool fresh air will wake her up. It's ok."* The husband looked at Veronica to comfort her.

Veronica couldn't speak. The emotions were running rampant in her body. She was trembling. There was a ringing in her ear, and it was excruciating. It kept growing louder. *What is happening to me?* she wondered.

Despite the ringing in her ear that was growing louder and louder, she could still hear Jim who was screaming at her. He hovered about, yelling and pointing while she sat lifeless on the floor below.

*"I could sue you!"*

Ring.

*"You and that kid of yours!*

RING

*"This is private property! Do you understand me?!"*

RING

*"Are you listening to me?!! What's wrong with you??!!"*

Veronica reached up to cover her ears.

# RING

Veronica looked up at Jim. She was no longer able to hear anything except the alarming ring in her ears. As she looked up to him, she realized that covering her ears did nothing. The ring in her head was inside her mind.

*Why? What was the purpose?* She looked around, at Angel, at the other mothers still in the room, at the rec room, the furniture. Then she looked around and saw the cat hole. *My God, Gloria would have barely fit in there. She would never hide in there. Unless... Unless, she wanted in there. What was it? What did she see? What did she sense?*

In her disorientation, she looked over and saw that the locked door was still open. She gazed in the room, the ring still constant.

The room was completely empty. She looked up at a bare concrete ceiling. A wooden shelf with only dusty mason jars on it. A few pipes running floor to ceiling. It was dark. No light. *No wonder Gloria was so scared.*

She could hear no one speak. Just the ringing. She looked from the floor and saw Jim now had his back to her, and he was screaming back and forth with his wife. She stood up. The ringing in her ear slightly softened.

# RING

She stepped away to head upstairs to check on Gloria.

# RING

She shook her head and fell backwards and was in the frame of the doorway leading to the empty room

# RING

Extremely disoriented, she didn't know what was going on. She tripped She fell a few feet backwards but wasn't able to see anything.

# RING.

In the darkness, she saw something shine from the light in the rec room. She stepped aside so she could focus better.

# RING

Off to the side, she got closer. She was maybe two feet away. She tried to focus in the dark, and to let her eyes adjust to the light.

The faint RING was almost gone.

Her eyes came to full focus, and she took a huge breath in and covered her mouth with her hand before she could scream.

There it was, exactly how Gloria had described it. Exactly how she had dreamed it. An old, wooden brown door.

# CHAPTER 28

# The Aftermath

Veronica wanted to scream. She didn't even know why she wanted to scream. She had no idea what this door was or what it meant. She only knew her daughter was petrified of it.

The ringing in her ear was gone now. She stepped back and turned around.

Jim didn't see her go into the room, as he was still in a screaming match with his wife.

"You don't threaten to sue guests in our home!"

"Her daughter went into my private space! What if she got hurt! What if she broke something?!"

"You tell me? What is in there that could be broken? Not like I know! You get crazy when I even clean down here! Whenever you're home, all you do is lock yourself away in there and leave me to tend to OUR children and OUR home while you do God knows what!! You've always been like this wherever we move! You always have a secret room and get crazy when someone goes near it. You come and go as you please at all times-tell me?? Are you a husband and father or just a roommate?" Angel was spiting and foaming at the mouth she was so angry. Her nose was running and her eyes welted from crying.

"*Hey, hey, hey! Guys, calm down.*" Veronica moved quickly to separate the fighting couple.

Veronica felt bile rise in her throat. She swallowed it back. Only when she felt the kind of terror she just did, did she want to vomit.

The couple stepped away from one another, and Veronica wasted no time to dash up the stairs and head to the backyard. She only had one thing on her mind—her priority to check on Gloria.

She ran outside and stopped dead in her tracks. She saw Gloria sitting up and awake. All the children were gone, and only a few parents were left. Even Reggie was nowhere to be seen. The couple who brought her upstairs had her wrapped in a big fluffy towel. She was drinking juice and looking at the ground. All the remaining parents around her were in a frenzy, talking about what happened. She was so relieved to see her ok. She briskly walked over to her daughter, who stood up, losing the towel, and ran into Veronica's open arms.

"*Mom!*"

Veronica wrapped her arms around her and nuzzled into the top of her head and kissed it. "*Baby, you scared me. What was that!?*"

"*I'm sorry about the ringing. It was the only way you'd look.*"

Veronica stepped back and leaned in to be face to face with Gloria. "*Gloria—that was you?! What was that it? How are you so calm now!?*" She was shaking her, and her eyes were shifting back and forth. "*Was that the door?*"

Gloria just shook her head, her face completely devoid of any unsettling emotion. *"Mom, I'm sorry. It's just that when I made you hear the ringing, I realized what else I can do. What I have to do here, and why I'm here. What brought me here. Trust me, mom, can you do that?"*

Veronica shook her head, nodding. She let Gloria go. *"What do you—"*

*"Excuse me! But we're not finished! Do you mind telling me what your little brat was doing in my cellar?!"* Jim screamed from the step of the back door.

*"Jim! How dare you?!"* Angel yelled from behind him, trying to stop her husband. She grabbed him by the shirt, and he turned to yell in her face.

At this point, Gloria walked forwards toward Jim, through the patio furniture and any parents still left.

*"No, no, this is my home. We have rules around here."*

*"Jim, stop this instant! She just had a scare, that's all!"*

*"No way. You wanna know what I think?"* Jim turned from his wife and found Gloria who was now just a few feet from him. He was viciously pointing at her in her face. *"You were down there and wanted to cause a scene. I've heard about you. I've heard about the trouble you like to cause. Didn't you almost kill a teacher?!"*

*"Jim!!"* Angel screamed from behind.

*"No way am I going to let some little trashy kid come to my house and ruin my party, and scare ___ ___ ___ ___ ___ "* Mid-sentence, Jim's mouth and body kept moving, but no sound was coming from his throat. When he realized this was happening, he stood straight and looked down at the centre of his face. He clasped his throat with one hand, not sure of what was going on.

With no apparent motive, all the parents—even Mrs. Holtom, sat at the closest chair and closed their eyes while they're bodies slumped. Gloria just stared up at Jim in the eye. He gazed back at her, eyes bulging. Veronica didn't move, unsure of what was happening.

*"It's very interesting, isn't it, Mr. Holtom? The mind is such a powerful place. It even controls every muscle in the body. Some we control. Like when we want to walk somewhere or want grab something."*

Jim was now paralyzed and couldn't move a single muscle in his body. He was frozen in place in the centre of his backyard patio.

*"Some we don't think about. Your eyelids, for example."* She raised her hand and touched the corner of her eye. *"They blink and we don't have to think about it. Our lungs, they just breathe."* She took the same hand and lowered it to her chest and placed her palm over her heart. *"Another fascinating one is the vocal chords."* She smirked and took the same hand and pointed to her throat. *"All just muscles that at some point get told by our minds to do something. The more I've been looking into the mind, the more I realize how easy it is to dig deep and see the part of what makes you tick, and even how to control your thoughts. Thoughts on moving muscles. I am only twelve, but this isn't words in a book. It's not something I have to memorize. It's pure feelings and emotions. Emotions can come easily to everyone, but especially kids like me. But, the reason I'm telling you that part is because you don't understand that. You lack emotion. You're like a blank slate, and all you see is what you want, and what you'll take."*

"Gloria, what's happening?" Veronica said, clenching her fists and crossing her arms. She was in a state of pure confusion. She looked around the patio at all the sleeping parents.

Gloria shifted her head to speak to her mom, but didn't break eye contact with Jim. *"I'm almost done here, mom."* Then she turned her face back. *"See, Mr. Holtom, my mom grew up with someone just like you. She didn't know that I knew, not until now. He hurt her. Scared her, **bad**. You know, it's sad I never get to comfort her, letting her know that I know what she went through. Everything. She told me never to pry, but her emotions are so strong that I can't ignore them sometimes. And when she sleeps, I see them."*

"Baby," Veronica interrupted. "Who do you see?"

Gloria was still staring in Jim's eyes as she calmly replied, *"Grandpa, grandma, my dad. I know it all, mom. I'm so sorry all those things happened to you. For what you went through. But I am so happy you chose to work things out, with me. I see what would have happened to me by now if you had given me up. Cathy wasn't wrong."* Gloria shook her head, eyes still locked with Jim's.

A single large tear rolled down Veronica's face.

*"So, Mr. Holtom, here's what's going to happen now. My mother and I are going to leave. We're going to go home. When we leave, you will not remember us. In your feeble little mind, I'm going to wipe clean that we were ever here. I've already done that with everyone, including the parents and students that already went home."*

Jim's face was a crimson shade of purple. The veins in his forehead were bulging, and those in his neck were too. His entire body trembled with rage as he tried to break free of the mental hold Gloria had on him.

"The parents here are all going to get up and drive home, not remembering any of this. Just that it was a lovely party your wife threw while you were still away on business. Your wife is going to go upstairs and lay down. When we leave, you're going to go in the kitchen and call the police to come because you have to confess to the horrible crimes you've committed. You'll take them to the basement, while other officers will wake up your wife and take her, Reggie and Oliver away. You'll never see them again. Not now or at your trial, and they don't come to your funeral after you kill yourself in jail. They too will forget. But in a few months, after the divorce, they never, ever think about you or they time spent with you for the rest of their lives. They get to go on and be happy, to fulfill their dreams. Dreams that every good person on this earth has the right to live out and succeed at too."

"What did he do, Gloria?" Veronica's eyes were wide, and her breathing was very shallow.

"But not all the women and men you have locked up in the basement get to do that, do they?"

"Gloria, there's people in that room? We need to get them out!" Veronica said.

"Mom, they're not all there. Well, all his victims are there. But just pieces of them. See, that's what he likes to do in there, mom. Behind that disgusting brown door. I didn't have to go in to see it. I could see through it. All the times he's marveled at his collection. Smiled and been proud of it. With his job, years of selling medical equipment makes it easy to have all the tools. And being on the road so much, no one every suspected him. How many are down there, Jim?"

Veronica's bile began to rise again in her throat.

"Mom, calm down." Gloria sent calming waves to her mother, settling her stomach. "You know, there is a term *being used for what you are. But it's not known yet, only in the FBI. You're what we will one day call a serial killer. But what makes you one of the scariest, is you don't have one type. What they'll one day call a pattern. You kill relentlessly because you get away with it. That's the thrill for you. Men, or women. Even some little boys down there- boys about Reggies age am I right?"*

Veronica felt disgusted by what she was hearing. She felt like she was reliving some memories of finding out what her father was.

*"So, I'm going home now. Your boys are safe, asleep in bed. And you're about to make your phone call. Is there anything you have to say before I leave? I'll let you speak, just this one last time."*

Beads of sweat were now pooling at Jim's brows. She let him only moves his lips, not his jaw.

"YOU LITTLE," he started to say, but then his lips were sealed shut once more.

*"Goodbye, Mr. Holtom."*

Veronica ran and grabbed Gloria's hand and rushed her into the house to leave through the front door.

They almost made it outside when a voice from the top of the stairs called out, "GLORIA!"

Gloria stopped in her tracks while Veronica kept running and lost her grip on Gloria's hand.

It was Reggie, standing at the top of the stairs. He wasn't crying, but he looked confused.

*"Gloria, what happened? I heard everything you said. Did, did my dad really do those awful things?"*

*"Reggie, how—how are you awake? You're supposed to be asleep."*

*"Oliver is sleeping, but when I heard you talking, I looked out my bedroom window and heard everything you said."*

"*Reggie, you should be asleep. This can't be.*" Gloria squinted her eyes. "*Reggie, come down here a second.*"

Reggie came to the bottom of the stairs.

"*Reggie, come closer.*"

As he did, Gloria held up both hands and placed both palms over his forehead. She concentrated a second and smiled. "*Of course.*" She lowered her hands and hugged Reggie hard.

Veronica, who was still just a few feet away, came running back to the doorway. "*Gloria, we have to go!*"

"*Mom, we have a few minutes, it's ok. Give me a minute?*"

Veronica just nodded and took a few steps away, still able to see and hear what was happening.

Gloria hugged Reggie tightly and placed one hand over the back of Reggie's head. She spoke calmly and softly into his ear. "*Reggie, sshhh, be calm.*"

Reggie's body relaxed immediately.

"*I'm going to miss you. You were a great friend. I understand why we were such good friends, and what drew me to you. But, you won't understand it for a few more years. You're going be great and powerful. I'll miss you. But you move with your mom to Cambridge next year, and we won't see each other again. Your memories of your youth will never haunt you, or your family. This I can do for you. Stay strong. You turn out to be a wonderful man.*" Then Gloria moved her hand from the back of his head and cupped it over her mouth into Reggie's ear.

She spoke something Veronica could not hear.

She let go of Reggie and took a step back, gently tracing her fingers over his face from forehead to chin. "*Now go sleep and be well, Reggie. I have to go.*"

Reggie closed his eyes as she traced over them and turned and went up to his room with a blank expression in his eyes.

Gloria ran to Veronica who grabbed her hand and they rushed to the car. Sirens were starting to ring from a long distance away.

# CHAPTER 29

# Awake

"After we raced home, I made Gloria promise to let me keep my memories. I told her that I wasn't afraid. She promised, and I am forever grateful she kept her word."

"What happened to the Holtom family?"

"Gloria was right about everything. The police came, there was a trial, it was all over the papers. His family was left out of the news coverage. I know Gloria still had something to do with that. I followed along in the papers for a few years, and the night before Jim's sentencing, he hung himself in his jail cell. Years later, Gloria's publicist removed all the records of it ever happening, so nothing would be linked to Kitchener, or Gloria. But, no one really knows about that story. And anyone still alive would have no memory of it either."

Both Richard and Veronica sat in silence. A few minutes passed, and Richard was letting the information set in. No wonder he had no memory of Gloria at the pool party. It all made sense. He was never good friends with Gloria, so he never thought twice as to why she wouldn't have come. A few more minutes went by, and Veronica's thoughts were distressing. She was feeling raw, having never shared so much with anyone

"Veronica?"

She looked up at Richard.

"Thank you. You have no idea how this has helped me. How it will help with what we have to do. I feel very privileged that you shared with me all that you did."

Veronica smiled. "It was just nice to have someone up here, someone I'd like to call a friend if that's ok."

"It's more than ok." He got up and walked up to her to grab her hand in a courtly gesture.

She placed her hand in his, and he kissed it and placed his other hand over top.

"Please, when this is over? Come see me again."

"I promise."

It was now very late and dark outside, and as Richard stood up, he heard the click of Sarah's heels coming around the corner.

"Mr. Matheson, are you both almost finished? It's late and Ms. Chastain needs to take her medication."

"I'm not a toddler, Sarah!"

"No, it's fine. It is late. And that was an awful lot to take in. I should get back to the hotel. Thank you again, Veronica, sincerely, thank you." He gave her hand one final squeeze and let go.

"Well, I guess I should get my beauty sleep. Good night, Richard. I hope what you now know helps."

"It will, I'm sure of it." He smiled.

Sarah came up to Veronica and helped her up. "Mr. Matheson, I'll have to call down for you and get an escort. Could you wait here for me, please?"

"Absolutely. There is a painting over there and I want to have another look at it anyways. Good night, Veronica."

"Sweet dreams," Veronica said and winked at Richard.

Sarah took her out of the room and her heels clicked down a long hallway.

Richard walked back to the Raphael and admired it a little more intently. He would never see a painting of this rarity, let alone value, again. A few minutes passed, and he heard Sarah's heels click back down the hall into the room.

"Follow me, please, Mr. Matheson."

"Lead the way."

Richard smiled. He knew everything he'd learn tonight would go a long way in his quest.

Sarah led him back to the front foyer and unlocked the door with her fingerprint. He hadn't noticed that on his way in. She helped open the door and ushered him into the hallway. He stepped outside and waited for Sarah. She led him back down the hallway and walked right past the elevator doors.

"Sarah, isn't this—"

"I need to see you, Richard. This won't take long."

Richard tried to read again her but made nothing out of it. She went to the other end of the hall, and there was only one other door on the floor. She opened it with her thumb print, and the door opened. She held it open for Richard, pointing for him to go inside. He reluctantly stepped in.

There was a small table with chairs at the door. There were monitors with security camera footage, and notes and photos were pasted all over. Richard tried to take them in but as far as using his intuition, he was still heavily sedated from the alcohol. The lights were all off, and he couldn't see anything else.

"This is my dwelling on the floor. I don't like to live with my clients directly. I always make sure I have some privacy. Being too close can interfere. Take a seat."

Richard did as he was asked and took a seat. "Interfere? With being a legal liaison?"

"Richard, you are here because of me. Because I allowed it. My employer is very particular and doesn't allow anyone to ever step foot here under any circumstance, only she is allowed to. Even though it's been four years since I've seen her, she is also a friend."

"She?"

"Yes. I work for Gloria. I have for years. Since we trained together after her high school years."

"YOU'RE SARAH? THAT SARAH?!!! How did I not see this?"

"I only let you read what I wanted to show you. I'm a lot stronger than you. You were supposed to think of me as her lawyer. But when the council reached out to me and told me you'd be coming, I let you in."

"Are you on the council?"

"There are many of us all over the world whom they consult. I am kept in a very discreet way, being too close to Gloria. But I helped form it in university. As the regular world started to rely on people like us more and more, we knew we had to work together to form our own sense of establishment. In case it was ever needed. Now with what is going on, the medical community is in the dark, and we are the only ones who can find the answers we need. The last pandemic, was a virus. Something Western Medicine could see and make sense of. This new illness, is one of the mind. Effecting our consciousness. When that gets sick, those kinds of doctors can't help. No, we are the ones who will figure this out. But we need her, we need Gloria."

Richard knew what she was saying and agreed. The whole council felt this way.

"None of us knew why we all felt it was the best way years ago, to keep the council secret, but now this is coming to light and it makes sense. I've always been a part of the council, but not in the open. Gloria knows of the council of course, but she has no idea that I have any affiliation."

"So why am I here? As in here with you? Shouldn't you want me to keep going?"

"Oh I do, but I couldn't help but see how clouded Reggie was in your mind. I think I know why."

"Because of the block Gloria put on Veronica all that time ago. I was there, in the Grade 6 class. He is blocked in my mind as well."

"Wow, the depth of her power never ceases to amaze me. Even after all the years." Sarah was staring at Richard in such marvel as she sat smiling across from him. "Even as a knowledgeable doctor in the field of psychology, you really have no clue, do you?"

"Clue of what?" Richard asked, sincerely clueless as to what she was talking about.

"Wow, even at her age she could do this."

"Do what?!" yelled Richard. So confused by what she was saying.

"Richard, or should I say, Reggie?"

Silence and stillness over took Richard. After a minute, he was able to speak. "What? No, Reggie was in my class."

"Richard, you have no memory of your father. You have no memory of your life before Grade 6."

"That's normal. A lot of adults don't. I see it all the time when I read people."

"Yes that's true, but you have nothing. No memory at all. It's blank. That's not normal. Haven't you ever wondered why?"

Richard's heart rate started speeding up. He looked down in thought. "Well, no. I haven't."

"Yes you have. You've looked for reasons over the years. You even had other psychics try to help you. They couldn't find anything of course. She made it that way, Richard. Look, I'm sorry to have to tell you this. But you know as well as I know that there are no coincidences. I know what to tell you to unlock it. But there is still some things I won't let you see. What your father did no one really remembers, so I'll leave that block up forever."

"This can't be right. I am not REGGIE!" Richard screamed and stood up from the chair, slamming his hand down on the table. His heart was now pounding in his chest. He'd never been around someone who could read more than he could.

Sarah sat back in her chair and raised her hand and spread her fingers. "RELAX!"

Richards's heart slowed down and he sat back down. A wave of calming euphoria took over him. "So that's how that feels firsthand."

"You are strong, Richard, but you never could control the body, just the mind. Compulsion is a strong skill with you, and it is still something some of us never master. There is only a handful of people who can push their will to motor function and memories. Look, you're going to be in shock. I will not withhold this memory from you. But you will wake up back at your hotel, feeling refreshed and ready for tomorrow. You will remember everything, including your life as Reggie. It's imperative." Sarah laughed, shaking her head, and leaned into a subdued Richard, placing her elbows on her knees. "I still am amazed you never picked up on it at all. You always went to Kitchener when you could growing up. You even took Linda there on your first date. You never left Ontario except for your studies. Always close by, always checking up on the internet, and still no inkling. But she did go deep on you."

Some of the memories started to become clear, and the shift in focus started to change. Instead of him looking at Reggie and Gloria sitting together, he saw himself sitting beside Gloria. Them doing homework after school. Playing and laughing together. Then the dark ones shifted back. Getting snacks at the lobby or Queensmount arena. Coming around the corner and seeing her touch Mr. West as he passed out. Watching his hair go white.

"More will become clear as you sleep. So sleep, Richard. Sleep deep. Remember. Focus. Now she will have to see you. The more you learn, the more you can hit deep, and awaken what she's buried deep and help the world. She won't see you coming. She doesn't know who you are. She won't see the block on you as it unbinds. I am the only person in the world who can do this. The only one she ever showed. I just never thought I would ever have to use it on you."

Richard was so sleepy all of a sudden. The weight of his body was sinking into the chair.

"She told me about you once, when we were young. I knew you existed, I just never thought I'd meet you. Strange how we're allowed to know certain things, and others the universe leaves even the most powerful psychics in the dark about."

Richard's eyes were getting heavy now. Sarah got up and stood over him. She leaned in and looked in his eyes.

"Do you want to know what Gloria whispered in your ear the last time you saw her?"

Barely able to answer, he used his tired breath to make out a soft, "Yes."

Sarah leaned in and cupped Richard's ear just like Gloria did and whispered, "I'm not sure I will ever see you again, dear friend. But, I hope one day I get to meet Linda, and tell her how lucky she is."

Richard blacked out at this moment.

Deep in his sleep, all his memories came back. Moving in his youth, never really knowing his father. Meeting Gloria and sharing a close bond with her right away. The memories Veronica shared were clear. It was his mental block blurring them out in his mind. He vividly dreamed for what seemed like days.

His eyes suddenly popped open, and he was lying across the bed in his hotel room at the Crowne Plaza back in Kitchener. He sat up, feeling energized and alert.

"Just like she said," he said out loud to himself.

He looked around the room to make sure he wasn't still dreaming. He saw his luggage as he left it, nothing out of place. He knew he wasn't dreaming. As he scanned his surroundings, he looked to his right and saw a note on the bedside table.

Dear Reggie,

I know you slept well. With our services, I got you home safe and sound. Good luck today. You're going to need it. But I foresee you succeeding. I am leaving the loft for a few days. I have a lead on something that may help us. Veronica is safe under watch with my staff here and will alert me if anything happens. Call me later tonight, and let me know what you find.

Sarah
519-555-4636

With no time to waste, Richard got up and got started. He quickly showered and phoned Linda at home to check in. He went down the lobby and ate really quick, and then headed to the front desk. A new attendant he hadn't met yet was on shift.

"Good morning, Mr. Matheson," the young man said. "How is your stay with us so far?"

"Stan, I tell you, I had the most interesting sleep of my life." He smiled, thinking of the serendipity of his life and how it had led him there.

"We do use the best of the best for our bedding and mattresses."

"No arguments there. Say, Stan, I need to get the key to my meeting space upstairs. And Stan, what time does the Forest Heights High School reunion start tonight?"

# EPILOGUE

As Mark wandered down the corridor of the police department, he mentally made comments like he always did. *What a boring building.* No colour, concrete floor, and florescent lighting. But what else was he to expect from this building? It wasn't designed to be aesthetically pleasing. Mark worked at Division 1 in Kitchener, located close to downtown on a street called Fredrick street. Growing up in Kitchener, he knew he always wanted to be a cop, and he would fantasize about working in this building when he would go passed it as a kid. Now that he worked in it, he couldn't be happier. But, he couldn't help but wish it was a bit more pleasing to the eye.

As he rounded the corner down the hall, he got to the break room. All the off-duty cops were there, having a break and talking about their shift. Every cop on the beat had to hand in their reports at the end of each shift, and most stayed around to blow off some steam and share stories. The room was just as clad and boring as the rest of the building, but at least it offered some oversized sofas to relax in. When Mark saw a few of his buddies there that day, he was excited.

"Hey, guys, how was your shift? Where is everyone else?"

Mark saw Ken, Dean, and Vic. A few of his fellow officers whom he had trained with. He wanted to know where the rest of their group was.

"Ryan and Brian are out back having a smoke," Sean answered.

"Ok, I'm going to grab them. Meet me in interview room 3—you won't believe what this kid is saying. I picked her up this afternoon for shoplifting at Fairview Mall, and I have to release her to her mother soon. So be quick."

Curiosity lingered in the room, and the guys didn't question it. They headed down the hall while Detective Mark went to grab officers Ryan and Brian to join the fun. Just off the break room were two heavy metal doors with thick glass windows. As he approached them, he could see his other two friends smoking along with some other off-duty cops he knew. He pushed open the right door and stuck his head out.

"Hey, guys, you have GOT to come check this out. We picked up this kid today day on some minor charges that we dropped, but after questioning her, I'm having some fun. Come check this out! Ken, Dean and Vic are already waiting, so hurry up."

All the guy around the smoke pit looked at Mark with excitement. It wasn't uncommon to grab one another to see an interrogation. Not just to help the investigation, but from time to time, it did have entertainment purposes for them.

His two friends, along with a few other off-duty cops followed Mark back into the building and down the hall. There was quite a group forming around the one side of the two-way mirror, all looking in at the young girl. She was sitting there, looking bored and annoyed. The expression on her face could not have been more obvious. Her arms were crossed, and her big black military boots were up on the table.

She had a hard look to her. One that most cops believed to be trouble. As all the fellow cops stared at the unsuspecting girl, they all thought she was suspicious. She wore a ripped metal shirt, tons of black bracelets, jeans with large rips that could be seen as she had her foot up on the seat and was resting her leg against the table.

While Mark originally interviewed her, he made comments in his notes about her heavy black makeup, black nail polish, and wild teased hair. *What a punk*, he thought.

"Ok, guys, I'm going in. I've been with her for only a half hour, but I've never heard such crazy shit. Seriously, we may need to get the doc from the second floor to have a chat with her before we let her go."

Some of his colleagues were just politely laughing, unsure of what to make of his statement.

"Mark, what the fuck are you talking about? She's just some punk kid," said Ken.

"I know, but give me a few minutes. Trust me. It's wild."

Mark straightened out his linen blue uniform shirt and took a deep breath in. He was still in his beat uniform and badge. He wished he'd taken a minute to have a quick smoke, but he was too eager to get the boys in on his fun. He opened the door and closed it tightly behind him.

The interrogation room was only 6' X 8' with a small table in the middle. A chair stood on either side with a two-way mirror on one wall. Mark sat with his back to the mirror, and a young girl of about fourteen sat wide-eyed and unimpressed on the other chair. He had let her out of the handcuffs he'd arrested her in after she was caught shoplifting down at the local mall. He picked up kids there all the time. Mostly for shoplifting, but occasionally for other things. He'd never made an arrest like he had that day. He found it odd how easily the girl got caught, and how she didn't put up a fight either. Most girls her age get wild, and most of all, cry. This was a first for the officer. She had just nodded her head and said, "let's go" when he got to the security office in the mall.

"Miss, please take your feet off the table," Mark asked in a stern manor.

She rolled her eyes and took her feet down. She then slouched in her chair, her elbows now on the table. "That better?" she asked sarcastically.

"Thank you. Ok, so one more time for the record, please."

"Are you kidding me?" The girl leaned back in the chair, raising her hands before crossing her arms again.

"No, miss, this is very serious. You have been placed under arrest."

"Arrest for what? You didn't find anything on me."

"We still found that you had vandalized some merchandise with the intent to steal."

"How many times do I have to tell you? I wasn't going to steal. I had to get you to come arrest me. That's what I was doing."

With that, all the men on the other side of the mirror started to notice her and really pay attention.

"What did she say?" asked Dean.

You could hear a murmur of gossip coming from the officers crowding around the one side of the mirror.

"So you wanted to be arrested?" Mark asked the young girl, condescendingly.

"No, fuck! Open your ears, would you? I had to get YOU to arrest me. We had to meet today," she aggressively answered.

"Why did we have to meet today? Why me?"

"I don't know. It doesn't mean anything now. Soon it will, just not today."

"So you're saying you had to go to jail today?"

"Does is look like I'm in jail? No. I am in a room talking to you which is what I planned. That's what I keep telling you, isn't it?"

"Well, I'm flattered, but I am a married man, and you are a bit young for me."

The group of men huddling on the other side started to laugh as quietly as they could.

"Go, Mark, go!" one of them said.

"You pig. I'm not talking about anything like that. Don't get me upset, you wouldn't like it."

"Is that a threat, Miss Chastain? I'm not sure your mother would like it if I tell her what you said. She was really upset when I called her and told her about your arrest."

"You didn't charge me, did you? No! That's because you know you have nothing on me! This is the last time I'm going to say this to you. I had to meet you. In a few years, this will make sense. Maybe by then your pea-brain will understand what I'm talking about."

"You seem a little worked up and confused, miss—"

"Gloria. I told you to call me Gloria."

"It's not professional of me to call you by your first name, Miss Chastain."

The men behind the mirror were laughing louder now. Even Mark heard them through the glass and held back his own laughter. He couldn't help but smile.

"Fuck off, would you? And tell all your other cronies behind the glass to fuck off too."

More laughter came from behind the glass.

"This kid is nuts! Mark was right!" yelled another officer.

"You know, Mark, I've been nice. Really nice. Pleasant as peach fucking pie. Now, why don't you let me go so you can get home to Racheal?" She leaned into him, a smug look on her face.

Mark stopped smiling and all the other men behind the glass stopped laughing.

"Excuse me?" Mark said in disbelief.

"Don't you want to get home to Rachel?"

"How did you know my wife's name?"

"I warned you. Don't piss me off. You're making a mistake by getting me going. Are we done here?"

"I don't know what you think is happening here, but I am an officer of the law, and you can't speak to me this way!"

"Don't say I didn't warn you..."

"You know, I have it in my right mind to keep you overnight. Perhaps send you to KW hospital to check your mental health."

"I'm done playing games. Let me go now!"

"Excuse me, but I'm in charge here, NOT you! I don't take orders from pushy, punk little kids like you!"

"You tell her, Mark!" Dean yelled from behind the glass.

Hearing that empowered Mark. She was just some punk kid to him.

"Dean, I think you should keep it down. Seems to me like your son, Mike, bosses you around a lot!" Gloria yelled, looking in the mirror.

On the other side of the glass stood Officer Dean Jenson. A big man of 6'1" with black hair. He'd yelled that out. He was in disbelief how she'd known his name, let alone that his teenage son, Mike, was a nightmare to deal with.

One of the other officers in the group pushed on Dean's shoulder. Officer Vic Sanche was a senior cop on the beat who loved to ruse the younger ones.

"Is that true, Dean? You let your kid boss you around?"

All the other officers laughed.

"I'm not sure you should poke fun of Dean there, Vic. After all—do your kids even talk to you since the divorce? No—neither of them do. Not since Angela told them about your affair."

"What the fuck is this, Mark? Some kind of joke?!" Officer Vic yelled at the mirror, ensuring he was loud enough to be heard on the other side. He banged on the glass with his hand.

Behind the reflection of the mirror, Gloria and Detective Mark could hear yelling and a few pounds on the glass.

"You guys are fucking unreal. Look, I'm going to go now because my mother is at reception waiting," Gloria said, pointing to the phone on the wall.

"We're not done here," said Mark. "When she arrives, they call—"

**RING RING.** The phone extension on the wall went off.

Mark got up in disbelief. He forcefully grabbed the phone off the hook, the whole while looking at Gloria.

"Ya? Fine." He slammed the phone down on the receiver. He looked at Gloria with fury. "Your mother is here."

"Like I said." Gloria stood up out of her seat and walked to the door. "See ya in a few years, Markie. Can't wait to learn why! Say hi to Rachel."

The door buzzed open and Gloria walked outside, a group of officers just standing in awe.

From the back, Brian yelled out, "FREAK!"

They all laughed and a few high-fived.

Gloria stopped and turned around. "Oh Brian, that's not nice."

"YOU ARE A FREAK," Brian said again.

"Well, that's not what you call yourself when you wear your wife's dresses when she's out at work?" Gloria smiled at him.

"The fuck?!" Brian said, looking pissed.

"Ya, your favourite one right now is the hot pink shiny number. You like how it makes your ass look."

"Brian, what in the actual fuck?!!?" screamed his partner Ryan.

"Oh now, Ryan, those in glass houses, right? Or should I say, those who smoke from glass pipes?" Gloria said, now looking at him, her brow raised.

Office Vic, being the senior staff in charge got serious. "Officer Ryan, do you use drugs?"

All the men started tuning on each other and voices were getting louder. They didn't see Gloria walk down the hall. A minute later, at the end of the hall, she turned around and smiled.

While walking away, she shouted over her shoulder, "Bye, boys, see you in a few years!"